"Who drinks first?" he asked. Neither Irissa nor Orvath moved. "Irissa?"

She met her grandfather's gaze, as dark as her father's and far more forgiving. "Yes," she said. She lifted the horn, frowning slightly at its somehow familiar form. Chill green gold touched her lips, then the borgia's potent syrup flowed—warm on her tongue and burning hotter as it surged down her throat. Irissa lowered the horn. Fascinated, she watched the frothy green pool slide toward her as slowly as a snake. She saw the Towlocs laughing, saw open mouths and half-shut hands . . . and heard nothing. She must say something, do something. Someone must . . .

"Don't drink it," Kendric ordered. White-faced despite his stooping, he straightened, bringing up Irissa's senseless, open-eyed form. Her silver eyes had turned the color of old borgia.

CAROLE NELSON DOUGLAS
HEIR OF RENGARTH
SWORD & CIRCLET 2

TOR *fantasy*

A TOM DOHERTY ASSOCIATES BOOK
NEW YORK

HEIR OF RENGARTH

Copyright © 1988 by Carole Nelson Douglas

First printing: May 1988
First mass market printing: August 1989

A TOR Book

Published by Tom Doherty Associates, Inc.
49 West 24th Street
New York, NY 10010

Cover art by Maren

ISBN: 0-812-50046-6   Can. ISBN: 0-812-50047-4

Library of Congress Catalog Card Number: 87-51407

Printed in the United States of America

0 9 8 7 6 5 4 3 2 1

For Betty Roney,

epicure, grammarian, fellow ailurophile,
quintessential columnist,
and great friend

PROLOGUE:
Pre-conceptions

THE GLASS BALL PINCERED BETWEEN LUDBORG THE Fanciful's sleeve ends plummeted to the floor. Crystal shards rocked on their shattered curves, then lay still.

"Read me a fortune, scryer," ordered a shadowed figure at the narrow window. Evening came to Edanvant, leeching bloody sunset into the day's cloud-clotted sky.

Ludborg's round form squatted nearer the floor, where silvered glass sugared the stones. "I may read awry. It is better that the seeker himself search the shards for a vision."

"Awry or not, read."

"And the daylight is . . . dying."

"Better it than you. Read."

Ludborg hastily pinched a larger slice of glass in one sleeve end and bent his hooded head.

"I see a babe."

The form shifted to bar the last light from entering the window and grunted. "Irissa's unborn one."

"Not . . . hers." In the silence, Ludborg's swallow was audible. "Yours."

The man whirled to face the room. "Liar! Jalonia has said nothing."

"Perhaps she doesn't know anything—yet."

The man paced, a slight hesitation in his step seeming more habit than necessity. "Then your duties double. Tell me the sex of the child."

1

"Which?"

"Irissa's, fool Rengarthian."

"None can accuse you of overdoting fatherhood, Orvath. Wouldn't you like to surprise Jalonia with a prediction of the sex of your own babe?"

"It's Irissa who bears the seeress's seed. I must know what breeds under my roof."

"Jalonia is unmagicked and yet bore Irissa," Ludborg noted.

Orvath froze, his silhouette muted against the darkening tower walls. The chamber's half-light glinted on the long parings of glass sprinkling the floor, on Orvath's opalescent eye whites.

"Then read the gender of both," he said finally.

Ludborg cleared the region of his throat. "There are— that is, I *see* . . . three . . . babes in my glass sliver. All told. One casts a mere shadow behind the nearer two— behind Irissa and Kendric's babe . . . and Jalonia and yours."

"I barely tolerate the chicanery of a reading, scryer; endlessly multiplying the absurdity does your welfare no good."

"I read only what is there to be read."

"Figments, no doubt." Orvath snorted his disbelief. "But that is what we Torlocs are reduced to in these latter days. Read the sex of all three, then, and prove your art's effectiveness to me."

"I am not even human, lordling, much less Torloc. I may read what is right awrong."

"Read."

"A daughter for Irissa."

Breath hissed between Orvath's unseen teeth.

"A . . . son . . . for yourself."

Orvath's shoulders loosened a long notch.

"And a . . . surprise . . . for the unknown parents of the third child. I can read no sex. This babe is not of Edanvant and casts a crooked shadow."

"Fie on it, then!" Orvath strode to the opposite wall

and laid his hand on it, some golden object glinting in his palm. Where there had been darkness, light flared. A green-flamed torch snapped at the harsh lines of Orvath's face.

"My lord Orvath does not seem gratified by news of his impending fatherhood," Ludborg observed humbly.

"*Grand*fatherhood," Orvath corrected. "That's what concerns me, for if Irissa bears a daughter, it will be a seeress like herself. Then our small community will be cursed with two of that sorcerous kind."

"Had Finorian lived, there would have been three."

"Finorian does live, in her inimitable way. A second seeress swelling our small number here in Edanvant means more contention between the seeress's inborn magical ways and the talismans of power we men have won. One seeress we might have survived, but two—"

"Perhaps Irissa will not bear a seeress."

"You said she carried a daughter."

"Not all daughters are born seeresses, even when borne by one."

"Mine was seeress-born, and that is more than enough."

Orvath flung himself at the window, like a tower-trapped gutterhawk seeking daylight. Only a crimson stiletto of light cut through the stone now. All Edanvant had grown dark.

"Aren't you interested in a further reading on your own child," Ludborg wondered, "or on the intriguing shadow babe that lurks behind the splintered smile of the glass?"

"I am interested in the balance of power, Ludborg, not the details of generation. Besides, you already said Ialonia will bear a son. What else is there to know about the birth, then?"

Ludborg clucked like a ruffled hen as his voluminous sleeves swept the broken glass into a glittering heap.

"You won't win plaudits from the ladies with that notion, Orvath. Some taint of the fallen wizard, Delevant, must still infect your bones, despite Irissa's healing your deformities with her Overstone."

Ludborg's hands, or what passed for them, clapped. A single globe floated in his grasp, its convex sides reflecting Ludborg small in the glass—and Orvath's distant figure even smaller.

The Torloc leader spoke measuredly. "Irissa did not heal my fears—of the future, of herself, or of what evil her powers may work here in Edanvant. We have not yet decided who will rule here—she or I."

"Irissa seeks no rule."

"So she is most dangerous. She seeks power only when she feels obligated to do so. I trust the greedy more than the self-righteous."

"What of your son-in-law? He is not greedy, either."

"Kendric." Orvath's attitude unbent a bit. "A sensible man, albeit stubborn. Yet he bears his own self-deceptions, and too great a share of Irissa's magical powers. He cannot help what he has fathered, any more than I can."

"Or Irissa or Jalonia can."

Orvath was silent.

The globe between Ludborg's sleeve ends winked aquamarine in the torchlight and vanished. "You are right, lordling, you distrust magic too much to read it right. Better to leave the future unread, then."

"I do not like surprises."

"That is unfortunate." Ludborg's parting bow never dislodged the darkness shadowing his hooded face. "From what I glimpsed in the shards, you are in store for quite a few."

Orvath moved to detain Ludborg, but the door—or the darkness—had whisked his homely presence from the chamber.

"Cursed weaseling floor-scraper, come back! You drop not only glass but hints, and such sharp-edged toys can cut you deeper than you think—"

Orvath scraped a dagger from its sheath, but the room remained empty . . . except for a single shard of broken glass. Orvath began to kneel as if to study it, then paused.

Instead, his boot heel crushed already shattered glass to fine grains of sand beneath his feet.

She passed the looking glass and paused.

The frame was a snarl of carved green-gold. The mirror itself seemed dull in comparison, smoke-surfaced. She didn't turn to face it, but slowly swiveled her head over her shoulder until the sweat-sheened whites of her eyes met an answering glimmer in the glass.

Other things glittered in the mirror—constellations of sparkle were strewn over her breast and glistened at her throat, earlobes, fingers, and wrists. Starlight cinched her waist and cascaded down the long, dark folds of her gown.

No one had forbidden her the use of mirrors. They lined her bedchamber, hung from the leather-embossed walls, and littered her dressing table and window seats. Even now, one small circle of mirror twisted slowly near her hem on the fine Iridesium chain that linked it to her waist. As she watched, not moving, the mirrors' winks softened and died.

She was motionless, looking into ill-lit shadow. She watched the pinpoints of reflection on her figure fade and vanish as stars forsake the predawn sky. She saw only the glitter of her eye whites now.

Her fingers moved to her throat, fanned and stroked down her body. Crustations of metal and stone interrupted the passage of her hands, impressing their reality into her palms. The mirror showed nothing but a swelling darkness.

And then it cracked—from top to bottom, side to side, diagonal to diagonal—dark hairline fissures fracturing into rivulets and finally into cracked-eggshell patterns.

The mirror showed nothing now but a dim veil of disintegration. She took a deep breath and moved on.

CHAPTER
1

KENDRIC EYED HIS SHADOW IN A WALL.

Blacker than the Iridesium metal that reflected him, the shadow stretched as long as Kendric's seven feet of height. It was complete to the determined set of his shoulders, the angled hilt of longsword topping his back.

Kendric drew that sword in a practiced twist that wrenched it from its back-borne scabbard. In the dark mirror of the wall, his reflection also cocked a naked blade.

Kendric's jaws clenched. Meeting a formidable foe sword-to-sword was nothing new, even if it masqueraded in his own likeness. Meeting something hidden beyond that— a sensed but unseen foe—with the invisible weapons of magic, came less naturally.

He lifted his weapon and struck the wall.

A discordant screech echoed in the empty woodland as Kendric's sword tip scored metal. A copper-colored scar trailed the sword's downward motion; the blade seemed to soften and glow slightly green. Around it, the wall wavered. The weapon pressed its advantage and pushed inward, downward.

When the blow was done, the sword had gone to earth and a long copper scratch in the wall bubbled corrosively. Iridesium metal burnt back from emerald-green flames as blackened parchment peels away before red-fingered fire.

A raw-edged hole roughly Kendric's size yawned before him. He no longer faced a shadow, only impenetrable darkness.

A quick chirrup made Kendric lift his face to Edanvant's lavender-blue skies. He studied the faint rainbow striations above, the trees at his rear, the swift pulsing silhouette of the bird directly overhead.

Then Kendric walked into the hole in the wall, sword-first.

Sound held its breath. A blue-green shadow world patched the dark wall behind him, making the long-dead surface into a living tapestry. But Kendric knew he could as likely retreat to that window of illusion as double back on his own past.

He had chosen the wall; now the wall would try to choose him.

In his hands, the sword hilt glowed through its wrapped leather thongs until light leaked red through the veins of Kendric's skin. Five colored stones—formed into a single smooth cabochon beringing his left hand's middle finger—glowed their lurid colors: copper, green, silver, black, and dull ocher.

Kendric waded deeper into the darkness, not knowing what to look for until it found him.

"Where is Kendric?" Jalonia asked her daughter.

Irissa stirred uneasily. "The forest. I would take him for a gameskeeper the way he scours those woods of late. He won't say why."

"It's a difficult time," Jalonia said. "Perhaps Kendric feels redundant."

"*I* feel redundant." Irissa glanced to her waist, much easier for her to see nowadays.

Her mother laughed, a silvery sound that finally found silent echo in Irissa's eyes. Jalonia lifted her minnow-fine needle from its darting forays into a tapestry.

"Irissa, all women feel redundant at such times. The babe you bear grows to its own pace. Your role is merely to give it as much space as possible. Besides, you barely swell enough yet to feed a flute with a single scale of notes. Wait until later."

"Apparently I have no choice."

Irissa lay the silken sash she sewed on her lap, her free hand moving to a falgonskin pouch cradled between her breasts. That was a common gesture with her nowadays, and gave her an ever-thoughtful appearance. The feather-scaled skin gleamed violet-green in the daylight pouring down from the hall's high windows. Swollen by an egg-sized lump, the pouch fit her curled palm as if designed to.

"I barely knew you as a child," Jalonia mused, stitching again. "I know you even less now that you are to bear your own child."

Irissa's hand fell to her lap. "Why not? I hardly know myself. I sit indoors and sew like the most contented country girl. I eat the disgusting gruels Dame Agneda prepares. I count stitches and days, yet my life seems ragged and cut from unraveling cloth. I am not made to wait."

"You are young yet."

"So are you. You will make a young grandmother." Irissa shook her Iridesium-black hair over her shoulders and stared at her mother until Jalonia looked up. A ruddy ring tightened on the amber of her mother's irises even as a smile tautened her lips.

"All these years without generation among us," Jalonia reflected. "Oh, it is not long to a Torloc, twenty-five years. But to humans, a little eternity. You should be proud, Irissa, to break the spell that held us Torlocs separate and sterile—first with your magic when you fought the outer evil that threatened Edanvant and became the force that reunited the long-divided Torloc men and women. Now you use the magic of your body to build a new being from the raw materials of your old one."

"I am more alone," Irissa said, "than I have ever been. So much for the Torloc unity. So much for human body magic."

Jalonia's face, so like her daughter's as to seem its twin, twisted sympathetically. Her hand covered Irissa's, obscuring a ring of five stones forged into a single cabochon.

"You are not alone," Jalonia said. "Kendric cannot share your burden as intimately as you might wish, but I can."

Irissa's silver seeress's eyes remained lowered, her figure stiff. Jalonia leaned inward. "Not simply because I am your mother, or have borne a child before you, but—"

"What?"

"I am to bear another!" Jalonia's honeyed eyes brimmed with possibility.

Irissa stared. "You?"

"Yes! Orvath and I are to have a child! A second child. I haven't told anyone yet—not even Orvath. I meant to tell him first, but you seem to need my knowledge and company more. So you see, Irissa, you are not as alone as you think."

"I see." Irissa drew her needle from the sash. A pinpoint of blood dappled the green fabric, looking like a ripe apple on grass. She lifted her pierced finger to her lips, but it paused at the Overstone pouch and lingered.

"Yes, you see," Jalonia repeated. "We will bear our burdens and our joys together."

"What will Orvath say?" Irissa wondered.

Jalonia sat back, thinking. "He will . . . be delighted. He and I can begin again. This time our union and parenthood will not be prematurely ended by Orvath's departure on some errand of Finorian's. It will be a second chance for us."

Irissa rose, slipping the sash over one shoulder and under the opposite arm. She lifted her shortsword from a nearby table and slung it through a knot at her hip.

"I have come to find anything around my waist confining," she explained.

Jalonia smiled indulgently. "Why wear a sword? Irissa, you are home now. Safe. We Torlocs have nothing to fear in Edanvant now that it's truly ours again. You're no longer a wanderer of worlds. Sometimes I think Kendric has adjusted better to a settled life."

"As Orvath has?"

Jalonia looked surprised, then nodded, smiling. "As Orvath."

Irissa turned from her mother and the table they had shared. Her palm hit the sword pommel, driving it into place at her hip.

"You ask a good question. Where *is* Kendric?"

Out of the dark came a lighter dark. Kendric's hands tightened on the sword hilt. A figure skimmed through the murk, then another and another—so many that they circled him.

"Welcome, brother," rumbled a voice familiar from Kendric's nightmares. Dead Valodec lifted his falgonskin gauntlet in greeting, dead Valodec his bond brother, whom Kendric reluctantly had slain in Rule.

Beside Valodec stood another, seven-foot-tall Wrathman. Though he didn't speak, Kendric knew his name too well—Thrangar, meant to wed Irissa but wedded instead to quick death at the undermountain keep of the sorcerer, Geronfrey.

"Some borgia?" a third, throaty voice inquired.

A woman's figure raised a dim goblet to sable lips. Though her eyes were shadow through and through, Kendric painted a remembered violet shade within their tilted lashes. This one, too, had perished in the retreat of magic from Rule. Her name had been Mauvedona and he had more reason than most to remember it.

Other, less vocal forms surrounded Kendric: Verthane, the Rulian sorcerer, now dead; Delevant, the overreaching Torloc wizard now twice dead; assorted lemurai Kendric had killed in the Inlands of Ten. Metal-studded jackets glinted on their hairy forms; the light was just bright enough to glimmer on saber-toothed faces and clawed hands and feet.

Shades of the dead Kendric could confront and exorcise; that was precisely why he had walked into the ambiguously endless land within the wall.

Then something he was less eager to engage resolved into view—a single-horned, ebonberry-black bearing-beast. Its eyes shone as midnight blue as the cut-velvet saddle cloth draping its hindquarters.

Perched sideways atop the bearing-beast was another dark being, a shadow woman with a glitter on her breast and a ground-sweeping black skirt concealing her feet. Her hands lay on her lap, for the bearing-beast bore no bridle. Occasionally one would lift to toy with the gemstones garlanding her neck.

Her eyes were opaque—dead black—and set in a face that was the exact likeness of Irissa's. . . .

"Very well," said Kendric, addressing them all. He emphatically tapped his sword point on the blackness at his feet. It hit—not with the dull thud that indicated earth, nor even with the ring of metal on metal—but it clicked as if rapping a brittle, glassy surface.

Kendric glanced down.

He saw himself glancing up.

He glanced up. He and his circle of visitors peered down at him. Darkness blurred their forms—and his—but they were there. Kendric was squeezed between a magically reflective floor and ceiling. Every move he made in reality would spawn a pair of shadow motions.

"Very well," he repeated, his eyes assessing a triple tier of attackers. "Who will be first?"

They all moved at once, toward him, tightening as inexorably as a rope on a condemned neck. There was not a figure among them that he would hesitate to strike in his own defense—again or for the first time—save Irissa's.

From below, a pack of snarling lemurai leaped at his knees. Kendric lifted the heavy sword, let it lower again and again to cleave fur, blood, and bone.

Brackish mist, not blood, poured out at his blows. Lemurai, sliced into slivers of themselves, still tore Kendric's clothing, still scaled the ladder of his legs with their nails.

A stench worse than a Marshlands bog enfolded Kendric. His defensive thrusts slit lemurai into shadows; shadows reborn came hurtling at him. Lemurai eyes, once bright hungry brown, twinkled sapphire blue on every side, scattering at each oncoming blow, reassembling at each backswing.

Blue-eyed, the great bearing-beast lowered its twisted horn to charge. Blue-eyed, dead Wrathmen and sorcerers surged toward Kendric. Blue-eyed, Irissa let her gaze pinion his and came catapulting forward on the bearing-beast's back.

The intense confusion mirrored itself in the reflective floor and ceiling. Kendric felt himself as the center of a contracting vortex. He seemed to be shrinking under a baleful onslaught of glittering blue eyes and past-shrouded memories.

His sword cleaved attackers, but it was like rending clouds. Faces and limbs severed, stretched, distorted—and conjoined again.

He delved inward, seeking a magic to repel them. He dodged and spun to duel a bearing-beast horn that grew between his feet . . . speared at his head . . . aimed at his heart—all at one and the same time.

Above and below the tri-level conflict, Irissa's image floated, her motion-tangled hair weaving its own black net. Kendric stumbled to avoid striking her, lost his balance, and fell to one knee.

A lemurai from below began gnawing it. Pain felt dry and icy—unreal yet effective. Kendric severed Valodec's head, then struck Mauvedona a fatal blow from shoulder to rib cage. He waded into dark, reflective carnage, never seeing blood, feeling pain but not believing it.

He could not stop them, and he could not stop himself.

The one thing he couldn't bring himself to do was strike Irissa.

"Smite her," a voice urged him the moment the thought flickered in his mind.

"No!" With gritted teeth he halved Verthane only to see the gentle old sorcerer shift into himself once more and push forward again with teeth bared.

Surrounded, hard-pressed, Kendric reminded himself that he had invited this encounter. If he failed, so be it. He vowed not to endanger even a parody of Irissa, not to use his sword against her even by proxy. . . .

"Smite her," the voice insisted.

No. Kendric didn't bother answering aloud who- or whatever called. He was too besieged to spare breath, or even thought. He would never attack Irissa, no matter the cost. Never, never—and did the enemy he sought to expel know that, too?

Fresh thought rinsed Kendric's mind clean. He paused midstroke, batting the nibbling lemurai from his consciousness as if bites from inch-long teeth were no more annoying than a marsh-mite's invisible nips.

Above him in real space—and below and above in the dark mirror of reality that enclosed him as leather binds the pages of a book—Irissa rode passive atop the charging beast.

Kendric spun himself and his sword toward the one target he had vowed most to avoid and lunged.

He had never intended making contact. He never had a chance to make contact. The beast reared, retreating. Over its high, churning shoulder, Irissa's face sank out of sight.

Kendric lunged again. The creature backstepped, its eyes shining balefully blue in its midnight face. Kendric spared a glance for his other attackers. They advanced listlessly, their eyes darkening to emptiness again. He paused to slay their airy forms with methodical blows.

This time they separated from their selves and did not regroup. Gloomy veils of mist draped the darkness. Kendric stood alone in dense black. No reflection peered back at him no matter where he looked. He was alone.

He lowered his sword point to the ground, letting the treacherous surface share the burden of upholding weapon as well as its wielder. The floor had a springy, earthen feel again.

Down the endless circle of hollow wall, Kendric heard the faint rap of retreating hooves.

"Who spoke?" he interrogated the darkness.

A pale figure, then two, resolved near him. The darkness lit their eyes first—gold and silver, respectively.

"We," said the man and woman, speaking together.

Kendric shook his head to clear it. "Ilvanis. Neva. What were you two doing within the walls?"

"Leaving them." Ilvanis stepped sideways and vanished to one thigh and shoulder.

Neva waited to take Kendric's arm and waft him personally into the barrier blackness. "Come," she said, smiling. "What you came to banish has fled."

Kendric heaved a tempestuous sigh of relief and stepped with her. Darkness wavered around him, then his eyes watered under the full power of an Edanvant sun again. He glanced back at the curved metal wall. He stood outside it, as before. Where his sword had smote, the metal was whole again. Healed.

"You can pass through the metal walls?" he asked the white-garbed couple watching him.

"We did when we were caught within the form of the Rynx. Now that we're ourselves again, we retain the same power," Neva explained. "Sometimes we find ourselves . . . drifting into it. Perhaps something from our unremembered past calls us. But why were you there, Kendric? You cannot walk through walls without the aid of a talisman. Irissa would chafe to know what risks you take."

"Leave Irissa out of it. I won't have her worried."

"Then don't take risks," Neva answered.

"Then don't report them," Kendric said, his voice hardening.

Ilvanis raised a silver-white eyebrow that sat oddly on his ever-young face. "Why did you challenge the wall?"

"There's something in it," Kendric answered.

"The same thing that usurped Irissa's magic when she cleansed the forest of the Torloc men's magical scourge?"

"Yes, Neva. The same thing, I think."

"I think so, too." Neva tossed her mane of frost-white hair, then took Ilvanis's arm. "I believe you banished it, for I felt as if a thread connected to my past had snapped. I thought for a moment of home."

"Rengarth?" Kendric paused in redonning his sword.

She nodded, the white woman of the woods, as mysterious in her fur-trimmed gown in broad daylight as she had ever been by night as shape-shifting wolf.

"I will snap every thread between here and there," Kendric vowed. "Every filament visible or invisible. And you two will tell Irissa nothing of it."

"You are most gallant," Neva said, "but I think you do Irissa no service by concealing danger from her."

Kendric frowned at Neva's serene tone and golden eyes, and glanced for support to Ilvanis.

"My sister is right," the young man said. "Were we still encapsuled in the animal form of the Rynx, we might tell you so more forcefully. But we are merely human now, and must argue with our tongues rather than our teeth. We thank you for rending the cobwebs of our past, nevertheless. What threatens Irissa also threatens us."

"How can you be sure?"

"We feel it." Neva linked her free arm through Kendric's. "How did *you* know that evil still lurked in the wall?"

"No magic. I am suspicious by nature."

Neva's golden eyes twinkled. "Then by nature you are well equipped to deal with Irissa's suspicions."

"Where have you been?" Irissa whispered to Kendric that evening as they sat among two scores of Torlocs at the communal dinner table in Citydell's great hall.

"Looking over this world of yours that is now mine."

"There is more to this world than woods. The city that surrounds the forest houses all the people."

"That's why I was looking over the woods," Kendric responded cheerfully, pronging a slab of meat from a passing platter. He offered the portion to Irissa first, but she shook her head. "You should not eat so daintily, especially now—" he began.

"It repels me. Please suit yourself."

Shrugging, Kendric lowered the food to his trencher.

"You're looking *for* something," Irissa decided, nibbling on a wreath of salad greening a wooden bowl.

Kendric's keen gaze swept the long table. "Only the salt cellar."

Irissa rolled her eyes, recognizing evasion even in the guise of earthy innocence. "Here is the salt, and answer my question, please: what are you hunting in the woods?"

He sprinkled a few emeraldlike crystals over his meat. The Torloc native shade, green, tinged almost everything in Edanvant—even the commonest items. While Kendric feigned a state of thinking, someone else had actually been doing it and now diverted Irissa's attention.

"Cousins," a voice rang down the board, "let us have a toast with this recently decanted borgia."

Medoc stood halfway down the endless table, a wrought Iridesium goblet lifted before the gold medallion on his chest.

Kendric invariably found the way he thought of Irissa's grandfather—and the way Medoc actually looked—disconcerting. Despite Medoc's obvious chronological seniority, the man himself appeared to be in the prime of life—an exact contemporary of his son, Orvath; even of his granddaughter; of Kendric himself.

Still, Medoc often donned the ceremonial leadership that the blunter Orvath had ceded. Now he made a fine toastmaster—and, incidentally, distraction.

Kendric gratefully lifted his goblet and looked uncharacteristically attentive.

"In the three months," Medoc began, "since Irissa and Kendric built the bridge between the walls that separated the men's and women's camps, we Torlocs have managed to share one roof after years of divisiveness.

"But I do not toast this fact.

"In these same three months, we Torlocs—for the first length of time within even our extended memories—have been denied the presence of the Eldress, Finorian, who gave the sum of her long life to repel the evil from Without that threatened our reunion. We must not forget that, despite certain . . . failings . . . on Finorian's part, she did not desert us at our direst moment.

"But I do not toast this fact."

A sigh riffled down the table. Torlocs, Kendric thought, might be longer-lived than humans; that didn't mean they tolerated long-winded speeches any better.

"No, cousins, what I toast tonight hails the future—*our* future as a kind that has resolved its internal differences. I bear news, news of a joyous nature."

Knives, forks, and idle chatter paused in expectation as diners hoped to hear the matter's nub at last.

"So tonight I toast . . . the forthcoming birth of the first Torloc to be born in a quarter century—"

Kendric glanced sideways to see how Irissa was welcoming such public attention to a condition that still sat stiffly upon her spirit.

"I toast," Medoc concluded happily, "the undelivered yet not unconceived offspring of Orvath and Jalonia!"

Amid the sighs of surprise interweaving among the women and the nodding grunts of the men, only Kendric noticed Irissa's silence.

"You knew?" he asked as her parents stood at the long table's head and borgia tilted into Torloc throats all up and down the board.

Irissa merely nodded as Kendric, too, drained his cup.

"Are you not drinking?" he asked.

"It does not agree with me."

"Little does of late."

Kendric eyed the distant couple. Jalonia was smiling and, perhaps, blushing. He was too distant to be sure. Orvath, like his daughter, seemed stiffer and more stoic. Odd, Kendric thought, how the two who were most alike were most alienated. Or not odd at all.

"Jalonia told me this afternoon," Irissa suddenly confided, smiling. "I used up all my surprise then."

"I . . . hadn't expected such news."

"One generally doesn't." Irissa's smile turned rueful. "At least now you have company in your condition."

"Apparently I shall need it, if you go ranging through the forest daily on anonymous errands."

"That again."

"That. You don't realize how difficult I find it to remain here at Citydell—immured—with months . . . perhaps years of it still ahead of me."

"You are perfectly fit," Kendric asserted. "Nothing keeps you from woodland wanderings of your own."

"I was not made to wander, but to go purposefully, as you do."

"Irissa, what I do in the woods is . . . exploratory."

"And I could accompany you?"

"Certainly." Kendric lifted his cup to a servingman. A thin stream of green liquor refilled it. "Someday."

Irissa's answering exclamation was sharp but almost inaudible.

"I know!" she went on, her silver eyes glittering. "You hunt the one-horned bearing-beast! You're still set on besting the creature that nearly killed you. Perhaps you cherish some notion of presenting it to me as a steed." Irissa considered further, resting a hand on her midriff. "Or to . . . it. As a pony."

Kendric laughed, long and hard.

"That *is* it, isn't it?" Irissa persisted. "You don't want me to know you take such risks. You spare me because of my, my . . . condition."

"Your 'condition' is more within your heart than within your body. Irissa—" He pressed her hand between the encompassing warmth of his. "Irissa, you are so conscious of the invisible babe you bear and the fact that you bear it. You remind me of myself and my burden of magic. We both make dubious vessels for uninvited wonders."

Emotions flickered over her features as quickly as multicolored threads of color swirled through the black Iridesium circlet banding her brow.

"Look at your mother," Kendric pressed on. "Look at Jalonia. I admit she's borne a child before, and most successfully, but she does not fret over what the future holds." Like most mistakes, his was an innocent one.

Irissa wrested her hand—fist—from his. "We are not alike, Jalonia and I! She sees no gates in rainbows, only mist and pretty colors. You should have heard her today, prattling how this turn of events will give her and Orvath a second opportunity to play out their alliance, how this time they will not be separated before the infant's birth. She thought once that *my* child would soften Orvath toward us both, and she was wrong. Hers will not do any more—perhaps less."

"You Torlocs calculate even such things as births so coldly?"

"So do humans," Irissa retorted. "We Torlocs differ only in that we know what we do—and say it."

Kendric drew back to see her better. "Irissa . . . would you deny a second child the chance you never had to know both mother and father, to grow up free of Finorlan's yoke—although I suppose another child need not be a seeress? Still, if it *is* another you—"

"Oh, hush!" Irissa's silver eyes flashed warning.

Kendric's stare matched hers until Irissa softened.

"I merely practice," she said gruffly, "for my forthcoming new role. I must be allowed my idiosyncrasies. There will be fewer if you avoid discussing my parents' affairs."

"I must be allowed my . . . deviations also." Kendric's amber eyes narrowed. "After all, I bear an unwanted weight of magic. I, too, will go better if you avoid inquiring into my where- and whyabouts."

Irissa sighed and shut her eyes. "Let us not debate. I am uneasy and cannot say why. I would guess that some sorcerous storm is stirring, but all my magical instincts seem blunted by my . . . condition."

"Your condition," he pointed out, "is my condition."

Irissa's eyes flashed open. "I wish you the same joy of it."

CHAPTER
2

THAT NIGHT THE WIND EBBED AND FLOWED THROUGH the open coldstone window of their bedchamber high in a Citydell tower. Irissa dreamed, stirring imperceptibly in the clasp of Kendric's arms.

She saw her younger self in the mountain cavern in Rule, finding the ember-bright egg of another, more dangerous dream, then looking up to see a white foaming tide of panicked moonweasels sweeping down upon her.

Kendric's arms snatched her from out of nowhere, holding her back, holding her safe. Danger flowed past, flood-fast. The foundling egg she clutched to her heart beat red against the soft shield of her breast.

It was the Overstone she clutched in this vision that mingled past dream with present reality, the thing of no apparent use that everyone coveted by rote. Irissa had taken it from the Inlands, but it was not hers. Yet it hung as heart-heavy from the frame of her shoulders, and beat as independently.

Her entire being throbbed to its rhythm. For a dreadful moment Irissa thought she had lost it. Then she pressed her hands to a triple heartbeat, and though the wonder of that multiplication frightened her with its implied alien alliance, still she accepted it.

She walked the land of Dream, after all, where past, present, and future form a six-pronged crossroad, and the invisible air of that world exhaled magic.

From cave to crossroad to . . . window.

The chamber's window frame arched above her, strong and subtly made. Both coldstone shutters spread their wings wide. The air came cold, as when it drapes itself over high, icy places. Below her, the night's moonlit shadow-work patterns wove a blurred plaid of countryside and city-top as far as she could see.

Beyond her, high in the cloud-patched black rags of night sky where stars thrust through like shining fragments of flesh, images shifted.

An old woman, bent nearly double, trudged down the heavens, wisps of white hair wreathing the moon of her face.

An entire company of the lost followed her pale wake—one was a woman whose slighter form momentarily merged with the moon until she seemed to bear it as a lu-minous offspring-to-be; another a windswept woman whose hair blew from horizon to horizon and whose eyes flashed order like steadily burning blue stars; a puff of smoke-black cloud across the moon that expanded into the likeness of a column—a tall, draped column crowned at its wider cap-ital.

Irissa felt her three hearts leap as one in recognition. The dark column surged toward her, floating on the ghostly night ether, solid as death among the phantoms of the sky—inflexibly unbending, endlessly oncoming.

It paused before her—high as a Torloc tower, dark as the shadow of all ten Citydell towers combined. She took it for a figure draped in night-black fabric, hidden except for a crowning circlet of jewel-strewn gold. And then it spread folded arms, sweeping wide the cloak, revealing its defini-tion, identity, familiarity.

No, Irissa said with the mute, frantic mouth of Dream. Nothing of her voice shook the silence except the triple heartbeat only she could hear. That was her sole talisman, her best talisman, she knew without knowing precisely how.

And the dark wings spread to welcome her, revealing an interior emptiness as vacant as Ludborg's oval hood.

She saw through the force, the forgotten enemy—through to the sleek black fall of fabric at its back. The folds smoothed with the easy undulation of rippled water quieting and gave back a shiny smile of dark reflection.

Irissa saw herself emblazoned there on the darkness, barely discernible save that the similarity to herself sang recognition through her veins, and her triple-timed fear pounded to the phantom beat of a faint echo.

Irissa stepped up to the windowsill. Her bare feet should have shrunk from the night chill on the stone, but they did not. She was being drawn as thread is through a needle's eye into a tapestry of another's patient design.

What was worse, her own self plied the needle, plunged her mind sharp and searing through the ragged fabric of time and space. Her will trailed after, a fragile thread that would follow where guilt-headed intention drew.

Nothing could stop her, though she did not want to go, could not go, had committed herself to every other element in her life except the leaving of it. . . .

She could not stop herself, her dreaming self so strong and yet so weak.

She could not save herself.

The window frame drew past her—or she pushed herself past it. She was about to step out onto the night, to step into the dark arms of the waiting empty figure with herself etched upon its deepest distance.

Then, without sound to announce it, her body expanded as with some gargantuan breath. She saw herself swelling like one of Ludborg's crystals, like Ludborg himself, into a great, light round ball gently bouncing against the window frame and as gently rebuffed by it.

The night sucked at her as if to draw her bones through a reed, were even that much space available. A whole window's worth of passage did not suffice—she had stretched herself thin, too high, too wide to pass. She floated, airy as a bubble against the frame as against prison bars.

Her heartbeat—be it one, two, or three—seemed tiny, muffled. The dark figure waited, narrowing and tautening as she watched. She could not pass through to it had she wished to, and she did not wish to.

It swirled into itself then, twisted deep into its own inner darkness until it was narrow as a nail. Each turn pulled upon Irissa's will and body. Each pull was gently balked by her sense of impassable bulk.

She rocked against the window and the night, watching all, able to act on nothing. Her eyes grew heavy with seeing so much and so little, and shut. Her dream ended there, with Irissa rocking, endlessly rocking, against the window of the future and saying—simply . . . no.

Someone was tugging the coverlet down to his toes—no brief chore—and should regret it.

Kendric awoke, alert by nature and by nature annoyed. The room reeked of chill; coldstone windows, splayed, banged in the wind that howled through the bed curtains and roughened the basin water into a small, insistently lapping sea.

He sat up, reaching for the sword that always lay beside him at night even if the position was as lowly as the floor.

Irissa hung from the window frame, he saw then, flapping like a curtain, her hands hooked around the hinges, her feet clinging bare to the stone, her hair whipping back into the room, then out into the night.

Kendric leaped up to aid her and found the wind repelling him. A gritty black dust nailed his eyelids shut; wind drove his hair into his face, pushed his body back as if it were made of straw.

He hurled himself against the chamber's stone wall as at a door to be stormed. The wind relented; perhaps it only forbade him the window. But once by the wall he could pull himself along its anchorage to the window.

Sometimes he clung by the handy hook of a torch

socket; sometimes only the unseen whorls of his fingertips seemed to hold him to a surface from which the wind sought to dislodge him.

Yet step by step gained inch by inch along the floor, Kendric battled toward the window so near in geography and so distant in deportment. Near the blinding, deafening wind-choked aperture he gathered himself, then spun that self into the wind's path again and forced his eyes to keep open.

Endless emptiness churned beyond the window. Foreign towers twisted like long grasses. Mountains shifted under rainbow-shaded suns, and darkness dappled everything he saw, so he could only be half certain of seeing anything.

Irissa still clung to whatever slim unseen lashes held her fast, her body bowing to the wind and then arching back as if about to be snapped in twain and swept into the greedy night beyond.

Kendric clasped his arms around her knees and suddenly sagged, hoping his weight would drag her out of the wind's direct sweep. She sank toward him, his grasp climbing her form, reclaiming more and more of her. He felt the gold underbelly of his ring digging into his fiercely clasped hands. Upon that ring sat the Shunstone, which had banished much good and some evil in its time. That stone he thought of, so plain and unremarkable, so much wanted in another world and then despised.

He thought of the Shunstone and only the Shunstone, intent on rejection, not destruction. Whether force benign or malign called he could not know. But it would find no answer here, not even an echo of itself.

Then he was crashing to the floor, Irissa falling with the full burden of her ordinary weight upon him. The wind released them, refused the room with a haughty final gust, pushing back upon them like a suitor who abruptly reverses his pursuit.

The water basin overturned, ringing brassy to the stones as it sprayed them farewell with a wave of icy liquid. Coldstone circles popped out of slamming shutters and splintered to the floor, rolling hard-edged into their shins and elbows. Irissa's dream and Kendric's waking nightmare ended in imprecations muttered against small injuries more deeply felt for their very superficiality.

Kendric finally rose to the accompaniment of heartfelt oaths and latched the sievelike windows.

"Parables are built around the act of locking shutters after the storm is past," Irissa observed from the floor.

Moonlight flooding through a vacant pane cast a cold core of light along Kendric's grimly set jaw. "How can you jest about such a matter?"

"How can you glower when we are safe now? Besides"—Irissa hauled herself up by the windowsill, then sat upon its edge—"I could never have been drawn through the window, for something made it into a gate for a moment. No gate will accept an unwilling passer—or passenger." Her fingers rested on her waist while she caught a relieved breath. "But I could have been buffeted to pieces before the gate repented and became an ordinary window to Edanvant again."

"Ordinary." The word assumed a mild imprecatory effect on Kendric's lips. He punched a half-dislodged circle of coldstone free and watched it plunge floorward and shatter into light-sparked fragments. "I suppose this was an ordinary wind as well."

"No." Irissa frowned. "Something waits Without."

"Without what? Without mercy? Without hope? Without fail?"

"'Without' as it means 'outside.' Outside ourselves. Outside Edanvant. Without the gate."

"What gate?"

She smiled ruefully. "Whatever gate we take next."

"Strange," he mused. "Were the word 'gate' opened with a letter but one place earlier in the alphabet. . . . There will be no more gates," Kendric declared. "You and I are no longer in a position to test gates, to seek answers. We must consider other things now."

"We did not ask for . . . other things to consider," she reminded him.

"Nor did we ask for other things to consider us."

Kendric turned to face the window, to press his eyes against the paneless frame and regard a cloudless night sky and frozen black and white landscape below.

"Our reticence will not excuse us. But"—Irissa's next words sounded wistful—"I cannot go, even if I would still meet my danger face-to-face. And there is nothing more of the world you wish to see, certainly," she added blandly, "no curiosity drawing you on and on. . . ."

"Certainly not!" He turned her from the window toward the wind-chilled sheets of the bed. "You're sure that this . . . it . . . could not have taken you, even if I had not awakened?"

"Sure as sunrise."

He nodded and drew her back to the bed, pausing only at the foot. Irissa settled wearily into the linens, knowing she would not dream again that night, and would never dream again what had just passed.

Kendric stood indistinct and suddenly uncertain at the bottom of the bed.

"What if it was a world without a sunrise? Or a sun?"

"What?"

"The place . . . Without." He waved toward the window. "Perhaps it had no sun, although I saw a train of them."

"'Perhaps' is the commonstone of words. Find enough of them and you could string a necklace long enough to throttle yourself. Come to bed; make peace with yourself, and you can begin by making peace with me."

"We are not at war."

"No, but we can pretend we have been. Truce is always the best part of war."

CHAPTER
3

THE CITY OF EDANVANT MARKETPLACE THRONGED WITH common folk selling and buying common things—fresh-roasted meats and bags of rainbow-colored tongue-sweets; wovenwear and leatherwork; hammered metal and the metal hammers to pound it with.

Kendric ignored the market's medley of enticing scents and sounds to plant his seven-foot height before a stand offering nothing that appealed to nose or ears. Its only commodity was a row of sunlight-silvered blue glass globes.

A handwritten sign above the stand's paisley awning advertised "Ludborg the Fanciful, scryer extraordinaire" in letters so tortured they seemed etched by the death agonies of a Gilothian fireworm.

Ludborg himself, extraordinaire or not, was nowhere visible. Kendric rested his palms on the translucent globes, unthinkingly warming his hands against Edanvant's autumn chill.

A curtain behind the display parted. Kendric's hands jerked from the globes as if burned.

"Welcome, my overextended friend," Ludborg greeted him. "How go things in Citydell?"

"As well as can be expected with so many Torlocs about."

"And how does the forest do? I often spy you passing by on your way to the inner woodlands."

"The forest goes as forests ever go: wild and willful."

28

Ludborg's rotund figure rolled forward as his voice lowered. "And your . . . ah, lady. How does she keep?"

There was a pause. Kendric's impatient fingers tapped a globe top. "You claim to . . . read . . . these things—for a price?"

"The casting crystals go as your forest, friend—wild and willful. But they have things to say to those who will see. And for you—no charge."

Kendric considered, his burnt-amber eyes narrowing. He pulled the boarskin purse from his belt and dug out a fistful of coins. "I have lordlings now, plenty of them—"

Black metal circles shone like charred suns in his grasp, the same rainbow colors that flashed from ice-clear coldstone sparking their more somber surface. Something else gleamed in Kendric's palm—a smooth silver droplet slipping like liquid among the brunette coinage.

"Lordlings I have to spare," Ludborg demurred. "But that other item—"

"No." Kendric's big fist closed on all his booty. "That is *my* talisman, Ludborg, and not to be bartered for."

A sound like a saw cutting overdried wood wheezed into the space between them. Kendric watched Ludborg's face-shadowing hood for signs of upheaval, but it remained oddly motionless. Still, he knew when he was being laughed at, no matter how surreptitiously.

"Forgive me, marshman," Ludborg finally sputtered. "I see you are the Twice-lands with their talis-this and talis-that. Talis-*things*, say I. Yet you carry the most potent talisman of all on your back and use it to hack and hit."

"My sword is mine to use as I will." Kendric shoved the fistful of coins back into their harbor. "Are you going to give me a . . ."—the word seemed to catch in his throat—"a reading? Or not?"

"Oh, not . . . not. Decidedly not . . . not." Ludborg drew back, his robed body parting the curtains. A blue globe had materialized between the pincered ends of his long sleeves, a fat wick of blue-worm burning at its bottom.

Kendric quickly counted the ranked balls on the counter. None was missing.

"Step 'round and come in," Ludborg invited. "I prefer quiet for a reading, and darkness."

"No doubt," Kendric grumbled, following Ludborg into the stand's rear. "Hand-sleighters always need shadows."

"Not this much," Ludborg's voice admitted from the utter blackness that blinded them both. His unseen fingers—or what he wore for such—snapped. "Blue-worms," he commanded.

The selfsame letters as decorated his exterior sign glowed blue on the darkness, then wriggled into hundreds of individual members. Threads of living light covered the entry curtains, brocading the simple surface.

Kendric regretfully eyed his only egress, now glittering obscenely, then looked back to Ludborg. Between the exiled Rengarthian's supportive sleeves, the globe reflected the blue-worms' bright pattern like an enormous iris.

"You will read yourself, friend?" Ludborg wondered. "It makes for more accuracy."

"I would read," Kendric agreed, "could I see sufficiently."

Another snap of Ludborg's unseen appendages. A line of blue-worms migrated from curtain to ceiling and crossed the upper blackness until they hung above Kendric and Ludborg. Quick as rope-dancers, they swung down from each other's forms—more and more swagging from the first—until they formed a chandelier of pulsing light.

Kendric studied the backs of his blue-washed hands and glanced at the midnight-blue shadow occupying the pursed hood opposite him. The crystal globe itself beamed doubly cobalt, its surface writhing with maggots of light.

"I'll read myself," Kendric promised, unwilling to trust any senses but his own.

At his words, Ludborg dropped the globe to the floor. It hit and smashed. Crashed. Slivered. Chimed. Shattered.

Impact sliced itself into infinite pieces as glass shards splintered like ax-eaten logs into thorn-slim fragments.

Kendric stared at the ruin.

"I have never known," Ludborg offered hastily, "the crystal to subdivide so thoroughly. There is hardly shard enough left for a blue-worm to read, much less a person of such stature as yourself."

Kendric went to one knee among the sapphire shimmer. His scraping boot toe ground shards to glittering flecks.

"Careful, you shall sand yourself," Ludborg warned.

Kendric was too absorbed to answer with more than a grunt. He had come to the shards to seek their meaning, and by Finorian's left elbow, he would find meaning somewhere in this mess.

He plucked the wholest piece from the ruins—a trapezoidal sliver as slender as Irissa's small fingernail. The fragment was large enough to curve slightly. Kendric held it between the jaws of his thumb and forefinger, pressing just enough to contain the sliver without fracturing it.

"The past was never meant to be confined to such a slender remnant," Ludborg cautioned.

"It is the future I seek."

"The future, as I've said before, springs from the past. The present is the illusion that bridges them."

"It's no illusion that your cursed crystal is piercing my fingertips," Kendric said. "Now be still and let me see what moves within this thorn of illusion."

Ludborg rolled more tightly into himself and was quiet.

Kendric stared into the narrow shard, seeing first himself writ large—the slow blink of an eye, eyelashes rooted like stripling trees along a curve that matched the shard's. . . . He sighed his disappointment and would have cast it away. Except—with Ludborg's casting crystals, there always seemed to be an exception in the making.

"I glimpse something."

"Good, good. What?"

"Turbulence. Wind. A . . . rainbow twisting back upon itself. A gate—I see a gate and someone passing in it."

"A gate. Most promising. You know something of gates. Is it one you have traversed?"

"It is a gate; it does not wear a sign, like your stall. It could be one of the two that Irissa and I have taken, only . . . it has an alien sniff."

"Excellent. A reading is all the more accurate for using your nose as well as your eyes. And you are as generously endowed there as elsewhere."

Kendric's eyes flashed into the bottomless hole of hood now opposite him. "You mock me, Ludborg. I would be mindful of your own nose. I may just push my sword hilt through your hood to improve it."

"A calm mind is more beneficial to a reading."

"So is a closed mouth—or whatever you use for one."

Ludborg was silent while Kendric contemplated the sliver of glass again. His expression tightened.

"I see more than a gate—a figure clarifies within it!"

"If you can see a figure in that mote of glass, you could use the eye of a needle as a magnifier."

Kendric ignored Ludborg. His free hand began patting the glass-strewn floor, traveling a geography of shattered glass in search of a piece large enough to latch on to.

In moments he elevated another slip of glass to partner the one still propping his other hand apart. Carefully, he wedged it into place, doubling his viewing area.

"It is a woman," Kendric breathed. "In midgate."

"Perhaps Irissa."

"Not . . . Irissa—though her long hair writhes in some midpassage gale. And . . . she is child-heavy. But far more so than Irissa—"

"You see the future, then."

"It is *not* Irissa," Kendric insisted. Grains of sweat were gathering on his forehead. A tall man was not used to crouching; a powerful one was not accustomed to exerting

the delicate force needed to press scintillas of crystal into
the mosaic of a mirror.

"The past, then," Ludborg suggested.

"I wish to know *who,* not what, I see."

"So do we all, but—alas—crystals come with labels no
more than people do. Something must be left to us."

"I see her clearly now! A tall woman clutching a cloak
around herself but concealing nothing, certainly not her
. . . condition. A woman holding a chain and a dagger and
a—it looks like a huge gold coin. The wind whips the cloak
over her hand, her hair over her face—quickly! Another
fragment."

Kendric's hand probed the broken pieces while his
eyes kept the scene fixed between his fingers. He had no
time for nicety, he sensed, ignoring the crystal's repeated
stings as he would the invisible bites of a marsh-midge.

Blood glittered amid the limpid crystal, and blood
threaded the next long needle of glass he raised from the
ruin.

"A festy reading, Sir Wrathman," Ludborg fussed. "I
did not know it would be such a bloody venture. Perhaps
you should let it go."

"I'd as soon let a moonweasel escape my sword in mid-
blow. I've bled before, more deeply."

Ludborg shrugged, a landmark gesture for him, but
one Kendric missed. The Wrathman's eyes had never left
the sorying glass pinched between his thumb and forefinger.

Now he coaxed the third shard into place beside the
first two.

"There is another figure in the gate!"

Ludborg's form drew up. "Another? Yourself? You
see yourself and Irissa in a gate again?"

"Another *not* myself! A man, though, and tall. Dark-
meined. Perhaps I conjure Torlocs, Orvath and Jalonia—
had Jalonia ever dared a gate to go with Orvath. Perhaps I
see what never was, and leap to conclusions."

Kendric's voice had grown darker, though his figure remained frozen in concentration.

"You see what is important to you, that I know. Whether it is what you *wish* to see neither you nor I can know."

"Perhaps this third piece, this new element in the scene, this man, will reveal something. He looks familiar in an unfamiliar way, as if I were seeing someone I knew . . . but *before* I knew him—"

A teardrop of sweat trembled on the brink of Kendric's eyebrow, swelled and plunged into his eye. He blinked. In that instant, a glass broke its back between his fingers. A shard drove into his thumbpad as the force which had held it snapped shut upon itself.

"Aiiiiii . . ." It was Ludborg wailing in sympathy.

Kendric remained stoic, even as he picked his fingertips free of the future—or the past—embedded in them. Kendric heard a crystal chime falling all around himself and stared down at the broken glass. Among the blue shards, a new array of clear gemstones twinkled.

Kendric elevated one. "A . . . coldstone. As Irissa weeps when she is so inclined. She is not here—"

Ludborg's sly sleeve licked forth to capture another of the small gems. "Coldstone is an item of great value in other places—the tear of a true Torloc seeress made concrete. And now, here, more coldstones, transmuted from the sweat of a true Torloc wizard. I have changed my mind, friend Kendric, and will take my payment now—"

Kendric's hands seized Ludborg's shoulders—or what he assumed to be Ludborg's shoulders. His fists sank into gelatinous emptiness punctuated by a shifting random hardness. The alien feel gave Kendric pause but didn't prevent him from shaking Ludborg—thoroughly.

"No one but I profits by my blood and sweat, magical or not, Rengarthian! Sift these unnatural stones from the glass by whatever means you possess and return them all to me. I'll pay you in lordlings, but not my own substance."

Coldstones clicked into a tidy mound. They levitated

between the two figures, remaining afloat as Kendric swept them three by four by five into the dark depths of his boarskin purse.

"And keep your . . . whatever . . . closed about this," he finished.

"The reading or the coldstones?"

"Both." Kendric rose and pulled Ludborg up with him until the Rengarthian hung suspended between his hands, his empty hood opposite Kendric's face.

"As usual with the weaselly arts of magic, Ludborg, your crystals produce more mystery than they solve. I'll keep my mysteries to myself, thank you, and solve them likewise."

"As you wish, Lordling. As you wish." A few blue-worms fallen from the chandelier blossomed atop Ludborg's hood and wriggled pathetically.

"I have never," Kendric reminded him, slowly lowering Ludborg to the floor and brushing fallen blue-worms aside with his bloody fingertips, "relied on wishes for anything."

CHAPTER
4

THE EYE OF EDANVANT LAY DEEP BENEATH CITYDELL, far below the ten tall Torloc towers, beneath the fortress's crystal-sung gardens of endlessly chiming water, under the beaten Iridesium pillars and cascades of white marble stairs, beyond outer semblance and public pomp.

The Eye of Edanvant had been closed tight for three months.

Since the men had sent talismanic power against the women's forest keep, no Torlocs of either gender had cared to look themselves in the Eye.

With the Eldress Finorian gone, the women had lacked the focus to try rituals of Torloc power. Irissa, their only remaining seeress, had never learned the ceremonial side of her inborn magic. And the men had scorned the Eye's ancient instincts, using it only to spy on the women or buttress talismans wrested from alien places and other wielders.

Now Irissa followed the downward path Kendric had described. She smiled to imagine him taking these dark crabbed turnings at the behest of Finorian's old cat, Felabba. The way was paved with everything inimical to Kendric's nature—mystery, magic, and few comforts.

When the rock-hewn tunnel opened into a vaster cavern, Irissa was prepared for the orchard of jeweled fruit trees that glimmered softly emerald and ruby as she passed. She missed—although she would never admit it to Kendric or anyone else—the wafting compass of a scant white tail to follow, missed Felabba's acid comments and surefooted feline certainty.

She missed—would she care to admit it out loud to anyone, even herself?—Finorian. Edanvant was infinitely blander without the Eldress and her erstwhile cat that was so much more than a cat. Irissa paused, sighed, and put her hands to her hips, perhaps to remember an interior duty, perhaps just to reassure herself of her sword's presence.

She brushed past the last of the sparkling trees and entered the huge central chamber that housed the Eye.

"Lost your way, Seeress?"

Orvath, her father, stood in midchamber, the half-light sparkling around his tall form like a samite cloak.

"No, I have found it. I am Keeper of the Eye now."

"The Eye has blinked." Orvath stepped back. "See for yourself."

Irissa approached cautiously—although Kendric had described the huge inlaid floor map that could assume any geography. For one thing, she found it unnerving that her boots took seven-league strides over alien continents that changed from highland to lowland even as she stepped upon them. For another, she did not trust her father, Orvath.

Apparently that conclusion was mutual. He drew back as she approached as if eschewing contamination.

"I thought you were more concerned now with the future than with the past." Orvath's fleeting glance paused at her midsection.

Irissa felt her shoulders clench. One of the more unsung but irritating side effects of her condition was exactly this: everyone took it as a right to remark upon portions of her anatomy normally and politely and wisely ignored.

"The future is the past," was all Irissa answered as she dropped to one knee to inspect the Eye.

"You sound like Ludborg, who calls himself Fanciful."

Irissa sensed her father looming over her bent shoulders and streaming cloak of hair. He was whole now, strong. She had cured him of the partial paralysis that had afflicted him since shortly after he'd left Rule before her birth. He had taken a gate to a hostile world. There a long-dead Torloc wizard had contended with him, and frozen portions of both his motion and emotion. Irissa had healed the physical, but could not change the spiritual. Now Irissa heard the disconsolate drip of subterranean water and regretted her mercy.

But Orvath had not lied. The Eye—a bull's-eye of deep green malachite inset into the polished stone floor—had darkened to solid black. She passed her hand over the malachite, surprised to see a faint reflection of her palm wave back at her.

Orvath chuckled. "The Eye has closed to us. Once we could glimpse things beyond ourselves through it. Now it will only reflect us back—and then darkly."

"Like the Nightstone. . . ." Irissa named another, more dangerous stone known only to herself and Kendric.

"Nightstone." Orvath nodded. "A good name for it. The Eye has gone blind. It is blacker than Iridesium, without the shifting threads of color that confuse the issue. It is, perhaps, our night that we read in it, our decline as a kind, we Torlocs. Our midnight sunset, if you will—"

"You are melancholy for a man who celebrates fresh proof of his manhood—"

He drew his breath in as sharply as another might unsheathe a sword.

"Jalonia told me, not the Eye," Irissa reassured him.

"You are somber for a mother-to-be," he retorted. Orvath was smiling thinly when she glanced up.

"Perhaps it runs in the family." Irissa stood, meeting her father's gaze until it fell again to the clouded Eye.

"No." His face sobered. "Jalonia is euphoric."

"Was she . . . before?"

"With you?" Orvath turned away before he answered. "Yes. That is always the way of women in that condition."

"Not I," Irissa mused to herself.

"Nor I," he conceded.

Irissa was surprised. "You thought that Finorian sent you on a quest before my birth to sever you from your unborn child. You even believed that Jalonia wished to separate you from me with a mother's jealousy. I should think you would rejoice in a new child, one you can perhaps possess fully this time."

"Perhaps. But in child-getting, one never knows quite what one will get."

Irissa regarded him with her own certain gaze rather than the indirect eyes of seeress or an estranged offspring.

"You . . . do . . . know what you will get, Orvath, don't you?"

His mouth tightened. "I have my suspicions."

"And I mine! You think to replace me finally, is that it?"

"By every force Without, no! I asked for neither event, neither birth, neither . . . problem."

Irissa brushed her hair back over her shoulders as if lightening a weight upon them. "We are alike in that, our reluctance. I, too, find Jalonia . . . overoptimistic."

"And your Wrathman, how does he find you?"

Irissa shrugged and bent to the Eye again. "As I am. He has always known that."

Her father was silent. During his pause she searched the Eye for activity.

"Do not brood down here overlong, Seeress," Orvath bade her at last. "It may turn things awry for you and your . . . progeny."

Amused, Irissa glanced up. "You think I will bear an odd-eyed one?"

"I know what you will bear. You will bear what your mother did for me—grief."

She wrenched her head to look over her shoulder, angered, but Orvath was pacing away, his boots treading the far reaches of the inlaid map.

When the echo of his last step had died, Irissa let herself slump over the Eye. Her long hair fell forward, veiling her peripheral vision. Wispy tendrils coiled on the ceremonial stones; she felt they trailed in water. She found her crouch taxing; already her body seemed less willing to double over itself. She resented the discomfort but ignored it. The Eye of Edanvant remained opaque.

"How do I use you?" Irissa wondered aloud, passing her palm over cool, smooth stone. "Finorian would know. Why would I use you? I might have known once, when I used to know how I would use myself. We change, Edanvant and I. All things Torloc. Even you. Orvath is like me; thus we fear each other all the more. Blink again for me, Eye, and window a brighter future than I yet see."

She bent lower, her gaze boring into the Eye, transmuting the solid viridian stone into a translucent skin, delving for lightness and brightness in its thick dark depths.

Surface colors began to flicker—green strengthened, waxing and waning with its own inner seasons. The variations in color mimicked the veining of malachite, the flecked patterns of a human iris.

The Eye of Edanvant quivered awake under the silver eyes of a Torloc seeress. Irissa sought deep within it for some vision that would clarify the events clouding around her. Images flashed—more in her mind than before her eyes.

She saw Kendric—falling deep into the Eye's obsidian iris, his separated sword spinning lethally beside him. She saw a city of balconies, bridges, and towers shifting from side to side as she watched, until its very boundaries blurred.

She saw . . . the Rynx—whole and white, melting into a snowstorm until its every feather and hair merged with the roiled flurries. She saw her mother, Jalonia, wringing her hands and mourning—what? Orvath? A lost child— and if so, one long since born or one not yet born?

She saw white-meined Ilvanis and Neva limned against

a woodland afire with autumn. They both caught flame and burned away in shades of orange and red, their tattered hair and garments licking at their forms until they vanished.

She saw herself—at last—in some alien place wearing the bulk of an unborn child instead of a sword, helpless, alone. . . . Irissa dashed the heel of her hand against the Eye. It sank to the wrist into some tingling, unsensed substance.

Irissa snatched back her hand. It came free despite her fear, but was gloved in sparkling green flecks that flaked to the floor. The Eye of Edanvant had turned rusty black. Irissa's arm ached icily to the shoulder. She knew she had reached into another world—or into a vision of herself in another world. Her hand had broken a barrier meant to be pierced by her eyes alone.

She knew of only one other person who had so transgressed a physical barrier. Geronfrey, the Rulian sorcerer, had reached through solid stone to touch Irissa in his revenge. His hands had been stripped to the bone. She shuddered and looked at her own hand. Despite a burning chill that manacled her wrist, her flesh was whole. Perhaps Irissa's motive in overreaching her powers was more benign than Geronfrey's.

Another call of the flesh roused her; cramps were squeezing their way from her legs to her shoulders. Irissa pushed herself upright, feeling unbalanced. She had learned next to nothing at the Eye of Edanvant, save that her father was as dubious as she about the redemptive value of acts of generation.

Irissa frowned as she retraced her steps. This time she ground half of Edanvant underfoot and never noticed the map, not even when her passing footsteps left a newly formed alien terrain behind them.

For all the sights she had glimpsed in the Eye, not one had answered her most worrisome concern: why Kendric prowled the forest and what he did there.

*   *   *

"You look tired," Kendric said.

Irissa bristled. "I am not."

Sunfall's first gilt was mellowing the falgon's-eye mullioned windows of their chamber. Soon they would join the Torlocs below for dinner. He took the coldstone-heavy Iridesium comb from Irissa's hand and plied it through her hair.

She softened into his petting as a cat does. "My shoulder aches," she volunteered, but when he asked further, she would not say why.

No mirror backed the small stand that served as Irissa's dressing table. She could have imported one, but had become used to not seeing herself after all the years the exercise had been forbidden her.

Now that her seeress's silver eyes could dare her own reflection in any medium, she found she was used to forgetting herself—or at least her external self. For a rare moment, though, she wished for a mirror. She could have peeked at Kendric's reactions in it.

"You visited the forest today?" she began casually.

He laughed, stroking so firmly through her hair he drew her head back. "No, the City."

"Edanvant itself?"

"What other city is there in this divided Torloc world of yours? Endless Edanvant, the city that circles its central forest—an unnatural arrangement, I say, for wildwood to be so contained and city to be so narrow yet pervasive."

"What did you do in the City?"

"Explored the marketplace. Looked into its high and low. Talked over old times with Ludborg. Ate."

"Ah."

"And you . . . what did you do today?"

"I . . . explored the Eye of Edanvant."

The comb's rhythmic strokes stopped. "And found—?"

"My father."

"Hm. What had he to say for himself?"

"He is not overjoyed by his impending second fatherhood."

"What would you expect from a man as cold as Orvath?"

Irissa shivered. "Perhaps I was fortunate that Finorian sent him away before my birth."

"No one is fortunate for the loss of a parent, however inept."

Irissa studied Kendric in the mirror of her soul and saw a new reflection. "You never knew your mother, that is true! She died at your birth. I think you so self-sufficient that it never struck me until now. . . ."

She could feel a renewed pull on her hair. "I knew my grandmother." His voice smiled as the comb curried the long strands to the very tips. "Jalonia will make a good one."

"But what kind of mother will she make? And I?"

"Irissa, you worry at the future like a moonweasel at its prey! Let go. You are what you are, as they were what they were—Jalonia and Orvath each. You mourn the past too much; that's why you fear the future."

"I mourn myself; it is my right."

"Then leave me out of it."

Irissa intercepted the comb on his next stroke, then his eyes. "And if I said that to you?"

His hands curled around her shoulders. "I should know you didn't mean it." His eyes darkened from honey to gall. "Irissa, I can't tell you what I do! I hardly know myself. But some . . . danger lingers in the forest—"

"You have no right!"

"What—?"

"You have no right." She rose against the dead weight of his hands. "You have no right to court danger anymore. You have courted me—and won. You owe me your safety."

"I will do what I must. And perhaps it isn't for your sake alone that I confront the forest. . . ."

That thought struck Irissa with even less favor. Her face drank deeper from its own pallor. "You would disquiet the mother to protect the unseen child? No wonder Finorian thought my father Orvath too overbearing an influence for his firstborn! Such solicitude—"

"Irissa!" His hands tightened on her shoulders as if he would shake her, but he didn't. "You bemoan the leash childbearing puts on you, but then turn and loop the same constraint over my head, don't you see—?"

"I see that we used to share danger and safety, we used to be of one mind, and now are of two."

Kendric's jaw tightened. Sometime in the last moments, his hands had left her shoulders. They clenched at his sides, then relaxed.

"Perhaps," he said, "we should each remain one."

"Simple enough for *you* to say!" she flared back, her face lifting defiantly.

Words balanced on the brink of his lips, a silent syllable forming there and freezing. He turned and left the room.

Irissa watched him leave, disbelieving that something so solid could melt so quickly from all her senses. He was gone—look, feel, sound, scent of him. The room seemed wrung of life. Regret rubbed itself around her ankles, a purrless cat, then rose and entwined her like a moonweasel.

Pride repelled the feeling, kept the room unoccupied and still, kept everything the same. And not the same, Irissa thought, her fingers playing across the comb's jeweled back. She picked it up, but it seemed too heavy, or her hair too long, or the idea of combing too pointless.

The sun was winking red through the windows. Irissa sat on her stool before the mirrorless dressing table to wait for dusk.

*   *   *

The table that night creaked under a weight of ewers, goblets, and trenchers. Serving platters of pewter and copper and rare green-gold flashed down the board under burdens of stewed, baked, roasted, steeped, and boiled crudités and delicacies varied enough to tempt any palate.

Now that the Torloc men and women were reunited, now that game reinfested the forest and could be harvested, now that separated Torlocs were not obliged to rely on all-vegetable or all-flesh fare, they feasted.

Normally, Kendric's plate was heaped with a sampling of all. This night, he was methodically chewing his way through a covey of city-bred puff-quail; their tiny bones piled into a lacy tower on his plate rim. He kept his shoulders hunched and his elbows on the table and his mind on his meal.

Beside him, Irissa sat picking at a slice of cold rhubarb-green pie. Except for a heightened color under her eyes, her face was as white and well-set as the custard that served as her main course.

Around the two, reunited Torlocs ate and talked and laughed and carried on with such camaraderie that their glowing good fellowship veiled Irissa and Kendric in the same taken-for-granted emotion.

"I am glad to see color in Irissa's face again." Jalonia dipped between them for a moment, her hands squeezing their shoulders in greeting.

Her butterfly-brief presence fluttered away, leaving Kendric's shoulders stiffer than before, and Irissa more violently flushed.

"I have found," Medoc announced over the clamor, "a special vintage in the undercellars of the forest keep."

"A special vintage . . ." Mclyconial, her off-color eyes now appearing to focus slightly off center, rose to rap a long wooden serving spoon on a platter rim. "A special vintage requires special attention. Silence while Medoc introduces his find.''

"From beneath the forest keep?" Jalonia wondered into the sudden stillness. "Finorian never spoke of wine stores there—"

"Nevertheless, I have found one keg of ancient Edanvant vintage.'' Medoc hoisted a gnarled wine cask atop the table. Platters up and down the board rattled like bones to the weight of its arrival.

"In the forest keep?" Dame Agneda's squat form drew up in disbelief. "The women's keep? I beg your pardon, Medoc, but I tended the larder when we women lived there. There was no wine cask."

"Perhaps you did not explore the farthest reaches of the undercellars, as Kendric did."

All eyes turned to him except Irissa's.

Kendric finally looked up from his plate. "I . . . thought it wise to take inventory, see what damage the flame scourge had left. I found that cask intriguing, and Medoc was more than interested when I brought it back."

"Why not? It is borgia, cousins." Medoc's hand pounded the keg's curved side. "First borgia, stored in a weepwaterwood cask so ancient it has turned green to match its heady contents. Perhaps our earliest ancestors made this rarest of libations."

Medoc alluded to an era distant enough to quiet even the time-oblivious Torlocs. In the silence, Kendric mumbled, "I forgot about it," to no one in particular.

"But I did not!" Medoc braced the cask on his cocked knee and set a drinking horn under the spiggot. "Nor the drinking vessel you found with it." The horn was an odd vessel, spiral-twisted out of some unknown root.

A gleaming stream of green poured down the horn's dark throat. Medoc shut the spiggot. Irissa watched him with dead eyes, seeing three teardrops of borgia dribble from the spiggot to the tabletop.

Medoc lifted the filled vessel.

"This is first borgia in the vessels of our forebears. On this, our first night of unstrained reunion, I propose that we seal our truce. Will Irissa, seeress and first among the women, drink a common toast with Orvath, her father and first among the men?"

Heads swiveled all down the table. Irissa watched their inevitable joint focus sharpen on her. She straightened, resisted an urge to glance to her left, then stood.

At the table's far end, beside Medoc, Orvath rose also, a look of sour surprise congealing on his features. Medoc looked at his son.

"Who drinks first?" he asked. Neither Irissa nor Orvath moved. "Irissa?"

She met her grandfather's eyes, as dark as her father's and far more forgiving. The horn in his hand tentatively saluted her. Such uncertainty in a man as self-certain as Medoc swayed her.

"Yes," she said, sounding defeated.

Medoc grinned and handed the horn to Dame Agneda, who passed it to the Torloc man opposite her, and he to the woman opposite, so the vessel laced its way down and across the board, from man to woman and Torloc to Torloc.

By the time it reached Irissa, the rim sparkled with spilled borgia and the twisted wood slicked her hand.

She lifted the horn, frowning slightly at its somehow familiar form.

"To Torlocs, and our new union of an old kind." A smile tilted her lips as she lifted the metal chased rim to her mouth. Chill green-gold touched her lips, then the borgia's potent syrup flow—warm on her tongue and burning hotter as it surged down her throat.

Irissa pulled the horn from her mouth.

"Too strong a vintage for seeresses?" Medoc eyed his son sideways. "Orvath will not refuse the challenge to taste the past."

Hands clapped and knife handles rapped the tabletop.

"Pass it to me," Orvath said. "What a seeress can do, so can a man."

Irissa lowered the horn. It suddenly seemed heavy, half slipping from her fingers.

A hand took it from her. A large right hand, ringed with a single cabochon stone made up of five colors. Irissa ignored the hand's possesser and watched the horn pass back up the table from hand to hand, woman to man.

She sat, her part in Medoc's surprise ceremony over. An aftertaste twisted her lips. She would have raised a cloth to wipe them of the musty residue of old borgia, except that her arms felt too heavy to lift.

Her eyes moved leadenly to the drinking horn. Its spiral torque made it seem to spin as it progressed from hand to hand. Borgia bubbled over the rim, spilled onto the table, and foamed into a lacy cloth that seeped around the platters and spread.

Fascinated, Irissa watched the frothy green pool slide toward her as slowly as a snake. She could feel her sip of borgia leeching into her limbs, the rhythm of her heart, the pulsing in her ears, behind her eyes. Her eyes widened. Sound had ceased. She saw the Torlocs laughing, saw open mouths and half-shut eyes, saw knife ends pound table-wood, and metal platters joust metal goblets in passing. She heard nothing.

Her fingers tightened and reached for her sword pommel. Something blunted itself on her palm, but her skin passed no judgment on it—it had no familiar shape, temperature, feel.

Irissa blinked. The motion left a veil of palest green over her vision. Beyond it, Torlocs laughed and a twisted goblet made its passive way to Orvath.

Her mouth opened, or she thought it did. She could no longer feel it. Her eyes focused on the goblet, to spill it, she thought. Medoc reached for the returned vessel and presented it triumphantly to Orvath.

In the soundless, senseless world within Irissa, emotions unreeled like ribbons. She must say something, do something. Someone must—

"Your toast, Orvath." Medoc watched his son elevate the vessel to his mouth and smiled.

Orvath's lips cracked. The horn tilted toward them. His head angled back.

A table knife slashed the long distance of the board and drove a knuckle deep into the hardwood just before Orvath. He froze and glared down the table. Only one figure stood.

"Don't drink it," Kendric ordered, his face brooking no resistance. Then he bent under the table.

"Is he mad?" Medoc whispered into a silence so profound that everyone heard him.

Kendric, white-faced despite his stooping, straightened, bringing up Irissa's senseless, open-eyed form. Her silver eyes had turned the color of old borgia.

CHAPTER

5

MEDOC STOOD LOOKING OUT A WINDOW ONTO BLACKEST night. Below Citydell, lights twinkled through the town in pale imitation of the luminous stars above.

"I couldn't resist," he said in a dead voice. "I drank a flagonful myself. First. Three days ago."

Irissa lay on the bed, still dressed, the skeins of her dark hair radiating around her like spokes from a wheel. Her green eyes were open, seemingly staring at the draped tester high above.

Jalonia hovered nearby. The braids circling her ears cast harsh shadows on a face already whittled by worry.

Kendric, his emotions so contained they seemed to armor him, moved from the bedside to Medoc and the window.

"Three days ago, you say? And—?"

"I felt no ill effects, Kendric, I swear. True, the borgia had a cloying taste, but it's *old*! Perhaps the first Torlocs made it differently—"

"It's obviously tainted, Medoc! How could you serve it?"

"But I drank it myself with no harm!"

Kendric's eyes shut for a moment, as if the dark night were too bright to watch. "Then the harm was put in after."

"You think . . . poison?" Jalonia whispered from the bedside.

"Look at Irissa! Had she not succumbed so quickly, Orvath would have drunk."

Jalonia clenched Irissa's limp hand more tightly and glanced to the chamber door. Through the hinge crack, a shadow paced across the flickering illumination of a wall torch.

"If I did not want to believe better—" Kendric began, his voice low and taut in Medoc's ear.

The Torloc turned to him, his head shaking. "No, I had no intent other than to foment peace. I would hack my arm off to the shoulder to undo it! I would hurl that cursed cask into the Swallowing Cavern itself and the ill-found vessel after it—"

Kendric's eyes glimmered desperately. "The vessel! Where is it?"

"Here, if you wish it."

"Yes, here, and the cask as well. Don't destroy them, Medoc—learn from them!"

Medoc left the window. He paused at the foot of Irissa's bed, then hurried from the room. Kendric paced back to Jalonia, then glanced at the pendulum of shadow sweeping back and forth beyond the ajar door.

"Orvath is shy of thresholds?" he asked.

Jalonia's eyes begged his for understanding. "He is oh, it's strange how one can wound another, yet flinch from the consequences of an outside blow to that same person! I can't explain it."

"Nor I." Kendric abruptly knelt by the bed. His fingers combed the finest, farthest tendrils of Irissa's hair. "Do you think he feels anything?"

"Oh, he feels. Orvath feels." Jalonia kept careful watch on Kendric's profile. "Perhaps he is ashamed to have escaped harm when she did not. He is . . . in a way . . . competitive with Irissa."

"Even to the death?" Kendric's tone was harsh though his moving fingers remained remarkably gentle.

"He is . . . consistent in his pride. It mortifies him that Irissa should be stricken under his roof."

"Citydell is all our roofs now," a new voice said. Dame Agneda's homely plump figure stood behind Jalonia, two vessels in her hands. One was the empty drinking horn; the other held its remaining contents.

Kendric rose to take them from her and place them side by side on the small dressing table. A moment later, Medoc lumbered over the threshold with the almost-full cask. Outside in the hall, a shadow still paced.

"Well?" Medoc asked.

They stood contemplating the tabletop, baffled by these commonplace items. Torches at the room's white stone perimeters beat like moths' wings against the dark. Torchlight lit their features in timid flashes, as if what lurked in their faces' deepest crevices was too awful to illuminate.

Then Kendric's finger dipped into the remaining borgia.

"No!" Jalonia hung from his wrist.

He lifted his hand into the light anyway, studying the pallid green drop on his fingertip. For a moment it seemed he would touch it to his lips, but his glance suddenly moved to the empty drinking horn.

He picked it up, turned it, let the light spiral around its twisted curves. Kendric turned from the others as if to consult the vessel privately. He paced with it, examined it, stroked it. At last he clasped the wide drinking end with both hands, suddenly aiming the opposite, pointed end at his midsection—daggerlike.

Dame Agneda screamed. Medoc strode forward.

But Kendric's self-destructive gesture ended just before connecting. He raised the vessel again as if to toast the greenish light. Then he turned the thing upside down. No remnant borgia dripped out.

"Horn, not wood!"

They stared at him.

"It's made of *horn*, not wood." His face burned with

the light of discovery. "I took it for weepwaterwood root, to match the cask. But it's made from horn—the discarded horn of a bearing-beast! Don't you see? I was gored months ago in the wood, when the Hunter came and sounded his horn so piercingly I felt its note stab my very soul. . . . Could the poison imbue this vessel? Medoc, from what did you drink your borgia?"

Medoc's dark eyes hollowed. "A cup. A carved stone cup. The horn had never been used. Until this night. I was . . saving it for the ceremony."

Kendric regarded Medoc, his face stolid. Sharp words whetted themselves on his tongue, but he couldn't accuse the man of more than Medoc himself did.

"How old do you think it—the drinking horn?" he asked instead. "As old as the cask?"

"Surely. Torlocs have not drunk from such primitive vessels for hundreds of years."

"Yet a bearing-beast of the woods gored me with a horn like this not many months ago. Perhaps some long-dead ancestor wore this horn. I haven't seen the creature I fought since, and thought it banished. Perhaps it shed its horn with the seasons. Perhaps it lingers. Perhaps the beast itself is the taint, not the borgia. Old or new, this horn has done its work. There is nothing left to do except root out the source."

"The source?" Jalonia had returned to the bedside and now stroked her fingers along Irissa's pallid cheek.

Kendric went to a low chest under the window and lifted his longsword. "The source is the woods, home to the dark force that usurped Irissa's magic, that has always desired to harm her, that still taints the things of this world. I drove it from the wall and out of the forest keep. It has run to ground elsewhere. I will whip it forth from there as well. I should have never rested—"

"Don't blame yourself, for my sake," Medoc broke in.

"I blame no one but the sorcerer Geronfrey. It is he who, once denied Irissa by herself, determined to take her from us for himself."

"Geronfrey!" Jalonia's eyes widened like a child's but her face had hardened. "I remember hearing of Geronfrey in Rule, a powerful archmage. He has hounded you two from world to world—?"

"He has hounded Irissa." Kendric slapped the sword upon the baldric over his back. "I now hound him."

"Wait for daylight, man!" Medoc raised a comradely hand to Kendric's arm, then thought better of it.

"Why? Geronfrey waits for nothing."

"Let some of us accompany you."

"You'll never pass where I am going." Kendric was at the door. He paused to regard Irissa, her body arranged as formally on the coverlet as a corpse upon a bier. His shadow-haunted face remained set.

"If she wakens and finds you gone—" Jalonia half rose.

"If she wakens, it doesn't matter if I never come back."

Kendric moved, blocking the door, the light—and then the door frame was empty. A moment later the hall light danced as he ripped the torch from the wall.

Out of the deeper shadow Kendric's departure left behind him, Orvath edged over the threshold into the room at last.

Medoc moved to the bed's other side to make room for Orvath beside Jalonia. "I had grown fond of Irissa, my never-seen granddaughter, despite her seeresshood." Medoc's fingers touched the Iridesium circlet banding her temples. "Irissa does not seem one to lie in living death, no matter the source. Perhaps she can help herself."

"If she could have, she would have warned Orvath." Jalonia buried her face in her hands.

"You believe that?" Orvath had come to stand behind her.

"She healed you once—why let you fall later?"

A scimitar of smile touched Orvath's harsh lips. "True. She is stubborn . . . too stubborn to fade before her time."

"But poison—and, Orvath, what of the child she carries?"

"Her fate rides with Irissa. I doubt either of them is done with us."

"*Her*?" Jalonia stared up at him, shock making her face into a gawking parody of itself.

Orvath leaned down to pat her shoulders. "I presume another seeress—or two—in the family. I was ever a pessimist."

Citydell's great hall with its forest of weepwaterwood columns receded past Kendric's attention. A hush infested the soaring spaces; no Torlocs could be seen and—what was more unusual—none of the many townsfolk who served them.

It was as though, with Irissa senseless, the entire vast fortress had surrendered its energy. Kendric didn't care what shadow her absence cast on a larger world. The smaller world within him contracted to a hollow core of heart-heavy rage. That their last words had been high-tempered only deepened his sense of unutterable loss.

Something whispered along the red marble stairs he approached. He paused, lifting his torch, ready to fight anything rash enough to accost him.

Perhaps the only one in Citydell who could safely do so appeared in a flutter of albino robes, approaching at an intersecting right angle. Kendric's strides paused, then resumed.

Steps pattered down the risers after him. "Kendric! What's wrong?" A stone would have heeded the concern in Neva's voice.

Kendric managed to turn impatiently, his feet bridging three steps. "Irissa has been stricken by some magical toxin. I go to the woods to find its sender."

"The woods?" Ilvanis's slim figure came clattering

down the steps, too. "You suspect the influences you banished from the wall the other day?"

"Yes. I cleansed the wall and the forest keep, but I neglected one last place because I disliked it more than the others." Kendric's boot toe tapped the marble riser, eager to be off.

"Where?" Neva's worry polished her eyes into beads of pure gold.

"The singing stones." Kendric turned and took the steps three at a time.

"And Irissa? Can we help?" Neva called. Her voice almost rose into the mournful wail of a wolf's for a moment. That gave Kendric another instant's pause.

"Perhaps. Try!" he shouted over his back, through his teeth. "Try anything!"

Ilvanis and Neva remained staring after him. With their elegant white garb drooping against the carmine stairs, they resembled discarded candlelilies past their prime. At the same moment, their hands reached for one another.

"Is there no end to woes here in Edanvant?" Neva wondered.

Ilvanis smiled sadly. "Kendric would say . . . only if we try to make one."

"But we are displaced, cut loose not only from our native world but our time in it or anywhere else! We hardly know who or what we are—other than brother and sister of the same ancient birth, exiles from the same lost land of Rengarth. How can *we* ease an ill among other people in another place?"

Ilvanis swung her hand. "We won't know unless we try. At the least we owe these people who have sheltered us a sharing in their grief."

They turned and ran up the stairs.

The hall outside Irissa and Kendric's bedchamber remained dark without the torch. Ilvanis's and Neva's ghostly figures wafted through it to the room beyond.

Here all light had congealed—tapers flickered atop

every surface and torches wavered along the pale walls. It seemed there was not light enough in Edanvant to illuminate fully the ghastly sight of Irissa lying entranced upon her bed, her silver eyes gone green even to the whites.

The Torlocs within the room stiffened as Ilvanis and Neva entered. They regarded the two Rengarthians as mystifying phantoms. No one had ever seen them eat, for instance; they never shared the dinner table with their hosts—or much else.

Ilvanis and Neva came and went like tendrils of fog, sharing a space with other people, but never occupying a concrete corner of their minds. That until recently Ilvanis and Neva had shared a single form—that of a creature with a white wolf's body and owl's head called the Rynx—disturbed even the magical Torloc kind.

So Jalonia, Orvath, Medoc, and Dame Agneda looked up from worry-locked faces and kept aloofly silent at the pair's entrance.

"Oh . . ." Neva's gilt eyes waxed green-gold in the torchlight. "So I came to a Torloc tower once, wounded and not myself. Irissa succored me."

She knelt by the bed, her fur-edged sleeves brushing Irissa's clothes, and took a slack hand in hers. Across the coverlet, Jalonia had drawn back. Orvath's long fingers curled fiercely into her shoulder.

"Is there nothing you can do?" Neva consulted every eye.

They glanced away from the eloquent sympathy of that steadfast look. Medoc spoke, his voice rusty from silence.

"We can wait and hope. She seems frozen, not dead. And we . . . cannot close her eyes. I tried."

"Her eyes." Ilvanis moved behind his twin, his youthful features sharpened by the violent torchlight. "I remember seeing eyes like that before—"

"Open?" Orvath inquired icily.

"Abrim with borgia to the lashes," Ilvanis answered, no reciprocal discourtesy in his tone.

"Where have you seen eyes like that?"

Ilvanis glanced across to Jalonia. "Neva and I have only ragamuffin memories of our past, a few poor tatters of this place and that person . . . but I do remember eyes greened by poison."

"He calls it poison! Kendric was right." Medoc sounded hopeful. "Perhaps his errand will destroy the evil at its source."

"Perhaps." Neva let Irissa's hand slide back to the coverlet. "But I can feel her deepest inner warmth ebbing. Medoc may be right; she is freezing."

Jalonia convulsively clasped Irissa's other hand. Moments later, she, too, relinquished it with a shudder. "Ice. Sheer ice. I cannot hold it. You said 'freezing' as though it were a process with an . . . end."

Neva nodded. "Look at her eyes."

Irissa's eyes were still open, still green-tinted.

But between the frost forming on her dark eyelashes, the irises themselves had turned milky under a thin skin of solid ice.

CHAPTER
6

GREEN FLAMES STREAMED INTO A BANNER BEHIND THE torch as Kendric forged through the dense night forest. Invisible creatures rustled on either side; he didn't even wonder what they might be or how dangerous.

Since he had walked the bridge from Edanvant and crossed the walls where they had melted during the Torloc confrontation, only trees surrounded him—and his own, thickset thoughts.

Half of those thoughts were litanies of regret for his behavior toward Irissa. The other half were self-flagellating itemizations of the thousand ways he had neglected to purge the forest of every trace of the sorcerer Geronfrey and all his works. And he had discovered—retrieved—the very vintage that had drunk so deeply from Irissa's essence!

Now Kendric drove as straight as memory could take him toward the one place he most wished to avoid in Edanvant. From there, he guessed, came the poison that had taken Irissa.

The woods weren't helping him get there. His path seemed interlaced with trees. Striplings whipped his exposed face and hands. His back-bound sword swung diagonally with his strides, tangling with the underbrush.

Kendric shouldered free of all impediments. From time to time, he'd try to consult the unseeable sky and study the undeviating trees. Night had him in its inexorable grip—night like the paw of a great black cat cupped over a

59

fruitlessly scurrying mouse, lifting only to press down harder again.

But Kendric was hunting for a darker piece of night, and hoped he could make it declare itself soon. Night! The notion stirred a new thought. He switched the torch to his right hand, then shone its light on his left one.

His knuckles gleamed green as leaf wax in the emerald glow, but his ring reflected back a tiny torch flame in its cabochon . . . a tiny torch flame and—on the darkest spoke of the masterstone's five-color wheel—a black tower.

The Nightstone of Geronfrey reflected the tower of Geronfrey—the Black Tower Irissa and he had found when first deposited in Edanvant by a rainbow gate.

Kendric gauged the direction in which the tiny tower pointed—east—and bore to his right. Striplings bowed to his blunt-bodied passage.

When a clearing came, Kendric had stalked well into open air before he realized it. Ahead lay a door of darkness, a shard of night so solid that he took it for an absence of structure rather than a shape—a hole in the fabric of Edanvant, eaten away by time and patience.

Kendric wedged the torch into a tree crotch and unanchored his sword from its scabbard. He glanced into the Nightstone of his ring and approached the blackness. As the image of a tower neared the actual emptiness in the night, it seemed to cast a shadow.

Coming closer, Kendric recognized the Black Tower he had seen before by daylight. It assumed its shape gradually, stones thrusting atop stones, rubbing each other raw and forming a crude, high edifice.

Kendric circled the foundation, surprised to find the curve of stone continuous. At any moment he expected a void—an ebony void brimming with some black libation.

There was only the tower, much as he remembered it—high and dark and round. There was no door, and that was how he remembered it, too. He recalled other, less plain facts—how Irissa had strummed the stones to discover they sang; how she had stepped into them and vanished; how he had followed and seen unwelcome things within the tower's inner curves.

He let his sword hilt swing against the stone. A gonglike sound echoed in the woods, raising a rustle of sleeping birds from nearby trees.

Kendric kicked the stone. His foot rebounded, smarting through the thick boot leather.

He finally let his hand feel the alternately polished and rough-cut surface, seeking the invisible cracks of a door. When his palm plunged into ice water, he knew he had it.

This time his booted kick slipped through stone as into pudding. There was a screech of discord. The tower's side amputated his leg to the ankle. Kendric finished the step and took another, each motion sawing raucous sound from the stones he passed through.

Night tired of toying with him and slipped him fully into its dark warm maw. Disconcerted, he felt a sudden absence of the wind that had whipped his torch flame all the way here. His hair flattened across his forehead, sticking. His clothes hugged his body and breathed when he did. Sound wound down, except for the thud of his heart blood. He was alone in the dark, and the dark knew it.

He waited, his joints settling, the sword weighing heavy in the hands he could not so much as see. His mind saw, though—saw a hilt-light beaconing through other times of dark and doubt.

As he thought, so it did. His ringstones glowed in the borrowed gleam leaking through his fingers. Warmth softened his face and lightened his heart. Beneath him was solid ground; his resting sword point dimpled it. Darkness recoiled somewhat.

Then the night yawned and decided to play games again.

A spark of light near his feet swelled until it illuminated the inside of the Black Tower. Kendric saw a circular series of archways leading to vistas of alien chambers. Each archway was like a mirror that reflected some segment of himself—a piece of shoulder or boot top, forehead or foot.

He seemed to be fractured and disappearing down numberless hallways into infinite rooms.

He wanted to run after his escaping selves—to grab a fleeting scrap of tunic or belt. He had already lifted a foot to take a step when he remembered his previous sojourn inside the Black Tower—and his conviction then that, other than a ledge around the perimeter, there was no floor, only deep, hollow vacancy.

He glanced down.

It was like looking straight into the Swallowing Cavern itself. The light he had seen, the source of the new illumination, was a lone glittering eye inset in the navel of some sprawling creature that inhabited the vast well of darkness below.

Kendric's back flattened against the tower's inner wall. He edged along the circular interior ledge, each step rubbing his scabbard on the stones. The beast below shifted its lolling carcass to keep its lurid eye on his progress.

Kendric kept moving, peering across the gulf at unfamiliar halls that seemed alike. He wouldn't perceive so many doors unless one was true, he thought. Magic, more often than not, he had noticed, was designed to distract one from something less magical and therefore more vulnerable.

If Geronfrey had an entrance to Edanvant in this tower—and Kendric had glimpsed sorcerous shenanigans here before—then the multiplicity of archways must disguise a single true opening.

See with all your senses, Irissa had instructed him more than once. See into and through and beyond a thing to find the truth of it. See thusly, and see through the eyes of magic.

Kendric knew not what to look for—other than hope, other than the slimmest thread of Irissa herself, a thread as long and resilient as one from her head.

Once, Irissa had plucked such a hair and fashioned a bridle for him to snare a one-horned beast beyond catching. Irissa's silver seeress's eyes were her rarest feature, but

Kendric couldn't bear to remember her eyes now, poisoned as they were by the lethal borgia.

He thought instead of her hair, black as Iridesium and, like the rainbow-tinted metal, lightened by its own inner fires of red, blue, and violet, especially when sun-struck.

A patch of darkness in a chamber opposite him shimmered as he edged into view of it. Kendric peered, letting his innermost senses see through the dubious medium of his eyes.

Something glossy lay tossed over a chair—a dark satin cloak embroidered with crimson, azure, and gold threadwork. The fabric shivered, shook, separated. A wedge of white surfaced through it as through a veil.

How had he not *seen* it before? He didn't stare into shadow or study forgotten garments! A *woman* sat in a corner of the chamber. Even now her pale face lifted from the fancywork in her lap to show him eyes of . . . silver . . . through the parting curtains of her long dark hair.

Irissa! And . . . not . . . Irissa.

He shouted her name anyway.

The singing stones around him trilled it back until the syllables died in sibilant echoes. The beast below writhed its long, segmented body, then dimmed its one eye to an ember.

Kendric's boot jolted when a piece of the narrow ledge beneath him crumbled and sifted downward in an ashen fog. The monster coughed, its half seen body bucking to its unseen extremities.

The woman across the pit from him—no more than a dozen strides away as Kendric would have taken them had there been a solid floor—looked up, directly at him, her face puzzled, as if she had heard something unexpected.

She was weaving a bronze wire net. It draped her midnight lap, glittering like scales. At each wire crossroads, a jewel winked—gems of every color, not only common crimson, ultramarine, and emerald green, but peach and fawn and palest peridot and topaz and pink and other clear winking colors Kendric had never thought to name.

All this delicate richness spread over the long skirt sweeping from her lap to the floor. Her fingers seemed almost caught in a cage, they were so entwined with the bronze skein.

A crack at his feet made Kendric sidle farther along. Stone broke from stone—basalt sheering off from basalt. Where he had stood gaped a hole a gigantic mouse could have nibbled off the ledge.

Retreat back to the tower entrance across that eaten ground was impossible. He would have to edge around the tower's entire inner circumference to reach the exit from the other side. That thought crossed his mind and receded. Something worse had happened with his forced movement. Irissa—the Irissa figure—was obscured now, as if she had turned him her profile.

This vantage proved that the figure was no near apparition, but uncannily like Irissa in every detail. The woman's waist swelled below an Iridesium-studded belt circling her rib cage. She, too, wore an Iridesium circlet—Kendric saw it glint between her highlight-bright strands of hair! And . . . he looked for one last telling detail.

In the hollow between the hills of her breasts, something lay—dark and oval, heavy and subtle. It was an onyx cabochon, not a falgonskin pouch. Fraud! his mind shouted. But why, how?—it asked afterward in a whisper of disbelief.

Like ice cracking, the basalt ledge crumbled toward his foot, forcing Kendric another step beyond the archway opposite where the woman waited and worked.

His balance suffered from the sword in his hand, its weight pulling him forward and down toward the pit. On his back it might have pushed him in the same direction. Either way, it was the wrong weapon for the circumstances, but he was saddled with it.

He sighed and tried to bestir his wits, well aware that thinking in the dark was not one of his shining skills. For most of his life, he had relied on the solidity of a warrior's world, the reality of bravado and blood.

Magic operated in an unreal realm, in feints of the mind and subterfuges of the emotions. There was nothing to hold on to in magic, in the dark.

All he saw of the chamber now was the woman's back. Beyond her, the wire web shifted from time to time, as if being handled, but Kendric couldn't see her move. From the rear, she resembled a discarded cloak again, and seemed thin and vacant, like a wineskin. She seemed not to be there, though his eyes told him he had seen her.

The basalt ledge to his right fractured again, forcing him to step left. In frustration, he banged the wall above it with the flat of his blade. He only managed to dislodge a hail of stones that agitated the monster below, which was now rippling its awesomely elongated form.

Kendric balanced on one foot to peer into the chamber he only saw a slice of now. In that mere sliver of sight, he glimpsed a long-necked decanter sitting on the floor. He hadn't noticed it before, but the thick green glow of borgia swelled the container's belly—was even now rising as he watched, oiling up the long pipe of neck as serpent venom siphons into healthy veins. . . .

He knew in an instant, by means that had nothing to do with logic and common sense, that it was Irissa's essence— Irissa's life, Irissa's magic—that he saw rising in the opposite vessel.

Leaning forward to see it, leaning over the empty darkness below into his own horror and disbelief, readying himself to bellow a challenge to the dark and distance, to name a name— Kendric simultaneously heard the ledge beneath his feet crack free and felt himself suspended in air.

Bonewood!—his mind shouted that name instead of the one he feared to name, made that idea into skin of a sort, and bone, then pushed it through the reality surrounding him, through solid basalt foundation. The stone cracked farther below him, but he was plummeting so fast it snapped in his ears even as he fell abreast of it.

His right hand gripped his sword hilt. His left snagged a sudden branching limb of bonewood. He wedged the sword sideways through the branches and hung from both of them.

Kendric dangled thirty feet below the ledge lip, staring up at distant archways through which he could only see vaulted ceilings pierced by intermittent windows. There was no Irissa to glimpse, no filling decanter of borgia.

There was only himself clinging to a branch of mind-made bonewood that had jutted from the cliffside at the last possible moment—and the beast below stirring and stretching, bristles along its immense bulk rising as if sensing Kendric's nearer presence.

Kendric concentrated his magic, making bonewood snap and strain and grow limb by limb. It spread beyond him like a thorn hedge, jointed fingers stretching and adding knuckle after knuckle, reaching up, bridging the open gap, and striving for the opposite ledge.

It built better than Kendric would have believed possible, given his rudimentary grip on the insubstantial reins of magic. He scrambled atop the chain of bare tree limbs, knowing bonewood to be virtually indestructible, and dragged the weight of his sword behind him. He didn't even wince when the naked blade rebounded off a bonewood gantlet of blows.

The way swung upward. Kendric spared a glance to the pit-dweller. The thing was coiling upright, segment by segment, its midsection eye beaming campfire hot. A weaving conglomeration of fetid flesh—not so much head as hump—rose within six sword lengths of Kendric.

He jabbed at it with the blade to remind it of his resistance and continued laboring up the thorny path he had created. The interwoven limbs meshed into a cradle that would catch him if he slipped. . . .

Air—icy to the point of breaking bone and shattering flesh—struck Kendric like invisible lightning. Frosted, his eyelashes, nostrils, and lips clung together, rendering him blind, breathless, mute. His ears shrieked their outrage and his fingers would have released the sword, but they were gloved in immobilizing ice.

The bonewood to which he clung had chilled until it leeched the air, the blood, the warmth and will and magic from him. Kendric felt whitened, bleached. The normal fluids behind his closed lids scorched his sight and sizzled through his frozen lashes. Stinging, his eyes tore open.

He clung to frosted silver branches. His sword blade was sheer ice, the hilt a lump of packed snow through which no light gleamed. His body burned with cold, but he forced himself atop a particularly thick limb of bonewood, his boots slipping on the icy surface. His own joints snapped like dead sticks at every motion.

Finally he crouched half erect on his precarious perch and surveyed his situation.

He stood midway across the bonewood bridge. Below him the creature roiled. Its maw had finally opened. He recognized that fact by the gleam of ice-dagger fangs. He looked to the ends of his bridge. The bonewood held— would hold—it was marvelously constructed, if he thought so himself. Broad trunks anchored each side, with the jointed limbs narrowing and interweaving as they met in the middle.

Odd, Kendric thought in the ponderous manner his numbed mind could manage, but magic had refined his most primitive instincts. The bonewood had shaped itself into a pair of interlaced hands. Kendric paused at the very crux of that joining, cold but encradled, worried but safe. He had not known his magic was so subtle, so symmetrical, so—

Then the bonewood fingers parted slowly, intentionally.

Kendric plummeted from someone else's empty hands into the deeper dark, down to the glacier-breathed monster. His sword engaged a bonewood limb as he plunged, then ripped free of his hand.

It fell alongside him—lethally spinning, still as frozen as he was . . . by surprise and by something that was not surprise at all, but tardy recognition.

Irissa was looking down at her own form from a high window, deeper inside herself and farther from herself than she had ever been, even during her most intense moments of self-seeing.

For a moment the tall, thin tower that held her second self jolted. The shudder threatened to shake her from the window, but she was bound by ropes of warm, thick borgia and they held.

Irissa heard a distant call, saw herself in a mirror for an instant, and was shocked. Her eyes felt as heavy as her head felt light. She wanted to close them but fought the impulse, as a watchman will battle that sneak thief, sleep.

It was vital not to close her eyes, Irissa's second self told her, and more important to heed the tug on her hair. Irissa looked down again; her hair was green and growing down the tower wall. An odd dream, she thought, and stared down at herself again.

Her self stared back from open eyes of borgia green.

CHAPTER
7

"THERE IS A WAY," NEVA SAID, "BUT I SENSE RATHER than remember it."

"A way of . . . Rengarth?" Medoc looked dubious.

Ilvanis's silver-gray eyes widened. "That would be the only way Neva and I would remember. Have we your permission to try—?"

No Torloc in the chamber responded; instead, everyone stared at the one person incapable for once of answering for herself—Irissa.

"We must try *something*!" Medoc's fist rammed his palm.

"Kendric will do it," Jalonia said confidently.

"And if he doesn't—or it's too late?"

Jalonia couldn't answer.

At last Orvath spoke, his uncommitted eyes fastened on Irissa's motionless form. "Send for Ludborg."

"Ludborg?"

"He knows something of this Rengarth. He claims to know something of the future. Let him make himself useful for a change."

Dame Agneda bustled out to find the scryer, eager to be of use herself.

The others waited, crowded into a room not meant to seat more than one or two.

In time, the beating torch flames and the ceaseless candle flicker came to flay their senses with shadow blows. The fickle light played hide-and-seek over Irissa's form, casting illusions of movement across her hands, onto the folds of her clothes, even into the icy glint of her open eyes.

When the chamber door finally creaked wider to admit Ludborg's rotund figure, a conjoined sigh of relief dampened candle flames and dimmed the chamber's unnatural brightness for one breathless moment.

"Ah." Ludborg's syllable embodied all understanding and all sorrow. He waddled lugubriously to the bed's foot. "My Lady Longitude lies stricken. What by?"

"We thought a scryer would know such things."

Ludborg swiveled languidly to confront Orvath with the faceless hole of his hood. "I know what I am sent to look for. This is an unforeseen event."

Neva and Ilvanis detached themselves from the white stone walls into which they had blended while waiting.

"We think we can draw off the venom—"

"Venom?" Ludborg spun into himself, thinking.

"Tainted borgia." Medoc lifted the cup holding the remainder of the draught.

Everyone looked away from the brew, but Ludborg skated over to drape his hood above the container. "Borgia," he intoned, "can be delectable when properly brewed; death when it is not. Accident or intent?"

"Kendric thinks intentional." Orvath's tone obscured whether he agreed or disagreed with the diagnosis. "He has gone into the forest to tackle demons whose names only he knows. I would have drunk from the tainted horn next had Irissa not collapsed so speedily."

"Ah, yes. She was never one to dawdle." Ludborg veered to confront Ilvanis and Neva. "Well, if you two know to do something, act on it. Rengarth is a seductive place and, like most seductive things, can poison as well as please. You two are of Rengarth, though twice removed, and are best suited to counter its evils."

"We are not sure what to do—" Neva began folding back her trailing sleeves with something of a washerwoman's abstracted efficiency.

"So begin most undertakings." Ludborg drifted back

from the bed. "So therefore . . . begin—we'll see what comes of it."

Shrugging, Ilvanis regarded Neva. "Hand-to-hand, I think."

"Yes, hands." She extended hers to him, then her free hand lowered to the coverlet to clasp Irissa's. Ilvanis mirrored her gesture, completing a linked triumvirate. Ilvanis and Neva glanced at each other.

"Poison leeches!" Ludborg's voice rose so high it cracked. "You are hereditary poison leeches—of course! The royal families of Rengarth always house a penchant for poison in one way or another. Then leech."

"We . . . we don't remember how."

"It must be an inborn gift," Ludborg fussed. "You are Rengarthians, after all, heirs of an overthrown Ruler and Reginatrix, no matter how many centuries have severed you from your roots. Poison-leeching is an instinct, a . . . quality of your very flesh and bone. Accept it and you will do it." Ludborg's robes fluttered as he rolled into place near Irissa's head. "I have never observed a poison-leeching."

"Neither have we . . . that we remember" Neva returned Ilvanis's gaze with a rueful smile. "Oh!" Her exclamation was the kind one would make if pricked by a needle.

"What?" Ilvanis and Ludborg demanded together.

Neva stared at where her fingers curled around Irissa's. The fingernails were slowly turning green.

"Mine also!" Ilvanis sounded triumphant.

Infinitely slowly, as if Ilvanis and Neva were vessels fashioned of clear crystal instead of flesh and bone, a green coloration soaked into their skins and up their pale fingers, even into the weave of their white sleeves.

Torlocs watched tight-lipped, once more doubting the Rengarthians' corporeal existence. The green spread so neatly, so methodically—as if it were being inhaled through a reed, as if Ilvanis and Neva were mere sponges.

The ice over Irissa's eyes splintered and cracked. Her

silver irises surfaced through green shards that melted into the bed linens.

Neva and Ilvanis had greened to their own shoulders now. The color began to run down their bodies in veinlike tendrils—melting, dripping.

Neva turned her head away from Irissa, from Ilvanis. A pulsing vine of green veined her white neck. "I fear . . . I fear we *share* the venom; we do not banish it."

On the bed, Irissa blinked. Her lips, more white than green now, parted. Her face seemed to be floating to an unseen surface, her profile breaking free of the poison. She struggled for breath until the pouch on her breast heaved.

"Ludborg, help them!" Jalonia beseeched. "Orvath, Medoc, surely one of your talismans—?"

"Nothing we have counters poison," Medoc said helplessly, his dark eyes fixed on the Rengarthians.

Ludborg spread his sleeves. A casting crystal was buoyed between them.

"A little late for reading the future, scryer." Orvath's smile was savage. "Time has taken the bit in its teeth."

Ludborg floated the object nearer the bed, letting it hover over Irissa's chest, then sink. In a moment the crystal had absorbed the falgonskin pouch into its transparent contours. Like a blue-worm the feather-scaled pouch rested at the globe's base, then slowly levitated.

The Overstone thrust its narrow nose through the pouch's drawstring end, emerging finally in full egg-shape. It floated within the floating globe, veins of ruby and blue pulsing within its ovoid contours.

Neva gasped suddenly and began gagging, her body writhing. Ilvanis started to console her, but choked instead. Half of their faces were tinged with bilious color.

"You have leeched, now unleech it!" Ludborg commanded. "Rid yourselves of the venom. Let it flow into something that will contain it without harm, something immortal—"

A disembodied sigh stirred the chamber hangings and shook candle flames almost off their wicks. Ilvanis and

Neva collapsed onto the bed, never loosening Irissa's hands.

The seeress's body rippled—once, as if buoyed on an invisible wave—and settled.

Vivid green lightning laced the Overstone itself, twining among the crimson and azure threads flickering with opal fire in its pale depths.

Ludborg's crystal cracked into so fine a pattern that it shifted into dust motes shimmering in the candlelight. Like dust, it glimmered and disappeared.

Released, the Overstone egg thudded to Irissa's breastbone, its vacant pouch atop it. All three figures began stirring on the coverlet. Ilvanis lifted a pale hand to his paler forehead. Neva massaged her pallid wrist with a hand like alabaster.

Lastly, Irissa sat up and brushed emerald dust from the far corners of her eyes. The Overstone egg rolled into her lap, where her quick fingers retrieved it.

She stared hard at her father, Orvath. "There was something I was going to tell you—"

Jalonia, laughing, caught Irissa's free hand, then Ilvanis's and Neva's by turns.

"Amazing." Ludborg dusted his sleeve ends together.

"A wonder," Medoc agreed, grinning.

"More trickery." Orvath stepped away from the bed as if fearing contamination.

"You'll be wanting," Dame Agneda admonished Irissa, "some dinner. You missed most of it."

Irissa blinked from one face to the next and smiled uncertainly. "I'll be wanting," she amended, "explanations."

   ❖

Within an hour, the excitement had ebbed. Dame Agneda's "dinner" congealed in a porringer atop the dressing table. The chamber was vacant except for Irissa, who sat before the mirrorless wall and studied the empty drinking horn.

All of the wall torches and most of the candles had been extinguished. Citydell and Edanvant slept. Irissa glanced to a night-dark window and tensed. A white face stared back from the murky surface—her own.

She released a nervous breath and lifted her hand from the falgonskin pouch it habitually supported. The Overstone weighed heavier now, she noticed. Pulling it from the pouch, Irissa watched firestorms of color shift within it. Sometimes the filaments seemed to weave into a shape, as clouds blend into imagined forms.

She studied the room again, recalling the relief that had filled it on her awakening. She smiled to think of the worry she saw scurrying from familiar faces; even Orvath had looked relieved. And everyone had a theory for her revival.

Ludborg had credited his crystal with her salvation. Dame Agneda praised the poison-leeching of Ilvanis and Neva. Jalonia maintained that Kendric had accomplished some unseen wonder at the very moment of Irissa's revival and would soon return to regale them all with the details.

Irissa felt no wonder, just a dull sense of having been half drowned. Their exuberantly told tale of the pale youths of Rengarth greening their very flesh and garments in her service seemed just that—a tale. And Ludborg was wont to make extravagant claims for his casting crystals.

As for Kendric . . . Neva had admitted that he had been secretly pitting his journeyman magical skills against an evil that he believed lingered in Edanvant's abandoned landmarks. He had already tackled the Iridesium walls and the forest keep.

Irissa lifted the comb on her dressing table, remembering how Kendric had slapped it down during the argument that had soured their last moments together in this chamber. She felt more than his absence, more than a certain remoteness after her own far more dramatic withdrawal.

She felt . . . nothing. It was as if a familiar tension had collapsed, as if something that customarily filled a space within her inner world had simply . . . evaporated.

That internal emptiness disconcerted Irissa far more than questions of whether the borgia was lethal, or whether the cask or horn was tainted, even whether she or Orvath had been the target—or neither.

Irissa rapped the comb on the wood, as if calling herself to attention. She could do nothing but wait until morning, and glanced to the windows again. Dark as ever, she saw, with no threat of dawn.

If Kendric didn't return by then, he wasn't going to. That knowledge arrived in the same intangible way that Irissa knew that something—someone—had left Edanvant that night.

The door creaked. When she turned, a blue-worm was wiggling through the keyhole. It dropped to the floor, then vanished under the wooden door as it swept wide to admit Ludborg.

"I thought the estimable Dame Agneda had ordered sleep." Ludborg lolled in and perched on the bed corner. The latchkey blue-worm emerged from his coarse brown hem, writhed up the fissure of his sleeve, and disappeared.

"Sleep cannot be ordered," Irissa answered. "It must be invited, and even then it sometimes makes a fickle guest."

"I worry, too," Ludborg confided.

"About what?"

His hood waggled from side to side. "This and that. Mostly that. The crystals have been reading most ambiguously for Kendric."

"He has gone to you for readings?"

"Some depend a great deal upon my scrying skills. Some pay very well for it."

"Kendric . . . paid?"

"Not in the currency I desired. He read until he sweated coldstones. Those I was anxious to acquire—very rare, rarer than seeress's tears. . . ."

Irissa had stood so fast the blood rushed from her face, leaving her slightly greenish in the pallid candlelight.

"What did Kendric read at so arduous a session?"

Ludborg curled his sleeves around his sizable girth and rolled back and forth on the coverlet. "Nothing, he claimed. Fraud, he claimed. What do my crystals know?"

"Perhaps as little as you say." Irissa had advanced on Ludborg, looking severe. "Stop teasing me with hints and say what you think." She turned and went to a nearby chest, elevating a green silk sash and shortsword from it.

"No need to get festy," Ludborg urged, his sleeves obsequiously patting the air. "It is my calling to be oblique."

"It is mine to pierce through that." Irissa gestured with the sword effectively enough to encourage Ludborg to dodge behind the bedpost.

"Would I have come here were I not inclined to aid you?"

"You are like Felabba; you come because you come and you go because you go. Oh—!" Irissa spun to the window, approaching her own reflected image. "I have been an utter fool!"

It was one of those statements that only another fool would comment on. Ludborg kept polite silence.

"I have seen the footprints of Geronfrey on this world since we came here and hoped they were another's," Irissa said. "My . . . blindness . . . allowed him to reach from someplace else and nearly usurp my magic, destroy my kind, and ruin Edanvant as Rule was ruined. He has haunted Kendric and myself since we left his undermountain tower in Rule. But I refused to see it, to believe that the mere act of choosing one man over another merited such . . . pursuit."

"Geronfrey is not merely a man, but a mighty sorcerer."

"Still, the disposition of myself is my sovereign choice. Even magic cannot meddle in that."

"No . . . but in the aftermath—"

"I know." Irissa paced, her face tautening with purpose. "The magic and the meddling come after." She sighed. "Where is Kendric, Ludborg?"

Ludborg's hood hung very still. "Not here."

"But where? In the forest?"

"Not . . . in the forest, I think. Not anymore."

Irissa's shoulders lifted, then lowered. "At the Black Tower?" When Ludborg's entire circumference jerked, she rushed on. "Neva and Ilvanis didn't know what Kendric meant by 'the one place he abhors most.' I do. There was a Presence in the tower, but I refused to see it so that it couldn't see me. . . . Yes, definitely a Presence there—"

"No longer," Ludborg intoned.

"And—Kendric?"

"No . . . longer." The hood inclined in the affirmative.

"Where?"

"Rengarth, I believe. That is where the . . . Presence flowed from."

"Rengarth." Irissa stood stunned. "But that is . . . you said it is a place that refuses to be found, that welcomes no one! You yourself are forever exiled from there—and Neva and Ilvanis as well. You've always insisted that there's no way back for any of you, that there's no way for anyone to get there!"

"Sad but true."

"Sad?" Irissa had stepped close enough to curl her fists into the puckered fabric of Ludborg's hood.

"Tragic," he amended quickly. "Perhaps you overexcite yourself for one so recently ill."

"If I am ill of anything, it is of implications and allusions. Facts, Ludborg; give me facts or I shall—" A suitable threat eluded her, then her silver eyes sharpened "—or I shall look into your hood and see your face."

"No, no!" The hood's material wrenched in her hands. "It is unthinkable. My privacy is my only defense."

"Knowledge is mine, pray share some with me, and not through the medium of your crystals."

"Very well. It is only speculation, but I believe your instincts are right; some mishap has befallen Kendric at the Black Tower."

"Mishap?"

"I believe your enemy calls Rengarth home now."

"How would Geronfrey get there if no one else can?"

"A gate to which he has the sole key?" Ludborg offered unconfidently.

"A gate would hardly be the means to so reticent a place. Gates are commonplace; gates go everywhere—" Irissa turned and stared at the darkened window. "Kendric saw something not long ago, in this very window, when a terrible force came to suck me through it. An alien land, he said, and three peaked cities—"

"Rengarth," Ludborg gulped. "I recognize the terrain. 'Two cities fair, and one to ensnare'—a rhyme of Rengarth."

Irissa's fingers slackened on his robe. She advanced on the window until—this time—she reached out to her own reflection, long fingers growing into meeting fingers. The gesture made a pale, jointed bridge between the two—between reality and image, inside and outside, Citydell and darkness.

Irissa whirled from the window, her black hair windmilling around her white face. "I'm going to the woods."

"Wait!" Ludborg lurched back at Irissa's expression. "Wait until morning," he finished lamely. "If the others lose *you* as well—"

"As *well*?"

She whirled again—to snatch a candle—and was out the door, her footsteps rasping down the long, empty hall.

If Ludborg said more to deter her, Irissa didn't hear it. She was striding away too fast, too intently. Her shadow preceded her down tiered staircases, along tapestry-hung walls, through pillared halls, and into the serene Edanvant night.

Irissa shivered as she hurried along the streets past bolted doors and shutters. Predawn expeditions called for a cloak, particularly perhaps in her condition. Voices of caution and restraint nipped at her boot heels like a pack of mongrels, but none spoke from her heart. Her "condition," she concluded, was graver than anyone suspected if what Ludborg had hinted was true.

Once beyond the city gates and past the dozing gate-keeper, Irissa discarded her candle. She felt breathless and her heart thudded resoundingly against her chest, perhaps a result of her poisoning. Under her palm, the emerald cabochon set into her sword hilt greened to life, casting enough light to enshroud her like a cloak.

Where once in Edanvant magic had infested such structures as the double wall or the bridge she and Kendric had magically manufactured, both landmarks were ordinary now.

The walls had melted into doorways where the bridge began and ended. Irissa crossed the bridge and wove through the fallen walls, remembering a time when she had walked into solid metal and the bridge had been built from nothing more substantial than what Kendric called wish-for-it.

Everything was ordinary now. The forest cackled with the predawn screech of birds. Irissa rustled through their leafy domain, alert for pounce-cats or treemonks, not magical beasts—no Rynx, no one-horned bearing-beast with a gold and silver coat. All the magic had left the beasts of Edanvant.

A flash of white streaked through the underbrush.

Irissa paused. "Felabba—?" she wondered. But Finorian's old cat was gone—had run off without notice, as is the way of cats. Felabba would not come back here, Irissa knew in her bones. That, too, was the way of cats. Though speaking was not. . . .

Thinking of Felabba brought thoughts of the cat's eternal verbal dueling partner, Kendric. While Irissa had lain senseless, had he been pulled into some irresistible trap? Irissa could hardly bear to think of such an event. She pushed through the untended forest, one hand holding the Overstone pouch secure at her breastbone, the other anchoring her sword.

Morning debuted by removing one gauzelin veil of darkness after another, revealing unrevealing woodland

and knotted roots. Birds grew brassy-throated above her; the occasional treemonk hurled a cone or nut at her head.

Then the forest stopped; foliage creamed like a wave in midcrest and froze. The trees opened onto a clearing and stilled even the shudder of their leaves. Alone, unguarded, the Black Tower commanded a grassy knoll. Raw new sunlight cracked like egg yolk over its glistening black stones.

Irissa stopped and rested, watching the tower watch her. It looked benign. She remembered the delight with which she had first viewed it, the pleasure she'd taken in its singing stones.

Now she approached it warily, and her palm hesitated before strumming the stone. The note she struck reverberated out of tune. She trailed her hand around the tower until it seemed to melt into the tarry mortar that cemented the structure. Her hand felt suspended inside an ice dagger.

Irissa faced the section that had taken her hand, then lifted her other hand free of the Overstone and pushed forward. She waded into—through—the stones, hearing an atonal wail as she passed.

Inside it was dark, as before. Irissa didn't like the look of the floor, as before. She saw more than before—mirror frames opposite her, all around the inner tower surface, each frame designed to replicate an archway. Each mirror reflecting a door.

Irissa looked for her own reflection, as before.

There was none.

The framed rooms were all empty.

She angled her hilt-light toward the floor. It yawned down into flat black darkness.

She risked calling. "Kendric."

Behind her, the stones wailed mockingly.

She decided to edge along the wall and stepped to her left. Her foot plunged into nothing. She balanced for interminable seconds on an unseen precipice, the small swell of her pregnancy alien enough to overtip her, the Overstone pouch swinging forward to add its infinitesimal weight to her precarious battle.

Something—perhaps simply her own human two-footed sense of balance—righted her. Irissa edged back to her right and her feet met solid ground. Her fingers clung to the stone walls, stroking muted chords from the surface they brushed.

If the tower floor were a chimney with only a narrow ledge around its interior, none of the reflected rooms were directly accessible. She would have to inch around the tower's inner circle, perhaps enter one frame backward.

As she moved right, the archways slowly angled past. Irissa paused, incredulous, to peer over her shoulder through one archway into the room beyond it and through an external window to a winter landscape.

Something slashed past the window, falling. A sword—Kendric's sword! Irissa reached for the vanishing glint, for the window she had seen, for the mocking, framed mirror-door—again she teetered over vacancy, her weight shifting from heel to toe, her knees wavering and hands flailing—

Irissa flattened against the wall, breathing hard, not caring that the stones snickered musically at her clawing touch. She hardly heard them for the blood-drum in her ears.

She edged farther right. Perhaps if she had seen the sword, she would spy its bearer. Another framed opening slid into view, this one a portal to darkness so thick she felt she could heft it by the scruff of its neck and shake it.

Light beamed in the darkness, firefly faint. It spread and separated into tongues of flame eating an unappetizing pile of dead leaves, rags, and torn parchment. The fire flared with the initial optimism of existence, illuminating the man who had made it.

Kendric was sitting on his heels, tumbling the familiar flint and steel back into the boarskin purse at his belt. Kendric—alone in the dark and looking like he knew it. Kendric seeming only a hand high from where Irissa stood, a homunculus trapped in a bottle kept closeted in the dark.

Irissa counted archways from where she stood. Seven,

eight—nine! She would edge nine frames forward and then—somehow—step into the unreal room. Despite caution, her feet slid right at a rapid pace. No more breaks in the ledge stole her breath. She didn't teeter once. The stones remained silent, as if holding their breath with her. Her mind tolled the archways while her hands felt the ornate frames swell and fade behind her as she passed.

At nine, she stopped. Instead of stones, her palms met cool, smooth glass. Breathless, she turned to face the wall. Every motion tilted her toward the abyss. When she faced fully sideways and had to swing one foot over the drop to turn herself, the moment seemed sliced into infinite pieces.

Her stomach seemed a barrier that kept her from clinging to the shiny surface. For a moment Irissa thought her grip on either side of the carved frames would slacken and she would slide like a spider down . . . down . . . down on a silken thread of death. . . .

Her cheek, fevered, cooled on icy glass. The mirror was neither light nor dark, but invisible, unreflective. And she faced it. Irissa peered into the darkness, saw Kendric far and small inside it. Her breath fogged the glass and he vanished.

She bit her lip, then focused on the nearer rather than the farther plane. It was so close it made her sight seem cross-eyed, it made her powers strike themselves and slide off, like dueling blades.

Her vision concentrated until it focused, then Irissa's eyes took in an invisible stitch in the invisible glass.

A tiny threadlike crack appeared in midmirror. Another stitch—longer, looser. Another crack. Cracks beget cracks. Irissa's silver eyes were flashing needles intent on slicing through a surface as gossamer-thin as the skin on water. The archway was veiled now by a fine, black crosshatching as well etched as Finorian's lined face.

Irissa spread her fingers and pushed—Nothing shattered into motes ground fine. Mirror or glass or illusion— the barrier broke. Her breath no longer frosted anything that stood between herself and Kendric. She grasped the archway sides and lifted her foot into the frame.

She didn't pass. It was as if the scene before her had retreated, or she had been knocked back.

She pressed again into the portal. Time shuddered and the stones on either side hummed with tension, but she did not pass. On her next attempt, she hurled herself with all her force into the gap.

The gap remained, and she remained on the other side of it. Not even the fingers of one hand would poke through.

Nothing by normal means—or magical ones—barred her way.

Nothing kept her from going where she wished.

Nothing stopped her but . . . Nothing.

CHAPTER
8

"I'M GOING BACK," IRISSA VOWED.

"There is nowhere to go," Jalonia answered, aghast. "Even you admit that Rengarth is unattainable. Wouldn't Ludborg have returned if he could? And he is native to the place."

"Perhaps it's easier to return somewhere if one is not native," Irissa said obliquely. Jalonia sighed in frustration.

"You cannot pass a gate now anyway." Dame Agneda lifted her eyes from the leather belt she tooled. "Even from a natural standpoint, such gallivanting is inadvisable to one in your condition."

"My condition!" Now Irissa seemed poised on the selvage edge of exasperation.

She looked around the great hall, in which were gathered all of those who had attended her during her dread siege of poison, all of those close to her—or who should have been. In midsurvey, that look changed from one of determination and even defiance to regret.

"I must try the Black Tower again. Otherwise," Irissa added, "none of us will see Kendric again."

"You cannot be sure," Medoc began. "Credit the man with ingenuity as well as courage. Kendric is hardly one to be snatched unwilling to another world without someone answering for it."

"I am not one to quaff a swallow of borgia and lie helpless until rescued. We—and he—face more than we know. The answer waits in Rengarth. I will go there."

"How?" Jalonia wanted to know. "You have failed once."

Irissa turned to her mother with a maternal smile. "I don't know. Somehow. There is always . . . somehow."

Ludborg, who had been following the debate with rhythmic swings of his hood from one speaker to the other, produced a sound midway between an ahem and a sneeze.

"They are all right, Lady Longitude," he said. "Even if Kendric passed to Rengarth through a gate we were unaware of, he was *drawn* through by someone of Rengarth. That is quite a different matter from storming the gate oneself."

"Perhaps I shall persuade the gate instead," Irissa answered, busily braiding her forelocks.

"And . . ." Ludborg paused lugubriously. "You ignore the main obstacle. You cannot take one unwilling with you through the gate."

"Kendric went unwilling enough, I warrant." Irissa was sweeping tidbits from the trestle table into a leathern sack.

"He was spelled most likely. That is not the same thing. You know what I mean."

Irissa paused. "Phoenicia apparently traversed a gate on the brink of delivery. Remember Kendric's vision in the shards after my battle with the shadow in the sky? Phoenicia was huge with child, yet she passed. I bear merely a hint of my . . . condition. What this Phoenicia can do—did—so can I."

"Phoenicia was a Reginatrix of Rengarth! Such have access to powers beyond the ordinary. Besides, we know the price she paid for her flight—death. No, my Lady Longitude, if you bear any wisdom at all, you will heed Scyvilla the Rengarthian and stay —"

"No!"

"—or at least . . . take your humble servant Ludborg with you." Ludborg (and when it suited him, Scyvilla) bowed until his hood tip drooped to his waistband, which banded nothing defined enough to be called a waist.

Jalonia pressed her palms on the tabletop and inhaled deeply. "What of you two?" she wondered, looking to Ilvanis and Neva, who sat the fringes of the argument. "You originated in Rengarth. Persuade Irissa to remain with us. We will do all we can to find and return Kendric—we have the Eye of Edanvant to employ, the men's talismans. . . ."

"We have not followed our own course for centuries," Neva said. "We could save Irissa from the tainted borgia, but not from the risk of following her own will. If we had reason to seek Rengarth again, nothing could stop us. Nothing stops us now, but our own . . . dislocation."

"She may never come back!" Jalonia's face grew anguished.

Irissa rose, half turning from the gathered Torlocs. "Neither may Kendric."

In the inarguable silence, Orvath finally spoke, his deep voice tolling in their midst with a certain finality. "Let her go. Have you not yet learned, Jalonia, that you keep only what you free?"

Irissa stared into her father's dark, unreadable eyes. Perhaps Orvath wished her gone and good riddance. She took him at face value anyway. "Thank you," she said quietly.

Irissa tied the food sack to the sash that held her sword, looked twice around the vast room, memorizing each and every face in it, then stepped quickly from the echoing hall.

Instead of taking the broad red marble staircase that led down to the outside, she climbed the frozen river of coldstone stairs that led up to one of the twelve towers.

The room she and Kendric had occupied lay becalmed, expectant. Someone had replaced the coldstone panes shattered days ago by the wind of Irissa's gate dream. Irissa had noticed, never wondering who tended to such mundane matters in Citydell.

Now she wondered.

Not long before, she had lain dormant on that testered bed. Reports of her poisoning helped her people the room

with a circle of worried, torchlit faces. She saw Kendric as
the others did—terse, grim, turning to his sword and stalking into the night to deal with a danger only he recognized.

The bed instilled no fear in Irissa: she had never seen
herself immobilized upon it. The bed held other memories.
She now saw Kendric as *she* had, sharing a sustaining
warmth that even now imbued the empty room, the perfume of her memory.

Irissa sleepwalked through the familiar scene, touching
a carved bedpost, pausing at the tightly latched windows,
letting her fingers ripple the stagnant water in the wash-
basin.

No one else knew how it irritated Kendric to grapple
with ambiguous pockets of alien magic, how he distrusted
his own inner powers and risked them every time he exer-
cised them.

Irissa felt an interior tug-of-war between pride and
hurt that he had never told her of his solitary campaign to
eradicate all traces of Geronfrey from Edanvant.

Geronfrey's magic was ancient and pervasive; even she
would never have dreamed of rooting it out. Kendric's
magic was unwanted, arbitrary, and amateur. Kendric's
greatest gift was the stubbornness to wield it against better
judgment.

A spasm of dread rippled through Irissa, as if in agitating the water she had stirred herself. If Kendric's magical
rooting had annoyed Geronfrey sufficiently, the Wrathman
could be beyond recall, could be . . . dead . . . even
now.

She might be leaving her. . . . Irissa stared around, realizing that Citydell and its occupants, despite their flaws,
were her home—too late. Nothing was home enough without Kendric, the droning ache in her heart told her.

She clutched the Overstone pouch, feeling the cold inner surface warm to her hand. Kendric had always scoffed
at what he called wish-for-it. He put his faith in his own
inexorably human will.

Now Irissa needed more than her inborn powers; she

needed a full rasher of Kendric's "will." Where he had gone—or had been taken—was forbidden to her by every law of the unnatural universe of magic.

No one came uninvited to Rengarth, or had in centuries, said Ludborg. No one could even *find* Rengarth to be refused it. Worse, the very proof of their union, the unborn one her body bore so quietly so far, barred Irissa from the passing of any gate, to any world. She could not take an unwilling person with her, even if that person be barely there.

Irissa unfisted cramped fingers and let her hand fall to the dressing table. They rested on a comb like an Empress Falgon back begemmed with coldstones. Irissa could still hear it snapping through her long hair, could hear Kendric's voice rumbling behind her—calming, encouraging, telling her the truths she least liked hearing and thus most needed. . . .

Her hand tightened around the comb until its tiny teeth pricked her palm—a pressure like a row of moon-weasel fangs. Irissa thrust the comb into her food sack—knowing the gesture was pointless, knowing that of all talismans, emotional ones were the least reliable—and yet sometimes the most effective.

She shook off fear, sorrow, and worry, resuming the brisk stance that had convinced those in the Great Hall that she knew what she was about and should be left alone to do it.

She turned, feeling the room's lure and its memories drag against her departure like a weighted train. Then she was over the threshold, as if Citydell were simply another place she had to leave.

The green-flamed torches beat against her lithe figure as it strode down halls and ran down endless stairways to the high entry hall that was her exit.

Citydell slid into her wake with every step. Each tall, sinewy pillar, its shining sides corded into the likeness of a weepwater tree trunk, seemed a guardian slipping into her past. She knew the number of the stones beneath her feet, felt the last light of the green-tongued torches soften upon her shoulders and then melt away. At the flight of stairs leading outside, she stopped and looked back.

Far behind gleamed an ember of light and life in the dark stone pile that was her people's fortress. For all the forbidding vastness of that place and the forbidding aspects of certain of those people, for the first time in her life, Irissa was leaving home. Perhaps, she thought, finding home is impossible until one leaves it.

Even as she wavered at the top of the steps, someone separated from weepwaterwood pillar and came toward her.

"Medoc! I won't be dissuaded—" She spoke forcefully to forestall the gentle force she expected him to exert.

Medoc raised a hand. In the palm shone a gold medallion. "Take it," he said.

"It's your talisman! I know at what cost the men of our kind sought such things. I do not need it."

"It was given me by Phoenicia in the gate, before you were even conceived. If she passed with her 'Willing One,' perhaps this bauble had something to do with it. I've never found a use for it.

"I only wish Kendric had not banished the dagger that held the Single Tongue of Flame. That, too, was Phoenicia's, and I can see more practical use for it, despite its fell powers. So take this, useless as it seems. It may save you from some future harm that neither you nor I can foresee."

Irissa extended her hand. Medoc let the medallion and its chain pool into her palm.

"It is light," Irissa said, "but not accepted lightly. Thank you, Grandfather."

Medoc's young features winced humorously in the faint light. "It's time you leave if you grow inclined to use such depressing titles. My regards to Kendric. We shall expect you both to give detailed accounts of yourselves on your return."

Irissa smiled at his implied confidence and looped the medallion chain several times around the hilt of her sword.

"I never saw another land but this and Rule," Medoc noted a trifle wistfully. "Mine was the easiest road to Edanvant, my talisman handed to me by a woman, not won from another man. I envy you your harder road, Irissa. Perhaps that is why we men always had short shrift for seeresses."

"Perhaps that is why there are so few seeresses left," Irissa answered, and ran lightly down the steps into the outer darkness.

Edanvant exited her mind as soon as she slipped through the city gate. She was in primitive forest again. The woodland sounds whispered of four-footed stealth and supernally sharp senses.

Her own senses quickened. She had not expected help from those in Citydell, but had owed them the courtesy of asking, the nicety of bidding them good-bye, especially when that farewell might be forever.

Irissa mulled her future—or that part of it that she could fashion at the moment. Somehow, she must pass into one of the impervious chambers ringing the inner Black Tower; somehow, she must follow Kendric to Rengarth, to Geronfrey.

There, she had named the enemy. Why Geronfrey should have taken Kendric she couldn't fathom. It had always been Irissa he had wished to reclaim, ever since he had claimed her in his undermountain tower in Rule. In the guise of Reygand, he had awaited Kendric and Irissa in the Inlands of Ten, and trapped Irissa in a mirror until Kendric had released her.

Now Kendric himself was mirror-bound and beyond her reach. Now she was hampered from pursuing him by her very body and the child that body bore in slow, secret ways. No matter how anyone cooed over the future, that awkward fact of the present could not be denied. Kendric's very stake in immortality could seal his mortality.

No! Nothing should stop her from reuniting with Kendric, Irissa resolved, burrowing through a thick hedge of underbrush, especially not the seed of their union.

"Aiiyiah-choo!"

Irissa's sword slid noiselessly from her sash, but the medallion chinked against the metal hilt. The emerald hiltstone gleamed hot green, illuminating a verdant circle of woodland.

"Show yourself," Irissa ordered, "unless you be a surreptitious, claw-footed beast of no name and less manners."

Leaves rustled prodigiously. Bushes underwent an ague. Berries plummeted to earth. Twigs snapped and branches groaned.

In moments, Ludborg's rotund bulk pushed through a shower of leaves. Ludborg's robes quivered, either from exertion—for Irissa was a fast walker—or in mute sympathy with the tremulous leaves all around them.

"You truly wish to accompany me," Irissa was dumbfounded.

"Wish . . . ah, no. 'Might as well' is more like it. Oh, I can't deny that Rengarth has called me since I put myself beyond the pale. But going back is a festy business, rife with rubbing things the wrong way. I have not the disposition for rubbing things the wrong way. I prefer, at my age, that things rub me the right way. No, I cannot say I *wish* to accompany you."

Irissa sheathed her sword through the knot of silk. "Then why do you lope after me in the dark of night?"

"Lope? Oh, indeed, my Lady Longitude, I am most distressed by your terminology. Scyvilla the Rengarthian was never known to lope, not even in his younger days."

"Lope or skip or slither, I care not. Why are you here?"

"Because I am . . . not there."

"Where?"

"Rengarth. Or Rule. Or merely . . . Citydell."

"Kendric would have had your throat slit by now—had

you a throat to slit, which you may or may not. Speak plain or be prepared to receive some rather pointed directions back." Irissa agitated the sword at her side.

"I come to . . . assist you, if I may. I do not know if I can. My role, of late, has been scribe as much as scryer. If you breach a gate to Rengarth, I may slip through on your tunic tails. If that is not to be, I may at least be able to tell those at Citydell that you have gone where you hoped to go . . . and were not eaten by wildwood beasts or—"

"Or aggravated to death by a loquacious Rengarthian. Do they all talk so much there? Poor Kendric. No, Ludborg," Irissa said more gently, "my path is only wide enough for one—and you make at least three. If I find a way to Rengarth that permits more traffic in future, be assured that I will find a way to tell you of it. I am, after all, the sole seeress of my Torloc kind." Irissa paused to consider. "For now. I am not helpless."

The hood swung up and down several times. "You, who have had so much chosen for you, must choose your own way in this. I shall be most impatient of news—you and yon Wrathman are among the more intriguing—in fact, the more consistent—of my . . . er, subjects. I shall . . . hmm . . . miss you."

"Oh, Ludborg, why is it that home only seems that way when one leaves it?"

"I don't know, but so I have found it. And lost it. My regards to Rengarth."

"You believe that I shall get there?"

"I believe, as you believe, that there is always a somehow, for someone."

"Then somehow you must find your way back alone and bid them all farewell—again—for me."

Irissa turned to the dark and moved on.

She smiled as she nudged through the forest's feathery undergrowth. It tickled her extremes, scratched for attention at her hands and face. The forest felt like a single, black-green beast curled upon itself for the night. She seemed but a flea burrowing at the roots of its long-leaved fur as it slept, indifferent to her kind.

Irissa forged through a wall of foliage and broke free of forest. She felt as if a wave had beached her and drawn far, far away, back to a deep-green sea she could hear seething at an unreachable distance.

A hole of night lay before her, empty. The heart of that hole, she knew, was the Black Tower.

Irissa approached it cautiously in the dark, pacing sideways as much as forward. Slowly, she spiraled closer, hearing the tower's subtle hum shake the ground beneath her feet.

It always sang, the tower, Irissa realized. It was never silent if one listened.

Irissa listened.

If the night forest was a sleeping beast, the tower itself pumped like some unattended, never-resting mechanism. Irissa could sense the stones trembling one against the other. A terrible tension held the tower's circularity to itself. It waited, taut and sprung, like a trap.

Irissa sighed and sat suddenly on the ground, thinking first to tent her knees, then deciding that she was better served by crossing her ankles. The earth, cold and hard and quite unseen, resonated with the tower's tangible percussion.

Irissa unknotted her sash and felt taut-drawn silk part from silk. She laid her sword with its hilt-strung medallion on the ground beside her, alongside the small food sack. Both objects pulsed when her hand rested atop them, a subtle responsive purr to the tower's presence. Irissa could feel her bones quaver to the same source. Her fingers shook as they reached under the dark of her hair to untie the cord that held the Overstone pouch.

She hesitated to lay it on the vibrant ground, yet wanted to remove it from her person. At last she laid it in the hammock her tunic made between her akimbo legs, so it touched neither her body nor the ground.

Finally—and with a reluctance so strong she feared her fingers would refuse her will's bidding—she tugged on the ring wedded to the middle finger of her right hand.

All of Kendric's might, all of Irissa's magical skill, could not dislodge the rings that had formed unbidden during their passage into Edanvant. Irissa didn't know what force within herself could accomplish the impossible, only that she must try it.

In her mind's eye, the single cabochon spun through each of its composite gemstones, their colors melding—Bloodstone, Shinestone, Skystone, Floodstone, and Drawstone. Red, gold, blue, clear, and plain. Faster the color wheel spun, Bloodstone and Shinestone blurring to orange, then Shinestone and Skystone to green, Skystone and Floodstone to palest azure, Floodstone and Drawstone to a watery yellow.

Her mind spun them faster, until even color had lost its boundaries. A terrific suction pulled at Irissa's ring finger. For an instant she thought it would be torn free of her hand. So be it, she thought grimly, bracing herself, if that is the price. . . .

The ring spat to the ground, glowing green-orange. When she extended her still-intact finger to touch it, the metal felt warm. Hot. Her finger jerked back, a band of searing pain marking where the ring had been.

But her hand was bare now, her person was purged of every talisman. Irissa didn't know how to do what she would attempt this night, but she would rely on her purely Torloc powers, on her uncompromised seeresshood.

All right, she told herself, shutting her eyes in the dark to open them to a deeper, inner dark. Very well. If she could not cross a gate with one unwilling, and if the babe within her was unable to speak or will for itself, she would farsee in reverse—peer deep inside herself to the incipient eye of her offspring itself. She would ask—plead . . . insist—that her unborn child permit Irissa to follow Kendric through a gate to Rengarth.

Irissa had not looked deep inside anyone in some

while—there had been neither time nor need for such introspection. As for herself, she made an unreliable looking glass, and now she was distorted by the presence of another—an unknown, unguessed-at other.

Still, Irissa quieted her doubts, cast question to the winds, and turned her gaze inward.

Interior darkness stretched as far as her mind could reach. It was not only her own dark, but the unshaped becomingness of another. Her inner paths were close, clogged. She moved within them as a solitary drop of blood pushed and pulled along an endless route, her own substance oiling the passage and diminishing in the very act of navigating it.

Overstone help me, Irissa thought, knowing that she had thrust much more concrete help than that far from herself even before beginning this journey.

She ached for a beam of inner light—some flicker of Torloc green, even the wink of Felabba's feline eye. But there was no natural light here, only warm, viscous dark, only the endless empty shadow of the self.

Irissa drove on and inward. The link with her outer self frayed. Her sense of herself shrank, grew sere, and blew away. Still some subtle outward tension held her whole, baled her thought and will together. Still she moved, farther, into herself.

The way defined itself now. She was not traversing a vasty cavern, as she had on other such occasions, but a network of thin tunnels. A mote beamed in the seductive distance. Irissa wafted toward its brilliance, warming herself as the glow became ruby. A globule of carmine light joined her path with its continuation, with a cross path Irissa plunged into it, through it, wrapped in redness for a moment before finding and following another thread of darkness.

Other crossroads of light awaited her—some golden, others blue, some merely bright, and others dull, ill-lit. The intervals at which the lights came grew rhythmic, like a pulsing. Irissa sped toward her innermost self, so distant from her outside semblance that it seemed worlds away. . . .

The lights winked by, lucid as flame-caught cat irises in the night, so fast they formed a congeries. Jeweled raindrops shredded the darkness. Irissa had arrived at an inner core of brightness that spangled the surrounding dark.

She hung motionless, sensing herself small in some unformed vastness. The beads of light were strung on a mesh of intersecting pathways. They glittered like stars above and campfires below—and to the side, like hungry forest eyes.

Yet this place was not wildwood, but of all places most sheltered, most internal.

A cauldron of color bubbling at its heart drew Irissa's attention, drew whatever passed for herself in this state. She neared it, remembering Kendric's description of finding a silver-ringed pool at Irissa's center on his own excursion into her essence.

No rings awaited; she had doffed rings and swords and other talismans. A throne awaited, a great, sunburst-backed ceremonial sedan chair, its carrying poles untended. Irissa strained her senses to discern some presence in this inner chamber, some person. She saw no pole-bearers, no royal attendants. Only an empty throne—empty save for a jewel-encrusted fan of fabric carelessly abandoned on the seat . . .

The stiff cloth shifted, rays of light winking from the gemstones. Two black jewels sparkled in tandem—matched, like eyes.

Irissa felt her thoughts clench. The throne was occupied! An oval of face above the opulent garment regarded her, a tiny pale face with eyes glittering jet-black. An even tinier hand—white fingers curled and almost lost against the richly crusted taffeta, a hand like a baroque pearl—lifted to acknowledge Irissa's presence.

Irissa bridled. Was she to delve to the very center of herself, only to find this overdressed puppet in command? She had almost forgotten why she came, or for whom.

"What do you ask?" the being on the massive throne said, its delicate mouth moving infinitesimally.

"Ask?" Dull resistance stirred the mote that was Irissa. She was not supplicant here, but—but . . . what she was eluded her. Ask, there was something she should ask.

"I must have permission," she blurted at last.

"Must you?"

A mocking note twisted the two simple words, reminded Irissa of Finorian's icy inquisitions or of the cat Felabba's sarcasm.

"I . . . need it." Irissa felt her way to expression, knowing she was stating her case badly, or too baldly.

"A boon?" the creature on the throne demanded in its high, imperious voice.

Irissa didn't like the implicit royalty in the word "boon." Irissa didn't like to play beseecher at her own altar. She studied the small, wizened face. It reminded her of Finorian's age-whittled features, or Felabba's pointed predator's visage. Who *was* this tyrant, to be judge of her needs, her wants? Who ruled Irissa's inner regions, some surviving piece of the Eldress? A spirit of the vanished cat, Felabba?

"A boon?" the creature repeated.

"A boon. A favor. An act of empathy."

"Ah, empathy. We know the word."

Again the royal "we." Irissa stiffened, painfully. She had not known such sovereignty dwelt in herself, and felt ashamed.

"Do you know empathy?" she asked back. "Do you know what it is to be reft of home, kin, world, surety? Do you know how it is to lose one upon whom your own oneness rests? That is my plight. And I have come . . . here, to ask . . . you, for a . . . a permission—"

"We permit the asking, certainly. The granting is another matter."

Irissa searched for her purpose, which seemed to have shattered into rays of light and slipped away. She no longer knew where she was, *who* she was, why she had come here, or for what.

"Speak," the being ordered.

"There is a gate I must cross, only—I can't."

"You need power."

"No, not power! I have power, so much that I must set it aside. Now, I need . . . permission."

"Our permission?"

"I . . . suppose so, if I knew who you were—"

"You don't know!" The tiny figure rustled indignantly upright against the massive chairback. "We *are* you."

"Surely, I don't need to seek permission from *myself*," Irissa began. Then thoughts cleared, memory rinsed her mind clean.

She stared into the tiny precise face, into the eyes that were not so much eyes as holes into the future. "You are . . . my child."

"Not quite . . . yet."

Irissa's outrage evaporated into wonder. "You are . . . should be . . . helpless."

"Not so much as you."

Irissa felt her form in this place smile, or something similar. "You . . . should be dependent, humble."

"Not if you must seek a boon of me."

"—unaware at this stage, unformed . . ."

"Appearances are deceiving, especially to the self-deceived."

"You would deny me?"

"The world is a reciprocal place, we are given to understand. Have you not denied us?"

"Not seriously. I keep you warm, fed, quiet, safe, hidden—"

"Ignored."

"You were not . . . demanding . . . until now."

"I was not in demand until now."

"Is to be a child only to seek for power?"

"Is to be a parent only to deny power?"

"I don't know. I have only been a child. I have never been a parent."

The stiff figure was silent and Irissa felt sudden sympathy for it. How alone it was, how lost in all its pomp and splendor! It was sovereign unto itself, yet its kingdom was an unpopulated inner realm that it could not rule until many, many years of powerlessness had passed.

Irissa considered her own childhood under the tutelage of Finorian. She was not sure she would wish parenthood upon a parent; she was even surer that she could never wish childhood upon a child.

She stared at the figure so distant, so alien. She searched its features for clue to its gender, and found none. It was total potential, a being utterly without realization. That would come later. For now, it had not the compassion to understand her quest; it owed nobody anything, least of all her, least of all . . . Kendric.

"I seek a boon," Irissa finally said. "I hope that you will permit me to cross the gate, if I find it, to Rengarth, where your father has been taken, if he has."

The little head stirred uneasily. Irissa saw now that only the stiff buttress of a high, wide collar supported its neck. "It is our right to refuse."

She nodded, mutely. She felt herself again, sensed her normal form gathering around her. The chamber no longer felt so dark, so lost, so abandoned.

"You could do nothing if we did nothing," her child asserted.

"Nothing." Irissa felt strangely serene, as if in renouncing will and power, they flowed around her spirit again.

"Shall we remember this audience, our decision?"

"I don't know. I think not."

"You revere fathers so much that you would endanger us both to pursue one?"

Irissa thought of Orvath and smiled ruefully. "I grew

without one and found it a loss. Then I found my father
. . . and I am not so sure. Still, one has only one father—"

"And many children."

"Perhaps," Irissa answered, taken aback.

"We are expendable."

"No, as I see now more than I ever did. But . . . why
do you speak in the plural form?"

"We are . . . still becoming. We are you yet, more
than ourself."

"Then I seek a boon of myself."

"Perhaps."

"Will I be merciful?"

"Perhaps."

"You will agree to a gate, cross of your own individual
willingness?"

"We suppose so. Oh, go away! You are a relentless
creature. We feel . . . surrounded. Do what you will. We
wish to sleep."

The fabric shifted, slumped. Tiny eyelids slid over
huge dark eyes—almost all pupil, Irissa realized, and not
really as black as they had seemed.

The scene was rushing away from her—throne, infant,
chamber—as if she stood on a carpet that was being rapidly
rolled up behind her.

The jeweled interstices of the darkness flashed past.
Irissa felt her mind reel, felt turned inside out. Giddy, she
reached for orientation. Her stomach lurched and she fell,
fell endlessly until the heels of her hands came up hard on
stony earth.

The earth resonated, purred under her palms. A night
wind brushed beads of sweat from her brow. Her ringless
finger burned as if branded. She reached for the ring and
pushed it on again.

The Overstone swayed heavy in its pouch as she retied
it around her neck. Her shoulder muscles tautened again to
take the burden. She reslung the sash over her shoulder

and under her arm, setting sword and sustenance back in their accustomed positions at her hip.

The notion of food gagged her senses like an oily rag. Leaning over the earth she could not see, Irissa retched unenthusiastically into the darkness. She felt oddly satisfied, considering her condition.

CHAPTER
9

THERE WAS ONLY ONE CONSTELLATION IN HIS DARK heaven—a grid of tiny lights twinkling directly overhead. How far away it was, he couldn't guess.

At his feet, the odds and ends he had scoured from the dark burned in a flickering, sour-breathed fire.

Kendric juggled the boarskin pouch holding the flint and steel that had sparked the embers. At least these small tools remained faithful.

His sword had spun away on the plummet through the mists, the first time in his life they had been severed, save at his decision. Kendric's shoulders shifted uneasily, his muscles resenting the absence of sixty pounds of steel as much as they did its presence.

Kendric sat on his heels to study what the meager flames were slowly consuming. Not encouraging. Part of a rotten boot. Scraps of vellum scribbled with an obscure, possibly unspeakable language. Some splinters of wood.

A glint caught his eye, so his boot toe scraped the object from the flames. Inspection revealed a man's ring, glowing red-gold . . . once a costly, handsome thing, not lightly relinquished.

Kendric eyed the ring on his left hand. The stones of many colors that composed a single smooth cabochon were deadened now, lifeless. Like the dark.

Discontent made Kendric stare into the distance until his eyes watered. The place—call it a dungeon—smelled of abandonment. He would have felt easier had there been

surly cellmates, ravening guard beasts, even lowly rats or a
moonweasel or two.

Nothing shared the space with him but the few, forgotten pieces of flotsam that had hidden in corners. Not even a
petrified bread crumb or morsel of cheese lingered. Kendric's stomach growled. It had better, he figured, get used
to it.

He knew he should be wondering about where he was,
or how he'd gotten here and who was responsible, if indeed
the entire thing wasn't a figment of his imagination.

He worried instead. About Irissa. No matter how dark
the surroundings, his mind's eye could lighten the tenebrous distance with the imposition of Irissa's unconscious
form as he had last seen it. So utterly still, so poisonously
tinged, so unlike herself. A dozen Irissas ringed him, each
a reproach. So much for bold forays into the heart of
darkness.

Kendric growled at himself—he lost, and Irissa still
languishing, no doubt. Self-recrimination made cold meat,
but he must dine on something—why not himself, since he
was ever the handiest? Especially here. Wherever "here"
was.

A sound above made him tense. The scrape repeated,
stopped, repeated yet again.

The illuminated gridwork was spinning askew. Kendric
saw a solid bar of light forming, within it, a dark oval
slowly angled into view.

"Empty," someone whispered. The word reverberated
through the dark.

"Not quite." He jumped to his feet, determined to
snag any passing attention that he glimpsed.

"Oh!" A grate, hastily loosened, clanked to the floor
of what made his ceiling. The face darted out of sight.

"Wait! Or don't wait! You're wise to flee this unoccupied pit of nothingness."

"Not . . . unoccupied." The voice had returned, although not the face. The tone was light, tentative. A child's
voice, Kendric decided.

"Perhaps not," he said.

"Perhaps? There's no perhaps about it. I *saw* you."

"Do you see me now?"

"No. . . ."

"Perhaps I am no longer here, then."

"But I still . . . hear you."

"Do you see me?"

"No—"

Moments later the shadow face reappeared in the square of light, rather like a dark moon glimpsed in daylight. Kendric smiled. Whoever or whatever this evasive person was, its curiosity could serve him.

"I see you!" the voice trumpeted. "You are here still. So—" The scrape again, and a fading voice.

"Don't go—!"

"Why not?"

He had to think. "Because . . . we seem to be the only ones here. We should compare notes."

"The only ones?" Laughter came, light, airy, and a little sad. "There are many more, so many. Not here, precisely, but that's only because nobody ever comes down here."

Dungeon, he knew it! And nobody ever came down here? Worse and worse. This voice was his only hope. "Are you Nobody?" he probed, madly thinking.

"Oh. I never thought of it like that."

"I must be Nobody, too, because I'm down here."

"You've got it all wrong." Annoyance weighed down the vocal lilt now, as if he had finally confused its possessor.

"No doubt. I'm often wrong. Aren't you?"

"I don't know. Nobody ever notices."

"Nobody again."

"Nobody *is* everybody. Why are you here?"

"I must have . . . fallen in."

"Oh. It's dark there."

"Yes. I don't like it much."

"I like bright things, too. See!"

Kendric blinked as a shower of sparks flashed across his dark firmament. In a moment he expected them to plummet hotly to his upturned face, but they didn't.

"Do you like it?" the voice demanded.

"Of course. I have something bright, too."

"That faint little fire at your feet?"

"That . . . ," Kendric admitted reluctantly, hearing deep disdain in the voice—and a tinge of boredom. How could he keep this quicksilver person intrigued? "And other, even brighter things."

"A jeweled sword? I like jeweled swords, though I carry only a dagger."

A dagger! Kendric's instincts honed themselves on that promise. His mind sketched in a person behind the voice— some spoiled boy, as ignorant as he was ignored.

"I had a sword once," Kendric said.

"Was it jeweled?"

"It was its own jewel."

"Oh." Metal grate scraped metal frame.

"You're not going?" Kendric demanded, beating back desperation.

"I shouldn't be here."

"Neither should I."

A pause. This person radiated an innocence that made deception easy. Kendric felt a trifle sheepish at gulling such a simpleminded tool, but a man must survive.

"I could come down and visit you. . . ." The voice spoke so reluctantly that Kendric knew it violated another rule by even considering such a thing.

"By stairs?" he wondered.

"There is a way. But it's dark down there. I don't like the dark. It's . . . cold, too."

"I have—" He considered reaching into the boarskin purse for his flint and steel. A few sparks might entertain this visiting magpie.

His big fingers pushed past the bag's narrow neck, feeling for the familiar shapes. They eluded them; above, he felt the presence's attention slipping away. A grinding sound like a stone coffin lid being bullied back into place paradoxically cheered him. The youth must have *some* strength, then.

"Wait!" Kendric's fingers snagged a small something and pulled it from the purse. It slipped his grasp, clinking to the floor and then rolling into deepest darkness.

A trail of silver fire flared behind it, momentarily blinding Kendric.

"Oh, why didn't you tell me? What is that?"

The face and upper body strained downward, darkening all the hatch now. Kendric saw sparkle rain from its neck and hang suspended.

"A Quickstone," Kendric said, astounded. He had forgotten he carried it.

"I want to see it!"

"Then hurry down. They don't call it a Quickstone for nothing. It . . . melts if you don't look at it fast enough."

"Oh, no . . . please! I'll be right there. Don't let it melt."

Hair rose on the back of Kendric's neck as he heard the rough shove of the grate shutting. Only the pinprick pattern of light remained, as if strained through woven fabric.

Kendric picked up the Quickstone. It lay on his palm like a puddle of liquid starlight. While his ringstones seemed quenched and drained, the Quickstone sparkled with undiminished fire. Perhaps that was because it had begun as one of Irissa's coldstone tears and bore a Torloc magic no other necromancy could outshine.

A nearby clank made Kendric turn hopefully to the dark. An unknown person with a dagger was coming—hostage, unwitting accomplice, or resourceful enemy despite the testimony of the voice?

Kendric decided he'd leave future-telling to Ludborg, if he and that evasive individual ever shared a world again. For now, he had himself to save, and Irissa to somehow find again and preserve.

"Oh, it is truly wonderful . . . !"

The oncoming figure was not so slight as Kendric had hoped. As garments rustled nearer, he could only discern a grayness advancing fearlessly upon him in the dark. Kendric didn't like that. He was used to giving strangers pause, a man just under seven feet tall and as broadly built.

This one never hesitated, but skipped up to him—foolish child or childish fool. In Kendric's hand the Quickstone glowed madly, mirroring his inner jubilation. Its brilliance reflected from a starburst of shimmer around the nearing form, making Kendric wonder if he had evoked a ghost.

Then the shape was upon him, drawn to the glitter in his hand. Fulsome skirts swirled at his boot toes. A dark head—as high as his breastbone—bowed so he couldn't see the face. Its eyes were only for the Quickstone.

On the dazzle of this person it was hard to see a dagger, for a jeweled green-gold mesh overlaid the robe. Kendric looked for larger jewels and finally found a gem-hilted dagger sheathed in an inner sleeve pocket near one elbow.

His fingers itched, rehearsing the swift, pitiless gesture that should seize it, free him. He didn't care what it was—man, woman, or child, a foolish one in any case. Warriors were eminently practical: he would use what he had, and examine honor later.

"It's the most marvelous thing I've ever seen," the creature breathed. He barely listened, hearing his own heart pounding secretly, feeling his nerves tightening and his body poised for a surprise attack.

Then it looked up at him, through the parting veils of long darkness-webbed hair . . . through luminous eyes of borgia green . . . through Irissa's face down to every curve, plane, and feature.

Irissa stared into the dark mirror, palm-to-palm, face-to-face with herself. For an instant the darkness inside the Black Tower confused her; her reflection wore a gown, not tunic and trousers, and its eyes shone subtly green now.

She breathed deeply. She'd been inching around the

tower's crumbling interior ledge since resting after her arrival. Each chamber she'd confronted had been empty, its window as vacant of view as any other part of the room.

This was the only one in which she'd seen anything. While she clung there, the image surged toward her. Instinctively, Irissa pulled back—too far. The pit below her exerted its eternal pull, as if by simply being there it called her with a Drawstone's authority.

Irissa tilted toward the wall and the mirror frame, feeling her balance counterweighted by a delicate, new clumsiness. Her stomach lurched, and something else within her. Before Irissa, her own face was nearing, enveloping her.

She had no choice: only up or down, forward or back, herself or the unknown. Irissa felt her body sway one last time—inexorably—in the direction it must overbalance at last.

She fell into the mirror—hands spread, mouth open, eyes shutting against the splintered impact.

A dry, feathery sensation pulled her skin, like wrinkles forming and melting away. She felt the mirror frame fracture and braced herself again—this time for impact with the chamber's solid stone floor.

Instead, she plummeted through stone as if it were porous, through space and darkness, conscious of an airy freedom she had not known since her wild ride atop the back of an Empress Falgon.

Now she was plunging into the pit, though no ripples of rushing air touched her. She fell as if floating—or not falling at all. Yet visions careened past her closed eyes—a plunging sword, Kendric's sword; herself tumbling alongside her; a tiny, barely begotten figure flickering at the corner of her eye; a falling white cat, tail rampant and claws splayed as if it feared not landing in the customary upright position.

"Felabba," Irissa called—in recognition or for help. The cat faded from inner sight like the other visions. Irissa was falling alone, to the pit of a bottomless stomach, through—

Irissa opened her eyes, amazed. She plummeted past a tapestry now—a far-flung scene of earth and sky. Sunfall-pinked clouds loomed around her; her body cut through their fog. Where broken glass and solid stone had not hurt before, the insubstantial clouds met her with slaps of entry and exit. The buffeting spun her around and around as she sank through each rosy petal of mist, the air shaken from her lungs until she thought they would shatter.

Below her—between a dizzying passage through the concrete clouds as if through a series of gates—a rainbow-shaded landscape glimmered and twisted.

Coldstone mountain ranges bit into the far horizon like saw blades, their icily glimmering sides ashimmer in shades of lavender, coral, and rose. The land itself seemed jagged, stepped. Tiers of falling water sprayed a sheen onto the air, and in that restless mist strange half-glimpsed forms cavorted. Tremulous meadows flashed ocher and amber—and violet and crimson.

No dwellings dotted the elegant landscape, and lakes of every color bedewed every hollow, as if the whole world floated on some vaporous, soft-shaded sea.

Cloud-free at last, Irissa sailed down toward her doom, enraptured by the view. "Lost, limpid Rengarth . . ." Ludborg's long-ago description of his birthplace echoed in Irissa's mind with an anthem's measured grandeur.

She knew no panic, only wonder, even as she glimpsed a high, jagged city glittering in the distance. She saw that the ground seemed to be smoothing and the vague masses of color were now flowers wearing faces. . . . She fell in solitary splendor, wondering if it would hurt to break through the wall of a dream, as through a cloud.

An aquamarine veil drifted over her face. Dry, gauzy, it webbed her in yards and yards of airy embrace. Jeweled creatures floated by, glittering needles of darting form with great, incurious eyes.

She finally settled, with infinite ease, amid a bower of trellised plants, upon an oval stone seat as luminous as a pearl.

The seat lurched and sent her sprawling to the pale ground. A snout poked from beneath the stone, then the entire bulk sprouted legs and waddled away.

Irissa shook her head, not managing to dislodge the odd, blue-green veil that swathed her senses. There was something so familiar about this alien place. . . .

Two great feathered oars dipped and rose above her. She looked up for a bird speeding overhead. A bird it was, and overhead, but there was nothing rapid about its ponderous progress. The great white wings fanned slowly, iridescence sheening every pinfeather. With its neck outstretched, the bird was perhaps as long as Irissa herself. It cast no shadow as it coasted above her.

Irissa looked beyond it, searching for a sun. Only a dreamy glow was visible—light without any sharp edges, light lulled to a soporific monotone.

Bewildered, Irissa stood. Her sword, Medoc's medallion, and the food pouch still hung from her sash; the Overstone lay in the accustomed hollow of her breasts, the ring circled her finger, and her Iridesium circlet banded her forehead. She'd not lost her boots or any of her belongings, her body was whole, her magic apparently unshaken, and her mind . . . well, that was another matter.

"Where am I?" she asked herself aloud, more out of frustration than any expectation of an answer.

"Wrong question," returned a voice at her feet.

Irissa looked down. A small white creature was crawling over the silver sand on stumpy limbs, its sour face bristling with whiskers at the muzzle and above the eyes.

"And I should be asking—?"

"How do I leave."

"How *do* I leave?"

The grizzled whiskers jerked up toward a soft white shadow beating past on wide, feathered wings. "Let the swanfish take you."

"Swanfish—?"

The elevated creature paused as if called and dipped toward Irissa. A long neck extended fully, its silver-gray bill opening to reveal a pale yellow tongue.

Irissa glanced to the bizarre little beast at her feet. "I'm underwater! But I can still breathe. Felabba—how? You, me . . . ?"

Whiskers twitched with feline self-congratulation, an expression that looked strange on the chubby, smooth-scaled face. "You were not Irissa of the Green Veil for nothing in your youth. You were born with an affinity for water, and it for you. And magical water most of all."

"But—"

The diving swan . . . swan*fish* . . . nipped Irissa's shoulder. The elongated head clamped her sash in its bill. Irissa felt herself rising, felt herself *floating* upward, through the dry, gauzy sea.

A blob of white far below grew blobbier. "Felabba—"

But she must be dreaming in midgate, Irissa told herself; Kendric had mentioned seeing faces from his past when he had crossed to the Inlands. Now she dreamed, and would not wake up.

Diaphanous folds of light and sensation slipped from her as dryly as sand. The sense of illumination grew stronger, warmer. Above her the swanfish's downy belly—all scales, she saw now, sleek opalescent scales—arched suddenly. The pressure on her left shoulder snapped.

Irissa was abruptly falling again—through a dark, viscous substance. Irissa was getting wet, her boots were swallowing water and pulling her downward. Briny liquid was flowing into her mouth and throat, into her lungs.

She bucked for air and found herself treading water instead of endlessly elusive veiling. Light was no feature of this state, only confused gray sinking. Magic seemed too remote to reach. She had fallen into a lake and dreamed before death, that was all.

Irissa felt herself catapulted upward against her will, like a cork from a bottle. Salt water joined with a lancing bright light to sear her eyes. Sound suddenly plugged her ears—she heard thrashing and gasping. Her own.

Then the waves around her exploded in ropes of droplets. Thick arms were reaching for her, dragging her from water to land, to dry land, to shore.

"Is it a wailwraith?"

Irissa coughed unabatedly, and pushed the wet hairstrings from her face.

"No, I think a ladyfish."

Irissa blinked her well-salted eyelids and wrung her tunic hem.

"It does not matter," said a third voice that sounded dull to her waterlogged ears. "I saw it; it's my prize."

"What's prize about it?" demanded the first voice.

"It may carry some valuable. . . ."

Something was pawing at the Overstone pouch. Irissa's senses reassembled instantly. She scrambled away from the touch and the sounds, her eyes streaming hasty tears that as rapidly changed into the chill hard shapes of coldstones.

"Coldstones . . . ," someone near her breathed. Irissa heard nails scraping ground even as she half-crawled, half-scampered away.

She dashed the last of the inner and outer salt water from her eyes, her ring nearly bruising her temple in the process.

Before her blinking vision, a scene resolved. The lip of a lake, washing gently, a white sand beach ringing it . . . a tangled mat of yellow grasses edging chest-high hedges . . . and four creatures—men—following the trail of her shed coldstone tears.

Irissa struggled upright, horrified to see their lumbering forms advancing on all fours. Overgrown nails clawed the coldstones into dirt-scabbed hands. Their massive shoulders shrugged one another away as they jousted for the glittering motes of stone.

"More," one growled to Irissa. "Make more."

She backed into a hedge and clasped her sword hilt. She still saw only the men's rough-haired heads. Though they were clothed in homespun tunics, Irissa didn't like the way they rasped across the sand in pursuit of her tears-made-stone, or their lowly avaricious postures and hidden faces, their vague, unsettling shapes.

Sword—or magic? Irissa toted their size and number, then cast the quickest illusion she could conjure over their groveling forms. Perhaps her recent immersion in the dry lake had influenced her. A golden net was slinging into the air, each juncture secured by a bead of unbreakable Iridesium.

It hung airborne a moment, as pretty and fragmented yet whole as a breaking wave. Then it swooped over them like an airy cloak settling. Four startled faces finally looked at her. Four . . . round-eyed, scale-skinned shapeless faces. Their clawing hands, she saw, were flippers; their dragging feet—were tails.

Menfish! Did every land creature have a marine counterpart here as well? Irissa wondered.

The menfish thrashed against the tautening net, which even now cocooned their entwined forms. A fishy odor swelled on the beach. Far out on the lake's calm surface, Irissa saw a pale form break water, then fluff and fold its wings and float swanlike, its long neck catching a sickle of sunlight

The net was consuming the menfish, tightening on them like a voracious moonweasel. It stretched its sinuous form—stretched it, shaped it, grew beyond it. The net serpent coiled and swelled. A mesh head rose in the sunlight, jeweled eyes twinkling at every joint. A mesh maw opened wide and swayed toward Irissa.

Unbelieving, she caught the red/cobalt/emerald flash from a fallen coldstone and raised it into a multicolored wall of flame. The serpent's head wavered over the snapping tongues of fire for a moment, then the expanding body—still growing—rasped over itself and began slithering into the lake.

Irissa glimpsed the three fishermen through a shifting

fence of flame: they were the brown flotsam the gilded net dragged back down into the water.

The serpent was gone, but Irissa—heat beating on her face until perspiration ran free—saw her fence was fattening. Her mind, ever slower than her magic, strained to contain the spell. The best she could invent was to set the flames following the lake's irregular circle of shoreline.

The fire leaped forward as if let off a leash. With an ear-rending hiss it sizzled along the sand, burrowing into the distance until it vanished. She waited, dripping in the sunlight, until she saw the red, dancing tongue of its return licking down the white sand from the opposite direction.

When the ring of fire was complete, it settled down to beating amiably, a subtle undercoloration of blue and green pulsing around and around.

Irissa sighed so heavily the Overstone pouch lifted against her breastbone. At least if her fire would not die, she had constrained it to an eternally limiting form. At the same time, she'd ensured that the creatures of the lake—including the horrific net serpent she had conjured—would remain restricted to their bizarre domain.

Irissa drew the sword at her side and regretfully eyed the food pouch. Her stomach was too salt-laden to accept food at the moment, so she began hacking through the gnarled hedge before her.

She meditated while hacking (always an ideal combination of activities) that her magic was proving as ungovernable as her instincts. Irissa knew she'd somehow crossed a gate. She didn't know if this was Rengarth, or if Kendric was to be found here. There was, he would say were he here, only one way to find out.

Irissa hacked forward with Kendric-like determination, ignoring the sweat that streamed from her face to bedew the severed undergrowth as coldstones. She had never perspired coldstones before. Other mysteries worried her more.

She wondered as she went whether the . . . catfish . . . on the lake bottom really had been Felabba, and if her fire-ring had sealed the cat's consciousness in that alien place and within that alien form. But that didn't really worry her. Felabba would just have to fend for herself, like everybody else.

No, what worried Irissa—the conundrum Irissa worried in the ragged privacy of her mind as her body beat its way free of entrapment—was this: what force had subverted her magic, so that what she made seemed to make more of itself before its maker's very eyes?

Now, that was a worry worthy of a seeress.

CHAPTER
10

SHE LED HIM ALONG A TORTUOUS MAZE, ONLY THE glitter of her jewel-netted train guiding him through the twilight.

Kendric followed, mute as a man enchanted.

The place was subterranean, as he expected, but she led him *down,* not up. That disquieted him more than the morose drip of water on unseen stone.

"How can you see in the dark?" he wondered once.

"I was born in the dark."

"So were we all, whether you mean the womb itself or the world that welcomed us."

She stopped. The gemstone lights ahead twisted into a multicolored rope as she turned. "I don't understand you. What is this talk of 'wombs and worlds'?"

"No one has accused me of being . . . difficult to follow before," Kendric stammered.

"I don't know what they mean, those words, and you are following *me*—not I, you," she added primly.

Spitting image or no, this was not Irissa. Kendric shuddered at the remote incuriosity in her voice. He thought again of the knife. How simply he could wrest it away now that he was no longer unnerved by her resemblance to— her duplication of—Irissa. . . .

The glimmering skirt was swaying forward again; Kendric followed, eager to find his bearings in this ill-lit labyrinth and then pounce.

It wouldn't be the first time a lady's dagger was some

man's key to freedom—nor the first occasion a man had promised nonexistent jewels to win a woman's cooperation in some clandestine enterprise or other, usually more ignoble than mere escape.

"You know where to find more Quickstones?" she was asking again, her voice hungry.

"Millions." Kendric was never one to moderate things, even lies.

"I could have a whole . . . cloak of them?"

"A carpet, if you like."

"Do they come from a mountain, like coldstone?"

A coldstone mountain? Kendric wondered madly. Both Torloc seeresses and coldstones, their hardened tears, were rare these days. How could there be an entire coldstone mountain? But one lie followed another by leaps and bounds, like a mountain a molehill.

"An entire mountain *range* of Quickstone," he promised.

"Ah." Her sigh was almost a purr.

"You've never mentioned your name," he said.

"Issiri," she answered. He could hardly tell whether it was a name or another jewel-besotted sigh.

Ahead, Issiri's light-strewn silhouette thinned as she entered a narrowing passage. Kendric prepared to edge sideways, soon finding a convoluted wall of rock at his back—and front. He mentally began berating the human architecture that ever fell short of his height and scant of his breadth.

He began—and stopped to put his mind to more urgent work. The walls narrowed as he pressed forward. He would barely squeeze through as it was. . . .

Kendric grunted and forced himself sideways, but brute force held little sway over solid stone.

"Aren't you coming?" Issiri sounded impatient. "I want to see the Quickstones."

"I'm . . . wedged . . . into the . . . wall," he replied, air sputtering from his lungs. "Squeezed . . . as if encoiled by a moon . . . weasel."

"I have always passed easily." She made no move to assist him.

Kendric wriggled as much as a man his size could, trying to maneuver a limb through the passage neck. Nothing changed, except the increasing force that ground his frame as a mill does pepper.

"Squeezed," he repeated with new insight. "The rock . . . chokes me. Some mechanism must trigger . . . it."

"I always pass this way and have had no difficulty."

"Perhaps . . . weight. Greater weight."

Kendric's shoulders pinched toward his spine; his ribs contemplated collapse. What did the dark woman have that he did not? Or he have that she did not? She obviously passed these hazards unaware. There must be *some* simple difference. . . .

The pressure tightened, not with the abrupt swell of a constricting moonweasel, but with an inexorable, almost indiscernible intensity. At least that gave Kendric a few grains of time, if he could discover what to do with them.

He didn't even have his sword to use as pry or brace— nor the comforting light of its hilt. Only a Quickstone glimmer hid in his boarskin purse, for his ring had lost luminescence here. . . .

"Quick!" he shouted.

"You found one? A Quickstone?"

"No, come . . . here—quick . . . ly."

She paused, her invisible form twinkling with gaudy stars but feet away.

Stupid, the creature was not only greedy but stupid! How had a semblance of Irissa been transformed into such a travesty?

Kendric irritably pondered the mystery even as the grains of time left to squander on wondering sifted away.

Two iron-gloved hands of rock compressed him. An idea flickered in the dark of his mind, but the boarskin purse was smashed shut against his side, and his right arm was wedged too tight to move anyway.

His left arm, however, was flung over his head, and he could just see . . .

Kendric saw the faintest gleam of ring gold. His magic or his confidence came squeezing up into his eyes; then they saw even better in the dark. He saw the two carved, man-high profiles he was being crushed between—aghh, the nose nudging the small of his back!

He saw the glossy dome of his ring, then reached into its depths and darkness and began pulling out strands of color no thicker than a hair. Sandstone, Gladestone, Lunestone leaped most readily to mind, thus copper, green, and silver glimmered in an interweaving net over the cabochon stone's surface. Filaments so slender that Kendric hardly saw them fattened to a glow and finally a blaze.

At his back he felt the pressure lessen and pulled a deep breath into his burning lungs. From then on, the crushing faces gave way a scintilla at a time. Kendric stood captive, breathing better every moment.

At last he creaked his frozen muscles into motion and peeled himself off the ebbing rock faces. Issiri still made a bright statue down the corridor.

"Are you through finally?" she asked, her voice curiously indifferent.

"Finally." He glanced to his ring. The restored trio of colors beamed there still, promising him passage through any trap that Issiri's jeweled overgown spared her.

In the dimness, Kendric's hand traced the profile of one crushing pillar. The stone was still warm from his body.

"Hurry," Issiri urged. "I'm most eager to leave here and find your Quickstone Mountains."

"I as well." He started after her with greater wariness. There was no predicting what other pitfalls awaited.

But the way was uneventful and the tiny assembly of gleams ahead of Kendric stopped at last before another piece of darkness.

"Here's the door," she said. "Follow me and we will be free of the lower regions."

Sweet words, thought Kendric, watching the lights of her attire press into the doorway's darkness and beyond. Kendric followed—and met a slick surface as black as any part of the maze.

Ahead of him, Issiri's glitter-defined form shimmered, shrank, glimmered out.

Kendric's hands traced the ornate frame of a mirror, then smoothed the chill, slightly swelling blackness of its surface. He saw the passage of his ringstone reflected there, saw the pale shift of his palm, a glitter from the curve of one eye white. He could never pass this hazard alone, he knew.

Issiri's promised "door" had been a dark mirror, one no magic could shatter unless the mirror's maker allowed it.

He knew, too, who made such mirrors.

Geronfrey.

It was a rumpled land, almost ruffled.

Irissa stood atop a hillock studying the shimmering landscape. Every hill descended into a valley, every valley into a stream. Foothills crimped the earth, and mountains—some solitary, others huddled into feudal masses—soared until their peaks bleached white and snagged the rosy clouds with their ragged edges.

Water plummeting from the prominences shimmered like samite veils in the distance. Water ran everywhere: down hill and up dale. Water pooled in every crumple of earth. From puddle to lake, the water reflected the sky in a spectrum of hues—soft and pale, color diffused to its subtlest shades.

The bodies of water reminded Irissa of opals flung across the countryside. Their liquid substance seemed the ghost of the black Iridesium metal, with its rainbow highlights now faded to silver and lavender, citron and aquamarine.

She glanced back to the vast lake that had been her

entryway to the land. A raging fire still ringed it, but from here the water looked wet and wind-rippled, quite ordinary.

Irissa returned to the overview. Three of the massed mountains looked more than that—perhaps the trio of peaked cities Kendric had glimpsed in Ludborg's scrying crystals once. Then this world was indeed . . . Rengarth.

Wind rippled the long grasses, showing a paler petticoat beneath the conventionally green blades. Wind and water made the landscape undulate. No roads drew lines across the vastness; with water pooling in every dimple of earth, no wonder. One walked where one wanted to—or could.

Irissa glanced up to mark the sunpoint so she could estimate the time of sunfall. Three blazing objects occupied the sky—a massive sun directly overhead and two smaller lights, paired like sconces on either side. Irissa started down the hill, aiming for the middle of the three cities only because she had to start somewhere, and it looked the closest.

Once actually traveling the landscape, Irissa found her landmarks sinking out of sight into the now annoying irregularity of the earth. The peaked cities would reappear whenever she breasted a hill, like fellow vessels glimpsed on the crest of a wave, but would vanish as her path dipped into a valley.

She never knew from moment to moment if she bore straight for her goal or not, and she breasted every hilltop seeming to face in a different direction.

Trees grew sparse and solitary. Irissa rested under one's lofty boughs to pull bread and radishes from her food sack. Shade was greater relief than she had thought. It had a wearing edge, this relentlessly full-sunned land, seemingly caught in the eternal high noon of a perfect summer's day.

Better than traveling in rain or snow, Irissa told herself. Kendric would point out, were he here, that endless perfection can weary one as much as unrelenting hardship.

Kendric, were he here—but, of course, he must be,

Irissa resolved, determined that her lone trial of a forbidden gate be worth the risk. Kendric *was* here. Rengarth exerted some unsuspected pull upon him; didn't it keep conjuring itself in his unwilling crystal castings?

As for Geronfrey . . . Irissa's reminiscent smile faded. He must occupy one of the three cities. Irissa realized that taking Kendric was one way Geronfrey might have ensured getting Irissa, that she was likely walking into a trap of that mage's design. A trap that might spring at any moment, in any form.

So Irissa rose and warily trod the up-and-down land, weaving around ponds and lakes, walking miles with little visible progress, one hand on her sword pommel and the other on the Overstone pouch.

A sudden tinkle of metal made Irissa pause in cutting through a hump-shouldered defile. The ground thumped behind her as someone vaulted down from the high ground above. Irissa spun and whipped her sword through the sash knot.

"A weapon! You bear a weapon," the newcomer marveled.

Irissa relaxed from her wary crouch. She confronted a woman like herself. A bejeweled dagger loosely crossed the stranger's palm in the way of a veteran knife wielder.

"I bear a sword," Irissa corrected, "with a longer tongue than your dagger." She pointed that tongue rudely.

The young woman's head tossed her contempt, heavy auburn braids beating her shoulders. She was delicately built despite her hostile stance, attired in an orange gown whose long skirt was drawn between her legs, the hem chained to her waist. Numerous implements chimed at each link—Irissa glimpsed a key; several metal bangles that looked half armor, half jewelry; a small mirror; a spoon, a cup, and a tiny book with scrolled cornerpieces.

"You haven't yet explained yourself—or your weapon," the woman prompted, sawing the air suggestively with the knife blade.

"Why should I?" Irissa said.

A thump and a second chime rang behind her. She whirled, knowing what she would find—another confronter. This one was male and, like the woman, slightly built. Still, the pair radiated a wiry confidence Irissa had no wish to test. As she so often—and fruitlessly—counseled Kendric, she would try words before swords anytime.

"I am Irissa of . . . of Edanvant," she said, naming her newfound home as home for the first time. "I have come to Rengarth . . ."—neither man nor woman blinked at this naming—"to find someone. I carry a sword because it is mine, because new lands offer new customs, some of them cutting, and because I would defend myself."

The woman lowered her knife. "She doesn't know."

"Know what?" Irissa twisted to see the man. He was shaking his fire-red head. His waist chain chimed with objects similar to the woman's.

"No woman in Rengarth may bear arms," he began a bit sententiously. Momentarily, he reminded Irissa of her grandfather, Medoc, though he looked nothing like the Torloc.

"What about *her*?" Irissa swiveled again to rudely point, rapidly growing dizzy. The day had been hot, the walk long, and she was . . . pregnant. There, no getting around that; she'd seen it with her own inner eyes.

"No woman in Rengarth may bear arms . . . unless she is an heir," the woman put in pertly.

"To what?"

"The High Seat of Rengarth in the city of Solanandor Tierze."

"You are a . . . an heir, then?" Irissa dubiously eyed the woman's outfit. "To this High Seat?"

"I am Aven, and I am heir."

Irissa kept her back to the grassy wall behind her as the man walked closer. "And I am heir also. Call me Sin." Irissa studied his amiably freckled face and found the juxtaposition of name and person disconcerting. "Why do you smile?" he demanded none too courteously.

"What a rough place this Solanandor Tierze must be,

that its heirs wander so far from their throne, in such rugged clothing, accosting strangers."

"Accosting?" The woman snorted, then laughed until she caught her breath and spoke again. "This is not accosting." Her eyes flashed burnt umber as her knife tip undulated through Irissa's silk sleeve. "Accosting draws blood. We merely investigate. Besides, the High Seat has been usurped."

"So you two are heirs to nothing."

"To everything." Sin's smile showed teeth whiter than the milky skin glimpsed between his freckles. "'Heir' implies potential. Almost anyone in Rengarth is a potential heir until a Ruler and Reginatrix are established."

"Can you both be heirs, though?"

"Why not? We are brother and sister." Aven leaned against the rocky wall, her knife point poking Irissa's side for conversational emphasis. "And our parents occupied the throne for a time. Unfortunately, a good many other people's parents occupied the throne at one time or another. That's why the Usurper has had it to himself for so long."

"But why stand here accosting strangers when you could be claiming the High Seat?"

"We raise an army." Sin lifted a wicked blade that was overlong for a dagger, too short for a sword, and obviously capable of doing the worst damage of both weapons. A mocking grin charmed his features. "An army of presumptive heirs. Very presumptuous heirs."

"I suppose," said his sister, tilting her head so the braids looped engagingly around her freckled face, "that we could make Irissa an . . . honorary heir. We comprise, after all, a majority of our line. Then she can still carry her Usurper-sticker."

"That would be most agreeable," Irissa noted with steel in her voice. "For I will not give it up except point-first."

The hilt of Sin's weapon bowed toward Irissa's forehead. She felt her magic stiffening around her into a protective cloak. But the weighted hilt merely tapped the Iridesium circlet at her brow, ringing melodiously.

"I name thee Irissa of . . . far Edan—"

"Edanvant."

". . . of Edanvant, heir apparent."

"Is that all?" Irissa wondered.

Aven's raisin-plump eyes gleamed. "Oh, being an heir is easy. The hard part is what comes next."

"Then I'll be on my way." Irissa pushed off the rocky wall, sword in hand. "I want to reach shelter, a city, by sunfall."

"A city for shelter!" Sin hooted until mirth doubled him over. He collapsed to the ground and began rolling. "What a quaint idea! Cities crawl with heir assassins and royal tainters."

"Which city were you heading for?" his sister asked more politely.

Irissa waved in a direction she hoped was accurate. "The, er . . . middle one."

"The middle one." Aven's eyes rested pointedly on her brother's face. "I fear you'd better avoid that."

"Why?" Irissa was becoming angry.

"Because it's not really there."

"I saw it!"

"It's a . . . reflection—of the other two cities, So-lanandor Tierze and Liderion. It isn't a healthy expedition, especially for heirs."

"Then I won't be an heir anymore!" Irissa, exasperated, spit out.

"Then give up your sword." Aven's eyes were placid but her voice was harder than the callused white palm she extended imperiously. At least she had already mastered royal gestures.

"Where shall a stranger go in this land, then, to find another stranger?"

"You search for a stranger. How . . . odd." Sin sat on the ground before Irissa, no longer laughing. With his lanky legs intertwined, he seemed more impish than threatening.

"A stranger to you and to Rengarth," Irissa modified. "Kendric is no stranger to me."

"Kendric." Aven joined her brother on the ground. "The name has a familiar chime—" She snapped a small bell on her belt.

"You've heard of him—here!" Irissa bent to let her gaze urge answers at them.

"What . . . lovely eyes you have." Aven's hand reached for Irissa's face. "I've never seen silver eyes before."

Irissa flinched away, remembering her seeresshood, her powers. What would happen, she wondered, if she forced entry to Aven's open gaze and sought answers firsthand?

"Very striking," Sin admired in a tone that first irritated, then surprised, and finally secretly pleased Irissa.

She tossed her own black forebraids back over her shoulders and spoke to them both. "What does the name 'Kendric' mean to you?"

Brother and sister consulted each other in the same head-turning, eye-meeting gesture, as if they were hounds trained to it. Of course, twins! No wonder they were "both" heirs, Irissa thought.

"Was it—Arndric?"

"Wenrick, I think," Sin answered his sister. "But that was several Rulers ago and we were . . . sleeping then."

"Ah. . . ." Aven's sharp gaze softened as her face saddened. "I would rather be awake." She glanced to Irissa, reading anxiety in her eyes. "Don't make silver so sad. We have heard a name similar to Kendric somewhere in Rengarth's ancient history. But we remember poorly.

"Likely, it was some deposed Ruler or other. They come and go like wind and water. Only the Usurper endures, endlessly usurping."

"The *same* Usurper?"

"So he says."

"And what name does *he* use?" Irissa felt the blood slow in her body, could sense the inevitable answer rising to her mind.

"That we know." Sin grinned broadly. "Geronfrey—as it was in the Beginning, is Now, and Ever shall be."

Irissa felt the ground rock, or felt something within her rock the ground. She sat back, roughly.

"What's the matter?" Aven wondered, sheathing her knife.

"Nothing," Irissa answered dully. "I have only found what I expected I would. Or at least half of it—the worst half."

CHAPTER
11

KENDRIC STOOD BETWEEN THE FACING PROFILES OF rock. Only a dim phosphorescence limned their features.

Force couldn't remove his ring of Inlands Stones, but he could twist it. He wrenched it around his finger, band-side out and stone-side in. Then he made a fist.

Immediately, the glow he had evoked in the cabochon vanished into the dark of his palm. At the same time, he could sense the parallel rock faces swelling toward him.

So simple, he thought. Issiri, allowed the run of the place—even its deepest, darkest labyrinths—Issiri passed without impediment because the jewels she wore disarmed some built-in defense. And not simply *her* jewels—any jewels.

Already the rocky noses were butting Kendric at front and rear. He steeled himself against their prodding and continued to evolve his plan. Were the moving rock walls magic or mechanism? If magic, they had responded to his own ringborne powers alone, as they did now.

If not wholly magic, but mere reality abetted by magic, they would move to another pattern. If the gemstones' *light,* rather than their magical properties, overcame the danger, the rocks might be a mechanism.

Kendric felt the stones press inward until he was wedged between them, then fanned his left hand. Freed, the light of the ring winked bright. He sensed a moment of ceased action—when the walls no longer moved but prepared to retreat.

He pulled free and darted behind the rear rock face, into the dark . . . and then through it—right through the rock walls, as easily as Issiri had come and gone in the cul-de-sac of dark mirror at corridor's end.

Kendric breathed relief to find himself in a dim niche—the vacancy created when slabs of rock had moved inward. Behind him, unstimulated by his presence, the slabs began to slide back. In moments, rock would fill the niche in which he stood, crushing him to so much slightly damp bone powder—unless there was a way beyond the stone pocket. . . .

Cursing the darkness, he felt its limits. Velvet cables swagged over his head. Velvet-muffled tracks inlaid the floor—no wonder the moving rock faces had made no sound!

Kendric's hand followed the cables to an endpoint, then fumbled over the wall face. Behind him the silent stone was gliding back into its place—a place his body occupied now. He realized his ring could only separate the opposing profiles as they met—it was now doing nothing to halt their return.

Kendric gritted his teeth, recognizing risk for the bit he had taken between them. If he failed to find an exit, the pestle and mortar of realigning rock face and nook would make mincemeat of him.

So his fingertips scraped rough stone in the dark, finding at last a velvet bellpull. Retreating rock brushed his back as he jerked the heavy cord, then an inrush of warm air drew him outward. His head banged a lintel, but he felt no irritation, only a surge of triumph. What mouse cares if the way out of a trap be cramped?

Blinking, Kendric stood in full light hearing a small door behind him snap shut. On this side was no crude passage, but a room of wood-paneled walls.

Kendric ran his hand over a rippling grain of deep green and silver wood. A plush nap tickled his palm. Even wood here was velvet, he marveled.

He spun to fully regard where his foolhardiness had

led him—into a most civil circular chamber lit by clustered tapers. Moss-lush carpets were figured with designs that shifted as his feet crossed them.

He moved as silently as the rock faces, as Issiri herself, to the single door exiting the room. A loop of velvet played handle. Kendric opened the door on muffled hinges. A second chamber yawned beyond, tapestries covering the wooden walls, yet as empty as the one he left.

From chamber to chamber Kendric went—sinking farther and farther into a luxury so diffuse it dazzled him. Gradually furniture appeared in the rooms—chairs shaped from the horns of unheard-of beasts and hides of exotic pattern; tables carved from rainbow-grained woods; chests banded in rare green gold and bright blue-green metals Kendric had never seen before.

Every room was deserted and windowless, empty and closed. The deeper he penetrated, the more he despaired of finding his way out, the more imprisoned he felt. The dungeon's discomforts began to seem clean, uncluttered. Peaceful.

Food began appearing atop the tables as he strode from room to room—not appearing as he watched, a form of magic he would have accepted, but waiting there unobtrusively, more in each succeeding chamber.

His stomach, having accommodated hunger silently for hours, stopped him at a food-burdened table. Fruit floated in a compote shaped like human forearms and cupped hands. Kendric leaned back and looked down to see if the rest of the figure didn't crouch beneath the tabletop, supporting it.

Such a vision, no matter how unsettling, would have soothed him with the presence of a person at least. But no one shared the room with him. His stomach growled, asserting its undeniable presence.

Kendric eyed the compote fruit—opalescent-skinned apples with emerald-green stems. Thorns speared forth from cockscombs of moist violet and aqua berries. Roots mimed the shapes of beasts Kendric had never seen before.

Tempted, Kendric ignored the fruit and moved on. The next room added wine carafes to the arrangement. Each successive chamber expanded the array of food, all of it untouched save by the nervous flicker of candle flames.

In each room, Kendric searched the array for the prize of a table knife. Despite platters of fish and fowl, bowls of vegetables and fruits, saucers of puddings and soups, not a spoon, knife, or fork was to be seen.

His pace had increased as his impatience gained momentum. Kendric was striding through the rooms heedless of their contents, searching for he knew not what, perhaps an end to them even if it should be another dungeon.

He burst through yet another velvet-handled door into yet another richly accoutred room and stopped dead.

Issiri sat on a stool with her back to him, her beringed fingers flashing as she worked a needle through a jeweled tapestry.

Dancing candlelight burnished her gem-caged figure with a firestorm of color, motion, and light. Kendric caught his breath, thinking to demand an explanation.

"Now, how did *you* get out?" an urbane, amused voice inquired instead.

Turning, Kendric saw a man he had seen before, looking much the same, yet unfamiliar at the same time.

"*My* business," Kendric gruffed back, swaddling his surprise in hunger-edged irritation.

"Sit," Geronfrey urged with a velvet-gloved hand.

Kendric studied the chamber, then stalked to a tapestry-cushioned bench against a paneled wall. He did not sit.

"You have walked some time," Geronfrey said.

"And some distance. What palace requires such a redundancy of rooms? You used to keep a plainer place."

Geronfrey laughed, easing onto an X chair with broad, wing-shaped arms on which to rest his elbows. Like snarled eyelashes, the brightest hairs of his golden beard caught the light. His eyes shone as serenely blue as ever, his pleasant face looked no older, and no younger.

"A plainer place," the sorcerer agreed, "was what I

kept in Rule. But this is Rengarth, and nothing is plain here."

"Except your dungeons."

Geronfrey smiled. "Your wit seems to have warmed since last we met."

"But my patience has cooled."

Geronfrey's black velvet gauntlets, scrolled with coiled threads as gilt as his eyelashes, met at the palms as he tented his fingers to regard Kendric over their sinister apex.

"You wonder why I need so many rooms. A fair question. Now I tell you that you passed through only one chamber on your way here."

"Only one! There were dozens—each tricked out with more lavish fripperies!"

"I can see why Mauvedona found your astoundment interesting." Geronfrey's forefinger lifted with one eyebrow. "One. You merely saw it in multiples, a piece at a time."

"I don't believe you."

"Look, then."

Kendric went to the door and pulled it open. A room lay beyond it, containing all the items he had seen stage by stage and step by step in the progression of empty chambers. He stalked over the carpeting, ignoring the altering pattern beneath his feet, and jerked the opposite door open. It faced into solid rock.

"Sorcery, I suppose." Kendric returned to the room where Geronfrey waited. The shadow Irissa plied her flashing needle like a sword, paying him no attention. He wondered if that was deliberate—an attempt to hide her dungeon excursion from Geronfrey—or utter indifference.

"Sorcery," Geronfrey concurred. "It suited me to delay your arrival until I was ready."

"For what?"

"Oh, sit! You are far too lengthsome to stand and glower indefinitely. I shall crick my neck looking at you."

"Not half what I would do to it."

"Threats mean more when you are in a position to ex-

ecute them. You are my guest again, and I would have you
sit. But as you wish."

"I suppose you have my sword as well."

"Why would I want the shadow of a shadow? It fell to
ice, I know not where—"

"You don't?"

Geronfrey shrugged. "I'll look for it." He rose and
went to a table spired with decanters, choosing the simplest—a long-necked one of clear glass. The liquid within
swirled mistily. Kendric saw pale rainbow shades coiling
within the substance.

Geronfrey poured a period-small liquid dot upon the
table. "Think about your sword," he said. Kendric hesitated, unused to orders, especially to orders he didn't understand. "Is thinking too much for you still, then?" the
sorcerer jibed. "I didn't say envision it; I said remember
it."

Kendric did, coming over as the fat water drop thinned
and spread into an opalescent pool. Its colors separated,
then reassembled, taking shape. He glanced curiously at Issiri, but her head remained lowered, her expression hidden. She was as dormant as any object in the room.

In the palm-sized skin of water, Kendric saw his sword
angled into an expanse of ice. A frozen lake, perhaps. He
glanced up to find Geronfrey watching him.

"I fear your sword has fallen upon hard times,
Wrathman. That is the Paramount Athanor at the Iron-ice
Mountains, a far-flung place even in this far-flung land.
Well, you asked a question. I didn't say you'd like the an-
swer."

"I'll ask another," Kendric ventured. "Why am I
here?"

"You *have* grown profound in your travels, or do you
refer merely to the common mortal curiosity of motives
that I find so tiresome?"

"You drew me here?"

"You brought yourself to my attention."

"In the Black Tower?"

"In my old tower under Falgontooth Mountain in Rule, first. Then in Edanvant, in the tower you call black. I call it one of my many doors."

"Doors? Illusions likely." Kendric glanced at Issiri. "As she is."

"Oh, she is no illusion . . . no, the contrary. Come, my child." The sorcerer stretched out sable-gloved fingers.

Something about that shrouded hand made Kendric flinch, but Issiri rose and came rustling over, awash in a jeweled glitter so pervasive she seemed some scale-armored reptile.

Geronfrey thrust Issiri's ring-heavy hand at Kendric. "Take it. You will see she is real."

He paused, remembering how this woman had melted into the dark mirror. Her likeness to Irissa no longer unnerved him unduly; her behavior was so unlike Irissa's, and behavior was the soul of a person, not some outer similitude.

"You avoided my fruit, as well," Geronfrey noted, "but foodstuff does not recognize discourtesy. She does."

"I disagree. She recognizes little but the gaudy flash of baubles."

Geronfrey shrugged. "She is young. Comparatively speaking."

"Your ring!" Issiri's exclamation quieted both men. Her malachite-dark eyes brightened to borgia green as she stared at Kendric's hand. She reached to touch it. Only his not inconsiderable will kept him from shrinking from her touch.

Her flesh felt cool, but was clearly living, or seemed so. A delicately nailed fingertip circled the cabochon. "Pretty," she said.

Kendric's fingers curled into a fist. "Useful."

"Beauty has use, too," Geronfrey said.

"And use, beauty," Kendric said adamantly.

"But she is real, you agree?"

"She . . . seems real enough, in a fleshly way. What is she?"

"Haven't you guessed?"

"I have speculated but will keep it to myself. I thought you'd enjoy confounding me with the answer."

"I do not enjoy confounding you, Wrathman." Geronfrey's blond brows knit as he paced away. "I did not even want you here in Rengarth—you least and last of all, if you only knew! But you insisted on . . . battering . . . at my exquisite sorcerous borders with your crude cudgels of magic. What a waste Irissa's Torloc powers are on you—"

"My sentiments exactly."

"And then you add insult to injury by failing to appreciate what has been bestowed upon you."

"I am more used to adding injury to insult," Kendric warned.

"You can do neither here. You are in my power in the most ironclad sense of the word."

"Possibly. Is she in your power, too?" He nodded to Issiri, who still gazed deeply into Kendric's ringstone, her eyes as glazed as the cabochon surface itself.

Geronfrey sighed. "A fragile construction, this. Woven from so little—and so much. A mere . . . sliver of an Irissa of another day—a slice of her virgin vanity, really—breathed upon the surface of my Dark Mirror in Rule, kept liquid and supple in the pool that bottoms the Swallowing Cavern. Coddled and carried and kept. Brought with me and unfurled. Tended and nurtured. Fed and watered. Watched and worried over. Kept . . . alive."

"You could not win the original, so you are content with this simulacrum, this . . . pale imitation you drenched in darkness? This shadow isn't Irissa! She holds none of the worth of Irissa! You fool yourself, great sorcerer. I almost pity you, that you deceive yourself so much with so little."

Geronfrey's face tautened. "*You* deceive yourself! I care nothing for the vessel, only its contents."

"Contents . . . ?" Kendric turned to regard Issiri.

Her dark head was crowned with the same rainbow circlet that sunlight ignited in Irissa's hair. She even wore an Iridesium circlet around her forehead, although the metal was dimmer than the vibrant, color-chased Iridesium Irissa wore. Everything about Issiri was Irissa dampened. Kendric saw only a tool, a dark reflection empty of character. "Contents?" he repeated.

"She bears a child—my child, as Irissa bears yours."

Shock rinsed Kendric from face to feet. He stood frozen, for the first time in his life wounded more fully by a word than a weapon.

"Child? But how—? She is . . . vapor, mist, you admit it yourself! It must take all your arts to make her move, speak, seem as real as this."

"All my arts and some imported ones."

"I knew you were trying to wrest Irissa through a hidden gate to your world, wherever it was; Rengarth, you say."

"And so it is."

"But how could you conceive a child upon a shadow?" Kendric stared at Issiri with equal distaste and distrust.

"I think you would not care to know." Geronfrey backed away dismissively.

Kendric clamped a detaining hand to his arm.

"Careful, man of Rule. I am in my seat now, my element. Any effort of yours—force or magic—is doomed."

"Vanity, then, sorcerer. Your breed is ever fond of that, as your shadow wife proves. Tell me how you did it. Boast a little. Surely you suffer for an audience."

Geronfrey smiled at the undampened threat in Kendric's voice, as a man of circuitous subtlety admires a foe's unabashed directness.

"If you will sit," the sorcerer said.

Kendric did at last, ungraciously, with as much creaking as possible, upon the bench. Issiri sank beside him, still coveting his ring, although her every finger and both thumbs wore rings thicker than metal gauntlets. Geronfrey's face flickered annoyance at her attachment to Kendric, but he returned to his chair and arranged himself to tell his tale.

"You remember the Inlands of Ten and my keep there?"

"I remember you wearing another face and name there, and inviting me to dine. I remember being lost in some spell of your devising while you lured Irissa up your velvet stairway. Now I decline to eat your invitings and have probably saved myself a stomachache for it."

"Have you never wondered *why* I drew Irissa to my many-windowed tower chamber, why you found her caged within a mirror frame?"

"I broke her free," Kendric answered fiercely. "I broke that dread dark mirror of yours forever."

"Only a shadow of it. And in that shadow, she . . ." —Geronfrey nodded almost fondly to Issiri—"she walked. I needed Irissa to breathe life into her sister image, to animate her to the degree I found necessary then. And so she did."

Kendric had never complimented himself for mental agility; it was not his specialty unless a matter of tactics. Now, unwanted, his mind was twisting acrobat-supple to a conclusion that revolted his spirit.

"Then? You . . . impregnated the shadow Irissa then? While Irissa herself was in the mirror?" Horror made his voice a whisper, as if Issiri were too innocent to hear. "How could you subdue Irissa so? Her magic was her shield. She resisted you in Rule, and would again in the Inlands of Ten. Even your spells couldn't make her violate her will."

"No."

Relief pressed Kendric against the bench back.

Then Geronfrey smiled again. "You helped me."

He started forward. "I? I was spelled below."

"You, yes. But not your image. I evoked your image for myself, evoked a night under Falgontooth when Irissa left me in my high tower, and came to you instead.

"That night she spent her maidenhood—and the magical powers she confers on the man she shares it with—on you. 'Tis only just that she aid me in my enterprise with this 'shadow,' as you call it. It is all she legitimately left to me—a dim image from a dark mirror. You do well to gawk; what I have accomplished is beyond . . . conception.''

Kendric stood, whole bloody oceans roaring in his ears, his mind thick with the image of four figures merged into two, of two simulacrums donned like a suit of armor, of a false Irissa and a false Kendric mating in Rule for a false, second time and thus fulfilling Geronfrey's ambitions from the first.

"Travesty!" Kendric's voice was low but it seemed thunder rumbled far away.

He stood, Issiri clinging to his beringed hand, and he flicked her away. She fell to the bench, a shadow sinking out of substance, her bejeweled gown rattling like hail against the wood.

Kendric's rage surrounded him like a fire he could spread but not quite feel, a power more terrible than any magical one.

One stride took him to Geronfrey's chair. His booted foot kicked the base, and the chair spun sideways. Unsupported, Geronfrey—an ordinary-sized man despite his powers—sagged in Kendric's grasp like a sack of potatoes.

Kendric stared into the sorcerer's eyes unafraid. He didn't want to kill him—either the man or the mage. He wanted only to drink deep of his own disbelief, see through the icy blue eyes to the depths of Geronfrey's ambitions and deception.

Without thinking, Kendric was plunging into the sorcerer's inner self. He felt resistance—strong resistance—but his rage-buttressed magic was like the iron prow of a ship. It cut so swift and deep it could have plowed land as well as water.

Into the cold blue inner sea he sailed, land a long-forgotten memory. Only islands sailed by, each remote, unimportant. One assumed the teardrop shape of the Six Realms of Rule. Another reminded Kendric of the Inlands of Ten . . . yet another of Edanvant.

More islands—alien and unnamed—floated past, many more blots of land that were only that to Geronfrey's memory. All were stepping-stones to one ultimate land, one almost unreachable shore.

Kendric saw it now . . . Rengarth. Lost, limpid Rengarth. The horizon fattened on it, and Kendric found himself inexorably drawn to it, as a fish caught on a translucent line.

And always in the water, Kendric saw a long, black snake undulating through the waves. A lock of dark hair, animated and driving mindlessly. Kendric led it, chased it, paced it, caught it as it curled around a stone rising island-lonely in the water.

On that stone sat a seed—a pale yellow seed with an eye-bright dot of blue on its surface.

Not Irissa's powers, Kendric knew now, though Geronfrey would have taken them in the bargain—but Irissa's self and the self of that self. That's what Geronfrey had always wanted from Irissa, something so common that it was ironic he required an uncommon woman to accomplish it.

The seed fanned open on the stone as Kendric contemplated it. A black tendril wove up from the sea, cleaving stone like a sword.

Kendric's mind felt as divided. Reality's sharp, dark blade halved his wits, severed his will from him. He was adrift deep inside Geronfrey's innermost domain—unguarded, undefended, unconcerned.

His rash delving swept away from him. The icy blue sea dredged up a mammoth midnight eel to leech onto his throat and wrest him through a shattered spray of waves, away from Past and Future, from Stone and Seed, and into the present.

He was standing in a blazing chamber, dazed, while a shadow melted into the edges of his vision. Before him, Geronfrey's fury-ridden form shrank as the room rushed away from Kendric in a rapid reversal of the same, interminable chain of stages he had first seen.

Carpeting congealed at his feet. Walls raced by as if borne by maddened bearing-beasts. A barrier of dark, ungiving rock raised at his rear. He felt himself being hurled toward the stone walls of his dungeon, knowing that this time there would be no gap to slip between, knowing impact would be swift, harsh, and final. . . .

His magic remained at wit's end with his will. Kendric couldn't tell whether the rock rushed to him or he rushed to the rock. He even began to sense the first yearning tremor of impact along his spine.

"Duck, you silly," a voice sizzled in his ears so imperiously that he lowered his head and shoulders. He felt a quiver as rock met flesh, and rock . . . melted. Liquid, black, it washed past him, soft as a Torloc seeress's tear before it hardens to coldstone.

In the endless black distance, Kendric glimpsed Issiri's moth-pale face, her cat's eyes burning momentarily crimson beneath the green.

Then everything was gone. Kendric found himself patting at the sleek opaque surface of an unoccupied mirror, only his own shaken face staring back at him.

He stood at the end of the labyrinth staring into bottomless mirror, remembering Issiri melting through it . . . remembering the admonishing, faraway voice . . . wondering if he had dreamed everything that had happened after Issiri had walked through a stone wall as through water, into glass.

CHAPTER
12

"*ONLY THE WORST PATH TO TAKE FOR ONE IN MY CONDI-tion*," hissed a nearby voice.

"What?" Irissa paused in scrambling up a rock-strewn bank to look for the speaker.

Sin's nature-dappled features peered over the ridge. "Nothing. I was just telling Aven that we'll never reach shelter by sunfall at this rate." He grimaced until his freckles converged into a suntan.

Irissa glanced to the dimming sky, knowing he was right, knowing that her lagging pace made him right. "I'm sorry. The land undulates like an Empress Falgon's spine—"

"Like a what?" Aven's impish face popped up beside her brother's.

"An Empress . . . oh, never mind. It's tiring landscape, that's all."

"That's what keeps Rengarthians safe and separate. Solanandor Tierze is four-pair-of-boots-wear from Liderion." Sin had hauled himself atop the ridge and sat with crossed ankles to wait for Irissa to climb the hill's sharp withers.

She might have concluded that Rengarth suffered from a lack of male gallantry, but Aven also arranged herself on the rocks to watch without offering assistance.

Irissa grasped the bare sticks protruding here and there from the hard earth and pulled herself up the slope. "Rest a moment," she pled when she mounted the ridge. Her heart knocked against the Overstone that nestled near it.

Sin, half risen already, sat again and spat at an almost politely distant rock. Startled, Irissa seemed to hear the spit sizzle as it landed. She smoothed her tunic over her knees and tried not to flinch at Rengarthian manners. Or illusions. First she heard a voice that wasn't there—at least no one else had heard it—now she heard spittle hiss.

She soothed her abraded sensibilities by looking to the land. As always, from a distance its roughness seemed charming. The three suns were easing toward what Irissa presumed was the Rengarthian equivalent of the west. The smaller bracketing suns burned new-grass green; the larger central one was an orange globe of dragon fire.

Sunfall dimmed the land's unceasing rumples into a darkly glimmering surface, like sunlight and shadow dueling over a discarded shirt of chain mail.

The peaks of the two outermost cities etched flat black spires against the luminous horizon. And the third city, the third was . . .

"It's gone!"

"What?" Sin and Aven clapped nervous hands to their chain-hung implements, as if pickpockets infested this wilderness.

"The city. You call it the—"

"Spectral City," Aven trilled into Irissa's sentence. The setting suns were at the woman's back, but Irissa could still read the dismissive merriment on her face. "It's called the Spectral City for a reason. You've just seen it."

"I've just *not* seen it," Irissa corrected.

Sin shrugged. "The Spectral City comes and goes. Either way, we find it best to stay away."

"Aren't you curious?" Irissa wondered.

"About what?"

Irissa stared from Aven to Sin and back again. A nimbus of riotous sunfall shades surrounded their oddly similar but different faces, overpowering for once the heady scarlet of their natural coloring.

"Aren't you curious about where the city . . . goes—and why?" Irissa said.

They shrugged in concert. "Where do the sinking suns go—and why?" Aven mimicked. "They always shine again in the morning. So it is with the Spectral City. It comes again."

"We are concerned with real cities," Sin added with superiority. "Great events stir in Rengarth. The day of heir-right is at hand. Soon will be shown to us the heir who will finally overthrow the Usurper and loosen his deathless grip upon our two cities and the lives of all Rengarthians."

"Geronfrey rules *two* cities?" Irissa's heart sank with the waning suns. Not only were Kendric's whereabouts less certain now, but clearly there was no sanctuary city for them to claim if . . . when . . . Irissa found him.

"Now and then," Sin said loosely. "Like the Spectral City, he comes and goes, too, but he always comes back."

"That's why so many royal families plague Rengarth," Aven said, laughing. "Each time, the Usurper is beaten back before he can beget an heir, and the winning family occupies the High Seat. The Usurper comes again to topple their heirs, ruling for a few decades until another family waxes strong enough to overthrow the Usurper. After all these centuries, almost everyone in Rengarth can claim legitimate heirship."

"And it continues thus?" Irissa marveled.

"As long as the Usurper has no heir. Something in his power wanes, very slowly. When he is weakened enough to be banished for a time, he goes . . . somewhere . . . and returns with greater power. But no heir."

"So it has gone for centuries," Sin put in, yawning. "And it seems as if we have been sitting here nearly as long. Darkfall has all but blinded us. Now that we can't see, I suppose Irissa is ready to hunt shelter for the night."

"Shelter—? Out there?" Irissa studied the landforms sinking into black velvet darkness.

The twins jumped to their feet, neither lending a hand to pull Irissa upright. She stood and teetered on the ridge, feeling she was about to plunge into a well of darkness, though she'd had enough of such things.

"Come on!" Sin loped down the hillside, vanishing after taking two steps.

Aven lingered to cast Irissa an encouraging glance. "We dare not remain out after sunfall. The grassweavers come."

Grassweavers didn't sound too dire, but rather charming. Irissa put palm to sword hilt, feeling the emerald pommelstone warm to her touch, just as the Overstone always did.

She found comfort in that consistency, those small, similar magics . . . and more comfort when her inner senses evoked a green light that spread far beyond the hilt.

This time, the emerald hiltstone preened until a great swath of light fanned forth. Every blade of trampled grass at Irissa's feet shone luminously green.

Aven and Sin paused in loping down the incline. Irissa saw their upturned profiles etched in a green edging of light that contrasted oddly with their red hair and auburn freckles.

"Does your sword always do that?" Sin asked, not waiting for Irissa's answer. "Hurry," they urged in tandem. By her newborn light, Irissa saw worry crinkling their brows with identical furrows.

The heel of Irissa's palm tilted the hilt forward to light a downward path, then she plunged into the sea of grass between her and them.

"Not so fast!" a familiar voice hissed beside her, almost as if curled around her neck. *"This seesaw countryside would agitate an urn of curdled milk."*

Irissa paused and looked around. No one walked alongside her. No one talked. She started forward again, then stopped, one foot frozen above the turf the way a cat will pause when it is too dainty—or too hungry—to rush things.

"Felabba?" she queried the breeze, the air around her, herself.

The question whistled away, leaving—as most unanswered questions do—a queasy, unsettled feeling at the pit of Irissa's stomach. That feeling stayed with her a good deal these days. Part of it was Kendric's worrisome absence. Another part of it was—might be—the unsung presence of someone . . . something . . . else.

At night, in the utter moonless dark, the Rengarthian winds gossiped in the grasses.

Irissa heard them arguing softly at the fringes of her existence. She walked two paces behind Aven and Sin; somehow three abreast made a party that never stayed even.

The two ahead chatted. References to the city, their friends, their plans, came whipping back to Irissa on itinerant tendrils of breeze. The pair seemed unworried about finding shelter, but they obviously didn't care to linger outside too long after sunfall, either.

Irissa's embarrassingly efficient hilt-light swelled like the land. It heaved to brilliance, ebbed to a shadow of itself, then brightened again. Her fingers couldn't quite encompass it; rays of green light leaked in all directions. The light fought the dark, both managing to intensify nature's native green to a lurid emerald-black excess.

Light beams glanced off crystal-dusted rocks, off the grasses' wet gleam, though there had been no rain since Irissa had fallen into this lavish countryside. Perhaps dew gathered early on Rengarth, she thought. Very early.

Her steps quickened, the Overstone bruising her breastbone as she walked. Some instinct kept her lagging behind her companions. She studied the light-shot landscape as she went, and nowhere saw any sign of shelter.

Other signs came first: A glittering loop on the meadow as uniform as an ink scrawl trailing a quill. A certain repetitive hissing among the knee-high grasses, as of a thousand serpents convening. A bowing of the upright grass strands, not in a single wind-driven line, but in all directions at once, as if plants were scattering from some presence, some . . . unseen presence.

The Spectral City, Irissa thought. What if the Spectral City is . . . moving . . . past us, around us, through us? Her magical senses itched but she could find nothing specific to scratch.

"Faster," some internal voice goaded. Her legs milled through the low growth, chasing the dark that the hiltstone light always kept several paces ahead of her.

"Slower," that other, inward/outward voice argued. *"Remember what you bear."*

"My child?" Irissa whispered to herself.

The only answer was the wise, mocking laughter of the wind weaving among the shifting grasses.

Around herself, around all three, Irissa saw the meadow's pattern alter. Grasses parted, braided, interwove into a fabric of unnatural constriction.

And the weaving was tightening upon them, like a hand fisting around a flower it wishes to pluck.

Then she saw them—grassweavers . . . distant translucent filaments working their stately warp and woof on the loom of night. Their motions made a musicless dance. Gleaming trails foamed in their wakes and their basket-weaving bodies swelled as they neared. Irissa perceived a great assembly of spectral serpents writhing rhythmically in the grasses.

She hurried to catch up to Aven and Sin.

"Are those your grassweavers?"

The pair stopped. "Oh, yes. Quite an upwelling."

"Will they harm us?"

"They are spectral, like the city," Aven said. But she sounded uncertain for the first time.

"So they won't harm us?"

Sin grinned. "Depends what you consider harm. No one has reported ill of them, but then, few have been present when they welter. Rengarthians stay locked in their cities by night, and seldom travel anyway."

"Not you two," Irissa countered.

"We had a mission," Aven said mysteriously, "to Liderion. Besides, it is easy to be brave when we face only legends. Since childhood we have been warned of grassweavers. Why fear a phantom?"

"These are not phantoms now!" Irissa pointed out.

Grassweavers roiled nearer, their delicate bodies swelling to gigantic proportions. Despite their size, they remained airy constructs, more the stuff of dreams than nightmares.

A semicircle of the things cavorted on the grasses, flattening the long slender stems, silvering them with threads of some sticky substance.

"'Tis said grassweavers live beneath the ground," Aven began reciting in the remembered singsong of childhood. "When the suns are rightly configured they slither by night to the surface to enmesh the unwary in the dead hair of grasses. Then these lost ones are woven deep into the matted fabric of earth, like dried leaves and dying birds. . . ."

"Hush, Aven. An heir does not believe such stories." Sin was backing away and pushing forward at the same time. "Shelter waits only steps away—"

Irissa let her eyes leave the spectacle of the assembling grassweavers. Behind the three stood only another grassy hillock, not impossible to climb—for them, or for the grassweavers.

She sighed heavily, then dipped her sword hilt to the dark turf. Its green light touched off the grass as if it were tinder. Irissa scribed an arc of light around the threesome, pinning them against the hill's sheltered side.

"What is the green fire?" Aven wondered. She passed a bold palm through the weakest tongue of flame. Irissa yanked her back by a thick braid until Aven squealed.

"The green fire is my magic, Aven, and may bite. Are you burned?"

Aven turned her hand to the lurid light. Irissa considered the twins rough and hardy, but Aven's fingers were finely made, as delicately jointed as an Iridesium gauntlet.

"Cold . . . The flames are icy," Aven marveled. "Whence comes your cold fire?"

"From myself," Irissa said. "From my own cool rage to survive." She gauged the pellucid serpent forms, then jerked Aven farther back to the base of the hill where Sin waited patiently, as if to outlast a rainstorm. "Do your legends speak of vanquishing grassweavers?" Irissa asked him.

"No. We have concentrated on vanquishing the beyond-world Usurper for so long that our native perils seemed tame and were forgotten."

"Apparently, they haven't forgotten you," Irissa answered grimly, loosing Aven's braid at last.

She eyed the gossamer worms growing green behind the low wall of pommelstone fire she had erected as a shield.

If only Kendric were here! Irissa thought. Kendric would not be clumsy, queasy, and more than a trifle impatient with fellow travelers who seemed ill-equipped to meet the dangers of their own world.

Irissa scraped her sword hilt in another arc on the ground. Where it touched, the grasses hissed, then broke. A second, inner wall of fire crackled, then leaped the gap to the outer one. Sheets of flame a stride wide shook into the air. Beyond them, grassweavers loomed high above the fiery fence, their great bubbled bodies glistening against the black and starless night sky.

More worm than snake, their blind, stumpish heads wove above it all, shapeless maws working. They nibbled the farthest flames, then plunged face-first into the trench.

All three watched the pommelstone flames sear the creatures' lucid sides, turn violet, and sizzle down the length of grassweaver after grassweaver, leaping from one to the other as if all were interlinked.

Still the translucent worms writhed inward to make the final knot in their landscape-wide tapestry. Irissa's defensive flames expanded into a conflagration about to collapse upon the very ground the fire defended.

"My magic overleaps itself," she admitted desperately.

"I can't understand it! Some force distorts it, gluts it, sends it amok." She regarded the two Rengarthians with sad frankness. "I fear your sheltering hillside shall be our pyre."

For answer, Sin turned to her, his face ashen green in the fire reflection. His hands dug into her shoulders as he pushed her hard into the grass at her back, so hard that the unseared strands brushed over her face.

She seemed to be drowning in seaweed. Why would Sin bother killing her when they all were so nearly dead already? A sad waste of effort—

Then cool air brushed Irissa's cheeks. Aven was moving beside her. The wall of green fire and the consuming grassweavers were gone.

Everything was dark and quiet.

"Shelter," Sin said, his voice as cool as the dark. "I knew the opening was there, but it sometimes takes its time in making itself evident."

"As do Rengarthians," wheezed a familiar voice behind Irissa.

They all turned into the dark, toward a flicker of blue sparks that draped a shape more round than square.

"Ludborg!" Irissa gasped in recognition, forgetting her fatigue. "You always swore Rengarth was forever forbidden to you!"

CHAPTER
13

KENDRIC'S WATCHDOG STOMACH GROWLED, ALERTING him to movement in the dark. He had no light, no sword, no expectations of deliverance, and he knew it.

He rolled from his accustomed place against the wall and waited for his visitor to betray itself. A sound of minute nails scraping the floor resumed. Kendric's stomach managed another spasm of hope at the notion of a meal-to-be. Few things were palatable raw, but hunger itself made a more bitter dish.

The scraping stopped. Kendric quieted his breathing and waited, his mind chaotic while he forced his body to remain motionless. He marveled that he was still alive, especially when he remembered how Geronfrey had pulled the rug of his existence out from under him without so much as a magical gesture. The dizzying series of chambers swam through Kendric's memory again, along with the curious pause before he could be impelled into solid rock.

Some hesitant, stirring force had *changed* the rock to the airy shadow of a dark mirror, saving him.

Had Geronfrey relented? Kendric doubted it, but couldn't be certain. He only knew that he had passed through a veil instead of crashed into a slab. Then the wall had hardened again, sealing him from everything but the dark labyrinth. In that inward exile, memories of the paraded foodstuffs from Geronfrey's chambers had haunted him to the marrow.

His fingers twitched in the dark. No matter the size of

the prey, the kind of the prey, the . . . consistency . . . of
the prey, he would capture it, kill it. Eat it.

A sudden rustling nearby became the breeze of its own
movement. Or its breathing. Kendric pounced on the dark,
on target. He wrestled a thing nearly as large as himself,
something wearing an outer skin thorny with spines and
wiry scales. . . .

A fang, a horn, gored from the blackness, sinking into
his upper arm as into rotten fruit. The shock of the wound
was less disabling than the blood slick running down his
arm.

He groaned and rolled sideways, evading another
glancing blow from the same unseen source.

Moments later, he pulled the stinger at its root—the
fist that held it.

A dagger lay in the palm of his hand—small triumph
when blood oozed down that same wrist and pain was taking throbbing residence in his good right arm. He un-
clenched his fist, hoping to slow the flow.

"Is it you?" asked a voice so benignly vapid that he
almost laughed.

"Who else?"

"I brought a light." Skirts rustled and jeweled netting
clicked. A pale circle of green light glowed on the floor
between them, illuminating Issiri's sweetly avid features.
The light source was a small metallic bowl—regrettably
void of sustenance . . . the kind of thing from which one
might feed a cat.

"How did you do that?" Kendric wondered.

Issiri's forefinger circled the bright rim. "'Tis made of
the finest green gold. Geronfrey imports it from . . . Outside. Some kinship exists between the metal and myself—
perhaps also with the circlet I wear."

Kendric glanced to the Iridesium that clamped her
temples. Luminous green sworls danced in its metallic
darkness. If Issiri were a pale shadow of Irissa, perhaps she
wore a wisp of the seeress's potent Torloc magic. He wondered if that notion had ever occurred to Geronfrey. . . .

Issiri touched each side of the circlet. "I've always had it, but I don't like this trinket. It ill becomes me and the metal is dull, ordinary."

"On the contrary—" Kendric gritted his teeth as he wrestled the leather baldric off his torso, no easy task with only one working arm. "The . . . circlet pays tribute to the color of your hair."

She seemed not to heed his gallantry. "And the shape is so plain, like the simplest of ring bands," she fretted.

"Elegantly . . . simple," Kendric consoled with grim abstraction. He wound the leather around his upper arm and secured it with his teeth and good hand. "At times simplicity is . . . the most flattering . . . accessory of all."

He sighed and fell back as the blood band took hold. He'd never preened himself on a courtly tongue. Why did one's weakest aspects always become vital when survival was at stake?

"You think so?" Issiri prodded. "That simplicity is becoming? I feel you wouldn't mislead me."

Kendric met her eerie green eyes with a shiver. Her innocence made a better weapon than all Geronfrey's power. Yet she looked too much like Irissa to manipulate as callously as he should. Still, she was a tool, a weapon, and he had to turn her to his survival.

"I must rest now," he told her. Weakness pulled him toward murky oblivion with an anchor's slow certainty. Blood still emigrated down his arm like a tide of ants, tickling. The blood band was not working.

"But there are things I want to know!" Issiri objected. She seemed unable—or unwilling—to acknowledge his injury at her hands. "I must know of the Quickstone Mountain you were going to show me. Of your many-colored ringstone. All my rings have stones of single colors. See?"

"Yes. But unless I staunch my wound, I will never show you a Quickstone or even a grain of sand."

"I don't want sand—"

He shut his eyes, forgetting her, forgetting less easily the image of a green-eyed Irissa lying dormant upon their bed in Edanvant. Perhaps some . . . shard . . . of Irissa's being animated this mockery. Perhaps an unsuspected link existed. Perhaps this shadow could help Irissa, could help even . . . himself.

Kendric let his eyes open and fasten on the alien emerald green of Issiri's. Then her outer form splintered into the darkness as he delved inward, searching for the lost reins of his healing powers. He had found them twice before—once at Irissa's behest to mend a broken lorryk leg; once again to mend himself of a mortal blow from a one-horned bearing-beast.

This wound was not so dire, yet untended it would suffice.

In the dark inner morass that was himself—that was doubt and confusion and pain— no glimmer of a path existed. He flailed through his unsorted memories, emotions, fears. No single thread of hope, or skill, or invention led him.

Sheared of sword and seeress, the two constant companions of his life of late, Kendric sank into the swamp-swallow of his unmotivated magic.

Perhaps his secondhand magic had never been enough, but a mere shadow of Irissa's inborn powers, like Issiri herself, he brooded. Perhaps *he* had never been enough without the crutch of his accoutrements, be they steel or flesh. Why did Geronfrey not kill him from the first, and why could Kendric not find a reason to save himself now?

The figure of Ludborg swiveled soundlessly and withdrew into the dark. Irissa, Aven, and Sin glanced at one another, then started after it.

In time more islands of blue-worms appeared—and more robed figures—congregating until azure glowed from the walls, floor, and ceiling. They had reached a cozy inner cavern equipped with the most comfortable of furnishings, save for any light source.

"Ludborg!" Irissa challenged their guide again. "Why

won't you answer? You were talkative enough beforetimes."

The rotund figure turned, revealing the same concealing hood that Ludborg had worn in Rule and Edanvant. "Because I am not Ludborg."

"Not Ludborg? But you are the very image of him!"

The conjoined wheezing that emitted from the robed
figures throughout the cavern would have filled an armada's
mainsails.

"This . . . Ludborg . . . is the image of us," another
said. "But the name is strange."

"He called himself something other once in Rule.
Scyvilla—I think. Scyvilla the Rengarthian. And this is
Rengarth, so—"

The robed figures flocked inward, buoying Irissa with
their disquieting flaccid bulks.

"She has seen the Lost Member!" said one.

Hoods nodded, the gelatinous forms pressed in upon
her. "Our last Lost Member. What a privilege; she must
speak at the worm-mating."

"Please." Irissa felt a compression that frightened her
beyond any threat in it. The heart of the Overstone began
to quiver on her breast, and she couldn't catch her breath.
"I must have room, air—"

Their voices separated and joined, words stretching in
and out of focus, sounds racing in and out of sight.

Irissa, overwhelmed, felt a sudden shock of place. She
no longer knew where she stood—indeed, she suspected
she stood somewhere else . . . somewhere dim, where
some dread pressure tightened its grip upon her soul. She
saw herself asleep, with open yet unseeing eyes of borgia
green. . . .

"Please! Aven, Sin—!" Her hands lifted to the
Iridesium circlet. The metal thrummed and heated under
her fingertips. Her right arm throbbed.

"Quick, the inner gate! Take it," that odd new voice
within her insisted.

"Gates require rainbows," Irissa murmured. "I can find none beneath the ground."

"Gates require gatekeepers and gatetakers. You are the latter, and you are required elsewhere. Go! We will guard the outer gate you leave open."

"We—?"

Other voices unraveled the fringes of her senses. She heard them speaking above her, far above her, as they had in Edanvant.

"She is pale."

"She sinks like one dead."

"We found her in the Daledowns."

"She is . . . Torloc! A seeress. See the silver eyes—but she is shutting them."

"Catch her!"

Irissa spun into herself, down through an unsuspected gate no larger than the pupil of an eye at the center of herself. She felt herself twisted thinner than a thread and sensed herself thickening again somewhere else.

Then other hands were upholding her, containing her. She glimpsed a vision of Kendric, lost and lone and fading, that almost startled her back into herself. But she was in other hands now, hands that held her as though they were used to it.

She saw the world again through the Green Veil she had worn as an untutored seeress. She saw herself in the mirror of her mind, and did not recognize the face. She felt the draw of her healing powers reaching to another who needed healing through the medium of yet another.

And then she saw nothing at all.

A cool compress settled on Kendric's fevered temples. It tightened, and as it did, he felt the blood band on his upper arm squeeze shut also.

There was firmness to this pressure, a calm, professional consistency. The icy band at his forehead clamped harder. His overheated thoughts scattered, broke into cold-stone drops, and rolled deep into the well of his consciousness.

He saw inside himself now. He saw the endless inner labyrinth and followed its convolutions, recognizing the terrain with awe. This was *Irissa's* inner depths he plumbed! He'd been here once before, when her magic had drained away and he'd sought to show her that some remnant remained.

How could he pace the internal limits of Irissa? He knew only that his mind, his memory, his magic, did just this now. And in the cavern at her center, where once he'd seen the pool of her diminished magic gleaming silver only at the rim, he came to a great, open eye of silver water in the dark. Its edges shone emerald green.

The thing that was himself walked into the only light it saw—into the silvery pool to the knee, the hip, the shoulder. Warm salt water washed over him, light as down.

Blood swished away. He breathed the underwater radiance, inhaling silver and green together, then sank like a wailwraith to the bottom of the pond. He walked across the bottom and up into vapid air again, missing the immersion, the light . . . and the lightness.

Kendric held his breath, trying to retain that heady inner ether. His sigh of exasperation exploded. The bands on his arm and head broke simultaneously. His eyes opened. Coldstone sweat glittered icily to the dungeon floor. Issiri's emerald eyes blinked her easily won delight.

"Quickstones, as you promised! Only smaller, clearer—not Quickstones. What are they?"

He watched her scramble across the floor in the lurid light, wetting her fingertip to collect the droplets in the hammock of her magnificently jeweled skirt.

Kendric felt no rancor. Issiri reminded him of a child chasing glass-caught rainbows across a wall—or of Ludborg the scryer poking through the shards of his casting crystals. Ludborg the Rengarthian, Kendric thought more sharply, he didn't know why.

He shook his head as if to dislodge a veil. His arm flexed, the muscle cording fist-solid. On his hand the Gladestone and Lunestone gleamed bright . . . green and silver in concert, the colors of his recovery.

He surveyed his outer self. Healed. Issiri sat on the ground with her legs splaying beneath her rich skirt, coldstones clicking in her hands. He must have done it himself.

"What are they?" she asked with a rapt wonder he couldn't deny. "They're not Quickstones."

Kendric smiled wryly and prodded the cache with a blunt fingertip. "Sickstones. Call them Sickstones."

She frowned. "They are oddly named, but they are pretty."

"I know where more can be found."

Her eager eyes glanced up. Kendric frowned to see a fading trace of true seeress's silver in them. Issiri still lusted for more of what she did not have; she still could be used.

"Only," he went on, wondering if it would work, "you must take me through the Dark Mirror at the tunnel's end, just as you made the rock a mirror for me to pass through earlier."

"Did I do that?" All innocence.

He nodded gravely. "I think you did."

"I remembered wishing that I could see the Quickstone Mountain, I thought of how . . . fluid the Quickstone seemed, how light. Then you went through the rock. Even Geronfrey had no Quickstones, and he has given me all these." She plucked at the gilt net caging her skillful of jewels. "Not one variety of gemstone repeats in the whole network."

"Admirable. But you have no Quickstones."

"No." Her voice grew sorrowful. "Unless you would give me yours."

He paused. "I can't. I hold it for another. But if you will lead me from here, I will find many more."

Her open hand reached out. Kendric stared at the glittering palm, the golden ring backs banding every finger joint.

"My dagger has many fine stones, too," Issiri hinted none too delicately.

"It is . . . dangerous."

"But pretty."

Who could argue with such awesome vanity? Kendric silently returned the weapon. Issiri slipped it into its sleeve-set sheath with the same satisfaction as another woman might stab a jeweled pick into her massed hair.

Unarmed but healed, he pushed himself upright. Bone and muscle—both hungry—protested the idea. He reached down to draw Issiri up, marveling at the lightness of her form. Irissa was bone-heavy and resisted assistance anyway.

Issiri's heavily gathered skirt, caught under her breasts, hid any thickening of her waist, but Kendric remembered the triply conceived burden she carried and found his thoughts darkening again. Issiri's very existence blasphemed nature and magic. Were she not vital to his escape . . . And yet, could he destroy even the image of what he held dear?

Issiri was blissfully unaware of the conundrum she presented to Kendric. She kept her skirt swagged so the precious coldstones shouldn't hit the floor, but her vivid green eyes stared bewilderedly into his.

"I feel I should . . . know you. What is your name?"

"Kendric." That seemed too simple, so he elaborated. "Once Wrathman of Rule, Wrathman of the Far Keep, once a marshman with sodden boots."

"Did you ever bring me jewels?"

"Only tears of amber."

"Oh, I have amber," she said. "Lots of it. You must see it sometime. I have an amber box with Iridesium hinges."

"Have you ever had tears?"

"I know tears." Issiri thought about them. "They are pretty, too, and bright. But they don't last. I don't think they're worth anything."

*   *   *

Blue-worms blazed dead center in the cavern. Multiplications of Ludborg gathered around it, rocking on scrolled blue-worm chairs. Despite the cool blue light, none of the shadowed hoods revealed a feature of their faces.

Irissa leaned toward a table to lift slabs of cheese and meat from a plate being passed by a troupe of more blue-worms.

"So Ludborg is famous?" she asked.

"Among us. Few of our kind incur the Usurper's wrath. Not that we don't attempt to overthrow him along with the other Rengarthians, but we look an innocent lot, and are discreet. Ludborg was not—hence his exile. He is well?"

"I . . . it's hard to tell," Irissa answered. "As well as you . . . look."

"Excellent." Hoods nodded sagely around the cavern.

"I'm sorry I was ill—perhaps it is my condition."

"Condition?" asked Aven, who reclined on her own couch of blue-worms.

A ludborg skittered forward until an empty hood peered intently into Irissa's face. "Breeding," it declared, stroking a long sleeve end over her hand.

Irissa gathered herself. Since her fainting spell, her thoughts came fuzzy. "Perhaps I underestimate the drain of it—my powers are peculiarly erratic. . . ."

"Or the poison," Aven put in matter-of-factly.

"Poison! That was in Edanvant, not here. And how did you know?"

Aven came and touched fingertips with Irissa, her ebonberry eyes staring deep into Irissa's silver gaze.

"Most Rengarthian heirs are poison leeches," Aven said. "I sensed some faint lingering toxin—borgia, was it not?"

"Borgia." Irissa found herself uncustomarily dazzled by another's magic. "I drank some tainted vintage in Edanvant, my . . . home; then Kendric went to the woods to challenge the one he thought had sent it—"

"Geronfrey," Sin put in, his youthful face grim. "Why would Geronfrey meddle with you in another world when he has all of us to battle in Rengarth?"

"Geronfrey is an . . . old enemy of mine. Ours."

"And ours," put in a ludborg. They so looked alike that names would be redundant. Irissa now thought of the original Ludborg by his Rengarthian name, Scyvilla, and of his kind as ludborgs.

"See." Aven smiled and lifted long fingers from Irissa's hand. They shone faintly green with a poisonous aura to the first knuckles. "No, don't worry. Only a sensitive like myself or Sin would notice it, and the residue will fade. So, you think Geronfrey has captured this Kendric."

Irissa nodded, all worry.

"You are lucky." Sin slapped the long dagger at his hip so it jangled against his waist chain.

"Lucky?"

"We spearhead an uprising and are almost ready to act. If this Kendric is here—and lives—we will rescue him. We'll storm Geronfrey's citadel, and if we don't drive him out one of his many infernal windows to another world, we will make this one intolerable for him."

Ludborgs murmured and nodded.

"Soon?" Irissa felt hope take root like a tree and shoot sunward at one and the same time. Weariness fell away. "I will lend whatever magic I can to the enterprise."

"Green fire?" Aven nodded appreciatively toward Irissa's pommelstone.

"Purple fire, if necessary," Irissa vowed.

Sin laughed, a joyous sound in the dim cavern. "Wait until morning at least to dispense your fires."

"Why?" Irissa wondered, wondering too where Kendric was and how he fared.

"We can't go anywhere with the grassweavers laying their webs—and besides, our allies won't arrive until then."

"Allies?"

But Sin just grinned and Aven only smiled and the ludborgs simply nodded their hoods.

Irissa gave up, settling into a blue-worm hammock that formed around her upright and then tilted horizontal.

The worms gave off no tactile sensations. Irissa felt she floated on a distant, disembodied tingle. With her eyes shut, she could almost hear the faintest high-pitched hum. Perhaps the blue-worms purred.

She sighed. When her mind turned to Kendric, she felt a sense of relief, despite her vague glimpse of him wounded. At least that glimpse had reassured her that he was indeed here in Rengarth, and alive.

Events were proceeding as quickly as could be expected—from her lucky encounter with Aven and Sin and her introduction to the entire flock of ludborgs, who seemed to be cloistered caretaker-scryers in this world, to the imminent worldwide uprising against her archenemy Geronfrey.

Irissa dozed, too tired to sink into deep sleep as yet. Her body treasured its buoyant rest, a sign that her "condition" had progressed sufficiently to weigh in the balance of her well-being. Her hands, crossed on her midriff, cupped a swell that duplicated the Overstone's egg-shaped contours in larger dimensions.

Irissa's hand lifted to shape that familiar talisman. The stone felt warm, even hot, and seemed to swell in tune with her body. Doubtless it was all a delusion of her unfortunate condition.

Drifting in the misty marshlands of near sleep, Irissa glimpsed faces between patches of fog. Aven and Sin's redheaded visages flared on the grayness like flash fires. Something about the pair troubled Irissa. So blithe, so certain. Perhaps it was just their youth or the fact that with only one world to know, they knew so much less of themselves.

Not so with herself and Kendric, who sometimes knew too much of everything.

Irissa tossed on a bobbing sea of blue-worms, feeling

the Overstone list against the swell of her breasts as she turned, feeling herself turning on a spit of her own concoction, on something ever level, always anchored within her. . . .

The babe. Irissa's heart beat in triplet. Sudden fear galloped through her half-slumbering mind. It was not enough to wake her, only enough to hold her in disturbed thrall.

The babe, that tiny imperious face sheathed in helpless self-sufficiency . . . it seemed hardly part of her—or Kendric. Had some freak of fate implanted a changeling upon her? Or were all infant selves so utterly self-centered? Could she love a thing so separate and yet so inextricably twined with her? Irissa felt a wave of reassurance, somehow taking the form of Jalonia's voice.

Of course, of course you will love the life you have given, even when it seems to only take. It has granted your boon, has it not? Awakened beforetimes in its safest sanctuary, it began its awareness by granting you a wish. Few children start out so beneficently. Even fewer end up so, the soothing maternal voice droned on.

Irissa felt her eyelashes struggle to part—and fail. That voice of reassurance—it wasn't Jalonia's, but her *own*!

"Quite the little mother, aren't we?" came a dry chuckle too near and yet too distant to identify.

"Who mocks me?" Irissa asked herself at the gate of dreamland. It was moon-shaped and guarded by an Iridesium gridwork that split in the center.

"You suspect someone other than yourself of that happy occupation?"

"It doesn't behoove a child to snap at the hand that feeds it."

"A child, no, seeress. But sometimes the child is mother to the woman."

"I had no mother," Irissa said, realizing the truth even as she said it. "Jalonia was ever distant, and Finorian as maternal as a rabid moonweasel."

"Testy in your old age. One would think you had some splendid example to follow."

"Testy, I? Tried, perhaps, but never testy. Now, Kendric could be testy—would he were here to so belabor me."

"Fear not. You have me."

"You? You are a dream. An echo of myself."

"You are a seeress and things are never that simple for your kind. You should know better."

"I am a pregnant seeress, and liable to be driven half mad by the undulations of my state."

"You mean your 'condition.'"

"Condition," Irissa corrected herself sluggishly. "Is it you, my unborn, that speaks?" The inner voice was silent. "Or my unbalanced body? My conscience? You speak for yourself, unlike the babe, and use no royal 'we.' Who is so sublimely self-sure but myself?"

"Self-sure! You are a morass of swamp-swallow, especially with your great silly Wrathman lost—"

Again Irissa's eyelids fought to open and lost the battle. This voice was too separate . . . too familiar . . . to dismiss. It spoke from the arrogance of age, not infancy.

Besides, Irissa knew her babe slept within her, as it should. She could sense it now—an unreadable space in the center of her being, completely its own growing self now, indifferent to her unless she moved too roughly or fasted too long.

"You know me?" Irissa asked the voice. The mists were parting, revealing a black velvet curtain of sleep behind them. Against the solid color, Irissa glimpsed a shred of lingering gray fog.

"We have . . . at times . . . been companions."

Irissa strained her eyes—the internal eyes with which she saw best. The patch of fog was thinning, growing white and wispy before it vanished.

"Felabba?" she whispered.

"Always too late with too little," the dry voice noted in parting. *"Why whisper in the corridors of your own mind?"*

"No! I won't have you visited upon me, too! Felabba! I won't have you. I don't need you."

"You need, as usual, more than you know. But, hush. The threshold of sleep yawns before you. Step over it and be done with keeping me up as well."

"Felabba." The word seemed a remnant of a memory. Irissa looked up to an inner black night sky. One cloud wisp drifted against the vastness. "I don't need," Irissa said to herself weakly, "another uninvited passenger."

There was no answer except the silence in herself.

In it, Irissa sensed again the profound otherness curling at her center. It slept now, as it would until the world awakened it—or it awakened to the world. It slept, as Irissa would sleep many times between now and the day of its delivery.

It slept, as Irissa was sleeping now—lightly, lost, alone.

CHAPTER
14

"I TRUST YOU SLEPT WELL." A LUDBORG HOVERED OVER Irissa, the featureless hole of its hood deeper than the sky.

She blinked awake, pleased to discover that no part of her ached or cramped—a circumstance alien to her of late. "I dreamed," Irissa remembered.

"So do we all." Sin and Aven were up and ready, their brown eyes confidently bright, their hands bearing breakfast.

"Marching rations?" Irissa asked, surprised to find her appetite hearty for the first time in weeks.

She struggled to sit and was immediately buttressed by the accommodating blue-worms, who wriggled her upright, then melted away.

Aven handed Irissa a mug of warm buttermilk and a bowl of curdled wheat thick with ebonberries. "This does not seem much to go to war on," Irissa grumbled. "The city looked three days' march away last night."

Aven smiled and collected the pottery dishes as Irissa emptied them. "We do not march upon our stomachs. Come."

Glad for daylight after the blue concave of the cavern, Irissa followed the pair through the tunnels. Behind them the ludborgs bounced genially from wall to wall as they thronged toward the exit.

The earth belched the entire party out of the hillside into open air. Irissa inhaled a cacophony of scents—dew, moist earth, and sun-warmed flowers. Nothing remained of

the ghostly grassweavers except the silver roads of their
tracks drying to dust under the triple glare of Rengarth's
suns.

In the distance, the profile of Solanandor Tierze
spanned the horizon like a spiderweb.

"So far . . ." Irissa noted aloud, imagining Kendric
languishing in Geronfrey's hands.

"So fast," answered Sin, lifting his arms to the dawn.

Irissa saw his long sleeves fall away like leaves. He
seemed graceful now, rather than boisterous and crude,
and serious instead of impish. Sunlight sizzled on the curling edges of his crimson hair.

Irissa recognized an upwelling of natural magic, robust
as the day itself. A sound of panting erupted around them,
above them—panting or rapid fluttering. She looked up.

The blue sky had blackened with moving forms. Shadows flitted across the suns and plummeted. Leaves from an
invisible tree that stretched sky-high spiraled to earth—
black snow on a summer's day. A cinderstorm.

Irissa tried to name the forms, and failed. They flew so
fast, and even now fell to earth with an audible impact.

She covered her eyes and ears by turns against the onslaught, blinking into a bewilderment of images. What had
begun as innocent magic seemed spelled into horror. Limp
necks and vacant eyes plummeted past her. Dead beasts
flapped onto the ground—dying, falling, feathered beasts.
Birds. Swans. Far too many for her to resuscitate . . .

Sin dropped his upraised arms, unconcerned. Then
Irissa stared as the fallen dead revived. Flaccid necks
shortened. Dark feathers fell away. Plucked wings elongated into credible arms, webbed feet into boots, billed
heads into grinning human faces.

A company of ordinary humans stood around them—
some old, some young, some men, some women. At their
feet piles of glossy dark feathers cast rainbow reflections
back at the sky. The swan-spawn that had sprung up wore
glossy coats of Iridesium mail and carried dagger-swords at
their Iridesium-chained waists.

"Our army," Sin announced a trifle smugly. "Victims of the Usurper in times past. I've retrieved their spirits from their animal forms for a time."

"A fine army," Irissa conceded. She pointed rudely to the tiny spires webbing the horizon. "But still three days' march."

For answer, Aven collapsed to the ground. She stretched her upper body close to the earth, spreading her arms wing-wide. Her red braids shone like tapestry threads in the sunlight as she turned her head ear-down to the earth.

All the thousands of fallen feathers trembled. Irissa felt a sympathetic tremor in her circlet. Feathers danced on the ground as if buoyed by the very exhalation of the earth itself, then fluttered to new life. Beneath them, the ground bucked, shifted. The feathers swept away, swept up like wings.

A huge jet-black swan shuddered free of the earth, an upthrusting hill of feathers, until it stood on ungainly webbed feet large enough to crush a bearing-beast.

Sin gestured to the dazed swan with its carmine eyes and violet bill. "Atop that, we can skim the sky and be at the city by suppertime."

"No." Irissa's head shook so violently she felt her neck crack. "No. I've mounted something similar before. Better a three-day march, especially in my . . . condition."

Irissa's reticence had no effect on the swan-spawn. The people surged over the giant bird's back, settling among the ruffled feathers and clinging to the delicate strands as if they were the sturdiest cables, as indeed they were at this size.

Aven turned her other ear to the ground. Forewarned, Irissa braced herself. Again the earth reverberated—at first with a distant, rhythmic rapping, then with an oncoming pounding.

Over the rumpled hills swarmed hundreds of fleet figures—it seemed as if the ground itself were surging toward the onlookers. Behind Irissa, ludborgs quavered, but she

waited with rising excitement to see what would come
prancing to Aven's call.

Hordes came. Dappled bearing-beasts with wind-
braided manes. Their feathered hocks flicked the waving
grasses, not so much trampling them as weaving through
like harmless wind. Swells of beasts burst over the hills like
waves thrown up from the belly of the sea over and over
again.

Irissa, no beast-rider by nature, found her heart catching despite herself. Then—she saw something else to make
her pulses stop.

"Aven! The rogue beast—there!" Sin's urgent shout
came just as Irissa saw.

A single dot was bouncing over the rippled landscape—too lone to more than tease, tantalize. Nearer it
came, at an intersecting angle to the herd. A new under-
tone drummed beneath the earthshaking pounding—a single idiosyncratic rhythm that played against the herd's
awesome harmony of purpose and motion.

"I can't lose them," Aven moaned between clenched
teeth, her eyes closed and her ear pressed to the ground.

Sin bit his lip, his hand fisting helplessly upon his hilt.
Ludborgs flocked to the three, either to give or seek protection.

Irissa studied the lone oncomer. It was a bearing-
beast, like the rest, yet unlike the rest. Where their coats
were long and rough, its was short and glossy. Where their
forelocks flicked against bare foreheads, its brow raised a
long, curved spiral of horn.

Even as Irissa groped to put a name and a place on the
intruder, she saw that the wicked length of horn was dyed
blood crimson almost to the root.

"The Hunter!"

"You know the creature?" Sin demanded. "It came
but recently to Rengarth and is like our beasts, but heeds
nothing that rules them. It has . . . killed."

Irissa hardly heard him. She felt herself call to the
beast even as if called to her, as ancient enemies will sight

one another across vast distances and among great numbers.

"I know it," she absently told Sin. "I contained it with the colors of my circlet once, so Kendric could capture it."

"Did he?"

"Yes, and no. Later, it gored him—"

"It still wears the bloody colors of that encounter?"

"Perhaps." Irissa didn't like to contemplate Kendric's lifeblood serving as anything's ensign.

Sin glanced to Aven's bowed head. Irissa, reading brotherly concern in his expression, suddenly trusted him despite his wicked name.

"Aven is vulnerable now as at no other time," he said. "She must concentrate on the Call, and keep this interloper from turning the herd—"

So, too, had the Hunter concluded. The beast's hooves bit turf, spraying clods of dirt, then it spun and drove straight for Aven's prone figure.

Her head lay cradled on long grasses, fragile as an eggshell, her ear tuned to the oncoming hooves of her destruction.

Then it was there, a charging, churning beast of shining coat and wheeling form. Irissa glimpsed blue eyes rolling in the equine head, rearing hooves—and Sin bounding into its path.

The Hunter had been a terrifying beast when Kendric had sought to tame it; against its rampant bulk a youth like Sin was merely a slip of grass to be swept aside. One milling hoof ploughed into Sin's shoulder and hip. The young man fell sideways, but the Hunter's balance remained unshaken.

It poised, rearing, above Aven's rapt, prone form. Behind it, waves of long-coated bearing-beasts wove into a living train. Foaming manes and pounding hooves formed a tide as merciless as the sea, and as unstoppable.

One impulsive leap took Irissa into the position Sin had occupied, confronting the Hunter. She had drawn her sword without thinking, the point aimed at the muscular chest wall hovering above her.

Not since the Empress Falgon on Rule had she encountered a creature so inherently intimidating. On four feet any bearing-beast loomed large—if not insurmountable.

Towering on two hind legs like a living cliff above her—hooves and head massive shadows against the sky— the Hunter roared out a whinny of rage. Her sword point seemed no more threatening than a quill tip filled with ink. Even her magic, Irissa thought, would move too slowly for those lightning hooves flashing above her.

She flourished the blade anyway, the pommelstone leaking light through her sweat-slicked fingers. The Hunter's blue eyes glinted with almost-human anticipation. Something clinked against the sword hilt and then rapped Irissa's knuckles, hard enough to bring a tear-smart to her eyes.

She glanced to her fist. She had forgotten twisting Medoc's heavy gold medallion around the sword hilt, but now it lay across her hand. A nuisance—just when she didn't need it! A distraction, a . . .

Irissa looked up again, sure she'd feel the shadow of the hooves descending on her head. But the beast seemed as frozenly poised as she.

For a long moment their eyes exchanged a look that didn't quite translate to the language of either kind. The Hunter's rear hooves churned the earth and then it was mincing away from her, step by step—dancing backward like a bearing-beast trained to perform at a fair.

Irissa followed—prodding the retreating beast not so much with her sword, but with the medallion. Emerald pommelstone light caressed the metal surface, turning it to green gold and fixing the Hunter's rolling blue eyes on the small circle of light.

As Irissa slowly lowered her arm, the beast dropped to earth. Front hooves touched grass, then pranced backward.

Its long head switched sideways, back and forth like a tail, as if to avoid her gaze, or as if fighting an invisible bit.

Trembling, tamed, the Hunter came to rest at last. The other bearing-beasts swept by at a canter, splitting ranks to thunder past Irissa and the Hunter. The mass pivoted to a wide-nostriled stop at the very brink of Aven's prone form. A polished hoof rested lightly on one of her splayed braids.

"Aven!" Sin limped over to pull his sister upright. Her head lolled on her neck and she seemed not to hear him. He shook her anxiously. "Aven, are you all right?"

"What?"

Sin leaned close to shout into her ear. "Are you all right?"

"Oh," she shouted back, nodding exuberantly like one deaf. "Yes. What a splendid herd." She turned to find a shaggy bearing-beast nibbling at her waist chain.

"And . . . Irissa." Sin hobbled toward her, stopping well away from the Hunter. "How are you?"

"You seem the one in need of succor," Irissa couldn't help remarking. "Best leave the beasts to us women. We seem to have a way with them."

Sin's wary dark eyes risked surveying the now-quiet Hunter. "So I see. I've heard rumors of this lone wild-beast, but he's never tried to wrest herd right from an heir before."

"How long has he troubled Rengarth?"

Sin shrugged, resuming his old blithe facade again. "Some little time."

"'Some little time.' Can't you be more precise?"

"Rengarth is an imprecise place."

"How long? A month—two, three?"

"What is a month?"

Irissa looked blank, never having had to address so basic an issue before. "A month is . . . thirty days." Sin met her explanation with his own blank stare. "A month!" Irissa gestured at the sky. "One transit of the moon through its phases—oh . . ."

"Moon?" Sin inquired politely.

"That's true. Rengarth has no moon. Well—" Irissa glanced to the medallion in her hand. "A moon is a round pale thing in the sky, about this size, visible usually by night, but not always. And sometimes one can see all of it and sometimes one can only see slices. From cycle to cycle is a month—"

Instead of looking enlightened, Sin appeared as if he had been struck by lightning. His mouth sagged open, his bright eyes had dulled to an expression of vacant horror.

But it was not her description of a moon that had disconcerted him. He was staring at the medallion in Irissa's hand as if it were the carcass of his sister.

"How did you come by that?" Sin demanded, still agape.

"This? A family heirloom, you might say, passed to me by my grandfather. How old it is, I cannot say."

"I can." Aven's voice still rang a trifle too loud as she approached the two, her fingers massaging her ear. "I heard your last words. Irissa, you hold the Usurper's token, which was wrested from him when he exiled the first Ruler and Reginatrix. It vanished into the tangle of heiring families that have come and gone in Rengarth and never was seen again. But we heard of it—something as remote to us as the moon you were describing."

"No wonder it rules the Usurper's offworld beast!" Sin eyed the Hunter with nervous pleasure. "If this creature is indeed a pawn of Geronfrey's."

"It originated in Edanvant," Irissa said. "That's why I wondered how long it had plagued your world, if it was the same creature."

"No challenger has ever interfered with my herd-right Call before," Aven said. "I could hear his iron hooves hammering, but I dared not stop keeping count of the rest."

"You *counted* the hoofbeats?" Irissa couldn't imagine an ear sensitive enough to number one bearing-beast's hoof from another's.

Aven smiled. "Why do you think I go half deaf afterward? If you would have an animal serve you, you must at least do it the courtesy of knowing it."

"And this herd will speed us to Solanandor Tierze?" Irissa focused on the frail city silhouette on the horizon, thinking of something less frail, she hoped. Kendric.

"All of us," Sin said cheerfully, "even the scryer folk. But what will you do with your conquest?"

They regarded the quiescent bearing-beast. Even with all four feet on the ground, it remained a frightening creature.

Suddenly, Irissa wrapped the medallion chain several times around her right wrist. Her hand lifted to the Hunter's flared nostrils, dropped to the downy hairs between them. Still as an impending storm, the creature submitted to her touch.

Her fingers slid up the long muzzle and nose to the forehead. Behind her, Aven gasped and Sin growled a protest.

But the Hunter accepted Irissa's mastery, even as its rolling sky-blue eye clove to the medallion clanking against her chain-twined wrist. Irissa grasped the root of its horn and tugged, pulling the huge equine head down, pulling the deadly horn tip toward herself.

She sensed a silence all around her. Not even the herd of bearing-beasts shifted a single foot. Her fingertip tested the point's blunted sharpness. Compared to honed human steel, it was a crude weapon. Yet it had sufficed to push Kendric's mortality to its very brink.

Now Irissa's magic gathered, lazily, into a force. Her magic worked best not used hand to hand, or person to beast. It served better in quiet aftermath in restoration rather than destruction.

Under Irissa's intent gaze, the red on the Hunter's horn coagulated, grew liquid again, slid down the spiraled surface into one dark drop, and hung like a great crimson tear at the horn's lowest curve.

Irissa cupped her left hand under the droplet. Dislodged by its own weight, it plummeted into her palm with a clink that raised every head and pricked every ear around them—hooded, human, or animal.

"Bloodstone," Irissa announced, lifting a pendant ruby as long as her thumb for all to see. "It matches the Blood-stone in my ring."

She pulled the Overstone pouch's mouth open and let the gem vanish within. "Kendric is not the only one to carry a talisman squeezed from another's substance. So." Irissa's head lifted. Her eyes' stern silver made her seem grim. "When do we meet Geronfrey? When do we find and free Kendric?"

"Now!" Sin was laughing with new confidence. "With the Usurper's creature docile on our side." Aven caught his sleeve and whispered quickly in his ear. "But . . ."—doubt sobered Sin's impish features—"but can you ride, seeress, in your condition?"

Irissa considered it, considered the chastened bearing-beast with the ivory-white horn. She twined her fingers in a long strand of mane and faced the creature's swelling side.

"Can you help me mount?" she asked in return.

Her answer was Sin's quick presence, catapulting her atop the creature's broad, bare back. Astride, Irissa found Rengarth less intimidating. The Hunter awaited her will, so she tethered him with the light web of her magic, wove an invisible bridle and reins, then took the lines into the palm of her right hand, where the spinning medallion and chain tinkled against her wrist like bridle bells.

She looked to the horizon. From her elevated perch, Solanandor Tierze and Kendric seemed well within reach. The black swan, lying on the landscape as dark as a lake, began paddling its huge feet over the ground. Steps became strides as the great pinions sawed into the air.

Despite its magic assemblage from the feathers of flocks of swans, the creature was ungainly as any of its kind as it ran toward the fine line of the horizon, flapping its massive wings and extending its long, thin neck. Irissa, watching the mute swan-spawn cling to their graceless mount, shook her head at the odd forms magic sometimes took.

Then the natural magic of swankind cast its own spell. The huge, unbalanced body was lifting into the air on labored strokes of matched black wings. Each rise and dip of the wings grew stronger, slower. The great black bird was sailing into the three suns' glare, toward the city.

Around Irissa, ludborgs were mounting unsaddled bearing-beasts—looking like drab balls bouncing among a company of children's ponies.

Aven sprang atop a dappled beast with an ease Irissa envied. Sin mounted last, and then the herd was sweeping back over the cloud-dappled land. Irissa looked up. A great black shadow had slid between her and the suns.

A black swan worked into a tapestry, she remembered, always represented destruction. And death. Whose? she wondered. Beneath her, the Hunter's coiled muscles sprang loose, and the ground spun away in a long, unrolling ribbon.

His wet palms patted the end wall's slick black surface. It felt oily, like Marshlands pond scum. Geronfrey's Dark Mirror door also felt bottomless, like the Swallowing Cavern. It felt like risk incarnate.

"Beyond here you can show me the Coldstone Mountain," Issiri asked again.

"In time," Kendric evaded, still unsure he could penetrate even one of Geronfrey's reflective constructions.

A sigh behind him indicated Issiri's ebbing patience. He stepped back from his own reflection. "You go first," he suggested, with a bow.

She regarded him suspiciously. "The last time I went first, you didn't follow."

"That was before I knew that you could alter the composition of the wall. Simply . . . think . . . me through, and I will be there."

"Thinking is never as simple as people say," she complained.

"How do you know?"

"Geronfrey would have me think too much, and I find it tiring. Once he had me sit up half a night imagining borgia rising in an empty bottle."

"Borgia? Pouring from . . . where?"

"From . . . myself, I think. I'm never sure. Yes, borgia—or was it blood? I can never be sure. There are times when I . . . fade."

"Don't fade now." His hands encouragingly squeezed her upper arms. Disconcerted, he felt her shrink beneath his touch, like so much marsh mist wrung empty of its thin-spun substance. His fingers loosened.

"I'll go through," Issiri decided abruptly, walking whimsy that she was.

"Think me through," he reminded her. "Remember me."

Her dark figure was merging with the blackness that bottled them. Kendric tried to imagine himself walking through the bottom of a flask of tavern wine, then thrust himself into the opaque patch of night.

Cool and sticky. He felt the mirror's surface cling to his clothes and plunged deeper into its dark to escape that initial impression. Issiri had vanished. Everything had vanished. Only himself and his dislocated sense of motion remained.

If she had tricked him—or simply forgotten him, as she seemed to do when he was out of sight—he might be mired in this tactile nothingness for eons. . . .

It sucked at him like an unwelcome kiss, then released him with a smack. Kendric stood in a hallway, turned, confronted himself in a conventional mirror, and turned again.

Issiri stood before him, and—behind her—Geronfrey.

STUNNED, KENDRIC LIFTED HIS RINGED FIST. ALL THE colors in the cabochon ran in a mad round of confusion. Geronfrey confronted him like a stone—an immobile icon of power.

Issiri giggled.

Kendric almost spared her a withering glance.

She laughed again. "That is not Geronfrey! That is his living signet, which he brands on any doorway he forbids me."

Kendric approached the image fist-first. His knuckles brushed a substance—half liquid, half veil. Nothing in the likeness reacted to him, though Kendric could swear he saw the richly tunicked chest breathe in and out, and the blue eyes narrow at his nearness.

"Doorway," Kendric repeated, absorbing the information.

He turned to study the chamber. It was as small as a tower top. He could picture some widening column of stone extending far below.

Behind Issiri yawned a black mystery that he assumed was the back side of the Dark Mirror to the dungeons. Each plane of the tower—for its circle had been faceted into an octagon—was centered with a window, or a door, depending on your preference or point of view.

"Finorian would find this a proper welcome for a Wrathman," Kendric grumbled under his breath, studying window after window in hopes of spying a real slice of Rengarth.

"Who's Finorian?"

"A . . . an old adversary of mine, now dead." Kendric smiled to himself. "Or disappeared, rather. Call no Torloc—or anyone—dead until you see the body. By all logic, I would have assumed Geronfrey deceased by now."

"That is my birthing box." Issiri, disinterested in Kendric's digression, pointed proudly to an object on the floor.

Kendric approached it, disturbed by the shape in a way his mind had not yet labeled. Issiri slipped down beside it before he arrived, laying her cheek along the lid.

Kendric studied it. The rectangular surface was polished, dark like a mirror of his acquaintance. His fingertips touched the lid and came away cold. Stone-cold. Whatever was in it, the chest was buckled shut with straps of woven Iridesium mesh.

In two strides Kendric had paced out its measure: six and some feet long; three feet wide. Its resemblance to a casket was not lost on him. Neither was its incredible . . . thinness. It was a mere lozenge of a box, despite its human size; flat to the point of ludicrousness—perhaps a hand's width deep . . . and not a Wrathman's hand, either.

"Birthing box." Kendric hated repeating the strange phrase. "Is that where you will . . . bear your forthcoming child?"

Issiri's green gaze slid to his face. "I was born here. What else shall be born here I cannot say."

Kendric shook his head to clear the hunger-fog. He dare not invest too deeply in Issiri's reality or he couldn't vouch for his reaction. He returned to the chamber perimeter. Two of the eight windows were pointless to try—one led back to the dungeons, another to the way obstructed by Geronfrey's signet-figure.

He approached the figure again, still expecting it to explode into challenge. Close up, he saw that a viscous film overlay the likeness. Staring sideways, Kendric looked through clarity, as into a crystal. The image—as richly inlaid as a mosaic map in Rule—underlay the surface as if seared there.

Breaking the spell the dead-yet-living image cast over him, Kendric moved to the next window. He saw another chamber beyond, empty, but with tables food-laden and tapers flaring. Too conveniently inviting to one in his condition, he thought, and stepped to the next aperture.

This one opened onto a vivid alien landscape. Distant turrets and pylons glittered, tightening in and out of focus even as he watched. A shadow swept the sky; storm clouds flocked into a black glowering edge. The shimmering city dampened to a mere patchwork of landscape pockmarked with shifting pools of water. Too chimerical, he decided.

The next window revealed a room he recognized—the weepwaterwood-paneled private chambers of Citydell. A female figure draped in darkness bent over a tapestry in a corner. Only one whipping green flame from a wall torch illuminated her work.

Kendric perceived the handiwork first—a worn tapestry of a man and woman in a forest. The woman was embroidering a gilt bearing-beast into the pattern, one with a single horn. Her dark hair ran like evening rivers over her shoulders as his eyes polished the only portion of her face visible—a white hummock of cheekbone.

Irissa—well again, waiting? In Edanvant? For him?

He should have known Irissa better. The woman turned to pull a lock of yarn from a basket at her feet. The face that swiveled into the emerald torchlight mocked Irissa's in every line, but the glancing light traced one silver strand in the dark hair and turned it Torloc green. Jalonia, Irissa's mother. Jalonia, worried and alone. What was happening in Edanvant? What was happening with Irissa?

Too haunting. Kendric pushed himself from the window that showed something he could only regard as the past now . . . Edanvant.

The next aperture revealed a massive hall. Pilasters marched in rows down vast spaces, every surface scrolled with fantastic figures blending animal and human.

Besides the common centaur, there was the Rynx—several of them, their owlish heads and wolfish feline bodies twisted into hind-legged postures more mock-human than the centaur's. Monkey-cats climbed the pillars and bird-lizards upheld the capitals. Swans grew mermen's tails and people wore wings.

Something about the display's grandeur struck Kendric as a trophy gallery. Too disturbing. He turned, disgusted, without even looking to the room's farthest end where someone small and indistinguishable sat on a high-backed throne.

Only two options remained. One had to offer straightforward escape.

But the next window was blank—not blackly blank, or whitely so, but utterly impenetrable. He could not call it fog, though he saw nothing through it. He could not call it a barrier, for it had no substance. It was a hole in physical reality that manifested itself as physical unreality.

Too vague, he decided, and confronted the next—and last—window.

This led to a hallway, plain and simple. He liked the look of it. Stone-built, taper-lit, spiderwebbed. It had all the substance he liked and none of the shifting insecurity of magic. This was the obvious exit from the tower room.

He didn't trust it, for all the obvious reasons.

"Are you leaving?" Issiri asked from the floor, her cheek still pillowed upon the sinister box.

"Yes."

"To find the Quickstone Mountain?"

"To find . . . myself first, then another. Then, perhaps, Quickstones."

"It sounds a long journey."

"It is."

Her hand stroked the chest's smooth stone side. Here, in Geronfrey's eternal tower room, all the glitter on her person seemed dampened, tawdry. Here, even Issiri had lost her sparkle—and her own fascination with it.

"Come back if you find the Quickstone Mountain, Kendric."

He stared at her, at her green eyes growing leaden and her white face that reflected as faintly as a wailwraith's in the stone casket lid.

The wide arc of her gown hid any fruitfulness in her figure, but Kendric had a sudden vision of Issiri as Geronfrey had made her from the slimmest reflection of Irissa. He saw her hidden within the slender casket, floating on her own reflection, fed by means too vile to contemplate.

Kendric came toward her, drawn by her undeniable reality even as he denied her right to exist. Here, in this many-windowed tower room lit by scenes from present, past, and future, he saw Issiri only as a product of Geronfrey's twisted ambitions. She was less sentient than a newt—a mere construction fueled by stolen moments. Her very existence cheapened Irissa's sovereign selfhood, mocked his and Irissa's union, mimicked the very real fruits of that union.

"Do you want to say good-bye?" Issiri asked, looking up at him with wide, unfrightened eyes.

"If I see it, I shall slay it."

Kendric's own words echoed in his head. That Geronfrey, denied Irissa herself, should raise up a substitute and nurture it to this point of self-reflection, struck him forcefully again as an obscenity beyond toleration.

"Good-bye?" he repeated, the word finally penetrating his agitated mind.

Good-bye. Now. Here. He could kill her, throttle her, perhaps. Kill the infant-false within her, strangle Geronfrey's hopes aborning. He'd killed before—foes, prey, once a bond brother in Rule. Never a woman. Never something helpless.

But was she woman? Was she helpless? Were women always—ever?—helpless? While he debated, Issiri waited. Did her existence somehow rob Irissa, himself, their child?

His hands flexed. Bereft even of his weapon, he would have to stoop to raw handwork; no hiding behind the noble sweep of a blow, a quick piercing cut to the quick. No, slow, crude killing and Irissa's counterfeit face wondering at him all the while. . . .

Irissa herself may suffer because of this, the thought rattled in his head. Irissa may be dying drop by drop from the borgia poison, needing only this release—her shadow sister slain—to breathe again.

He didn't know. He could guess, could writhe against the possibilities and their ill-born ramifications, but he could never, never know for certain.

"Don't tell Geronfrey where I've gone—or how," he barked so suddenly that Issiri started.

"The Quickstones are our secret?" she asked.

"Our secret."

"And will you come back?"

"Not if . . . I can help it."

"But you'll send me a Quickstone?"

The eager light that flared in her face couldn't be denied. So Irissa might have looked if she were dying.

Kendric found himself reaching into his boarskin purse and pulling out something smooth—Irissa's coldstone tear turned to pure silver in midgate. It had been his talisman through two worlds, but he tossed it to Issiri as he would a thighbone to a dog.

He last glimpsed Issiri scrambling over the floor toward a rolling silver spark of fire. Then Kendric stepped onto the sill and through the window that led to an ordinary hall. Perhaps something in Geronfrey's lair was what it appeared to be.

CHAPTER
16

THE HUNTER'S HOOVES NICKED THE GROUND, CUTTING free a fine spray of earth.

Bearing-beasts thudded alongside, the ludborgs mounted upon them battering their backs at every wrinkle of countryside.

Aven and Sin, natural riders as they were naturally everything else, rode at the outskirts to keep the party shaped into one advancing force.

Above them all the black swan oared through the clouds, casting a shadow vast enough to darken half the visible landscape.

Irissa kept a hand twined in the Hunter's coarse mane; the other clasped the Overstone, which threatened to knock her breastbone back into her spine, it jostled so. Despite good intentions, her legs' curved grip on the Hunter's side threatened to pry loose at any instant. How the wild ride was affecting her "condition" she didn't want to know.

Still, she felt herself reining in the lead of her magic. At her inner reticence, the Hunter's head lowered as if drawn back by literal reins. Irissa willed his gait to slow, rejoicing when his hoofbeats softened.

She even detected a new upward inclination to her seat—perhaps Rengarth went uphill for a while. If it did she never felt it. Irissa seemed to float on cloudscape now, the Hunter's airy, even stride measuring lengths of sky, not land.

Then she glanced . . . down. Down?

"Irissa!" Aven had reined in and was waving. Aven, who sat on her mount *below* Irissa. On the ground.

Irissa stared wildly around, leaning over her mount's neck and then regretting it. She saw land receding beneath her. The Hunter was cantering up an invisible incline, rising higher into thin air with each step. Panic darkened Irissa's mind, and the Hunter's gait leveled as if her unease had subtly signaled it.

Sin—who now looked the size of a walnut mounted on a mouse—waved cordially, as if to congratulate her. From this height, the ludborgs looked like so many casting crystals gone opaque and jolting off to market on donkeyback.

A nearby agitation made Irissa glance sideways. The huge black swan's wings beat not many feet beyond. Swanspawn—ever mute, ever polite—turned their bland, pleasant faces and smiled before the great wing nearest Irissa drew up, up, up like an ebony wave to hide them.

Irissa willed the Hunter to sheer off from the swan and glanced down. The slow pace permitted a glorious view of Rengarth. Irissa glimpsed gilt pyramids among mountain foothills, noticed huge crystal bubbles at the bottom of ponds and lakes, ferns the size of castles and castles the size of bread loaves, herds of rabbits—an infinitely more varied panorama than she had suspected from her first, earthbound survey of the land.

Pleasant as the view was, observing Rengarth from the back of the airborne Hunter was far more terrifying than seeing Rule from atop an Empress Falgon. The winged Falgon—a legendary reptile of Rule large enough to carry a small army, like the swan—offered its own relatively level landscape to cling to, however scaled and feathered and uncertain.

The Hunter defied the element he traversed as if it were a mere meadow. Despite surmounting of natural law, he remained a stiff, unwinged thing—bird-puny amid the heavens' vastness. Falling seemed a momentary likelihood.

The Hunter was unafraid, however, and strutted up and down the unseen skyroad as if on parade.

"An apt pupil, is it not?" Irissa's alien inner voice inquired tartly.

Irissa, startled to hear anything so well with the wind whistling in her ears, clutched the mount more tightly.

"Cat got your tongue?" the voice went on sardonically.

Irissa didn't dare voice her deepest suspicions—they might be true—so she asked the obvious. "I suppose *you* taught the Hunter to tread thin air."

"Of course." Smugly. Then . . . *"It makes a smoother ride for all of us. I should think you would thank me."*

"Give me a name to bless and I shall."

Silence.

"Perhaps you prefer to remain anonymous," Irissa jibed.

"Perhaps I have not been named . . . yet."

Irissa shivered, suddenly aware that the air grew icy at this height. No, she would not accept the voice's implication! She refused to believe that her unborn child spoke to her.

She might have breached the wall between mother and unborn child against all nature for one necessary moment: she doubted that any magic, no matter how strong, would allow that unnatural link to remain unbroken, least of all the babe's own mysterious state of inner hibernation. Unless some other force had used the occasion to slip into the scheme of things and alter them. . . .

"I think I know you," Irissa answered at last. "But I won't name you. Most things lose power when named. I think you *gain* force by being named."

A chuckle—self-satisfied but marginally approving—rolled around in Irissa's head like a loose pebble in a shoe.

She frowned and tightened her grip on the Overstone. What if the voice came not from inside herself, but from the strange Inlands talisman she wore? Anything was possible and only one thing undeniable: something around her, *in* her, grew and gathered strength. . . .

"Oh—!" Irissa clung harder as the Hunter began turning upward-winding circles. Not only motion had changed, but sound; she heard its hooves hitting phantom stones.

The Hunter continued as if climbing a winding stair. Below, the shimmering outline of many edifices shifted into sight and out of view as quickly. And far, far below, the bearing-beast herd flowed through a delicate maze of byways and walls, tearing through them as if rending a veil.

Only the Hunter obeyed the rules of the semivisible city. The Hunter was climbing a half-there staircase hoof by sure, resounding hoof. Other architectural details resolved and dissolved briefly in and out of focus. Now his hooves echoed off a long outdoor gallery. Now came an archway of glittering opalescent stone . . . too low for her—!

Irissa caught her breath and leaned over the Hunter's neck as far as her thickening waist would allow. The earthy scent of the Hunter's sweat flooded her nostrils, strands of his mane blew into her eyes.

They cleared the archway, but another loomed. The Hunter trotted straight for the glimmering side walls, seeking to brush Irissa's legs off its belly and unseat her.

So she tightened her inner control, fought the earth-defying beast for mastery in the sky. She willed it left, then right, guiding the Hunter through a spectral geography of bridge and rampart and one portal after another. If she ever eased her control, the beast attempted to crush her against some part of the ghostly architecture.

None of the bearing-beasts below were so nice as to tread this parti-present structure on its own terms. They still flowed through the ghostly byways and buildings like water, their riders untouched by the danger and dread Irissa faced.

For the Hunter traversed the Spectral City on his own, intricate terms. Perhaps his powers stemmed from this ambiguous site. Irissa found her every magical nerve tautened as she interwove their way through a shifting maze of . . . illusion.

The worst was the faces and forms she began to see

behind the windows and in the far-below streets: pale, fleeting images, oddly familiar.

Finorian flitting by a window, the Eldress's blanched face, hair, and garb grown whiter still. An alabaster statue of an owl-headed wolf—the Rynx! The image stirred as she passed, then blinked hollow white eyes. . . . Other forms, half dreamed, half forgotten before they had been remembered, glittered into view and vanished.

The Hunter minced to the end of a sketchy battlement, hesitated, then stepped onto empty air again. Irissa flinched backward, eyes closed, expecting a literal fall from grace at last.

Instead, the Spectral City winked out of sight behind her—as thoroughly gone now as it had been partially present before. The Hunter was walking a long straight highway of sky, its gait soft enough to cradle coddled eggs. On the horizon, the reality of Solanandor Tierze loomed larger—a towered, dark-meined city that glowered at the foot of a mountain range.

On the plain below, Sin and Aven drew their short-steeled blades as they saw the city take shape. Silver flashed off the metal and echoed in the sun-struck steel blade that Irissa drew and lifted to the sky and the city at the end of the sky. Kendric was there, he had to be! Perhaps this patchwork party could help her find him, free him, after all.

The party rode on whatever level given them, covering great distances in whatever element they traversed, toward Geronfrey's ruling city.

By an hour or two before sunfall, they all stood outside the gates. The great black swan had sunk to the ground, tucking its head under one wing and resembling nothing more in the twilight but a dark, rumpled upthrust of earth. Even the Hunter's hooves were anchored again on Rengarthian soil. Now the only strangeness left to confront was that of Solanandor Tierze.

"I've never seen a gate so intimidating," Irissa confessed to break the long silence.

The barrier before them was a sheet of steel that reflected their dour faces in wavy verisimilitude. In the surface's lake-water ripples, every bearing-beast stood on scalloped legs and the ludborgs looked like a series of dislocated fence posts.

"Such a gate must be incredibly heavy," Irissa added when her first comment drew no answer. "How shall we open it?"

"It is some new impediment of Geronfrey's invention," Aven burst out. "The former gate was only timbers and strapping steel. We could have easily overwhelmed it. But this—"

"Apparently Geronfrey suspected your uprising." Irissa quieted the Hunter from churning in a circle at the sound of its master's name.

"Of course Geronfrey knew of it!" Sin, too, sounded out of sorts. "The crystals predicted it all, as every uprising is foretold. And the Usurper is always banished by the sheer force of the people uniting against him."

"Apparently Geronfrey doesn't intend to 'banish' this time," Irissa noted. "Why undergo this upheaval if the outcome is always known—and always the same?"

A ludborg at her rear wheezed politely for attention. "Yes?"

"This time the crystals were somewhat more . . . promising, although ambiguous. They showed the man-beast—four-footed and two-horned, for instance, and the coming of an ancient heir in unlikely guise, not to mention the strange vision of the Unborn One with two shadows—"

"Gibberish!" Sin cast himself off his mount and began pacing, his reflection rippling in the steel wall that remained a closed gate. "Portents always excuse those who avoid acting."

Another ludborg bounced indignantly from his mount and rolled toward the young man. "What of yourselves? You and Aven were seen in the crystals."

Sin snorted his disbelief, but the ludborg lifted his hood to the darkening sky and intoned, "'The Eternal Twins shall be seen again in Rengarth.' Even you must admit that your like has not lived here for hundreds of years; no twins have been born here since; no family remains to keep your throne-claim alive. Yet your fiery hair speaks of the clan of Brenhall, who was the first Ruler dethroned by the Usurper—longer ago than even the crystals can show."

Aven threw her leg over her beast's withers and slid off to support her brother. "You don't deny our right as heirs?"

"No, no—" The ludborg's hood trembled its disavowal. "But neither can you and Sin deny that you . . . appeared . . . amongst us—hale, whole, hearty—yet with no memory of how you came here, or even of the earlier part of your lives. It's as if you were born only recently, full-fledged."

"Who cares about our pedigree?" Sin fidgeted, his fingers nervously wringing his dagger-sword hilt. "We are here, we have used our beast-bonding powers to muster a force to overcome the Usurper, you follow us—"

"Perhaps," a ludborg still mounted put in, "we follow the *new* heir." Its hood nodded solemnly in Irissa's direction.

"We named her heir," Aven said angrily, "as a courtesy to excuse her weapon. She is an . . . outlander, and no party to our quarrel save as onlooker."

"I wish no heir-right," Irissa put in hastily. "My quest is purely personal. I do not wish so much to overthrow the Usurper as to free my lost companion, Kendric. But does it matter where we each stand in this contention? We stand here, before Solanandor Tierze and a gate of sheer steel. How will we surmount it?"

"Fly your air-treading beast over it," Aven suggested ungraciously.

"The swan-spawn could better do the job swanback, and then open the gate from within," Sin said.

"Use your magic," a ludborg volunteered.

"Our magic only commands the beasts," Sin objected. "What good is it to have them all here at our behest if we can't make a simple mechanism bow to us?"

Irissa leaned forward to tap the Hunter's shoulder with the flat of her medallion. The beast immediately went down on its forelegs, permitting Irissa a quick and graceful descent over its neck.

"Very pretty," Aven said, "but tricks won't open yon gate."

"*My* magic might," Irissa said tersely, moving toward her own shattered reflection in the huge steel wall. "I am not limited to living things—or dead."

The closer she came, the more her image scattered into shards of light and dark. The steel was too dull to act fully as a mirror. Its pewter depths turned reflection—after the first, superficial impression—back on itself, muddying the first impression into a deception.

Irissa lifted the medallion to the metal gate, seeing its yellow glint spin in the steel expanse. If the medallion commanded Geronfrey's creatures, it might exert power over his inanimate creations, too.

As the golden circle swung back and forth by the motion of its own weight, the gate of steel wavered, then bowed to its small swaying on a larger scale. Steel slit into foot-wide bars that flashed open and shut to the same rhythm.

Gasps behind her told Irissa that the others had glimpsed the same slivers of a city behind the flashing metal gate that she had—people and animals moving, streets and byways, clustered buildings.

"If we could somehow hold the view beyond," Irissa began. "The gate wavers, but a greater force is needed to breach it. Aven, Sin—?"

"You seem to be doing well on your own," Sin grumbled back.

"Not well enough," Irissa answered. "And I dare not unleash any greater magic. I find my powers . . . ungovernable of late. To open a gate, I may bring down all the city walls—"

"So be it!" Aven trumpeted.

"It is only Geronfrey you challenge," Irissa reminded the hot-headed twins.

She sighed, exasperated that the shimmering wall required her attention, that she had to converse with her back to the others, that dark would soon require magical light. In all her travels, one fact remained unshakable: reliable aid was hard to come by.

The medallion's torque was slowing. Even the gate slits opened less wide less often. Behind the metal barrier, the cityscape was hardening into something like a static tapestry seen from far away, its people flattening.

"Quickly," Irissa urged. "If someone does not lend a hand, I shall lose the slender opening I have—!"

Someone did lend a hand, quite literally.

As a slit flashed open, a fist punched through, then another. The slit remained ajar even as the metal solidified on either side.

Then the hands—large and determined with fine dark hair dusting the knuckles— pushed the gap wider, pleating metal against metal until a man-high slit remained.

The hands grasped the edges and forced the opening even larger, a begemmed ring upon one knuckle gleaming as brightly as animal eyes at midnight.

"Kendric!"

Irissa's party watched bemused as she shrieked that one word and vanished into the wink in the metal wall.

Sin and Aven dashed after her, then hesitated at the mangled opening. Assorted ludborgs came next, their versatile but globular forms stymied by the narrow gap. Swanspawn, agape and silent, gathered around last. Only the beasts did not cluster there, but remained milling at the city walls.

At the peephole, the onlookers gaped almost as openly as the hole in the gate.

Inside, Irissa—braids and locks flying—was whirling about in the arms of a tall, broad man in travel-rumpled clothes.

"The borgia didn't take you!" he was shouting joyfully.

"Geronfrey didn't keep you!" she was returning with equal glee.

Then they noticed their audience and Irissa regained the ground to lead their gateman through. He stood blinking in the fading sunlight, days' worth of beard sooting his jaw.

"Are you all right?" he asked suddenly, turning to Irissa with tardy concern.

"Are *you* all right?" she echoed more quietly.

"Fine," he said heartily. "Except . . . hungry."

"Fine," she said. "Except . . . too often *not* hungry."

They laughed together as if alone.

Sin couldn't keep himself from striding up despite the stranger's somewhat ferocious appearance.

"This must be the man you sought," he told Irissa. "Now that you've settled the contrary state of your stomachs, perhaps you'd care to consider the state of our revolt. Geronfrey must be aware of our entire party by now."

"Geronfrey's always been alerted to your . . ."—Kendric turned from Irissa to the people with her—"your, ah . . . party. By all the swamp-festers in Rule, Ludborg has multiplied his self-importance since last I saw him!"

"They're not Ludborg, only like him," Irissa explained.

Kendric nodded uneasily. "I hope Geronfrey hasn't spawned such self-magnification here."

"You've seen him?" Irissa asked anxiously.

Kendric nodded. "Briefly. Long enough for me."

"Did he say why . . . he pursues you, me—?"

"He looked the same as ever," Kendric answered obliquely. "But then, I was never fond of his face in Rule, either. He rules a fortress at city center—and an array of guards of every description. I did not stay to inventory their differences, but they left a mark or two upon me."

He displayed jagged rents in his clothing to the awstruck ludborgs and gathering swan-spawn.

"You have escaped the Usurper's lair?" Aven demanded, her voice taut with disbelief.

Kendric nodded brusquely, staring at the woman and her fire-haired brother, both of them exceptionally striking in the reddening rays of sunfall. Then his eyes surveyed the bearing-beasts cropping the long grasses, resting at last on a rangier form. Everything about him stiffened.

"That beast—"

"The Hunter," Irissa confirmed. "From Edanvant."

"How did it get here?"

"Originally? I can't say. But from the place where we found it to these city walls . . . I rode it."

"You?" Kendric's shock could have insulted Irissa's riding ability . . . had she not understood his deeper concern.

She lifted her wrist so the metal round caught the suns' last glimmer.

"Medoc's medallion, which he had from the woman he met in midgate!" Kendric identified it.

Irissa nodded. "He gave it to me as a travel token, hoping it might prove useful. It did. As a lost talisman of Geronfrey's, it tamed the Hunter. Medoc would be pleased—"

"Hang Medoc! *I* am pleased. Otherwise, that beast and I should require another encounter. I would not be so sparing of its mortality again, after it gored me near to death the last time."

The Hunter, discussed but unruffled, bent his wickedly horned head to the turf and picked a long bouquet of flowers with loose equine lips.

Kendric shook his head at the mild demeanor of this once-deadly beast, then remembered present dangers.

"Where were you and your party headed?" he asked Irissa.

"To find you," she answered promptly.

Kendric surveyed the massed swan-spawn and ludborgs. "All this—for me? I am impressed."

A ludborg sidled forward. "You are an heirling, after all, and we Rengarthians adhere to our native heirs. But our purpose was greater even than you, gentle sir. We are here to repel the Usurper into the great Without whence he came."

"Heirling I'm not," Kendric said impatiently, "nor am I a fool who thinks one or many can banish a sorcerer of Geronfrey's longevity with an army of"—he gazed at the surrounding company—"an army of simpletons. . . ." Here he looked at the swan-spawn, who, it is true, seemed only half there. "Mobile dustballs"—the ludborgs bristled in unison—"and a set of rather rusty twins."

Sin's freckled fist was on his sword hilt despite his inferior size to the seven-foot-tall former Wrathman of Rule.

"Aven and I are as legitimate heirs as you, Kendric whatever-you-call-yourself. We are Brenhalloy. You clearly hail from the Far Keep—your extreme height reveals that—though your line was believed perished for more than twenty years, ever since Ajaxtus was slain and Phoenicia disappeared during the Usurper's last reclaiming—"

With one hand Kendric pressed Sin's sword hand to his hilt; the other lifted the Rengarthian by his tunic folds to within whispering distance.

"What do you mean—Far Keep? Those words were a meaningless formula in my homeland of Rule. What do they signify here?"

Aven was clinging to her brother's side like a moonweasel, trying to pry Kendric's fingers loose. "If heirs fight each other we shall never overcome Geronfrey again! Let Sin go!"

Kendric no more heeded Aven than he would a fly. Irissa stepped into the fray, putting a hand atop Kendric's.

"Sin will tell you what you want to know. Only let him down. He is quite harmless."

Such description did little to mollify Sin, but Kendric let the youth's own weight draw him back to Rengarthian ground.

"Not a prepossessing name," Kendric muttered.

"A nickname," Aven interjected. "I doubt anyone would be fond enough to bestow an endearment on you."

Kendric laughed. "No, by the heavens, no one has had the temerity to do so. You have made me aware of an unsuspected blessing, Rengarthian lady."

"Don't 'lady' me," Aven answered. "I'm as much an heir as Sin is. Perhaps more. I am the elder—"

"By only a minute," her brother put in hotly.

"Pray you, stop." Kendric patted the air with his huge hands, instantly winning their attention. "Tell me—gently—what is this Far Keep? It's a phrase I have used myself in another place without knowing why."

The twins' auburn eyes bored into each other, then they began speaking in rapid explanation.

"The Far Keep is . . . far from here," Aven said.

"At the top of a mountain of ice and silver," Sin added.

"—called the Paramount Athanor "

"It once was the home of the Phoenix clan."

"But the clan dwindled through the years, although Phoenicia carried true heirling blood. She wed Ajaxtus, our last Rengarthian Ruler before the Usurper's latest upcropping."

"No one *lives* on the Paramount Athanor now," Sin added. "It has become too inhospitable without the warming magic of the Phoenix clan present. It is a . . . remnant from Rengarth's past."

Kendric stood as one dumb absorbing this mass of meaningless information. Then he looked up to the snow-sugared peaks at the city's rear.

"My sword—"

"Yes, where is it?" Irissa wondered. "I saw a vision of it falling away from you, of you falling endlessly."

Kendric shrugged, a gesture that emphasized the lack of a sword across his back. "My sword and I were parted in the Black Tower. Geronfrey showed me it impaled in an ice rift. But . . . I was thinking of my original sword, the one I carried in Rule and left drowned in a lake there—" He turned to Aven and Sin. "Was there ever a forge at the Paramount Athanor?"

"Forge? No forge." Aven and Sin looked truly perplexed. "Just the ancestral liquid fires of the Phoenix clan," Sin went on. "They were adept at warming the world around them, until they became too few and the heights' cold too much for them. They . . . died away, most of them. Phoenicia was the most illustrious survivor. She alone could have revived the line. 'Tis said she bore an heir when she vanished, but that was nigh thirty years ago."

"And Ajaxtus had been overthrown by then," Aven reminded him, "so such an heir was moot. We have better to do than mourn the eclipse of the Phoenix; our Brenhalloy clan is the stronger now."

"None of you are strong enough if Geronfrey still sits his citadel," a ludborg put in.

Kendric stirred as if waking from a dream and turned to Irissa. "Enough of such confusing talk. I wish to retreat somewhere for a meal where I can make sense of all that's happened. And you, Irissa, the borgia—how did you get here?"

"Ilvanis and Neva drew the borgia from me, then I confronted the Black Tower to find you and . . . came here." She wasn't ready to tell him about falling into the dry lake or the circle of fire with which she had ringed it. Or the catfish that spoke, or the swanfish and the flying giant swan—

He stared deeply into her silver eyes, past all the trivia of their separate adventures, in search of the poison-hurt as well as the heart it had taken to bring her after him. One he would heal and the other would heal him.

"Would we had never left Edanvant!" Kendric said fervently.

Irissa smiled. "Kendric, I remember a time when you regretted bitterly that we ever came to Edanvant."

"I had not seen Rengarth then," he said promptly.

"Rengarth is a most . . . ingratiating land," Irissa answered.

"You have not seen the half of it—and I hope you never do. We must find a way back to Edanvant."

"Does this mean you won't help us?" Aven asked.

"No," Kendric answered for them both. "We are strangers here. Your battles are your own. We have no right to tip the scales."

"A pity," wailed a ludborg.

"We don't need unwilling allies." Sin drew the dagger-sword at his hip and stepped toward the opening Kendric had forced in the gate.

Kendric regarded both weapon and wielder with amusement. "You'll need more than that against Geronfrey, but good fortune to you."

A ludborg skittered behind the Wrathman to tug at the back of his sleeve. "A most toothsome inn, gracious sir, awaits on the other side of the wall. Perhaps you and the lady would retire there while we manage our uprising. You did mention a state of hunger, and our kind is most sensitive to such deprivation." A sleeve supported Kendric's hand while another sleeve dribbled some square metallic coins into his palm. "Alms for the hungry. Say nothing of it."

The ludborg vanished into its fellows, leaving Kendric stunned and Irissa nearly as disconcerted.

"An inn," Kendric agreed heartily, closing his fist on the Rengarthian bounty. "We will meet you there after your triumph and hear all about it, no doubt."

"No doubt," ludborgs murmured in concert, rolling en masse toward the door in the gate that Kendric had made. The simpleminded swan-spawn followed, and—with a last fiery glare at Irissa and Kendric that reminded them of the sunfall's hot farewell branding the faces of everyone there—Aven and Sin.

CHAPTER
17

PEPPER BLANKETED THE SOUP, THE FOWL FLESH HAD A purplish cast and sour odor—and the beer was the color and texture of molasses. Kendric consumed it all in quick succession anyway, finishing up with a hasty pudding that must have sat on a shelf for at least a week.

Irissa watched with an odd blend of fondness and guilt.

"What worries you?" he asked between sips, bites, chews, and spoonfuls. "This world?"

She smiled wanly. "The old one."

"You should have stayed. As you can see, I would have found my way out anyway."

"I do not *miss* the old one, only worry about it."

"You worry too much." He swigged a mouthful of the thick-headed ale and made a face. "Perhaps that's a result of your condition." Irissa stiffened. "I shouldn't have mentioned it, but you—"

"Look more so in my condition than ever." Irissa smiled less wanly. "I know that 'my condition' is inescapable. I faced that fact when I was alone in Edanvant. And I don't worry *about* Edanvant, I worry that I *don't* miss it."

Kendric stabbed his knife into the smoke-scented tabletop. "You should miss it! We were safer there." His voice lowered as other guests of the Rengarthian inn cocked bushy eyebrows in his direction. "*You* were safer there."

"I seem quite safe here," Irissa said, grinning and looking around. So far the city of Solanandor Tierze was unremarkable, much like the city of Rule in her native world. More men than women patronized the tavern, but that was the way of any world. And the people seemed as unchallenging as the bulk of folk everywhere. "You're the one Geronfrey pursues now," Irissa pointed out. "Do you know why?"

"He said I meddled with his magic in Edanvant. Apparently, drawing me to Rengarth was an accident, if one is inclined to believe Geronfrey's explanations. What's clear is that he's quite at home here, and that we should be gone through any gate we can find as soon as possible."

"You forget." Irissa toyed with a six-pronged fork, prodding the knotted noodles on her plate. "Geronfrey may reign here, but he's only a Usurper and is about to be overthrown. Avon and Sin made *that* even clearer."

Kendric paused in inhaling his dinner to snort dismissively. "That childish rabble could no more dislodge a sorcerer like Geronfrey than extract a tooth with a fingernail!"

"*You* got away," she answered. "He can't be that omnipotent."

"I had . . . help."

"Oh?"

Kendric lowered his head and applied himself to mauling three sequential forkfuls of tough fowl meat, so he couldn't speak for a while.

"And those . . . ludborgs, as you call them," he commented finally when his eyes met Irissa's again "Ludborg has proved amusing at times, but an entire nest of them would be most . . . festy, to borrow a word. At least that troublesome cat has had the decency to dog us no more in yet another world—"

Irissa twirled her fork tines on the tabletop. Kendric stopped talking, then he stopped chewing.

"Felabba," he resumed hopefully, "is nowhere to be seen, that is right, isn't it?"

"To be seen . . . no."

"Irissa—are you evading me?"

"You were vague about your . . . help."

"This is different. Is Felabba here or not?"

"I don't know. Only, sometimes, I . . . hear . . . a voice."

Kendric lowered his eating utensils and rubbed his eyes, then scrubbed his worry-crinkled forehead. "You hear a voice. If anyone else said that, I would recommend a long retreat in a Soarian monastery. When do you hear this voice, where?"

"When it chooses to be heard. From . . . within."

Kendric contemplated the implications. "You don't mean to say that . . . that insufferable, meddling cat has somehow attached itself to your—our—child?"

"I don't think so. Our child seemed perfectly self-sufficient when I—"

"Our child? You've seen it?"

"Only symbolically perhaps. Don't stare so; I couldn't cross a gate without its permission, remember?"

Kendric sat stunned. "You . . . farsaw into your unborn child? No wonder Orvath was less than enthusiastic about his impending second fatherhood. Truly Torlocs are a breed apart. No mother knows her unborn child."

"In that I am typical. I would never claim to know it, only to know that it is there." Irissa laughed as she patted her widening waist. "It's rather hard to ignore. But don't blame me for accomplishing unnatural things. Perhaps the *child* is the wonder-worker who allowed me to visit my future in my present to save my past."

"Or . . . the unborn had unexpected help. Felabba." Kendric shuddered and drained his tankard to the gooey bottom dregs. "Well, we may need old bitterbones yet. Geronfrey is far from done with us, Irissa, that I know, if I don't know why he allowed me to blunder my way to Rengarth. Perhaps your laughable rabble can conquer him—"

"Oh! I promised I would help them—" Irissa looked anxiously to the inn door, as if she would be off.

Kendric's hand captured her wrist. "No. It isn't safe

for you to go anywhere near Geronfrey. Better I go back and aid them first."

"But—"

"Do you remember our last words in Edanvant, how close we came to letting such harshness stand as a hedge between us forever?"

She nodded into his sober ale-blond eyes, regretting her restless discontent, the discontent that seemed to brood within her entire kind.

"We must never let such unconsidered words separate us again," he said. "Our best magic lies in our power to remain unsundered. Even Geronfrey cannot counter that reality."

Irissa smiled again. "Don't you think I knew that the moment I awakened from the horgia sleep and found you gone?"

"Of course. Sleep always renders one sensible again. And sometimes separation. At least our faint-visaged friends, Neva and Ilvanis, were of use to revive you. Had it been left to Torlocs and . . . er, ludborgs, I fear you would have withered like Finorian before anyone saw your eyes blink true silver again."

"It's odd. . . ." Irissa thoughtfully but unconsciously pulled the last of Kendric's hasty pudding toward her to dip into the mess. "I seem to have heard of this ancient Ruler, Brenhall, before."

"And of Phoenicia and Ajaxtus and all that lot," Kendric agreed. "Rengarthians are a long-memoried folk for ones with such throat-choking names. I wonder if our original land of Rule with its Six Realms and Six Wrathmen and Six Swords sounded as fusty as this. I can keep little of it straight."

"Oh, I can keep it straight, all right," Irissa said with narrowed silver eyes. "I just don't quite see how it all curves together."

"It doesn't." Kendric's palm slapped the table. "And

that which does not join together hurls apart. So good riddance to it."

A sound of distant thunder rolled over their heads just as the inn door clapped open. Against the dark of night an even blacker form loomed in the doorway.

A servingman scurried from table to table, leaving flames afloat in small dishes of oil in his wake to brighten the torch-shadowed inn chamber.

The stranger, dry but wrapped in an air of impending storm, thundered step by stiff step to a nearby table. The icy wind of his passage beat the flames low along their oily seas.

Kendric's back was to the fellow, but Irissa saw him and surprise dawned in her face before she could hide it.

Around them, voices whispered, a husky chorus that sang one word in round. "Icewraith," the word hissed and lisped around the dusky inn chamber. "Iccccewraithhhhh."

A terrified townsman stood, overturning a bench behind him and a full tankard before him. The metal container executed a long, hollow death rattle along the floorboards and was still.

Open, the wind-shaken inn door drummed against the wall like nervous fingers. The north wind's frosty breath whistled inward as through its own icy teeth. Shudders racked the tavern-bound Rengarthians; chills touched Irissa to the hot, living core of her being.

Kendric alone remained unnumbed. He straightened as if an unheard voice had named him, and turned his head over his shoulder to view the new arrival.

"Icewraith," wailed the people, overturning tables to huddle against the room's four walls. Clouds of frost poured from the lips of their abandoned tankards like a frozen exhalation. Ice plumes feathered every surface— wood, metal, cloth . . . flesh.

A tavernmaid screamed at her frost-braceleted forearm, then retreated from the ice-white tankard she had dropped on the floor.

"Geronfrey has raised the icewraiths," someone warned through lips that froze into sudden silence.

The figure stepped into midroom, glittering. Though it resembled a human—head, arms, legs—no part of its form was supple. Instead, it was harshly angled, as if hacked by the dull edge of a blade into its present shape.

Kendric stood to face it. Irissa watched him rise to full height, seeing that fabled stature unfold—merely to match the icewraith's own seven-some feet of height.

She found it shocking to see Kendric's height made moot in a non-Torloc world. Irissa, at six feet, had grown used to towering over ordinary people, to seeing Kendric towering even more. So it was an inevitable contest—the Icewraith and the Wrathman. Only Kendric was strong enough to challenge the icewraith. Or perhaps herself. . . .

"Let boys be boys," a familiar voice hissed into her mind. *"They are always most amusing unhindered."*

"He has no weapon," Irissa hissed back, enjoying the vehemence such delivery gave her words.

"Tsk, tsk. They only relish such odds. Besides, you have other matters to tend to."

"Other matters?" Irissa surveyed herself, noticing that the emerald pommelstone at her hip had frosted over in the icewraith's draft. She drew the sword by its chilly hilt and tossed it toward Kendric. "A weapon," she advised.

He caught it instinctively and switched hands just as instinctively as the weapon's new cold began to freeze his fingers.

"Weapon? More like an ice-dagger toothpick," he complained. Sweat—or melted ice—was squeezing between his fingers as they warmed the hilt. His ringstone cycled brightly through its range of five colors. "But this sword has served me before to deal with vermin—remember the scaled thing between the walls in Edanvant?"

"I remember." Irissa, worried again and not wanting to be, clutched the Overstone out of habit. Habit became surprise. The stone lay dead-heavy and ice-cold against her heart and palm—how had she not noticed that before?

"See," the cold voice rasped beside her, a bit of north wind bound and given speech. Or was it *in*side her? *"You fret about an outward danger when the inward one is where your responsibility lies."*

Awestruck, Irissa slumped back into her seat like a spectator. She clawed the Overstone pouch open. Once-supple falgonskin felt iron-stiff. Even the exterior feathers and scales were brittle and flaked off as she wrestled the bag.

At last the Overstone itself lay in her hand, its opalescent sheen dulled to a stolid expanse of blanched ice—the veins of color had faded to a frosted anatomy of leaf-bereft trees. Irissa clutched the talisman in both hands. When it chilled her blood, she willed her blood warm again—over and over again—until the Overstone should heat itself in the oven of her folded fingers.

Like a wounded bird it fluttered in the pulse between her fingers, freezing and thawing in fast succession. Its native hues came and went. Irissa felt the ice flow farther up her limbs with each advance. Each time it ebbed back into the heart of the Overstone and away, only to flow again, and be repelled.

She didn't know why she fought so tenaciously for the Overstone, only that it was a burden she had chosen and she owed it all she could muster. She had not carried it this far in vain.

And so they throbbed in sympathy—Irissa and the Overstone—fighting the icewraith's freezing presence, racked by waves of fever and then chill. Always, always she felt the force that sought the heart of their separate natures burrowing inward and being cast outward.

Kendric barely noticed the half-frozen figures around him, or that the wind was forking the flames in the oil lamps into serpents' tongues of flickering light.

He saw only the figure before him, its eyes mere shards of ice-glitter, its fingers long and sharp as ice daggers that drip from spring eaves. The tiny lamp flames' light gleamed in the inhuman crevices of its craggy form. Kendric saw skulls illuminated at its shoulders, hips, elbows, and knees—as if the gristle of human lives oiled every joint.

Pieces of lost armor jutted from its limbs, half embedded in its icy contours—leathern greaves along its shinbones; rusted . . . or bloodied . . . mail on its stiff torso; a broken jaw plate from a helmet dangling from one ear.

It moved in his direction, clattering, cracking, as if seeking the only heat to be had.

Kendric felt cold sweat tickle down behind his ears, down his spine, his hands. Despite the sound of cold in the howling wind, the look of cold in the frost that was webbing everything in the room, Kendric himself felt like a furnace. His heart was fire in a blizzard, and his breath was a bellows pumping heat into the blasted inn.

In his right hand, Irissa's dainty sword blade was turning red-hot. The metal itself was wavering, curving in and out in serpentine fashion. In his palm, the emerald hiltstone glowed deep ruby.

The icewraith hefted an ax—an ugly, unbalanced ax, if Kendric had stopped to think about it. He didn't. His overheated, supple limbs were busy dodging the descending weapon.

It hacked into the hardwood settle behind him. He heard it bite and then the wood cracked from end to end. Looking back, he saw ice fissures expand the wound, breaking solid heartwood into splinters.

Kendric spun into midroom and snatched up a huge pewter platter for a shield. The metal set his fingers aflame with sudden cold, then he mustered the heat within himself to reverse the effect.

The pewter shone only with its native silver now, but the icewraith's next blow was in middelivery. Kendric ducked behind the platter shield just as the ax edge shivered into it. Solid metal shattered like glass and fell floorward.

Still too cold. Kendric retreated behind a supporting pillar—a thigh-thick timber bolted into place. The ax curved toward it . . . and him . . . on a chill whistle of motion that brought goose bumps to his forearms.

The timber buckled, and Kendric dodged falling rafter supports as the inn crinkled upon itself. Against the walls, the people cowered, quite literally frozen. Kendric moved into another corner, drawing the icewraith farther from Irissa. She sat stiff in concentration, her figure pulsing from chill white to hot silver to warm fleshy peach from second to second. Around it the green haze of her magic in motion wove a fragile web.

Kendric nodded grimly to himself. If the icewraith was an emissary of Geronfrey's, both of them were under attack. The inn was iced in magic; he would have to counter the wraith's chill powers with his own more human, molten ones.

Moving when no one else would or could, he let the creature drive him deeper into the corner. There the roof sloped sharply, leaving not enough room for a midget to stand straight. Kendric could bend and had proved it on many occasions.

Could the icewraith?

Kendric slipped away from the wall at the last moment, spun away from the descending ax. He ignored the weapon's frosty roar as it smashed the wall and touched his red-hot blade tip—the mere tip—to the icewraith's shoulder.

A scream like the heart of the north wind being torn from the roots of the world reverberated in the tiny inn. It was a roar—deep and cold-bellowed, a grinding kind of agony.

Where Kendric's sword had struck, an ice-water gash glistened, and through it. . . . He recoiled from the sight of burned flesh, of blisters swelling to the surface of the skin like beads of sweat.

Striking with a brand rather than a blade had never been Kendric's preference. For the icewraith was vulnerable flesh beneath the suit of stiffened snow that clothed it. Despite its inhuman appearance, that flesh wept, seared, and charred as Kendric struck blow after blow.

He flailed away with the red-hot blade of Irissa's short-sword, melting the icewraith's formidable exterior in flaying inches, exposing and scaring the flesh beneath it in painfully slow segments.

His final blow hacked off the ice-bound helmet.

Eyeballs blinked in the blistered face, then the icewraith fell—not stiffly, but in collapsing curves, limp at last.

What lay on the floor looked as inhuman as what had thundered into the room. That was only because it had once been human. Knowing that made defeating the icewraith only a remote form of suicide.

Kendric cast the sword to a nearby tabletop. The hot metal sizzled, branding its shape into the wood to the hilt-stone. Sweating, shivering, he moved icewraith-stiff toward Irissa.

She was blowing softly across her cupped hands, as if nursing a burn. For a moment he wondered if some wild blow of his had somehow singed her.

Then he saw the surface of the Overstone peeking between her fingers. Irissa straightened and stroked the stone's curved side as gently as the breast of a bird.

"It almost died, I think," she said softly.

Kendric sat across from her on what was left of his once high-backed settle—a bench. "Irissa." He almost whispered he spoke so carefully. "That's a stone. A piece of solid rock. It has no life to lose."

"It has life," she insisted, raising her eyes.

He was astounded to see tears in them—plain, wet human tears. They rolled down her face without freezing into the coldstones a Torloc seeress's tears commonly became before they reached the ground.

He glanced to the unlovely form warming the floor. "So did it have life—once. I had the oddest feeling that I somehow killed myself."

"And I! I had the strangest certainty I saved myself."

Kendric shook his head. His own battle sweat dripped to the tabletop. He studied the raindrop-sized blotches, realizing that they, too, remained liquid. He had gotten used to producing extraordinary excretions since Irissa had passed her magic to him.

Apparently neither had drawn on inward magic in their own separate battles—or had they drained their magic, until only human heat remained?

CHAPTER
18

OUTSIDE, IN THE DARK, THE INN SIGN CREAKED IN THE wind.

Kendric balanced the icewraith's ax in his hand. Slowly, so gradually that it seemed an illusion, the ax blade grew luminescent until a soft silver sheen beamed forth.

The glow lit Irissa's admiring features. "Once your magic came and went at its own command," she told Kendric. "Now you call it to you like a tame moonweasel."

"There's no such thing," he retorted, "any more than there is tame magic. It all bites when least expected." He sighed and regarded the swaying signboard. "The . . . 'Fecund . . . Phoenix.' Strange name for an inn. Strange land."

"Strange sword," Irissa put in ironically, lifting her blade to show Kendric how his use had altered it. The once-straight steel still wavered, frozen into its new shape by contact with the icewraith.

Kendric winced at the evidence of his handiwork. "Perhaps our magic can straighten it later. For now, I see that we cannot avoid what I hoped we could—joining the others in overthrowing Geronfrey.

"I have no interest in driving him from his roost here. Yet if we remain hidden at the . . . Fecund Phoenix, who knows how many vagrant sendings of his will find and challenge us? I hoped to keep you from something at Geronfrey's fortress, but—"

"Still?" Irissa slipped the altered sword into the sling

at her hip and shook her head. "That's how you came unwilling to Rengarth, by trying to keep something in Edanvant from me. Where shall your protection take me next, to what dire pass and dread land? If you continue to 'spare' me as efficiently as you have so far, I shall be the first Torloc to perish of an ordinary human life span!"

He couldn't help laughing, though trouble still roiled in his eyes. Then he glanced down to thrust the ax handle in his belt and those eyes grew child-wide.

"Runes! Rengarthian runes edge this ax blade! These same-style runes were scribed into the hilt of my sword. Ludborg always prattled of such scrawlings, but—"

"But you didn't want to believe him. Well, runes require deciphering, and even a magically shining ax blade doesn't shed light enough for that. Perhaps Geronfrey has a torchlight or two in his demesne—"

"Tapers by the dozen, roomfuls of them," Kendric confirmed promptly.

"That settles it," Irissa said. "We do not so much go to war as . . . go to market. We need light and Geronfrey has a corner on it, in more ways than one. Let us visit."

Wind blew through the dark streets like water—chill, rushing wind. Unseen things brushed Irissa and Kendric as they bowed into the teeth of that gale; it seemed even the light from Kendric's ax and Irissa's hiltstone was driven back into their wakes. Limp, wet forms twined their limbs, then slipped off. Wind-snagged flotsam of the city streets whipped at their garments and stung their faces.

"We swim against a dry tide," Irissa shouted into the mouth of the gale. The wind swallowed and merely whispered the words by the time they reached Kendric's ears.

"Dry tide?" he finally gruffed back. "You know more of this land than I'd like to."

"That's my name for this watery wind that repels us. I fell into a dry lake on arriving. And—remember the wind at our chamber window in Edanvant that drove you back?

A gust from Geronfrey's world, most likely. He must command even the air here."

Kendric signaled understanding by pinching her elbow and dug his feet into the uneven ground more fiercely. The pair found themselves walking ever harder to get nowhere, up an endless incline. Strange lights flitted past, hissing and snapping like sparks.

Kendric snared one in his fist, but when he opened his palm, only a mote of charred paper lay there. Irissa paused long enough in her upstream struggle to study it by hilt-light before the wind flapped it away.

"Geronfrey is burning his spellbound volumes," she diagnosed. "He must be losing—hurry!"

Her words put new heart into Kendric's feet. He lowered his head to the wind like an ox to the yoke and drove forward a stride at a time, his sheer spirit pushing Irissa onward.

They may not have known where they were going, but instinct told them that moving against the spectral wind must impel them toward Geronfrey's stronghold.

In time the eddies of sparks thickened and the wind abated. Filaments of light leaked through closed shutters on houses all around, the only sign that this city of sudden recluses was populated.

"Apparently," Kendric huffed, "the city dwellers have witnessed a Usurper overthrown before and stay well out of the way. Perhaps we should find some example in that."

"Look!" Irissa pointed at a bright whirlwind in the darkness ahead. The vagrant sparks had congealed into a mass, and now were churning into a turret-high column. Something else rolled in the pillar of bright motion.

The swan-spawn were climbing the motes of dancing light, drawn up as lightly as feathers caught in a spiraling spring wind. Behind the light-mote ladder, a dark close-faced fortress glowered as a mountain frowns behind veils of morning mist.

The citadel's forbidding facade gave Kendric pause.

"I never looked back as I escaped," he admitted.

"Geronfrey builds his seats to last, as under Falgontooth Mountain in Rule. And that 'army' of Sin and Aven's— they're *floating*!"

"Why not?" Irissa said. "I saw them called up. They're made of swans-down."

Kendric uncorked a skeptical look she had not seen on his face for too long.

"Where are the torch-haired twins?" he demanded next. "I thought they commanded this fools' onslaught."

His answer came in a shower of brilliant blue sparks that rained through the night. The sudden lightning-lash showed Geronfrey's bat-winged fortress sprawling against the pale background of snow-dappled mountains.

A congeries of ludborgs was hurling at the mouth of the edifice, a living battering ram wrapped in a cloak of blue-worms that burned through wood and metal with acidic sizzle.

Aven and Sin's scarlet hair caught blue fire to match the metallic sheen of their naked dagger-swords. Ludborgs piled up like stacked casting crystals, then their sheer mass buckled the door.

Contrary elements hissed into conflict as icewraiths poured out to attack and blue-worm-girded ludborgs tumbled in to repel. In the mayhem, Sin and Aven vanished.

"A fray. A simple, hand-to-hand fray," Kendric observed with relish.

He strode forward, the ax drawn from his belt.

Irissa hesitated a moment to consult her "condition," but found no dissenting voice within or without—either hers or anyone else's. She followed Kendric, as confident in their united force as she was in their disparate magicks.

A battle waged within the stone halls of Geronfrey's headquarters. Icewraiths melted limb by limb to the floors under the hot, hissing touch of ludborgian blue-worms. Once down, the dead beneath the ice-forged armor writhed under a new siege . . . triumphant maggots of azure light.

A waist-high creature with leathery crimson wings, small maroon hands stationed along the length of those ap-

pendages, and fingers like dried fire-peppers came flapping
down a stairwell. It squawked into their midst, long-clawed
hands tearing at clothing, at flesh, as it attacked foes and
fallen icewraiths equally.

It strove with a blind, unintelligent fury. Kendric
aimed his ax at the body behind the dragging wings, but
Irissa, with her more precise sword, managed to hack off
one of the grasping hands.

"No!" Kendric turned away from battle long enough
to catch her eyes. "I encountered one in my escape. The
hands work independently—"

Severed, the fingers pinched along the floor, clutching
ludborg robes at the ankles. If ludborgs *had* ankles, Irissa
reminded herself. She *knew* that she and Kendric did, and
shuddered to imagine those bloody fingers clawing at their
boot leather.

Irissa pushed her braids aside with one forearm and
thought of magic instead of trivia. Her mind, confronted
with too many new sights, fastened on a simple image: a
ball, round as a casting crystal, only heavy—and Iridesium-
dark.

It formed in the room, a dull metallic globe like a
small faded sun, and dropped precisely on the disembodied
hand. Pinned, the appendage stopped, save for an intermittent wriggling of claw tips.

But a row of intact hands still remained along the
wings' cutting edges, grasping as the creature flailed awkwardly, slashing Kendric's thigh, slicing past a ludborg's
whirling figure, cutting *into* the edge of a ludborg's hood

Irissa gasped at this breach of the ludborg's impenetrable form. Somehow, the shapeless robes that swathed it
were the ludborg. In time spent with the original Ludborg,
Irissa had learned to regard the inside of a ludborg as invio-
lable.

Yet the coarse-woven robe tore easily. And from the rent
torn in that dark, always-shaded hood into which no one—
Irissa, Kendric, or anyone—had ever seen . . . poured a

slit of solid light white beyond imagining. It was like staring into the heart of a sun, or metal when it's molten.

Blinded, Irissa and Kendric, icewraiths—even the blind winged creature—turned their heads. Light sealed them like hot wax, molding them motionless. In that suspended state, Irissa saw the creature's leathery wings shrivel as if all liquid and life were being sucked from them.

The entire beast shrank, curling into a form serer than a fallen leaf in winter.

Nothing moved in the stone-walled chamber.

"Ahem," said a mild voice. "You can look now."

Their eyes, wiser than their ears, resisted staying open as their heads turned. The . . . wounded . . . ludborg stood unharmed, a cross-stitching of blue-worms drawing his rent hood shut, as if he had lost an ear and that's all.

"What light was that inside your torn hood?" Kendric, ever bold, asked.

"Heartfire," the ludborg answered. "We usually burn blue, but when the ice-forged sword enters the Salamander Tewel, even the Paramount Athanor feels it."

"More dribble-drabble from a lipless walking riddle," Kendric muttered to Irissa, not bothering to conceal his discontent.

"Come!" a fresh voice shouted from the stairs. Aven stood there, dripping sweat, blood, and half-severed braids. "The swan-spawn have cleared the upper chambers. Geronfrey's domain is ours! Brenhalloy reign again."

Her call rallied the ludborgs. Irissa and Kendric followed, drawn more by curiosity than any sense of victory. They had seen Geronfrey shake an entire mountain apart to defend his pride. He was hardly vanquished because some icewraiths had melted or a feather-dusting of swan-spawn had swept through his inner chambers.

Kendric and Irissa sprinted up the stairs after the party, their rings chiming together.

"Magic," he advised her softly, "not might, from now on. Mayhap these young hotheads can imagine themselves victors simply because their enemy chooses to remain invisible, but we intrude where Geronfrey would have had you from the first—within his grasp."

"Yet you draw me along," Irissa answered.

"You are right. Keeping you from facing what waited has served neither of us. Perhaps confronting it will."

Torchlit halls and taperlit chambers intersected as Kendric and Irissa wove through them. Swan-spawn dashed from one room to another flourishing golden-bladed swords. Threads of blue-worms writhed in the ludborgs' wakes, wriggling on the rich figured carpets and burning sinuous holes into the fibers. Aven and Sin could be heard directing a search from chamber to chamber far ahead.

Leather-winged creatures shriveled in the sumptuous surroundings, and sudden slippery puddles on the uncarpeted stones between the rooms reminded Irissa and Kendric of the possible presence of icewraiths.

But except for a few signs of Geronfrey's fallen defenders, the fortress was strangely deserted. They could detect a rising frustration in Aven's and Sin's distant ringing voices.

"I remember walking the endless empty rooms of this place," Kendric said softly, stopping. "Now I sense the same half-seen futility. Geronfrey can roll out rooms like dough, and reshape them as easily. I think we search an illusion for an absence."

"Here! I hear something—!" a voice burst in. Footsteps pounded stone and padded on carpet. Then Sin erupted through the doorway like fire, his hair sweat-coiled and his fair face crimson with effort.

"Only the outlander and her oversized companion," he announced dispiritedly as he saw Irissa and Kendric. Aven came so fast behind that she nearly collided with her brother. Ludborgs piled up behind them—and swan-spawn—all looking spent, disheveled, and empty-handed.

"Is this how one overthrows a Usurper in Rengarth," Irissa wondered, "by running about the place announcing one's presence?"

"It's how one does it when said Usurper refuses to

present himself." Sin scabbarded his dagger-sword in its rune-stamped leather sheath.

"What can we do?" Aven demanded. "We've run from pillar to post and have seen nothing except the creatures Geronfrey sets forth as his guard. No one ever prepared us to face an enemy that won't face us."

"Our most serious enemies are always the least visible," Irissa said. "Perhaps *I* can draw Geronfrey into view."

"I will not let you use yourself," Kendric warned.

"Who is better qualified to decide my use?" she answered. Then she was pacing around the room—first along the perimeter of the large carpet, then along the stones bordering the wall.

Tapers flickered at her passage. The others drew to the room's center like sheep, allowing her free range. Kendric, dubious, stood between the central clot and Irissa's ranging figure, anxiety lurking behind his eyes and taut mouth.

He looked beyond Irissa and her immediate actions, trying to sense the sorcerer Geronfrey. Urging every particle of his being to alertness, Kendric felt his magic gather into a knot of uneasy, undirected force.

Irissa paced the room, her head cast down. Candle flames polished the blackness of her hair with rainbow-colored highlights, touched the similar surface of jet-black Iridesium circling her temples.

Her hand cupped the Overstone pouch to her breast. Kendric found himself soothed by this contemplative posture, by Irissa's calm withdrawal from the tensions roiling around her. She reminded him momentarily of her mother, Jalonia. Some serene, earthly magic had suffused her with its unsensed powers. Even the new fullness of her figure seemed proper, seemed . . . natural.

Kendric could no longer remember an Irissa of less luminous maturity. He saw her now as fully apart from her Torloc kind, perhaps even from himself. She seemed to stand more solitary than she ever had, despite the ironic multiplication of herself in another within herself.

The mute intricacy of it all confused him. He watched with the rest—hopeful, willing to be helpful, grateful.

Irissa paused at a wall, her head still bowed to the floor. Her closed fist, clutched around the Overstone, knocked softly on her chest as she thought.

Kendric heard the throb of the mock external heartbeat and tensed. Something hovered in the air—a breath of wind . . . held; a scent of storm . . . stilled; a rising heat of hope . . . suspended.

"Here," Irissa said, facing blank wall as if introducing herself. Her free hand tapped the smooth stone blocks. "A door into future-past."

"Gibberish," Aven said, her face haughty with youthful impatience. "We must search further." But she didn't move to go, nor did her brother, Sin.

Irissa sighed and touched the stones.

Their surface shifted to bright black—a slick ebony hole in the wall shaped precisely to her form, like a shadow without distortion thrown there.

An "ah" of surprise wafted through the chamber. Kendric frowned, his gaze drawn by the new whiteness of Irissa's face, her pale hand as it clutched the Overstone. The Iridesium circlet's dull black surface had lost all color.

In the darkness cast by Irissa's figure, a tiny whiteness flickered on the shadow.

"My child . . ." Irissa lifted her right hand from the Overstone to reach into the wall.

"Wait!" Kendric thundered. No flame reflections danced in the circlet's dark metal. It had become opaque and absent, a thin ribbon of nothing girding Irissa's temples. Seeing through the slim band of blackness, Kendric glimpsed the stones of the wall beyond Irissa—

"Wait!" he begged some force Geronfrey, who waited, or Irissa, who dallied, or his own magic, which debated. . . .

The decision was not his. Irissa suddenly tightened her grasp on the Overstone, settled her shoulders, and walked into the now-pale silhouette of herself.

Kendric, arriving too late to stop her, bruised his knuckles on healed stone. Stone powder dusted his palms, but the adamant blocks remained set in place, as they ever had.

Kendric turned to the others with a look of stony surprise.

Irissa walked a corridor she knew from dreams. She felt her self peel free and pull behind her into a train of thoughts that slowed her progress. Many selves trailed her, hanging from her shoulders in cloaklike folds too heavy to disregard.

The dark was softening and her shape was expanding to include walls, ceiling, floor, and—far ahead—a darker oblong of door.

She moved toward it, the Overstone still heating her palm, her feet icy with dread. And no wonder. The dark door never lightened as she neared it. Instead it grew thicker, black to the point of vanishing into its own deepest corners.

It was sized to fit her frame as a gauntlet is molded to a fist—six feet high and much narrower by contrast. Despite the lack of light, the black opening gleamed wetly. Her fingertip tried it, pushing into emptiness. The darkness dimpled. Cold ringed her forefinger and would not let go.

She wanted to retreat. She saw no reflection of herself in that eminently reflective surface and leaned away. But her fingertip was caught, snared. A cool dryness sucked on her until she was floating facedown into the doorway. Floating, she fell. Dry as the lake and darker, the aperture dove down forever, taking Irissa with it.

Then her world spun. She floated on her back, gazing at a midnight sky devoid of stars and moon. The horizon cracked at her side, levering open on a stone sky lit by flames strung along its perimeter.

Irissa saw it all through a foggy gray veil. When she tried to lift her hands to brush aside the veil from her vision, she felt them float limply beside her, weighed down by the dark, viscous pond in which she lay.

The face of Geronfrey rose on her horizon, his blue eyes darker than she had remembered, more caring than she had hoped and less cared about than she was willing to see.

Another face hovered over his shoulder, raven threads of hair unraveling at its edges. It was her own face—green-eyed and vacantly curious.

"She looks dead," the Irissa behind Geronfrey complained in a lighter voice than Irissa's own. "And . . . slimy."

"So did you once. You will have to draw her forth yourself. I can only bring her to you by one means or another; you must imbibe her of your own will."

"She is less than I." The face lowered to the side and then lurched inward so quickly Irissa would have blinked, save that her eyes seemed mired in ooze and could not close. "And she has nothing that I would have—no jewels, no light about her person. Why do I need her at all?"

"She is your inner self—or the seed of it." Geronfrey's voice came from fathoms away. Irissa sensed him like some ponderous beast swimming in the depths of the unopened doorway to herself. "She can make you whole."

"And I, why should I want to meld with this plain, unspeaking creature? She looks no thicker than an eyelash and has only one poor necklace to her name. What *is* her name?"

"Ask her," Geronfrey's disembodied voice urged, fading as if he vanished even as he spoke.

Irissa felt her mired lips moving, felt marsh-thick water lap against them. "What is *your* name?" she managed to ask first of the pale visage bending over her.

"Issiri," the creature replied, her green eyes widening with pleasure at the sound of herself.

Somewhere a dark cruising shape shuddered angrily. Irissa felt waves pummel her floating form, felt something rattle in the hollow at her center, felt the Overstone egg lose heat in her hand.

Still, she lay like an effigy on a tomb, frozen into the last position someone else had chosen for her—all open eyes with only one eternal view . . . up.

Stars seemed to fall from nowhere, dipping into the surface of Irissa's dark universe. The glitter paused, draping the darkness, almost veiling Irissa's face. She saw that a rich labyrinth of jewels hung from Issiri's neck.

"Your eyes are Quickstones," Issiri charged, as if somehow that fact cheated her.

"What do you know of Quickstones?" Irissa felt the thin surface of herself inquire.

"He gave me one."

"He?"

"The man in the dark."

"What dark?"

"The dark beneath."

"What dark am I in, then?" Irissa wondered.

"Only your own." Issiri's head turned as she studied the larger, well-lit world behind her that Irissa barely glimpsed.

"It is bright here, but there . . . where you are, where I was—" Issiri shivered. "Geronfrey said I must keep you there, or else take your place. Will you stay, will you promise to stay?"

"The man in the dark had a Quickstone and gave it to you?" Irissa probed.

"What a shallow, stupid thing you are! I said so. It is *my* Quickstone, my only one. I'd show it to you, but I'd rather have your Quickstone eyes instead. But Geronfrey said I wasn't to touch you, only . . . talk to you."

"Why talk to one as insufficient as I? I have no . . . jewels, no substance, you say. Only my eyes."

"What can I do with one Quickstone?" Issiri complained. "A ring, I suppose, but I have rings enough." Her fanned fingers flashed above Irissa, glittering with gemstones and gold. "With three I might make a pendant—"

"Why did the man in the dark give you the Quickstone?"

Issiri shrugged. "They give me bright things, that's all. I should have them. Do you think I am pretty?"

Irissa felt her stiff mouth stretch in a smile despite the difficulty of altering her position. "You should consult a mirror for that."

"Mirror? What's that?"

"You don't know?"

"Yes, I know . . . only not quite."

Irissa thought. "A mirror is a shadow of yourself, a window to your own Without. A mirror shines, and in shining lets you shine back at it. A mirror is . . . your friend, or enemy, or something in-between. A mirror is a gift and a curse. But it is always dangerous. Geronfrey is right to keep you from a mirror."

"I have not seen a mirror; I don't say that I am kept from seeing one."

"Perhaps the mirror is kept from seeing you," Irissa suggested.

"The mirror could see me?"

"Of course. It could see you much better than I do. It could see every flicker of your jewels, every eyelash on your lid, every fleck in your eye. And if it sees you aright, then you will see yourself in it."

"Oh! That sounds so much better than I thought. How do I see this mirror?"

"First . . . you must show me your Quickstone."

"I have not even shown that to Geronfrey. It is the only thing I have to myself, and he gave it to me, the man from the Quickstone Mountains."

"If you don't show me your Quickstone, I can't show you yourself," Irissa warned.

"Oh, no, please! I am most eager to see myself. I've

been sewing my habiliment of many jewels for so long. Here . . . here it is."

A hand enlarged in Irissa's limited range of vision. Kendric's Quickstone—originally Irissa's tear—hung between the pale hovering thumb and forefinger.

Irissa cast her consciousness searching along her body. Every limb hung heavy with lassitude. Yet she floated, feeling a new lightness that increased from minute to minute. Even the Overstone egg lifted from her chest, buoyed by the dark liquid that covered her.

Words seemed cast free, too, bobbing away on a placid tide with her roaming thoughts. Magic was a few slender strands of seaweed twining her ankles and weighing her down.

She floated here facing a flat sliver of herself. Now she must convince that separate self to share a jewel formed from Irissa's own inner anguish—to share it with . . . herself.

Irissa's tears formed a new barrier over her eyes. She fought to focus through their distorting clarity, then fixed her gaze upon the Quickstone. How it had come from Kendric's hand to Issiri's she could not know. But it was here, to be used, perhaps the only thing that would answer to her eyes alone.

Irissa's vision deepened, and darkened, then strengthened. Only the Quickstone shone for her, until it spread like a silver cloud and covered the sky. It was sky, sun, earth, rain, and wind. It grew, blotting out Issiri, inserting a reflective thin wash of pure silver between them.

Through it, Irissa saw a shadow of herself draw back to view herself—excited at first, then dismayed as the Quickstone swelled and swelled. Too large to suspend itself, the silver sank into the dark tide, webbing Irissa with its chill clarity, pushing her deeper into the dark behind her, propelling her back—in space, in time, in safety.

She reassembled before herself again—her figure precise in every detail—Kendric's hands clawing at her back, gathered ludborgs and swan-spawn gaping.

Before her eyes, the duplicate of herself softened into a sheer silver silhouette that reflected nothing. Irissa thought she read confusion in the quicksilver circles of her own eyes. She heard the faint lost wail of a failed child, then silence.

Quickstone peeled off the solid wall and crumpled to the floor, more made of veiling now than stone. Irissa bent to fold it against her middle, compressing endless yards of airy fabric into tighter and tighter squares.

When she was done, a single small dot of liquid brightness lay in the palm of her hand. Kendric's Quickstone.

CHAPTER
19

KENDRIC CLAIMED THE QUICKSTONE BEFORE IRISSA could offer it to him.

"I shouldn't have given it away," he said gruffly. "I'm afraid I tricked Issiri and, feeling remorse, overpaid her gullibility."

"Her gullibility has been given back." A slight sadness altered Irissa's face. "I tricked her, too, to recover this. It's easy enough to do."

"I know." Kendric's fist closed upon the Quickstone, as if its light illuminated too much. "I'm sorry you saw her."

"She saw me first. And perhaps I have always seen her."

"I would I had *never* seen her!" he answered fiercely. "Geronfrey oversteps even the bounds of sorcery to distill a person's essence into another vessel in such a manner. I would have slain this mocking shadow—"

Irissa's breath caught, she could not say why. "No!"

"I didn't." He slid the Quickstone into the boarskin pouch at his side. "But should have. Irissa, she has no existence to call her own! She is stolen from you—from an untapped, barely present part of yourself perhaps—but she remains a thing of perfidy, no matter how much she resembles you . . . or doesn't; no matter that she is Geronfrey's long-sought consort and shares the act of bearing with you. She brings forth yet another stolen soul—"

"What are you saying?" Sin was beside them, and beside himself with shock and fear. "Geronfrey has a secret *consort*? One who bears an heir? Then he can't be overthrown! It was what he always lacked, an heir. Something in the ancient balance of Rengarth requires an heir. Geronfrey's rule has always been as sterile as he has been constant; why else can we drive him off time and again?"

"Geronfrey has an unnatural consort," Kendric answered. "A half-being—or less—culled from some slice of Irissa captured two worlds away in a Dark Mirror of Geronfrey's construction. His 'heir' breeds from the same slim-souled stuff—it has been skimmed off the past, off Irissa's and my more natural union. It feeds on her and our unborn."

Aven gasped, but Kendric didn't pause.

"I can feel the fact of it gnawing at my core. I should have killed her, Irissa's opposite reflection. But"—he turned to Irissa, his eyes asking understanding—"this shadow self helped me escape, out of ignorance, of course, but she controls a primitive magic of her own and—"

"A *magical* consort!" Aven wailed, coming over. "And an heir. Worse and worse. We are ruined."

"Nonsense!" Irissa's eyes flashed. "You fear an uncertain shadow when you have me present in the flesh? The abundant flesh, I might add," she said humorously, adjusting the sash over her thickening waist. She turned to Kendric.

"My simulacrum is a virtual simpleton, a pitiful creature led by the tug of bright gemstones or minds brighter than her own. She is not great enough to be unmade, but her maker must be overthrown—he who conceived her and then conceived a child upon this shadow spawn. By this act, Geronfrey makes himself *our* Usurper as well as Usurper of these Rengarthians. He has taken more from you and me than mere rule—part of our sacred, sovereign selves."

"We engage him on his home ground," Kendric

warned, "and your magic may wane with your condition. My magic simply waxes and wanes, as it always has."

"He has no right," Irissa said, her face white in the taperlight. "He has no right to call me into the back of his Dark Mirror to provide reflection for the shell of myself. Once—unwitting—I fed his mirror with the skin of my fledgling vanity. He has nourished my one misstep into a thing with a life of its own. I begrudge not the tool, but the wielder."

"The heir must die," Sin said with a voice of iron. "It is the way of Rengarth with the Usurped." When Irissa and Kendric turned to him, amazed, they saw that his callow face had hardened to alabaster. "So it will be done to Aven and myself if we lose."

"Perhaps," Kendric put in mildly, "we should overthrow the Usurper before we decide the fate of his offspring. Still, I find this parallel Irissa and child too close for comfort. It may be they will fade, as shadows are eclipsed by sunfall, if Geronfrey loses his throne."

"High Seat," Irissa corrected absently. "Oh, Finorian forgive me, but I wish Felabba were here to advise us through this maze of rights, wrongs, and forbidden magic!"

"Felabba forgive you for calling on Finorian," Kendric added, chuckling. "At least we know that Geronfrey has invisible ways through these too-visible walls. 'Tis merely a matter of finding a gap in his stones wide enough for the rest of us to pass.

"This time we all search in our separate ways. You . . . the swans-down folk—take to the air and hunt for a tower circled by windows! Ludborgs, send all your . . . worm friends into the grout between the blocks in every chamber of this place!"

"What shall *we* do?" Aven demanded.

Kendric stared into her hot brown eyes. There was something familiar about her and her brother, many times removed. He often found them rash, overeager, and tiresome, but Irissa said their magic commanded beasts.

"Since so much is at stake for you two—all Rengarth and the ruling of it . . . and welcome to it—call the small beasts that inhabit this fortress," Kendric told them. "Mayhap the spin-webs and crumb-snatches will reveal a hidden chink in Geronfrey's architectural armor."

The pair promptly fell to their knees along the wall, their fingers probing the crevices between the stones.

"Och!" Irissa waved a rapidly descending spider from the web of her hair and fled the vicinity where the twins concentrated. "They are most literal adepts. We shall overwhelm Geronfrey with a flood of vermin."

Kendric sidestepped a small scuttler that threaded between his boots and joined Irissa in the next chamber.

"At least I've kept them all busy. Now you and I can direct our attention on finding Geronfrey." He glanced around the vacant, well-lit room. "This reminds me of his undermountain keep in Rule. An unassuming place as well, mostly empty. Geronfrey has a way of appearing and disappearing in his own domain. Remember how his wrath ground us from the stony-jawed tunnels under Falgontooth?"

"I remember that— and more," Irissa answered. "But how will that help us here?"

"Perhaps we cannot find Geronfrey *in* his fortress because he *is* his fortress. He's lorded it over Rengarth for a long time, despite frequent intermissions."

"Intriguing." Irissa approached the walls, lifting her hiltstone to the stones. The emerald reflected like a glassy flame.

"Look, the vapора!" Kendric warned.

One by one the flames dancing atop the candlesticks burned grass green. Then the stones of the wall shifted into a spectral form, as if only etched into place. Solid walls melted into mere veils to brush aside.

It was as if, once seeing through Geronfrey's magical method, Irissa and Kendric could look into every twist and turn of his illusion with little more than their native magic to guide them.

Irissa stepped through the melting walls first. She had seen the Hunter tread the Spectral City's spun-sugar rooftops and more readily accepted that which was half there.

Kendric forced his larger form through, expecting solid resistance. He encountered only an odd change in temperature.

"Colder," he said.

"As Geronfrey is older than he should be," Irissa said. "His decay infects this edifice, particularly the unseen ways within it."

"And well unseen they are," Kendric asserted, gazing at dim corridors leading into a gray, unlit maze of rooms. "No banquet tables burdened with foodstuffs, no cushioning carpets and flickering tapers enchant us here. Only cold stone walls and emptiness. Why covet Rengarth if this is all that the ruling of it means?"

"Why covet life," a deep voice tolled all around them, "if the long living of it always comes to dust? Welcome, again, to my abode."

"Your welcomes always carry stings in their tails, Geronfrey," Kendric retorted.

"You used to carry a sword; where is it now?"

"You know as well as I that it was cast into ice and snow. I bear other weapons now."

"So does she beside you."

Irissa stiffened as she felt the weight of Geronfrey's invisible regard. "No new weapons—" she began.

"You bear a weapon as old as humankind itself. Your body sheathes it as a sword."

"A child is only idle possibility," she objected.

"That is why it is *all* weapon," the voice answered. Despite the formality of their debate, it sounded mellow, unchallenged. It sounded as ungiving as a wall.

"*You* have made a weapon of our child!" Kendric challenged. "And yours. What is Rengarth to you, to be worth such a dislocation?"

A laugh infused with so much weariness and pity that it brought shivers to Irissa and Kendric echoed down the gray, uncomely hall.

"Ask rather what Rengarth is to you, Wrathman, that it has brought you here to your doom, and hers, and to the end of all that is yours and some things that are not."

"Doom!" Irissa chided. "You have dogged us from gate to gate but never significantly harmed us. Even Edanvant stands safe from your meddling. What doom can you give us, you who have been condemned to limp from world to world, to retreat from Rengarth time and again, to build an heirship on someone else's shadow?"

"Behold your shadow." The voice had swelled and so had the corridor walls with it.

The narrow passage expanded into a great circular room. In the center of it—at the very eye, the navel of it— an object sat, so small it was difficult to discern.

Irissa and Kendric began moving toward it, each recognizing something of themselves in the mote at the middle of Geronfrey's chamber. They walked faster, and farther, and still the object remained barely visible.

Yet they could see it more clearly with every step.

They saw a stepped dais crowned by a high-backed throne. A small figure sat there, some lavish gown swaddling its lower limbs so it seemed legless.

The figure clutched something to its breast—not an Overstone egg, like Irissa, but another small figure, which in turn grasped an effigy of a yet smaller self.

"My child," Irissa said, stopping. The scene hovered at the same distance as always, irretrievably misty. "Issiri *is* my child—"

"No." Kendric's voice fell like an ax, severing Irissa from past and future and pinning her painfully to the present. "Issiri is a means, not an end. Geronfrey's means, not ours. Issiri may be born of you, but not by natural methods.

"He stored her in a closed casket; she showed it to

me—a thin, black slice of stone made to keep life out, not in.

"Since when does what you see in a mirror breathe for you, Irissa, think for you, live for you? Geronfrey has only a shadow, why else would he need you to feed it? Believe him, believe that he has more than that, and *you* become his shadow queen."

"He offered me much once; now he threatens more," Irissa said. "If I can feed my shadow self, why can't his shadow heir batten onto our unborn one and suck it dry before it sees the light of day or dark of night?"

Kendric's hand curled into her shoulder. "You feel such a draw?"

"No . . . but the drain might be invisible—"

A laugh echoed around them. "Now the mighty seeress knows not even what might be dawning in her own inner domain. Fear not, my son does not need your petty powers, your unwillingness, to thrive."

"Son?" Kendric asked sharply. "How can you know?"

"Because I made it thus. Rengarth has always been my first seat; I wish it to be my last, and a son will see it so. Do you think Irissa's infant Torloc powers were why I coveted her in Rule? No—but they made her a suitable repository for my heir. The inheritance with which he has been lavished requires a rare receptacle and Irissa . . . or her shade . . . is that indeed—"

Another laugh resounded in the enlarged chamber— Irissa's. "Ah, vanity. I begin to see its twisted, ugly shape. I had so little vanity that you were able to skim its residue like fat from barley soup and brew a shadow consort from it. But yours—your vanity—is wider than a world and buried deeper than a failed ambition. You will reap what your willfulness has sowed. Your son shall inherit the chaff of your ambition—"

"Words were ever a seeress's least effective means," the voice responded. "My acts will stand when your words are empty echoes down the farthest corridors of time. I am tired of playing with you. You may have attained Rengarth, despite all likelihood, but I cannot be dislodged as long as I sire an heir."

Audience over. The distant throne was receding into the dark as if drawn by the anchor of its own past. Stones blurred past Irissa and Kendric. The very corridor seemed to be rolling up parchment-fast, flicking Irissa and Kendric from its surface as a dog would dislodge a flea or two.

"Wait!" Kendric turned to face backward, spinning Irissa in the same direction. He joined hands with her—unringed right and unringed left, leaving their ringed hands free to reach the retracting walls.

"Wait!" Irissa echoed, placing her palm against the receding stones despite the apparent speed of their withdrawal.

By any natural law, the skin should have shriveled from her hand as if scraping the ragged edge of a whetstone. Flesh should have been honed to mere bone, and bone to powder by the rough retreat of the walls.

Instead, she felt only a warm tingle, reinforced by Kendric's palm-touch to the opposite wall. The illusion lost impulse, then speed. The Nightstone on Kendric's ring, the Lunestone on Irissa's, shone intensely black and silver. Then the narrow neck of darkness that pulsed past them vanished.

They stood in a light-washed circular chamber, windows of every size and shape careening around them. Geronfrey held the center, the linchpin of this revolving wheel of windows. Beyond him hovered briefly glimpsed scenes both various and alien

In one, swan-spawn rode a huge black bird against a rainbow-opal sky. In another, darkness rained on Edanvant In a third, sunlight glanced off ice and snow until only reflection shared the glory. More windows unveiled scenes less recognizable.

"You haven't changed," Irissa marveled, confronting

the bland, too-handsome features behind the mask of Geronfrey's golden beard and azure eyes.

"Would I could say the same of you," the sorcerer returned cordially. "You are both the worse for wear, both shadowed by your unrequested burdens. Issiri takes to her new state with more grace."

Irissa glanced to the dark-robed woman perched on a low casket in the room's center. Despite the rich girding of a network of jeweled threads, her figure seemed dampened, its energy poured into the tension of a pendant raindrop about to tremble free of its support and fall.

Still, Irissa shuddered to see her second self face-to-face without the intervention of a magical medium.

"How can they exist in the same space?" Kendric wondered.

"They cannot, for long. But see—" Geronfrey's hand, gloved in ruby velvet to the elbow, gestured gracefully. At its motion, Issiri rose from the chest and the casket lid levitated, equally obedient.

Water dark as new-turned earth lapped the edges of the shallow box. On the rippling surface a scum of fallen leaves swirled. Leaf attached to leaf and then assumed a form—Irissa's. At last two birch leaves eddied into place and stilled, turning up silver undersides precisely the color of Irissa's eyes.

"You have left an imprint of yourself on my Dark Mirror yet again, seeress," Geronfrey said. "Repeat yourself enough, and nothing of the original shall remain."

With a stride, Kendric was at the casket, the heel of his hand slamming the lid shut. The sound was so harsh it seemed the stone would sunder.

"And you, Wrathman once of Rule, you still reach for rash action as if it were a sword. That habit, too, will diminish you. Issiri, being only surface, has little to lose. You and your Torloc have everything to lose."

"Why did you bring us here?" Irissa wondered.

"You are here of your own wills. Your talismanic rings

broke the illusion of my rushing walls. It's true, I could have drawn your essence from Edanvant and used it to plumpen Issiri, but you were too stubborn to fade, seeress, even when the ancient borgia sank into the sponge of your body."

"You sent that poison!" Kendric charged.

Geronfrey's head shook, a bit wearily. "You overestimate me, again. That brew tainted of its own great age. It came to Irissa's lips from the chance of your finding it and Medoc's making it the means of a celebratory toast. I have no need to set snares so deep within the past that even I don't remember arming them."

"But you know what happened in Edanvant, and you pulled me through the gate into Rengarth!" Kendric persisted.

"Only because you insisted on pushing at the gate."

"And you separated me from my sword—"

"Only because your sword had its own fate. Only those things return to Rengarth that came from it once."

"Not I," Irissa intervened.

"No." Geronfrey's subtle face grew sober. "You were not invited—at least not in your complete state. There is room for only one shadow queen in Rengarth. I fear your presence confuses the issue."

Geronfrey's gloved right hand raised, an Iridesium ring on one finger shining brighter than a black rainbow right after a rain. Before he could complete his gesture, Kendric had the Quickstone in his hand, swollen into a silver shield to reflect Geronfrey's magic back on himself. Issiri lifted her head.

"Oh! My lost Quickstone!" With a cry of dazzled recognition, Issiri rushed between sorcerer and shield.

"No!" Geronfrey commanded. Unleashed magic refused to heed verbal recantations. A lance of lethal light transfixed Issiri through shoulder blades and breastbone.

She hesitated on the brink of a final step, of speech. Then she puddled into her jewel-caged gown and sank toward the floor. No one would have caught her, had Kendric not.

He stood there sheepishly, upholding her stricken form, looking from Irissa to Geronfrey with an expression of mute horror.

"Lay her on the casket lid," Geronfrey suggested, no tinge of regret in his voice.

"You've slain her." Kendric's words were neither accusation nor condemnation, only statement of fact. He knelt quickly to install Issiri where the sorcerer had indicated.

"I didn't intend to."

"You meant to slay me," Irissa accused without rancor. "You have come some long way from courtship."

Geronfrey's straight figure slowly circled Issiri, his robe hem rasping over the stone floor. "All courtship ends in the death of something—usually expectations."

"Is she dead?" Irissa wondered. Antagonism seemed to have suspended in the chamber.

"Not dead, merely . . . lifeless."

"You quibble," Kendric put in, "like a sorcerer."

Geronfrey smiled, new lines graying his face as script muddies parchment. "Like yourself, you mean."

"I'm not a . . . sorcerer." Even as he said it, Kendric realized that having magic made him exactly that, even as carrying his sword had made him a warrior for so long.

Irissa came to look down on Issiri's limp form. "Why did you say 'lifeless' rather than 'dead'?"

"Only those who have truly lived can truly be said to have 'died.'" Geronfrey edged away from the low chest with Issiri arrayed upon it.

"You had me touch her hand," Kendric said, "to prove her reality."

"Reality alone is not life."

"What is life, then?" Kendric demanded.

For the first time, Geronfrey looked . . . shrunken. "I don't know."

"You have outlived the span of your own mortality," Irissa charged. "You of all people who live should know."

"I have accumulated powers, seeress. That doesn't mean I have obtained wisdom. There is more to life than the living of it, even over many hundreds of years. There is a core to life, a seed at the center that will not be denied. It can be taken, or extended, or ignored. But it cannot be changed, not even by magic."

"Yet Issiri, who was never truly alive, carried life."

"You see, Wrathman, wisdom manifests itself where it will." Geronfrey smiled mockingly and settled against a narrow interstice of wall between his circled windows.

On one side, the black swan cruised a sky ablaze with three suns, so its gilt beak looked like burning gold. On the other, wind scoured snow from ice to reveal the homely leather bindings of a sword hilt protruding from a drift.

"I am not wise," Kendric disclaimed, "only curious. Does the heir Issiri bears hoard the true seed of life, or is . . . he . . . another simulacrum of yours? So much mumbo jumbo and trickery, as is usual with you?"

"True life, Wrathman." Geronfrey's eyes glittered cobalt bright as he answered. "What I wove from secondhand wool spins raw straw into thread-of-gold, into substance and whole cloth."

"Your loom is stricken," Irissa put in, her voice oddly flat.

"Stricken." Geronfrey moved from Issiri as if he, too, might be stirred by her plight and dare not be. "Well and subtly put, seeress. Issiri was such a mere shadow of you; she would never see the loom, much less the warp and woof she wove."

"Irissa's right." Kendric straightened his shoulders and looked deeply into the mage's glorious eyes. "You seem uncommonly calm for a man, a sorcerer, a ruler whose hopes of self-succession now lie lifeless at his feet."

Geronfrey, edging along the windowed walls, paused.

His eyes met Kendric's with azure fire. "So could I say of you."

"I have nothing to lose."

"Because you have lost it already."

"What do you mean?"

"What have you lost?"

"Only—" the word struck Kendric as woefully inadequate. "Only my . . . sword, torn from my back as I plunged from Edanvant into that dark dungeon of yours."

"Your sword *is* your life!"

"You mean my livelihood."

"I mean your *life*. It is bound under the leather that hides the runes. You are the last symbol of the string. Separated from your sword, your life hangs by a hair to be snapped at the first truly lethal threat."

Irissa advanced, her fist on her sword hilt. "Why are you lying?"

"I have lost all I had hopes for; why should I lie?"

"You're a sorcerer," Kendric put in, his voice thundering with contempt.

"As well accuse yourself."

"Besides," Irissa said, advancing to Kendric's side, "he left the original sword in Rule. The one you severed from him was a shadow sword, mind-made in the Inlands of Ten."

"Shadow or not, the runes carven upon the hilt carry the same fate. Your fate hangs from you, marshman, much as the sword was slung from your back. The two of you uphold each other, and together fall."

"I've met and bested an icewraith of your sending, with only Irissa's sword for weapon. Where was my sword then, when my life outlasted that of a piece of animated death?"

"The threat was not severe enough." Geronfrey smiled sadly. "But why take pains to convince you of your own peril? Walk into it, cursing sorcerers and yourself even as you perish."

As the men debated, Irissa had knelt suddenly beside Issiri. She reached up and wordlessly took the Quickstone, shrunken to its normal size again, from Kendric's fist.

In Irissa's palm, it swelled to a teardrop-shaped mirror of peerless clarity. She brought the Quickstone looking glass to Issiri's senseless face, to her open eyes the color of milk emeralds.

Kendric frowned to notice Irissa nearing her counterpart, but didn't take his eyes from Geronfrey.

Leaning closer, Irissa looked into the mirror. For a moment light rays seemed to rebound from her eyes to Issiri's lifeless ones through the silver medium of the mirror.

Then Irissa saw Issiri's face resolve in the limpid surface. Where her eyes should be were only holes of utter blackness.

"Lifeless," Geronfrey confirmed.

Irissa looked up at him, directly. "You don't sound as forsaken as you should."

"I have outlived lust and, to one of my long years, love is dust-dry. She was an . . . experiment of mine. I accept that experiments will sometimes fail."

"She was—!" Kendric's indignation boiled over into words. "She was . . . something. Even I could not in cold blood kill her. How can you accept her . . . ending . . . at your own hands with such resignation? Surely, at least the child she carried bore some of your hopes with it?"

Irissa looked up at Kendric, her eyes narrowed to slivers of quicksilver that reflected every window in the room as if they had been squeezed into a single plane.

"'The child she bears'—Kendric, what ninnies we have been!"

"Ninnies?" he began, offended.

"Nine-times-enfeebled ninnies. Why does Geronfrey grant us the field, edge along his wall, and speak so softly? Because if Issiri fails him, if she 'dies,' his heir perishes. He has no heir now! He has no talisman against losing his rule yet another time—"

"Enough!" Geronfrey's velvet-gloved hands pushed him from the wall. A tone of command slipped over that one word like a gauntlet. "Let me bury my expectations, at least."

"Bury?" Before Kendric could challenge the impossibility of such a plan, Geronfrey had stepped to the head of the dark stone casket on which Issiri lay.

Irissa immediately rose and backed away, wanting her enemy no nearer than necessary. Kendric pulled her to his side.

"He lacks a consort now," the Wrathman said grimly, "as I lack a sword. He may have ambitions of converting you to his purpose now that his cage of glitter and illusion has faded."

"I honor my dead," Geronfrey said, "even if they were never among the living. They who serve me shall not be abandoned."

His gilt head bowed as he stared at the box, his face parallel to Issiri's shadow-pale features. For a moment her motionless form appeared to levitate slightly above the chest's shining stone surface.

Certainly, a shadow of her body impressed itself on the dark granite. The phenomenon silenced even Kendric. To see a shadow thing cast its own shadow manifested a magic born to silence skepticism.

Irissa wordlessly touched Kendric's arm, standing as spelled as he while the replica of her self floated in a net of jewel-strung gold. Then the illusion shifted. Issiri sank back to the casket lid, sank *into* the gleaming dark stone as if it were pond water.

All her jewels glimmered out like stars plunged into a swamp. The empty holes of her eyes merged with the dominant black of the stone. Her hands melted away, narrow finger by narrow beringed finger.

Nothing was left but the sleek, empty surface of the chest that had consumed her shadow, line by illusive line.

Irissa sighed. Kendric noticed for the first time that despite the many views through the encircling windows, no sound came through.

Geronfrey cleared his throat, causing both Irissa and Kendric to glance sharply to his face. His blue eyes shone sapphire-bright.

"Even sorcerers can dream," Kendric admitted.

"And scheme," Irissa said, something stronger in her voice than Kendric had heard before.

Kendric turned to her. "What do you mean—?"

"He has no heir now! He has no hope of winning here. That's why he doesn't challenge us head-to-head, magic-to-magic. He can't. His hands are . . . gloved and tied. He's helpless for the moment!"

"Merely a man in a tower?" Kendric's face lightened. His advancing boot sole scraped stone. "I'd like that. I'm tired of meeting your sendings in many guises and yourself in disguise. Perhaps you can answer to me now, this 'sorcerer' nonsense aside—"

Geronfrey raised a red velvet palm. The gilt threads that decorated the gloves had clotted into a circular symbol at the very heart of his hand.

"No!" Irissa started, her eyes focusing to unravel the thousands of tiny stitches on Geronfrey's palm.

Kendric reached for the sorcerer's arm, ready to rip the offending glove from its anchorage.

Threads snapped stitch by stitch, but it was too late. Sound broke through one of the unreal landscapes the windows overlooked.

Kendric and Irissa heard hooves thudding up the spine of the sky. The Hunter's blue-eyed head loomed over the windowsill, wind whipping its mane into a snarl of gold and silver strands. Its single horn pierced the plane of the unshuttered window. Air shattered into veins, like broken glass.

Geronfrey catapulted forward, one foot on the casket lid springing him to the window. His gloved hand grasped the intrusive horn. With a twist of his robes he was astride the Hunter, who tilted his head to show reddened eye whites. Where Geronfrey's glove had touched, the twisted ivory-white horn ran red. Tendrils of fresh blood meandered around and down its spirals.

Kendric felt a death blow again, and whitened, then the sheer shock of it leeched into the touch of Irissa's hand on his.

A moment later she was rushing to the window, a gilt medallion banging idly on her upraised wrist. "This talisman recalls you, Hunter!" she shouted into the snapping wind.

The Hunter was prancing away on an invisible stair of sky, its hooves echoing demurely. Geronfrey, a figure too small to show his eye color, lifted a crimson palm to wave farewell.

Irissa hammered Medoc's medallion on the windowsill in frustration. "When I left the Hunter by the city wall, I left him free as long as the medallion was with me. Geronfrey has used a . . . a shadow of the medallion to command his creature. I should have known—!"

"You knew his weakness," Kendric consoled. "That is enough with a sorcerer as strong as Geronfrey. He fled, but has no heir. Your second self is free at last. You are free."

Irissa turned from the window, her face alabaster. On either side, views of Rengarth showed opposite poles of the place—icy cold, airy warmth, swan-spawn and city dwellers.

"If Geronfrey can call death mere 'lifelessness,' then his brand of freedom is likely to be as hollow."

"What do you mean?"

Irissa smiled ruefully. "You look a man of strength, Kendric, once Wrathman of Rule. Lift Issiri's casket lid and tell me what you find within."

Kendric glanced askance at the somber box. "Look? In there? Who knows what horrors from what Dark Mirror of what Swallowing Cavern Geronfrey has left behind for us?"

"I do." Irissa had never sounded so certain, never seemed so sad. "Lift the lid. I am too weary to waste magic on so futile a task. See what Geronfrey has left us."

Kendric bent to grasp the casket edges until his knuckles whitened. "I cannot guarantee what she'll . . . look like now that she's . . . dissolved."

"If you can lift, I can look," Irissa insisted.

Grunting either assent or protest, Kendric let his broad shoulders shift. Stone ground on stone, reminding him of the grating Issiri had moved above Kendric's dungeon keep. He had found her shallow and feared her very existence, but he had no desire to see her . . . dispersed. Perhaps, being a mere shadow, she had undergone no mortal dissolution. . . .

The lid pried open, Kendric's jaw gaping with it.

Not emptiness or earth filled Issiri's coffin, but a dark lapping width of shallow water. And in it —or on it—lay nothing but their own reflections, his and Irissa's; his dumbfounded, Irissa's . . . wise and weary and terribly resigned.

CHAPTER
20

"GERONFREY?" SIN DEMANDED.

"Gone," Kendric said.

"The Hunter?" Aven asked next.

"Gone with Geronfrey," Irissa said.

"The heir?" a ludborg inquired astutely.

"And the consort?" Aven put in, reminded.

"Both . . . vanished," Kendric said, "into thin water."

"We are not amused," Sin said, stalking around the tower.

The scenes visible through the windows had faded since Geronfrey's departure, like drawings on water. Now the windows offered an ordinary vista of Rengarth from an ordinary tower in the extraordinary city of Solanandor Tierze.

"We have reclaimed our ancestral seat," Aven pointed out, "but have been cheated of vanquishing the Usurper ourselves. It is good that you two are merely honorary heirs in our land. Custom holds that the heirs who personally banish the Usurper hold the High Seat. After all our labors, Sin and I could be usurped, had either of you any right to rule in Rengarth."

"We told you," Irissa answered, "Geronfrey is merely gone, not banished. No one should sit easy on the High Seat until he is accounted for."

"And no one sits on the High Seat," a ludborg put in, "until we consult the casting crystals and determine why strangers not of Rengarth should defeat the Usurper."

"Luck!" offered Sin.

"Mere chance," Aven added redundantly.

"Such things do not occur by luck and mere chance." The ludborg's robed form glided around the empty casket. "And succession in Rengarth is handled correctly. Our order has ensured that for more years than there are seeds in a pod."

"At least," said Sin, bowing gracefully to display the undoffable cap of copper curls that topped his head, "let us thank our offworld allies and offer them our most royal thanks for their assistance."

He and Aven swept from the room, if two such hoydenish individuals attired in belts that clanked like cowbells could be said to sweep.

"Success can have strange effects upon its victims," a ludborg offered Kendric and Irissa under its breath—or hood. "They are young, these Brenhalloy, and overconfident. Come to our celebratory feast anyway; you will learn more of Rengarth, including your future in it."

"Which will be," Kendric said swiftly, "to reclaim my lost sword and then leave."

The ludborg was quiet, then its dark hood shook soberly. "Alas, it is harder to leave Rengarth than it is to find it. I fear you have found a home."

"I fear you underestimate us," Kendric answered.

"I fear I . . . tire," Irissa put in. "Could we rest someplace?"

The ludborg bowed as elegantly as Sin, making Kendric and Irissa long for its festier and less formal forerunner, Scyvilla—once called Ludborg the Fanciful. It almost made them long for Edanvant.

Their chamber was floored in milk glass in which colors pooled like sunfall clouds. Hairpin-thin fish in water beneath the glass swirled from Irissa's and Kendric's exploratory footsteps and flitted up the walls, which were made of glass to hip-height.

"Does one lie on this or hold worship here?" Kendric inquired when he faced the bed—a series of lucent risers crowned by a circle of opalescent metal covered with a knee-deep comforter.

"Swans-down." Irissa sank gratefully into the quilt and worked an airy black feather through a stitch hole. "Birds seem vital here."

Kendric was stomping across the fragile-looking floor, his mighty strides causing nothing to tremble but the trailing fish fins beneath his boots. He stopped to look glumly into a large bathing well. This appliance reversed the bed's approach: its steps cut deeper and deeper into a limpid circle of slightly agitated water.

"They seem fond of birds—and fish," he noted. A flitting form lifted from the water to twitch a pale blue mouth at him, then waggle the curlicued feelers above its magenta eyes. "A ewer of plain unoccupied water would be more welcome than a whole pond that's previously taken."

"Customs vary," Irissa said, sighing at the ceiling. Then she dug her hands into clouds of comforter and tried wildly to struggle upright again.

Kendric was there instantly, his hand on his ax. "What's wrong?"

She pointed speechlessly. The ceiling was swagged with thread-of-silver netting. Beyond the gauzelin, birds of every size and color flitted fishlike from perch to perch, chattering softly in a musical scale of sounds.

"I can think of more practical things to lie under," Kendric said. "Imagine how often the bed linens have to be changed. No wonder they make a bath the size of a fishpond! What is the point of such luxury?"

"A ludborg said we were honored guests," Irissa answered demurely. "Heroes."

"You perhaps, not I." Despite reservations, Kendric sat on a puffy edge of comforter. He sank as if into swamp-swallow. "Well, that does it. We can't attend the celebratory banquet tonight since we'll never be able to lumber out of this bed again. Besides, what's to celebrate?

Geronfrey is gone but not vanquished, and the Hunter's free to strike again."

"And I do not feel like celebrating," Irissa said soberly.

Kendric pushed himself upright. "You are unwell?"

She considered it scrupulously. "My boots pinch. And my legs seem swollen, as well as my hands." She massaged her middle finger where the ring had impressed welt lines. "I have just confronted an antagonist who tried to lock my spirit into a casket and then slew a reflection of myself. And what I have battled most urgently through all these recent trials is an unabating need for a privy."

Kendric regarded Irissa with new eyes. She looked disheveled, as he had never seen her before—disheveled, worn, and somehow diminished.

"What you require lurks beyond the fishpond they call a bathing pool," he said promptly. "Thrash toward me and I'll help you rise."

Irissa flapped on the buoying feather bed like a bonefish removed from water, finally wiggling close enough for Kendric to lever her upright. She was laughing when she stood, at herself and their overwhelming surroundings.

Kendric smiled but did not release her. "Something else troubles you."

She looked to the darting birds overhead as if seeking escape among them, then glanced back to him. "I have seen myself slain—"

"Issiri was never truly living; even Geronfrey admitted that."

"Still, she was a . . . sliver of myself somehow swollen into a reflection of it. We shared a . . . condition."

"Better that Geronfrey's heir . . . vanish," Kendric said grimly. "We've seen little of Rengarth, but I don't doubt that it deserves better than to fall under the on-and-off thumb of a foreign mage."

"It reminds me that—" Irissa paused and studied the top of Kendric's ring, which was utterly dormant now.

He could guess what she felt, because he felt it, too.

"The loss of Issiri reminds you that . . . you yourself could perish, or the child within you? From Geronfrey's revenge?"

She shrugged. "Geronfrey is not a man who lives well with losing his heart's desire."

"He will not get you," Kendric swore, his grip tightening on her until that pressure outdid the heart-soreness within her. "Nor . . . our rightly borne child."

Irissa pressed a palm to her gently swelling middle. "Our child may slay me," she reminded him, "not by any magical means, but through mere birth passage. I feel suddenly mortal, and am not accustomed to considering myself as such. I see that bearing another makes one vulnerable in unsuspected ways."

The notion of Irissa's perishing in childbirth hadn't crossed Kendric's mind. She was so supremely in control of herself, of everything around her.

"You are a seeress," he reminded her. "You can heal others of mortal blows; you can heal yourself. Why should childbearing pose any threat that you can't turn back upon itself?"

"It is a purely natural process, and as such extracts its own, inalienable penalties. I doubt even my magic could intervene in this birth fate of mine."

"Then mine would!" he swore.

She smiled suddenly and touched her hand to his hair as if comforting a child. "Yes, you would. You have delved deep within to draw your own mortality up by a thread through the eye of a needle.

"But now I hang from thousands of years of happenstance, no different from any woman, Torloc or mortal." Irissa sighed and laughed at the same time, and regarded the twittering birds. "My head aches and my feet hurt and I have never seen magic as more redundant than I do at this moment. When it comes down to the rock at the bottom of the well, even all of Geronfrey's sorcerous machinations were aimed at a result the simplest mortals can accomplish in their sleep."

Kendric grinned. "Before their sleep, or after it. And that's a difference. Where there's diversity there is hope."

"I have never felt less Torloc," Irissa announced glumly. "Where is the privy?"

He nodded in the proper direction. "Er, be wary of fish in the water bowl."

"Rengarthians must like suspense. Perhaps it's due to the Usurper's constant comings and goings," Kendric speculated at the banquet that night to a nondescript ludborg on his right. But then, all ludborgs were nondescript. It was part of their charm.

Irissa, her hair glossy from washing and her spirits almost as shiny again, attempted a gesturing conversation with one of the mute swan-spawn across the small round table the four occupied.

The banquet hall was furnished like an inn: many tables set for a few rather than the isolated eternity of one long board more designed to separate guests than accommodate them.

Best of all, Kendric thought, the intimate arrangement permitted readier access to the communal platters. He pronged another slab of what seemed to be venison while Irissa was distracted by the swan spawn, then turned politely to the impenetrable hood on his right. That was another comforting thing about ludborgs: one never had to struggle to read their expressions.

"What do you mean about loving suspense?" the ludborg asked.

Kendric gestured to the vast cloud of silver netting beneath the hall's high ceiling. "With so many birds abroad, surely it's only a matter of time before the . . . soup gets an exotic seasoning."

He checked his own bowl—rose petals floating in an amber fluid he called bee broth—to ensure it hadn't been adulterated while his attention had been distracted.

The ludborg wheezed its merriment. "What a drollish

fellow you are! The birds are hall-broken, and whisk out the clerestory windows to relieve themselves. Surely, all animals practice such nicety in your native world?"

"Er . . . not exactly," Kendric replied, suddenly feeling cheated. "I do see that Rengarth has many . . . advantages, though I have always relished the forthright odor of a bearing-beast enclave. Too much nicety might make the pudding bland."

"We have no pudding on our menu, but however you wish it, friend Kendric," the ludborg reassured him. "Rengarth can accept almost any perversion so long as it harms no one."

"Honest dung is no perversion," Kendric returned indignantly, remembering—perversely—many unpleasant scents he suddenly missed now that he suspected they might be only memories in future: the after-rain earthiness of Rulian soil, rancid swamp water, sour milk, the medicinal reek of herbs that cured if they did not perfume.

"Already weary of our world?" a light voice asked.

Kendric turned to find Aven standing behind him. Combed out, her braids rippled into a blaze of red-orange hair that made her face seem a carved opal set in carmine gold. The cumbersome chain still swagged her waist, dangling tools and weapons in a bright metallic array, but she had let her skirt down for the banquet.

"Only tired, as is Irissa," he answered.

The Rengarthian woman gave the oblivious Irissa a slow smile that warmed Kendric as much as Aven's flagrant hair. Now that the twins had evicted Geronfrey from the city, their inner fires seemed to have dampened, their impatience to have gentled.

"Irissa is indomitable," Aven mused. "The swan-spawn will return to their feathered forms by morning. They were always only half here. No one has ever been known to elicit a word from them."

"Irissa may," Kendric said confidently. "But why must they revert to swan-shape? And how?"

"They must because they are spirits of long-dead Rengarthians. And the potion they drink—that Sin spilled his power to call before serving it—will permit them to become again a flock and to speak to one another in the clouds again."

"In honks," Kendric put in.

"Music to their ears."

"And what is music to your ears, lady?" he asked politely.

Aven smiled again, looking girlish and looking—he hammered at his recall for the reason—so familiar his heart almost stopped. He had seen this woman before: in another place, another . . . form. He had spoken with her before.

"It's enough to know that I will live my life as I was meant to," she said. "We—Sinavli and I—found ourselves in Rengarth only recently, without recalling how we had come here in full-grown form.

"Oh, we knew *who* we were—Brenhall's spawn and the old legendry; we knew about the conflict that has shaken Rengarth for centuries. But we seemed half spelled ourselves, and everything we have done here has been as if in a dream."

"Perhaps life *is* a dream," Kendric offered. "I know that I have done things in it that I never dreamed of doing. Especially since I met Irissa."

"You and she journey on your own tangent. Sin and I are preordained to our path. The royal runes that scribe the High Seat speak of a man and a woman come from afar, who do not quite know who they are, exiling the Usurper for eternity. Sin and I can't escape our fate. We found ourselves here and did what we were destined to do.

"I suppose that now we have reclaimed the High Seat, we should worry about mating and marrying and child-getting to ensure we keep it. But"—Aven glanced again at Irissa—"it is alien to me, what she does and that she does all she does despite it. I sometimes feel I am fading. . . ."

Kendric stared at the robust young woman. Her brown eyes danced with ruddy luster struck from the lit tapers and the conflagration of her own untrammeled hair. Taperlight softened her freckled skin to the color of skim milk, so she seemed newly elegant in a way foreign to her. It occurred to him that such a vital creature should have no difficulty finding a mate, nor should she quail at the notion of bearing a child.

Irissa had, yes—not from fear, but because of the unbraided freedom within her. He suspected that some part of Irissa would always remain surprised that she had succumbed to something as commonplace as begetting a child.

Aven was different. She *knew* somehow that ordinary paths were closed to her. Kendric could almost see the ways darkening before her as he watched. She shook her head to shake herself free of reverie. Dark crimson hair trembled like a mane, reminding him of his lost mount of Rule, Willowisp.

"I'm certain," Kendric found himself consoling, although he was more than ever certain of nothing, "that you and Sin will find your fates taking the proper path."

Aven shrugged indifferently. "We have won our battle. That was the challenge. The rest is . . . boring." She tossed her hair for good measure and jangled away, skirts swirling briskly at her boots.

Across the small table, the swan-spawn's face was growing nobly pensive despite Irissa's efforts to coax some response from it. Kendric looked more closely. The swan-spawn's face was growing *longer*. He stiffened to notice a frill of black feathers edging the young man's jerkin sleeve. Moments later, the fellow lurched upright, abandoning Irissa in midgesticulation.

A rustle of departing swan-spawn sounded throughout the vast, talk-noisy hall. In the arboreal roosts, birds flapped like fish, cawing their disorder in a dozen avian dialects.

The swan-spawn, massed and looking oddly blackish despite their human dress, lumbered up some coldstone stairs.

"Their Call ends," the ludborg next to Kendric intoned between hiccoughs. He had partaken deeply of a libation Sin called groggy-bottom wine. "You notice they ate nothing, said nothing. They came only to lend the power of their presence to the battle."

"But they did little!"

"That they were called is enough. The Usurper tallies enough victims to people more worlds than Rengarth. Those who opposed him, he banished to animal form or slew until the sheer numbers of his quarry swelled into the ghostly citizenry of a city. To confront him with proof of his perfidy exerts a kind of magic against him."

The ludborg subsided to his groggy-bottom brew, draining the drinking vessel with an audible slurp. Across the table, Irissa's placid expression altered rapidly.

"What's the matter?" Kendric wondered, leaning inward.

"With me, nothing. But this . . . oh, it is too much!"

"What?"

Irissa shut her eyes, threw back her head as if tranced, and laced her fingers over her midriff.

"Surely it's too soon!" Kendric said, horrified.

"All too true." Irissa's silver eyes flashed back to his. "I hear my inner voice again."

"Your voice?" he whispered.

"It is in me, but not of me."

"What does it say, this elusive oracle?"

A pained expression flickered across Irissa's face. "It says the food here leaves much to be desired—"

"Felabba! Somehow that . . . soul leech . . . has fastened onto you yet again! What other creature would complain of the fare when it is not even present in person to sample it? Begone . . . riddlesome, magic-ridden, carping feline! We never invited you to the last world and you are twice unwelcome in this one!" Kendric finished by pounding the table for emphasis. "Well?" he asked when his tirade was done.

Irissa smiled wanly. "Perhaps my stomach was only growling. I seemed to hear one last word."

"What word?"

"Frostforge."

"Frostforge. 'Tis cryptic enough, and that suits Felabba for a parting phrase. I hope."

"I may hear an inner oracle other than Felabba," Irissa warned.

"I suppose that means our offspring is magic-burdened."

A frown imprinted itself beneath Irissa's Iridesium circlet. "I don't know. I wasn't able to tell. I think Orvath feared our child. Perhaps that's why he fathered one of his own."

"Such matters are not up to Orvath," Kendric said, "or any of us." He drank thoughtfully from his own tankard. The liquor within was a kind of mulled ale—thick and bittersweet. "Irissa, when you . . . delved . . . within yourself to ask permission of our child to cross a gate, did you . . . discern . . . anything about it?"

"It was so disconcerting to plunge into myself and find another." She leaned her pale face on her hand, fingertips brushing the circlet where it banded her temple. Kendric watched the metal's rainbow colors pool at the point where her hand touched, as blood will run, until they clotted into a gaudy blossom.

Irissa seemed oblivious to the shifting phenomena that radiated around her body like an aura. Her expression softened as Kendric watched her revisit her innermost secrets.

"What would I discern about something as unformed as an unborn child?" she wondered.

He took a quick swallow of ale-wine—too quick—coughing as the syrupy brew coated his throat and refused to slip past.

"Kendric—what are you asking? I hardly sensed anything, only a sovereign presence that was separate from myself. And weak, far weaker than myself. And far stronger. It was . . . contradiction incarnate. As I am, in my way. And you in yours. I cannot tell you what it will be, only what it is. And is not. And for now, it *is not* as much as it is."

"Riddles again," he gruffed through his clogged

throat, sorry he had ever asked a question he was unwilling to phrase plainly.

Irissa watched him gravely and suddenly began laughing. "Why am I wasting my time explaining the inexplicable? You don't want to know the profundities of my voyage to my unborn passenger! You want the facts. Has it magic? If it does, will that make you happy or sad? What . . . what gender is it? *That's* what you want to know! Something so simple when everything else is so complex—"

"I want to know what to expect, that's all," he said shortly. "I don't really care about the particulars, I just want to know them."

Irissa's laughter was softening to understanding. "I never thought to inquire into what *it* was. I was more concerned with you at the time, and myself. Our survival. Such things as magic and gender didn't seem to matter."

She leaned across the table they shared alone now that the swan-spawn had gone and the ludborg had waddled off in search of more foggy libations, and took his hands. He noticed her fingers were cold, not with nervousness, but as if the blood were being better used elsewhere.

"Kendric, *not* knowing what to expect is what makes gates worth taking and long-lost homes worth leaving and unborn children worth having. I must admit that my . . . unexpected condition . . . surprised me."

He grunted his all-too-natural understanding.

"I must admit I find my magic arbitrary," she went on, twisting the ring around her finger, or attempting to, "and my body even more willful since I began sharing it with another.

"I can explore myself again, seek another audience, try to come back with answers. What do you want to know—sex, magical ability, eye color, ultimate height? Can it carry a tune or a sword, weave bramblemats like your grandmother or shred garden greens like its own? Will it be left-handed or right? Will it be hale, whole—?"

"Stop, stop!" he urged in the face of this loving litany. "You are right. I do not wish to know these things. I've always said I don't need to know the future. I see that to keep too tight a grip on the past is to take the future by the throat and try to make it sing. It will be as it will be, as we will. It's just that I thought . . . if you were there, you might have . . . noticed."

"If you were there," Irissa answered softly, "you would have noticed that there was nothing to notice. I violated a veil between life and death, Kendric, when I went to my unborn one and asked it to play mother to me—and to you indirectly. I don't know what we will reap from such an upheaval of the proper sequence of things."

"You risk more than a warrior without even drawing your sword," he said, staring into the calm quicksilver of her eyes. She had changed, and was changing, he saw, as he was and would.

Irissa shrugged but looked pleased that he understood the depth of her courage that sometimes wore such a different face from his own. To mask her pleasure, she leaned and inspected his almost-empty tankard.

"Is that bittersweet brew all they serve in Rengarth?"

He recognized a request when he heard it, and went to the libations table to fetch a goblet of persimmon-colored wine. Despite all the talk of High Seats, a Rengarthian banquet was an informal affair, with participants serving themselves.

Kendric, passing the comestibles table, spied an unclaimed brandy-basted drumstick and appropriated it. Rengarthian table customs served him well, he decided on his return to Irissa and . . . who- or whatever else . . . waited at the table.

CHAPTER
21

"HOW DOES ONE," KENDRIC WONDERED IN A WHISPER that seemed to carry halfway to heaven because of his notable height, "determine the head ludborg?"

Hoods throughout the ceremonial hall turned to stare.

"Hush," Irissa advised under her breath. "Perhaps they take turns."

If so, the ludborg of the moment was holding forth upon a dais centering the circular chamber to which everyone had withdrawn following the banquet.

With its stepped, sunken floor and stepped, soaring ceiling, the place resembled nothing so much as the interior of a globe.

"So must the groggy-bottom wine be feeling in our dinner partner's stomach right now," Kendric muttered to Irissa. "I myself feel like a bit of undigested cheese."

She rolled her eyes, but couldn't fault Kendric's unease. The surroundings were disconcerting, to say the least, and the forthcoming ceremony looked to be intolerably long, to judge from the leisure with which the ludborg was holding forth.

Irissa occupied herself by studying the gigantic chamber—first the circle of pillars that supported it. These were shaped from glass and filled with water. Within them a graceful flotilla of fish churned in constant display.

Whether the liquid itself had that clear, rainbowed shimmer Irissa had noticed in Rengarthian waters before, or whether the Iridesium-scaled fish added their own glam-

255

our, was moot. The pillars gleamed with a muted, vibrant light, serving as long, liquid lamps.

Kendric kept glancing to the pillar on his right, as if daring some finned inhabitant to meet him eye-to-eye. For the fish all had eyes—exotic, multipupiled eyes; eyes winking from their scaled sides and impressed into the gossamer of their trailing fins.

Many wore patterns in the guise of feathers. The great eye that ends a peacock's tail came undulating past unescorted by the rest of the feather. A long sable variety of fish oozed by Irissa's ear, its scales mimicking the thick, rich texture of utterly dry velvet.

Some pillar-dweller finally took up the gauntlet of Kendric's stony stare and darted to eye level with him. The offender was a checkerboard-patterned fish as large as his fist, with a square body, minimal fins, and a glaring, mauve-gold eye.

Kendric intensified his stare, then jerked back when the fish, faster than a wink, turned fin and floated away.

"Think of them as fireflies in a bottle," Irissa advised.

"I'll think of them as dinner," he responded. "That usually encourages members of the animal kingdom to take humans seriously."

"Speaking of being taken seriously, what do you think of the High Seat?"

Kendric's eyes moved to the needle of carved stone driven into the room's center. It reminded him of the stalactites and stalagmites filling the Oracle of Valna's cavern in Rule.

This column was a single such entity, growing as much from ceiling as from floor, to judge by how it widened at its points of attachment. Yet it had a pearly, polished surface, as if water- and wind-worn for centuries, as if both wet and dry elements had taken turns at shaping it.

Pierced by whatever had shaped it—perhaps even the intervention of Rengarthian hands or ludborgian sleeves— the pillar rose like a long thighbone, gleaming, majestic, and somehow hollow. Where it thickened slightly at the top, a seat had been carved, or worn, out.

"High it is," Kendric conceded. "Too high to get to comfortably. Too high to be heard from easily. Too high and emptily mighty to tempt me."

"Its purpose is likely ceremonial," Irissa answered.

At its foot, which splayed to the floor like the trunk of a weepwater tree root, the ludborg continued his oration. The toll of names known to Kendric and Irissa from tales told in Edanvant rang oddly unreal even in their native land.

Centuries-since-slain Brenhall was eulogized; the coming of his conqueror, the Usurper, was bewailed. The Usurper's name came and went by fits and starts as the roll of Rengarthian royalty was called.

In the meantime, the guests stood. These were predominantly townspeople now, invited for the public celebration, and the ubiquitous ludborgs.

Kendric sighed gustily, drawing a servingman to refill his goblet. Irissa lifted hers as well for replenishment.

"At least they cater to us now that we are hopelessly trapped," Kendric grumbled thirstily, quaffing from his now-filled cup.

Irissa yawned in answer and let the numbing names float over her head like an audible veil.

"—and with the last perfidy," the ludborg was intoning, "the bloody murder of Ajaxtus and the casting of the Reginatrix Phoenicia into some animal form so obscure that no hint of its nature or her whereabouts has ever been found. . . ."

Kendric's frame straightened, if that was possible. "They got *that* wrong. Phoenicia was not in animal form when Medoc saw her in the gate—"

"Tell them."

"And prolong matters while they debate the hows and whys? No, thank you. That will remain our secret. I found

Ludborg the original a trifle talkative, but his cousins are an even windier lot."

"After this bloody crime," the ludborg continued with oratorical relish, "which took an heirling in the making from us as well, we thought ourselves under the Usurper's yoke for eternity."

"I'm beginning to think they deserve it," Kendric muttered to Irissa.

"But then the star-sent twins appeared among us—neither specters nor phantasms, neither knowing their past nor their future, and through their desire we see our High Seat among us again—free of the Usurper."

In the resultant roar of approval, ludborgs the chamber over raised their long sleeves and flapped them like wings for silence.

"Sinavli and Aven," said the ludborg, "fulfill the ancient runes carved into our High Seat and into our very bones. Two came, not sure of their past or their future, and banished the Usurper—forever, as it is rune-said."

A deafening roar made Irissa clap her hands to her ears. When she released them, the room was quiet . . . utterly quiet . . . and the ludborgs were congregating in the depression at its center. Onlookers ringing the higher levels had a perfect view of the proceedings.

"I can't believe I'm saying this," Kendric said, "but I could use a good magic trick by now."

The orating ludborg let his reedy voice carry to every crevice of the chamber. "Now, Rengarthians, we move to prove the curse ended forever. We cast the Crux Crystal, wherein meets Past, Present, and Future, to show us all the truest path we can take."

The ludborgs' plain brown robes pressed into a wad far below, agitating so voraciously they resembled overweight ants struggling to move a grasshopper carcass. The insect analogy wove deep in Irissa's mind. She saw a parliament of spiders weaving a joint web, or some other communal project under way.

A humming rose from the pillar's bony foot and

wafted up the many risers to the pillars. Fish fled the outer contours, clotting in the center while the opalescent water roiled at the fragile glass containing it.

Below, the clustered ludborgs drew back. Something trembled at their center—a huge, luminous bubble that grew even as they ebbed before it.

"Who will break a crystal that large—and how?" Kendric, ever practical, wondered.

"It is their world," Irissa reminded him, "and their worry. We are truly audience now."

Kendric grunted, not unpleased, and folded his arms to watch.

The declaiming ludborg's voice lowered respectfully. "We see the scene which holds the seed of our final triumph now. That which none of us know—working in obscurity and silence—has brought the present to pass and will turn past to future for all of us. Anyone here who reads anything into what we will see must speak, for in that speaking the spell that has held Rengarth for hundreds of years is broken. Now let the Crux Crystal perform!"

Ludborgs, suddenly awash in blue-worms, leaped back as if violently repelled. The crystal stood alone—or floated really—as diaphanous as the Spectral City Irissa had crossed atop the Hunter. Perhaps two Wrathmen high, it made another, translucent room within the larger room.

Irissa found herself reminded of a womb, then dismissed the fancy as a phantasm of her condition.

Yet there was a *becomingness* about the Crux Crystal, a sense of something shaping itself from empty air even as one watched. For once, Kendric gagged his skepticism, regarding the phenomenon with the same utter silence as the others.

Nothing happened in the crystal, and everything.

Irissa found the Overstone pouch clutched in her hand without thinking to do so. An answering thrum within the hidden stone made her sense again how the entire chamber rumbled, even the soles of her feet tickling slightly. She wondered if Kendric's soles tickled, and then decided that they wouldn't dare.

Still, the silence and the waiting and the infinite becoming continued. Everything strained without moving, like a breath that is held to its breaking point.

Then . . . so slowly, so . . . delicately that it seemed to fade even as it appeared, a scene resolved inside the translucent sphere.

Irissa saw an arm, a bare white woman's forearm clutching a cloak pin. Then Irissa's dark hair, caught in an unfelt wind, swirled before her eyes and obscured the vision.

Irissa raised her hand to bat away her windblown locks—and found her own hair sedate and unshaken. The hair she saw streaming was *within* the Crux Crystal.

Blinking against the wind that was not but which she felt in her soul, Irissa strained to make the image within the crystal coalesce. A tall male figure appeared—she first took it for Kendric and clutched his arm to ensure he still stood beside her. He did, rock-solid and as mute as she.

Then the face grew clear—not younger but somehow less taut than when she had first seen it not so long before. . . .

"Medoc!" Kendric whispered disbelievingly beside her, his voice so low its rumble added to the general tremor.

Pennants of long dark hair and the folds of a crimson cloak surged at the sphere's center. Medoc, looking as real as he had in Edanvant, stepped toward the woman's half-evoked image, pain and confusion contorting his face. He offered her his hand—that much was plain.

The wind plastered her cloak back, pinned her saffron gown to her figure, which belled out like a wind-filled sail.

In Medoc's palm appeared not the extended hand of one he would assist, but a dagger. Unpinned, the scarlet cloak was blowing back with the woman's hair. A flash of round gold crossed Medoc's palm next. He opened his mouth, spoke soundlessly in the silence of the sphere.

The woman's face focused enough for a moment for everyone to see it—her sad, driven eyes, her barely moving lips that mimed barely audible words.

The image poised there, at its most mystic and most poignant—Medoc locked into his angry helplessness; she pinned to her mute need; the dagger and medallion flashing in Medoc's palm with more reality and life than either of their two frozen figures.

The breath held in the hall escaped in one universal sigh.

"Here," said a ludborg, who sounded sacrilegious for even speaking, "lies the key to our future. Here is a piece of the past that acts even now upon our present. Who can decipher it? Surely it must mean something to these two, our reborn heirlings, Sin and Aven, who came to repel a Usurper and now must claim a High Seat with the turn of this key before them, before us all."

Ludborgs waited. Townspeople waited. Irissa and Kendric waited. Aven and Sin . . . waited.

"It . . . means nothing," Sin confessed, the admission thrown at his feet like crumbs for birds he resented.

"It means everything!" the ludborg exhorted. "Think! You and your sister claim a certain memorylessness. You can no longer afford that. You must explain these figures within the Crux Crystal, or the salvation set in motion by the scene remains . . . unfulfilled."

"Nothing," Aven echoed her brother. Even at the top of the tiers, Irissa could hear the swallowed sob in her voice. "We have done our best. We are what we are, but we cannot say what we were. We cannot *remember*!"

"Remember!" the ludborgs chanted in unison, adding another thrill of almost musical vibration to the tension-racked room.

Aven's and Sin's fiery heads shook in joint denial, mutual failure.

A small thunderclap shook the silent chamber—Kendric's foot taking a first, definite step toward the Crux Crystal.

"We can't remember what we have never seen," he said, "but we can describe what we have been told. Irissa and I know this scene secondhand, by hearsay."

"Then say it to us," a ludborg urged.

Kendric turned to find Irissa moving down the riser to join him. People parted like wheat from wind as they passed.

Each step brought the figures in the crystal nearer to life size. Yet the closer they came, the less the woman's features resolved. She seemed made of wind and water, painted on these gypsy elements as clouds are smeared across the shifting sky.

Standing before the crystal, Irissa found herself awed by its otherness and the utter separateness of the scene within it . . . another time and space caught within a bottle and beached on an alien shore. How was she—or Kendric—to translate what was written therein?

Kendric began, as usual, with the concrete. He pointed to the man's unmoving figure. "Medoc. A Torloc. Once of Rule, now of Edanvant. Irissa's . . . grandfather."

Ludborg hoods nodded in sage unison. "Living or dead?"

"Living," Kendric said.

"And the woman?"

He frowned. "The infamous Phoenicia, much heard of and little seen. Even Medoc admits he only glimpsed her in the gate—this 'scene' supposedly took place almost thirty years ago within a gate from Rule to . . . wherever. Medoc ended in Edanvant. I know not where the woman went."

"Phoenicia . . ." The name wafted around the room on a sigh.

"So she was not cast into beast form," Aven interrupted. "She escaped. And with her—"

"The heir," Sin finished, his voice flat.

"Another heir, of clan Phoenix." The ludborg who spoke stepped apart from his fellows to confront Kendric as taleteller.

"Rengarth is awash in heirs," Kendric noted, "but not

this one. Medoc said she hovered on the very brink of birth and death, that woman. He never knew where she went, or in what condition she arrived there. She must be . . . dead, and her 'heir' with her. Even her likeness here is only half present."

"Yes," the ludborg agreed. "The figure is semipresent, unlike the living man's, this Medoc." The fathomless hood turned to Irissa. "Seeress, you are kin to this man, perhaps also to this woman in some way."

"I am kin only to Medoc—and the medallion she gave him, which he gave me." Irissa lifted her wrist, letting the light touch the gold at her wrist.

The crowd gasped to see a crystal image in true form.

"The past does not forge links to the present without a reason," the ludborg insisted. "Why do you have the medallion?"

"Medoc gave it to me before I came here. He hoped it might protect me. It's a talisman of the Usurper that Phoenicia must have taken as she left. I can use it to control the Hunter, but—"

"Try it," the ludborg urged, hoods nodding all around him. "Use it on the Crux Crystal. Unless someone enters the icebound scene and sets that moment in motion again, even for an instant, our true fate can never unwind itself from the reel of the past."

Impelled by their need, Irissa raised her arm, knowing Kendric moved to stop her. She chimed the medallion into the curved bubble-bright surface, expecting her wrist to pass right through.

Metal rang on rock and the sphere remained intact, untouched.

Kendric was pulling her hand back, but Irissa simply smiled and let the medallion dangle at her wrist again. "I could have told you, this token controls the Hunter, not wombgates to the past."

"You have other magic," a ludborg said.

"Yes, but the wrong magic could destroy the Crux,

could set the moment in motion awry, making everything far worse."

"What of the dagger?" Sin asked. "Did this Medoc take it, too?"

"Phoenicia *gave* him both tokens," Irissa reproved. "She begged him to take them. She said they kept her from passing the gate, that magic weighed her down when she was taking an Unwilling One through."

"Besides," Kendric added, "the dagger held a fire demon that nearly ravaged Edanvant. Medoc would have nothing to do with it after that, so I threw it blade over hilt into the heavens until no one saw it anymore. It's as gone as gone can get. Pin no hopes on that demon's steel tongue."

"You *threw* it away! A thing of Rengarth?" Aven was indignant.

"You threw it so far than none could retrieve it?" Sin was worse than indignant; he was scornful. "You are an oversized man, Kendric, but that is hard to believe. It must have landed somewhere."

"We saw it vanish," Irissa said, "quite literally into thin air. Besides, we had no desire to retrieve it. It nearly destroyed all that we loved."

"Rengarth is all that we love," Aven argued. "You come here as strangers and obstruct our need to find the truth of our past so that we may live our future."

"We are not against you," Irissa began.

"I have magic," Kendric interrupted, answering Sin's accusation. "I can do many things I would rather not, and some I occasionally find useful. That is how I rid Edanvant of the dagger. If I wanted to, I might even breach this bubble of yours—"

He reached with his ring hand to the crystalline surface, meaning merely to rap it with his fist.

Perhaps it was the ringstone—all its colors were melding madly. Perhaps it was his indifference, his lack of trying. At any rate, his hand and forearm passed through the Crux Crystal as though it were vapor.

"The key!" a ludborg shouted. Voices all around picked up the chant, except for Aven's and Sin's. And Irissa's.

"No key but ill luck," Kendric demurred, trying to retract his hand. It would not come.

Inside the crystal, the figures stirred. Phoenicia's hair and cloak began drifting leadenly through the mist, as if moved by a ponderous wind. Her face, still vague, turned toward them, the features sharpening even as they watched. She had a slightly aquiline nose and eyes of pure amber.

"Help her!" a ludborg urged. "She calls."

"No!" Irissa cried into the crowd that was chanting "The key." The ludborgs were urging them like chattering treemonks. She started toward Kendric too late.

He had not so much moved into the Crux Crystal as it had swollen to encompass him.

He now stood within it, looking as real, as alive, as Medoc—a startled, intrusive third figure pushing into the past. He turned to regard Irissa and the others beyond his invisible yet impassable wall.

Already Irissa's questing hands were smoothing the curved glossy surface desperately seeking a crack. Her eyes waxed lucid silver to draw lightning strokes of power down the impervious surface.

Kendric pressed his palms to hers through the barrier. It was as if they touched through someone else's skin—in contact but still separated. Mutely, his eyes urged calm. She read no fear in them, which quieted the panic in hers.

Nodding, Irissa stepped back. He had watched many times while she had met magic head-to-head. Now, for some reason, the role of watcher and waiter was hers. Now, perhaps, she trusted herself enough to ask no more of herself than that—and no less of Kendric than she had expected of herself.

Oblivious, the two evoked figures within the giant crystal confronted each other. Solid as he was, Kendric was able to approach them, saunter around them, nearly touch

them without drawing so much as a glance from either of
their emotion-stamped faces.

Shrugging wryly at Irissa, Kendric circled them once
more, patting Medoc lightly on the back in passing.
Medoc's shoulder twitched as if dislodging a large insect
that had landed there, but otherwise he took no notice of
Kendric.

Kendric studied the woman next.

Although the wind still whipped her long hair past her
face, his shorter hair remained unruffled. Yet when he
paused to touch her shoulder, she shivered suddenly, and
looked wildly around, blindly past his all-too-obvious form.

Her hand, still pressing the two talismans into Medoc's
palm, jerked free from Medoc's at Kendric's touch. Medoc,
who looked so real Irissa half expected that he and Kendric
would exit the crystal together and join them, curled into
himself leaflike from the edges and vanished.

Kendric stood within the crystal, blinking like the
watchers outside the crystal. Phoenicia lifted her empty
hands, curved them as around an invisible globe, and
brought them to the sides of Kendric's face.

What he felt no witness could say.

Irissa saw him freeze in further astonishment and almost jerk away. Phoenicia gazed intently into his eyes—
and beyond his eyes—as if staring down an endless tunnel
into utter nothingness. Her mouth, slightly open to permit
her labored breaths, suddenly shut with determination. A
look of agony etched itself into her strong features.

Her head rolled back on her shoulders and then she
was sinking into her scarlet cloak to the ground. Kendric
bent without thinking to uphold her—and reared back
when another figure uncurled beside her on the ground to
catch her.

Yet another man occupied the crystal now—a man
with a warrior's width of shoulders and brawn of arm but a
milder cast of features . . . a blunt-featured, ashen-haired
man whose moss-green eyes warmed with sympathy and

wonder. Not a proud man, like Medoc, or a self-sufficient man, like Kendric. Simply a man.

The crystal floor was no longer anonymous ground, Irissa noticed, but reed-fringed and wet. Kendric glanced down, aghast to see the orange sillac hide of his boots slowly darkening to brown as if dampened to the knee . . . yet he stood in no visible water.

Despite his perplexity, he didn't look to Irissa, to the world outside the crystal, but only to the world within it.

Suddenly, his hands flew to his eyes, spread before them, and waved as if to attract his own attention. They clapped his ears next, as to assure that his ears were still there.

His leg jerked to take a step—and froze. Then he moved no more, but stood statue-still as if stripped of every sense.

Irissa charged the Crux Crystal again, ignoring the multitudinous pluck of ludborg pincers on her arms.

She slid off its impervious, glassy sides that curved subtly enough to forbid her any grip on it. The crystal evaded her inner sight as well; try as she might, it presented no image of itself in her mind. Perhaps she chased a bubble in time itself, which slipped from her grasp even as she closed upon it.

"He has altered the Crux Crystal!" a ludborg whined. "He is the key. He must be allowed to unlock this door."

"This door consumes him!" Irissa returned.

She shrugged off the lullings and circled the crystal, her hands sliding along its contours. A further anomaly revealed itself. Although Kendric's figure shifted naturally as she circled him, from side to back to side to front, Phoenicia and the man's forms remained always facing her—whether she stood behind them or not!

"He is real," Irissa muttered to herself. "It is they who are . . . not real."

Blinded, Kendric turned around in the crystal, perhaps even sensing the pull of Irissa's circling power.

His powerful figure diminished—not like Medoc's, utterly—but it, too, curled into itself limb by limb as his legs buckled slowly and his arms embraced himself and he sank upon the reeds that bowed before him into a bed.

Irissa beat the flat of her palms on the glass. It would not so much as chime, even at the touch of her ring band.

She pressed her cheek to the surface she felt as an icy veil rent before her. Her eyes' silver intensity sharpened until she saw a faint, silver reflection of herself. Her power rebounded from self to self, striking her eyes shut even as they pierced the barrier.

Time made a mirror of itself, and an impassable barrier to her.

No one within the crystal fared any better.

Kendric, rolled into himself, struggled silently on the mat of reeds. Phoenicia writhed as if mortally wounded by the wind that racked her flying hair. The unknown man hovered, seeing only the woman, his face beset by indecision and concern.

Phoenicia was dissolving, her cloak spreading into the bloody waters of a marsh, spears of reed shooting up through it. Her hair was dissipating to mossy strands adrift upon the murky water.

The man, as startled as any witness by Phoenicia's fleeing substance, dredged the water for her fading body and at length wrested something wet and wriggling from the mud.

The ruddy water that was Phoenicia swelled, tickled the edges of Kendric's still form, then lapped higher and higher, darkening his clothes with its wet tongue.

"No!" Irissa shouted outside the crystal, pressing her Iridesium circlet to the glass. Rage and its twin, despair, rushed the barrier, pooled into that one point of contact—metal and glass.

Irissa felt her will entwine her magic and drive toward the same focus. A third eye of sheer silver bloomed in the center of her circlet. Her own eyes rolled up in her head until they felt beyond recall.

Her fingers spread on the cool, unseen glass. Rage ran

down one arm and despair the other. The collision of their
unguided passion with that icy contained surface nearly
jolted Irissa free of the contact.

But something kept her pinned there, the circlet
branding her forehead, the hot regard of her single inner
eye focused to a dagger point.

Her fingertips took the glass for their own. She felt it
soften under their silver-white heat. Then her fingers rent
the very fabric of time at the same moment the Iridesium
circlet exploded at her temples in a riot of color and sound.

Glass gave on a scale unheard-of—it fractured into
shards and pieces and splinters and slivers of splinters. It
rang loud and soft and sharp and chiming. It shattered like
rain on a slate roof, it slashed itself to pieces like snow-
season ice daggers melting from the smile of the spring sun.
It glittered and heaped into a shining silver pile on the
chamber floor.

The pile stirred, then parted like a fountain.

Kendric rose from the ruins, brushing glass dust from
his hands and face.

Around him to the knees lay a mound of pear-shaped
droplets smoothed innocuously into cabochon gemstones.

Irissa waded into the softly clicking pile to reach him,
to see herself seen in his eyes, to feel her arms caught in his
hands, to hear her name on his lips.

Around them, ludborgs clucked, or perhaps the shining clear stones did.

"Amazing," someone announced.

Irissa and Kendric, reunited, were blind and deaf to
anything outside themselves.

"Coldstones," the same ludborgian voice marveled. "I
see, My Lord of the Longsword and My Lady Longitude,
that you have accomplished your greatest wonder of all and
brought Scyvilla home through time at last to Rengarth."

CHAPTER
22

"HOW?" KENDRIC WANTED TO KNOW. HE STILL LOOKED as though he had been through the gullet of an Empress Falgon the wrong way.

"Why?" Irissa wondered instead.

Scyvilla, the object of their questions, had settled onto the coldstone mound beneath the High Seat. He was happily filtering tear-shaped gems through his sleeves as if conjuring miniature casting crystals.

"Never has a Torloc seeress spent so liberally of her power to break so impossible a barrier," Scyvilla mused. "These remnants of the Crux Crystal should by rights be dagger-sharp, but the seeress's passion and compassion have combined to blunt them into harmless tears of glass."

Kendric and Irissa sighed in loud mutuality.

"How," Kendric asked again, "could I ever have confused *this* ludborg with the others? Never was so aggravating an entity housed in so unpretentious a package. He is nothing like anything I have seen before or since."

"I am glad to see you again as well, Wrathman," Scyvilla returned slyly. "But I would like to see the rest of Rengarth better."

"Later," Irissa suggested shortly.

Only the trio shared the deserted ceremonial chamber.

After much awe, fuss, and wonder, the others had been persuaded to leave and meditate on the evening's events. Now the exhausted survivors of the Crux Crystal put what was left of their addled heads together to decipher the mess.

"Well?" Irissa prompted when Scyvilla remained silent. "Why could you come to Rengarth now, when it was forbidden to you for eternity?"

Scyvilla's homely hood nodded to the spot that the Crux Crystal had occupied. "I returned on Phoenicia's cloak-tails, for that was how I left it." The hood twitched to survey their amazed expressions. "Oh, yes, I was a Willing One and could traverse a gate with her, even unknown by her. I always itched to see more of the worlds than Rengarth."

Scyvilla directed the dark of his hood at Irissa. "In Edanvant not long ago I asked you to take me with you. I had guessed by then that only a pregnant woman of magical power can ease me through a gate. You refused, becoming the ultimate instrument of my arrival nevertheless.

"When you engaged the Crux Crystal, I found myself . . . sucked from my peaceful abode in Edanvant and through a Citydell window as if by a passing wind. After much twisting and turning through indeterminate space and time—aided no doubt by my general shape—I found myself where I had been before: concealed beneath the windswept wings of Phoenicia's cloak. I was hence pulled home again by the Wrathman's blundering into the crystal and your breaking it. I thank you both."

The hood bowed profoundly as Irissa hissed her exasperation. She was not minded to serve as unwitting vehicle for yet another unsuspected passenger.

"Irissa alone didn't ease you through *this* gate," Kendric put in suspiciously.

"No, I owe that honor to Phoenicia again The . . . reenactment of her passage permitted me to . . . reattach myself and be . . . delivered here. How fortunate that the key scene to Rengarth's past and future should be one in which I was a low-profile participant."

"And what is that key?" Irissa demanded. "The Crux

Crystal almost stripped Kendric of his soul as surely as Geronfrey's Dark Mirror sought to swallow mine—"

"Oh, no . . . oh, no—" Scyvilla's rotund form rolled on the coldstones until the gems slid out from under it. His laughter echoed from the high rounded ceiling and came back to haunt them all with its many-throated echoes.

"Dear and most unfesty friend, dear seeress, you are mistaken. The scene in the crystal did not diminish Kendric's life and force, it *amplified* it. Few men are so honored as to be born twice, much less to witness it even once . . . or witness most of it."

"Born?" Kendric sounded more dubious than ever.

"What else? What man aided Phoenicia in the marsh?"

"Were he older," Kendric admitted reluctantly, "he would resemble my father, Halvag the Smith." The even greater reluctance of unwilling revelation flavored his next words. "You are saying that Phoenicia came through the gate to Rule! That my *father* found and aided her as she lay dying?"

"As she lay *birthing,* my roundabout friend. A simple mistake. There is little difference between the two, save a span of years that many reckon too short."

Kendric sat down, suddenly, on a riser. "I? She? He?"

"I quite often reduce grown men to single syllables, and I always named you Master of the Short Phrase and the Longsword. Yes. *You.* And *she* who bore you. And *he* who found her and delivered you, keeping you to rear as his son."

"He said my mother died at my birth," Kendric intoned slowly, as if hearing the sentence from his dead father's lips and repeating—although not understanding—it.

"So she did. Did he say else of her?"

Kendric kept his eyes on the throne of bone dissecting the darkness growing all around them. "No."

"Then—" Irissa began, unable to keep herself from interrupting. "*Kendric* is an heir of Rengarth! He is . . . *the* last legitimate heir. Geronfrey always knew that, or suspected it, and pursued Kendric as much as he did me!"

"Better," Scyvilla allowed. "You are thinking again. It is a festy business, but necessary at times."

"No!" Kendric roared, standing without any apparent preamble. He towered over Scyvilla on his shifting pile of coldstones, over Irissa sunk on the first riser, her chin propped on her peaked knees and her face a blank pale slate with worry written all over it.

"Enough!" Kendric continued just as thunderously. "Enough of your weaseling in and out of worlds and threading time back and forth through the same eye of the same needle! I am who I am. I don't need a rewritten pedigree or a refound land or an enemy more ancient than my own ancestors. I am a man of Rule, and that's final."

"Yes, yes," Scyvilla nodded his hood as if gnawing on a bone while he spoke. "A former Wrathman of Rule as well, that's what you are and what you were. The Wrathman of . . . what was it you called that place in the phrase you spoke without knowing why—?"

"—the Far Keep," Kendric growled ungraciously.

"The Far Keep. Amazing how magic will plant its seed even on unwilling ground. Perhaps I should say . . . unwitting. Some . . . spell of Phoenicia's must have canted that phrase into your unborn self, perhaps merely the inheritance of generations. You should go to the Far Keep and see for yourself what your true heritage is."

"Go there?" Irissa lifted her face from her knees.

Scyvilla shrugged. "'Tis only a long journey away, through the Quickstone Mountains to the Paramount Athanor. There is a map inlaid on some floor in this fortress."

"Quickstone Mountains?" Kendric was so aghast he forgot to thunder. "I . . . invented . . . them to enchant that idle Issiri—"

"Oh, indeed, and sometimes—the best times—we

make up the truth without knowing it. Besides, the mountains have many names. The oldest is the Frostrim."

Kendric sat again, heavily. His face matched Irissa's for pallor. When he put his hand upon her shoulder, she sank almost imperceptibly at the weight of the gesture.

"But you both are tired and I chatter," Scyvilla apologized with little regret. "The lost lamb returned to the fold ever did bleat out of turn. My order wishes to hear my tale—actually, my order will *insist* on hearing my tale. They will be far fiercer sticklers than Wrathmen or seeresses. I suggest you repair to your chamber and refresh yourselves. Turning time inside out shakes the innards."

Irissa and Kendric lurched upright, still dazed.

Scyvilla's hood tilted fondly toward them. "And don't be surprised if you begin . . . seeing things. That is the way with a trip through a time crucible. I myself am quite confused as to exactly how many of . . . myself . . . are here in Rengarth."

Kendric paused in mounting the risers, Irissa at his side. "Too many, Rengarthian, far too many."

The wonders of their alien chamber had become the sweet security of home by the time Irissa and Kendric reached it.

"I feel as if I had journeyed to the Swallowing Cavern and back," Kendric said, staring rather vacantly at the fish cavorting beneath his feet in the glassy floor. "How did you break the crystal and free me? Us, that is."

Irissa collapsed atop the swallowing comforter, unconcerned if she could ever lever herself upright.

"I don't know. I saw that you were being caught in a caul of time, so I delved to the Swallowing Cavern within myself, the very pit of my magic. All my talismans became intersections for that power, as I myself seemed to be. I went blind, like you, for some moments. Then I *saw* with an alien inner eye . . . perhaps the Eye of Edanvant. I—don't know."

Kendric came to look down at her. She could trace

Phoenicia's eyes and nose in his face now, as well as traits of a father she had never seen except for a captured image in a crystal. For all that she specifically knew Kendric's antecedents better than ever, he had never looked more of a stranger to her.

"Are you . . . unhurt?" he asked cautiously, and that Kendric she knew.

Irissa nodded, not wanting to repeat her litany of "I don't knows."

"And your . . . condition?"

"Remarkably unaffected," she answered with a smile. "It never seems to hamper me in matters of great moment, only in ordinary tasks and by embroidering the fringes of my magic. My condition is like Felabba, ever-present and arbitrary."

Kendric's boots creaked as he crossed the luminous floor, tiny fish lips nipping at his heels through the milky glass. He hefted a decanter from a feather-upholstered table and poured a thin carmine stream into a goblet.

"Ale-wine." Kendric held the glass to the muted light. "It's not . . . undrinkable. May I suggest some?"

Irissa struggled to sit up, and managed it despite the stubborn resistance of her midsection. "Indeed. I'd even sip marshwine at such a time, in a grubby tavern of Rule."

"Even in the Green Bottle?" Kendric grinned in remembrance.

"Well, perhaps not a place as grubby as *that*. It's a good thing I collected you there; you looked well on the path to idle drunkenness."

"It's a good thing I found you at Rindell; you seemed even further on the way to pining into a vanishing mist like Finorian and the other Torloc dames."

"I found *you*!" Irissa reminded him forcefully, "and *you* were wounded."

"You were wounded as well," he answered. "I see that now as I didn't then. You had been cut off from your kind without warning or reason. So, apparently, had I, not even knowing it. Nothing of Halvag and Rule is in me," he added bleakly, "but the rearing of me."

"And that is everything!"

"Then why leave Edanvant, where you found again your kin and your beginning?"

"Because *you* are my chosen kin, and my ending!" she flared in exasperation.

Kendric, who had sat on the circular metal rail containing the bed, leaned back to look at her. "So kin and birth-belonging are not the most important considerations?"

"Sometimes," she answered. "Sometimes not."

"Hmm." He handed her a goblet of ale-wine and sipped consideringly from his own after pulling his ax from his belt to set it on the floor. He reached out and drew Irissa's sword from the knot at her side, then set it alongside his weapon.

Disarmed in more ways than one, Irissa found herself uncommonly thirsty; jousting with the Crux Crystal had set a fire raging in her body, quenching her natural reserves.

"You don't like Rengarth," she offered.

"Like it? I've barely seen it. And did I like the Marshlands of Rule, in which I never felt at home and now see why?" he asked bitterly.

"So, too, I felt about Rindell."

"And did you find your people's home any better?"

Irissa moved her head from side to side while she considered, skeins of dark hair shadow-bruising her face.

Kendric was shocked at the hollow knowledge in that face now; Irissa's features sharpened as her body blunted. He saw the strain she carried as surely as he had once borne his sword, only her burden was invisible and living—and self-inflicted.

"I might have liked Edanvant better," she finally confessed, "had there been other folk than Torlocs in it."

A pause, and then he laughed richly, seeing the mischief outshine the weariness of her eyes. "So now you admit it—a contentious, high-handed, magic-flourishing breed!" His expression sobered. "So may be Rengarthians—or worse."

"Quite possibly."

"You seem calm at the notion that you may be abandoned here, consort to an unwilling Ruler, mother to an indifferent heir."

"At least I am certain of a title."

"Title?"

"Reginatrix," she pointed out, demurely self-mocking. "I like the ring of it."

"A Torloc would. But—" His face twisted again, to wrestle with the past. "No, it is too ridiculous! Leave Rengarth to the Rengarthians. Geronfrey is not even exiled yet, and Aven and Sin looked downcast as they left the hall."

"Ah, you noticed."

"Why shouldn't I have noticed? I am not as stolid as you think. They now see in me a rival where before they saw only what I was. What I wished to be."

Irissa sighed and sipped again. The bittersweet blend of ale and wine left her as liquid as the brew itself. A new mellow warmth stole through her magic racked limbs.

"They see in you a rival unrivaled," she said at last. "What they feared from Geronfrey—a consort, an heir— was already accomplished with you all along."

"Aven said she felt as if she were fading." Kendric frowned. "I am not here to replace anyone. I was drawn here unwilling—!"

"Scyvilla would say that you were always drawn here, and always unwilling, because you didn't know your origin and fate."

"Rubbish! Geronfrey drew me here because he wanted you—"

"Or he wanted me because he knew it would draw you. He must have known who you were from the first. He must have always feared your knowing it, too."

"He would have killed me, then."

"Perhaps he intended to, but you escaped."

"I am not that lucky."

"You are not that unprotected anymore," Irissa added.

"Hmm." Kendric quaffed and considered.

Irissa smiled into her goblet rim and sipped again.

"I . . . really . . . saw myself born?" he asked suddenly in a quiet tone.

"You saw less of what happened than the rest of us. But you were present. I only hope our unborn one is not as large and lusty as you when it arrives—"

Kendric shuddered. "I . . . couldn't do that to anyone, any . . . woman. I don't know what I saw, but I felt. I felt that woman's agony and desperation. Her pain. I felt myself . . . hurt her."

He turned to Irissa suddenly. "If there's any way to abbreviate your condition, stop it now. Will it away, wish it away—" His hand on her knee was hot with urgency and tightened almost painfully.

She released a shocked breath, then remembered her own early speculations on that very notion. She sighed, choosing her words as carefully as Issiri might pick the jewels for a new necklace.

"I felt Phoenicia's struggles, too, along my every nerve." Irissa swallowed as a revenant of that excruciating pain rose in her throat. "I cannot say I was . . . taken with how the body fights to spit out its successful seeds, and perhaps there was a time when I could have undone what was only beginning. But—"

She glanced to find Kendric hanging on her every nuance. Only the magic of utter honesty would serve them both at this moment, Irissa knew.

"But time pushes us down a narrower and narrower corridor," she concluded, "like babes resisting birth, and there is finally no room left at all in which to turn around. I have become used to the idea, Kendric. I have journeyed within and found someone mysterious and sovereign there. I owe it my gratitude; certainly I can risk an encounter with pain to protect it—"

"Phoenicia *died*!" he interrupted. "I killed her. Now I could be the means of killing you—"

"I do not kill so easily, I think."

"But do you *know*?"

"No. No one can, not even a seeress."

"What use is your magic, then? What use was hers? Only to have herself persecuted unto death! That is a legacy I don't care to pass on."

Irissa struggled out of the encompassing covers, somehow managing to rise without tipping her goblet. The fishes swirled under her feet, making her feel the room whirled as well. Kendric still sat on the bed's edge, hands hung between his knees, head lowered, looking like nothing so much as a large, morose bear.

"Kendric, look at me." He did, raising eyes redrimmed with fatigue and a strong dose of ale-wine. Irissa's head began to spin from her abrupt shift in position, but her words came straight and precise.

"I have changed," she said in a firm but somehow pleading tone. "It is visible even to a blind man. I can never change back, just as you cannot strike out the memory of what you saw and felt in the Crux Crystal.

"You were granted a great gift—to see yourself as few humans or even Torloc do—as you passed wet and spitting from the cocoon of your mother's body. My body spins its own web now, and we will share the gift of seeing someone unknown come to us to become itself and learn to know us. We may not like it, or its risks, but . . . the crystals are cast. Let us trust we will read them right."

"Speeches," Kendric answered finally, cradling his head in his hands and slightly blurring the first *s*. His empty goblet clicked to the floor and rolled noisily away, herding a flash of fins before it. "More ale-wine?" he asked.

Irissa looked up to see the nets sparkling silver against the ceiling. No birds flew or chirped, all having roosted for the night. The ceiling spun into a light as bright as the three suns of Rengarth, then came wisping down upon her head. She felt her knees sag, felt Kendric pull her down to the bed, felt herself sink onto a cloud of down . . . white swans-down wings wafted up and down ever so gently under a silver sky. Something fell from her uncurling fingers, clattering far, far away.

Then she felt herself released. Kendric snored softly beside her.

Irissa, drifting with the swan-spawn in a sea of clouds, had the serene conviction that they had said immensely important things they unfortunately would not quite remember in the morning.

She hiccoughed, a reaction that set her stomach in spasm.

"I beg your pardon!"

"I should be begging *your* pardon." Irissa giggled softly as another hiccough shook her.

"You have been somewhat intemperate," the speaker returned. Its voice resembled the dry wheeze of leaves blowing down a stone corridor.

"So have been the events of this evening. Some—" Hiccough. ". . . what."

"What will you do?"

"Sleep. . . ."

As if called, a profound drowsiness rolled over her like a great dark cloud blotting out the trio of suns. She was so exhausted, so worn, no matter how brave a face she put on it. She had drawn on the deepest strands of her power, and some of the oldest threads clearly had frayed. . . .

Another, amplified hiccough shook her. *"Not yet, ninny! There's more before you than smashing a Crux Crystal to Torloc tears. There's Those Without to consider, as well as those within. And Geronfrey—where is he, and doing what? And that great lummock of an heir? He requires wise guidance now as never before, and never has been so bereft of it. No time for sleeping now!"*

A kick in Irissa's ribs made her eyes jerk open and took her breath away. She raised her shoulders and pressed her fingers to her midriff.

"Felabba, is that you? It's so unfair for you to worry

me from within when you were barely civil to me from without. If my firstborn has whiskers I shall give it to Aven and Sin as an heir, then Kendric and I will leave Rengarth and where will your predictions and your reason for interfering be then? Well?" Irissa demanded of her stomach.

Kendric jerked upright and stared at her.

"I was . . . feeling a trifle unsettled," she explained. "I thought I heard a voice."

"Yes. Your own." His eyes shut wearily. "I think we both have had overmuch magic and Rengarthian ale-wine. Let us hope that we wake in the morning to find it all a bad dream."

He settled down again, pulling Irissa against him to lay an arm over her hip. His hand rested naturally on the growing swell of her stomach, a fact she found equally disconcerting and comforting.

"Sleep," he droned seductively in her ear. "In the morning we'll find it all a bad dream." His low, slow tones lulled her into exactly the state he urged. In a moment she had drowned in the curly white wool of a giant cloud bank of sheep.

Kendric could feel Irissa's breathing deepen, could feel her body soften against his. He fondly patted her stomach, something he'd never dare do were she conscious.

"A bad dream," he consoled Irissa again in her sleep. "Like Felabba."

Something kicked—hard, admonishingly hard—into the palm of his hand. Kendric jerked fully awake, startled, in a sudden, coldstone sweat.

CHAPTER
23

A FINGER-LONG FISH WITH GOSSAMER FINS CIRCLED IN the bathing pool, then darted inward to nibble at Irissa's toes.

She swatted it away as she would a forward fly. "I'm considering not wearing clothes again," she announced.

Kendric, his hair water-darkened at the nape, sat on the risers leading to the bed and pulled on his boots. "Dressing while still damp is discouraging," he acknowledged, "but why forgo clothes forever?"

"I am on the brink of nothing fitting."

"This, too, will pass," he suggested, standing to stomp his feet more firmly into the boots. "The only thing worse than falling asleep fully clothed is waking in that condition. For once I appreciate the decadency of indoor bathing."

Irissa splashed idly in the water, her ebony tresses trailing like despondent marshweed.

"Here." Kendric pulled a brightly woven shawl from a settle and tossed it to her. "A Reginatrix deserves new raiment. Look at Issiri, and she was only a Reginatrix Apparent."

Irissa laughed as she rose from the bathwater and swirled the fabric over her shoulders. "With all the hardships we have faced, why must we compound matters by treating a soft billet like a night in the Rocklands?"

"The contrary nature of the Torloc and the human. We have traveled too far to trust to comfort at this stage."

Irissa had readily donned her gray silk trousers and

tunic. Now she gathered the newfound fabric over one shoulder, securing it with the sword sash at her waist.

She marched barefoot to a long slice of mirror—one of several inset along the wall at intervals.

"Even Finorian would not come to odious conclusions about my condition if she saw me in this," Irissa declared, turning to show how the fabric disguised her swelling form.

She pulled open the falgonskin pouch at her breast and tugged out the Overstone egg. "I wish I could see it in daylight; it has not only grown heavier, but its surface highlights have deepened."

Kendric clumped over and stationed himself before the silver stiletto of a mirror. "I'll perform a piece of sleight of hand then—magic, if you will."

He placed his palm upon the sharp apex of the point-topped mirror and twisted his wrist. The mirror panel flicked open, revealing a plain wooden face on its opposite side. Beyond it gaped a similarly shaped slit of molten bright daylight. Birds swooped past the opening like schools of fish in airy transit.

"Oh . . . the shutter reflects the *inside* of the chamber instead of the outside." Irissa approached the window, then thrust her hand into the daylight. "There's no windowpane! Why . . . if the floors are paved with glass?"

"Ask Geronfrey. He's probably had the most to say about the place's interior arrangements over the centuries. He never did like overlooking ordinary, unadulterated country."

Kendric moved beside Irissa, staring past uneven roof tops to the rumples of tilled land surrounding the city.

Irissa laughed and pointed to the horizon. "You call that ordinary?"

Kendric looked. The line of distant clouds ringing the horizon glittered in the suns' light. For a moment it resembled falling water that froze crystalline-smooth in mid-plunge—the force of its onward hurl appearing to pause and turn a liquid element into an immutable one. Like a ruffle the silver-white substance flounced the distance.

Then . . . Kendric realized what it must be. Not clouds. . . .

"The Quickstone Mountains?" He sounded incredulous.

"I think so."

"The Far Keep—" The words drew his thoughts to the mystery behind the phrase even as his eyes lingered on the frothfoam edging the horizon.

Irissa lifted the Overstone egg to the light. It balanced perfectly in her palm, heavy side down. The surface seemed smoother than ever—almost stretched, like skin, with a scaly, pearlescent gleam. Meandering veins of crimson, azure, gold, silver, and emerald sparkled in the indirect daylight.

"Issiri would have loved to add this to her collection," Irissa mused. "See how the colors pulse—"

Kendric frowned at the talisman. "You're right; it has . . . changed. Put it away. Remember how you risked your life in a similar window, when your father fought you for possession of this same token?"

"I am more unbalanced than then," Irissa said ruefully, "but less precariously placed somehow. We have grown together, this talisman and I, and grown separate. I think I could let loose of it now without endangering my life."

"Don't try!" Kendric closed her long fingers around the stone and pushed it back into the feathered pouch.

"Kendric, once you would have had me return this stone—as soon as possible!"

"I have changed, too. Even a Wrathman may change—his mind, his magic, his manner. Keep the stone as you were meant to. If not even a father can take it from you without stealing the very life force he helped give you, you have no right to play lightly with it."

"But if you're right, I may be condemned to wear it forever—heavy, cumbersome thing that it is!"

"That," Kendric answered, closing the shutter so their own figures were reflected again, "is ever the problem with collecting stray objects on a journey, as I have told you before."

Irissa shook her head, both in reproval and to whip the last water drops off the end tendrils. She let the Overstone pouch purse its mouth on the drawstring as it dropped leadenly against her breastbone.

"This could be a more intrusive burden than the other, which at least has a time limit."

"Indeed." Kendric advanced to the feather-scaled table to tap his fingers upon it. The tabletop was the proper length to support a sword—an exceptionally long sword, Irissa noticed.

"The Paramount Athanor is in the Quickstone Mountains, Scyvilla said," she pointed out.

He objected to her implied statement, delicately. "My sword is impaled in what Geronfrey called the Iron-ice Mountains, also known as the Frostrim."

"Your sword bears the answer to your fate in the runes upon its hilt, Scyvilla said."

"My sword bears my lifeline in its steel. Separate from it, my life frays. So Geronfrey said."

"They said. What do *we* say?"

Kendric's shoulders straightened as he regarded her with daylight diluted amber eyes. She could almost see an invisible weight settle upon his back, as if some shred of Felabba might have curled onto his shoulders.

"We say," Kendric answered, "I say—let's settle this heir business and get on with our own. Whatever it is to be."

Where the night before a banquet had tenanted the tables, the large hall was nearly empty now. Only naked tabletops greeted Kendric and Irissa.

They threaded through the festive arrangement until they reached a lonely enclave of breakfasters—Aven and Sin, their faces looking as rumpled as the land they sought to rule, Scyvilla, and an anonymous ludborg.

"I've slept on it," Kendric announced without sitting or preamble. "This heir nonsense is simply that. Aven and Sin are welcome to whatever throne or title they wish to claim."

A dry smile flickered across Sin's face, then caught fire on Aven's.

"Oh, stranger who would remain so, it is too late to withdraw," Aven said. "We all saw the scene in the Crux Crystal. We all see that you fulfill our prophecy—you and she: those who reluctant come because they have been called. What is to contest, except our role in your new rule?"

"Whatever you wish!" Kendric said hastily. "Ah . . . regents, chancellors, whatever name you have in Rengarth for the people who actually run the place. I grant you clear title here. I know nothing of this Phoenix clan you claim is mine! If I *am* a child of Phoenicia's, she might as well be a thousand years dead as thirty. I grew up a man of Rule, which is gone as I knew it, and have no desire to claim another land as unpredictable—or more so."

"He is very good at renouncing," Scyvilla confided to Irissa.

"Yes, and at denouncing as well."

"Excellent traits in a ruler."

"I am not a ruler!" Kendric interrupted. "I am not *your* ruler!"

"Nor are we." Sin's voice was firm. "We have sat up all night, Aven and I, thinking and talking. We see we were somehow . . . released upon this land only very recently. We see we are not . . . complete somehow. Had this been a thousand years ago, we would have taken what we had a right to then. We are mere echoes now, fading with each feeble repeat of what was once a mighty shout."

"Don't say that!" Irissa's hands impulsively reached for Aven's as if to capture her warm vitality. The woman's skin was smooth, chilly, colder than the Overstone. Irissa withdrew, rebuffed.

"Our inner fires fade to embers." Aven stretched her

long white fingers and regarded them sadly. "It has become more pronounced since the Crux Crystal. Once we saw that the scene within it had nothing to do with us. . . ."

"But you can't be sure!" Irissa argued.

"We are sure enough that we will offer our aid in whatever enterprise you wish," Sin interjected. "If it is to renounce Rengarth, so be it. Perhaps we were always fated to leave Rengarth with you."

"Leave?" the ludborg squeaked. "But we shall have to begin an heir search all over again. There will be a gap, and the Usurper was ever adept at leaping into gaps."

"We have banished him for good," Sin announced with a flare of his old certainty.

"Perhaps," Kendric said. "Whatever is decided, I cannot leave this land without what I came here with." Two hoods tilted in silent question. Aven's and Sin's eyes were more directly curious. He smiled at their bird-bright expressions.

"My missing sword. Geronfrey implied that my lifeline winds 'round its steel blade and rune-carved hilt. So I gratefully accept the Brenhalloy's offer of assistance and propose a journey to the Quickstone Mountains to reclaim it."

"The Frostrim is forbidden." The ludborg's voice resonated with shock. "Not since the Phoenix clan betrayed Rengarth by admitting the Usurper through the navel of the world atop the Paramount Athanor has any living being gone or come from there. That is why clan Phoenix dwindled to naught but Phoenicia in the end; they were forbidden generation as recompense for their betrayal."

"Yet you would allow an offworld spawn of such to be your ruler?" Kendric was equally shocked. "Rengarthians are a forgiving sort."

"We cannot deny a bloodline that has surmounted such odds," the ludborg admitted. "Then, the Crux Crystal was clearly blind to Aven and Sin—as if they did not exist in the scheme of Rengarth, despite their claims on clan Brenhall. However diminished Phoenicia was, she was Reginatrix, and recently so. Her will delivered you from sure destruction, or at least transformation into some inimical form—perhaps a . . . house cat. Think of that, Kendric; you could have lived your life on some low animal level—"

"Say no more," Kendric intervened. "There is no lower animal level than that of a house cat, particularly one that remembers and aspires to some higher state. I will do what I can to set this land aright, but first I must have my sword. If Aven and Sin will help, and if you ludborgs keep Irissa safe in . . . Solanandor Tierze, I will find the Paramount Athanor and my sword—perhaps even the Far Keep."

"Safe?" Irissa demanded.

Kendric turned placatingly. "Your . . . condition," he explained. "A long journey to a forbidden place into the icy teeth of the unknown is hardly a Reginatrix's role."

"Only royal women in Rengarth carry weapons," Irissa reminded him. "How long will you strive to spare me by being unsparing of yourself?"

"I am a warrior born," he explained.

"I am a seeress born. My weapon is my eyes. I cannot use them if I am not there."

"I am . . . used to hardship and grave danger."

"I will soon be facing both in ways that no man has mastered."

"We do not even know when you will deliver."

"Not until I decide to."

"I would feel more secure if I knew you were secure."

"As would I. And you will if I am with you."

"If you were not with child—"

"If you were not without sword—"

Their dialogue had ended in a mutual glare, feelings brittle as tinder primed for the incendiary spark of a hot word.

"Both will go," the ludborg intoned, "as both engaged the Crux Crystal. It is his fate that twists into a tapestry of whole cloth, but her hand guides the thread as it turns upon the spindle."

"And we also will go," Aven put in eagerly. "Who, after all, will keep them from each other's throats?"

Kendric's and Irissa's glares turned to Aven, then—slowly—softened.

"Another journey," a voice purred into Irissa's mind. *"And just the worst variety of wilds to traverse. Snow. Cold. Wind. Crevices. Ice. Hidden caves. Frostforge. Who knows what monsters await? Mind you go gently, seeress. You have others to consider than yourself."*

Irissa gasped, half surprised and half exasperated. She had been hoping the previous night's visitation had been an ale-wine-abetted dream.

"Is something bothering you?" Kendric asked with a bit too hopeful solicitude.

Irissa saw herself reporting an unprovable phenomenon and confined to Rengarth for the madness of a gestating woman.

"Nothing bothers me," she answered stoutly, ignoring what seemed like a knocking for egress in her lower regions, "but delay. If we go, let us go."

CHAPTER
24

"NO ONE HAS EVER GONE TO THE FROSTRIM."

Sin, squinting into the glare of Rengarth's three suns, eyed the far crest of white with equally pallid enthusiasm.

"What of this Phoenix clan, to whose line I am sentenced to play the final period?" Kendric asked instantly. "They evidently sprang from these icebound ranges."

"No one in *recent* generations has gone there." Aven's coppery freckles glittered pence-bright as she studied the saw-toothed mountains.

"That would make it a perfect retreat for a deposed Usurper," Irissa said. Unlike the others, her silver eyes did not blanch under the combined assault of bright daylight and white mountainscape.

The four travelers stood atop a ridge of Rengarthian earth. At their backs the city of Solanandor Tierze poised, a towering stone wave halted forever in midsurge. Before them, the Rengarthian landscape tumbled and swept and eddied in untidy profusion as the constant winds combed the grasses.

Kendric's back was no longer bare, being burdened with a knapsack of travel rations supplied with rather smug mystery by various ludborgs. Aven carried another provisions pack between her shoulder blades. Sin had added several edged hand weapons to his waist-hung garland, but Kendric had refused all else but the icewraith's formidable ax.

Irissa carried only herself, her sword, and whatever

else had chosen or had been selected to ride within her person. She liked to think that she and Sin had been spared bearing duties because of their superior weaponry—physical and magical. She knew instead that someone had to lope ahead to scout the way—Sin—and someone had to admit diminished agility for any kind of exertion—herself.

Still, Irissa felt an inner thrill spurred by the notion of civilization at her back and empty leagues of possibility at her feet.

"Frostrim." Kendric tasted the phrase, then spat it out. "Everyone calls these distant stepping-stones to sunfall a different name. Geronfrey's 'Iron-ice Mountains,' Issiri's 'Coldstone Mountains'; now 'Quickstone Mountains,' thanks to me. If they're that mysterious now, when did my . . . forebears, these Phoenix folk, live there?"

"Ages ago." Aven dismissed the notion of great time with the entire Phoenix clan. "Even in our day, the Phoenix clan were degraded, banished from the Frostrim and living on the edges of other clan claims."

"Even in your time?" Irissa challenged.

Aven's eyes blinked with a bird's expressionless acknowledgment. "I don't know why I know that. I . . . fear that Sin and I are displaced somehow, that we remember a Rengarth that existed many incarnations of the Usurper ago. Or we forget it, rather," she added ruefully.

"So," Kendric observed with a certain satisfaction. "I am the last in a line of landless nobodies that not even the uninhabitable ice realms still claim. Well enough. All I ask is to find my sword somewhere in these cold wastes."

"And nothing else?" Sin wondered. "Aren't you curious to trace the footsteps of your ancestors? Phoenix clan will stand in more high regard—although they were always overtall—now that one of their own is Rengarth's ruler."

"One *said* to be one of their own," Kendric corrected him. "And call no one a ruler until he—or she—has ruled. It's hard enough to rule one's own fate, much less anyone else's." He glanced to Irissa, relieved to find color warming her cheeks. "Ready?" he asked.

"Always," Aven and Sin swore in tandem.

Irissa nodded briskly and moved down the incline in step with Kendric to demonstrate her readiness. Four made an awkward party, so they went two by two. Sometimes the men led; sometimes the women. At times Irissa shared the path with Sin while Aven paired Kendric, her leaping, lorryklike steps designed to match the Wrathman's ground-eating stride.

An odd, magical quality infused their route. Even when they crossed tilled lands, yoked oxen and reins-hung farmers kept at an anonymous distance, like figures knotted into a tapestry or painted into a calendar of seasons.

Metallic clouds of bees buzzed in the just-untouchable distance. Butterfly wings wrought from rainbow hues wove among the bobbing grasses just beyond the walkers' path. Even the blossoms nodding on their stalks seemed unreal.

Irissa examined her odd notion that anything she reached out for would shrink away. Perhaps she and Kendric—and Aven and Sin—traversed some bubble-domed tunnel of space, passing imperviously over Rengarth's earthiest elements.

The tri-suns catapulted up the wild blue arch of sky, pausing directly above to incinerate the crowns of the travelers' heads. It was all too idyllic, too temperate.

Life itself seemed to be flowing at a tempo so increasingly fast it began to repeat itself: the same peasants plowed the same field behind the same withers-humped oxen; the same bees droned over the same swaying flowers; the same grasses snapped under the same passing boots; the icebound walls of the Frostrim kept the same, cold distance.

A metallic drone burst into full-throated song all around them. Kendric instinctively clapped a hand to his back, clasping a lump of burlap instead of the leather-wound hilt he expected.

"Grassweavers," Sin whispered.

Quick as a cricket, Aven bounded atop a small mound,

her pack pounding her shoulder blades. Her blithe endurance stirred Irissa's wistful envy.

"Grassweavers . . . thousands of them!" Aven announced.

The others scrambled up after her, Irissa lagging.

A swelling ocean of untilled grass tossed as far as they could see, even to the ever-present ring of white mountains. The grasses' vibrant green—and every hue that echoed it—flaunted their colors in wind-rippled waves.

Slowly, a darker pattern scribed itself onto the random fields of motion—angular lines that curved to intersect each other. Figures the size of fallen Empress Falgons etched themselves among the grasses—wove themselves *from* the whispering grasses.

"An E! It looks like an E," Irissa declared. But the symbol braiding itself from broad-leaved bladereeds, thorny swans' whisker stands, and whips of witchweed turned back on itself and left off the expected crossbar.

"Not letters, *runes*," Aven pointed out. "And grassweavers have never *written* anything before, much less appeared in daylight."

"Coincidence." Kendric scoffed all the louder because he recognized runic shapes from the hilt of his lost sword.

Coincidence stretched into an invisible writhing grassweaver and stitched the grasses into one last form—a meandering line that ended in an arrowhead.

"That way lies the Bubblemeres." Sin frowned in the overhead suns' light, his youthful features grotesquely shadowed. "One can only sink or rise there, and either state is equally undesirable."

"Naturally, we are directed there," Kendric said. "But do we have to take this direction?"

"Of course not!" Aven sounded prettily emphatic. "Grassweavers knot their patterns to trap prey. Their random undulations carry no meaning."

"A line ending in a barb has meaning in any language," Irissa differed. "It points to a path, as a path points to a place. Do you see the dark patch on the white cliff face? It resembles a black eye."

"It resembles a patch of rock among the ice," Kendric said, less imaginatively and more definitely. "And that is where the woven arrow points us. Perhaps it shows a way up."

"Go as you please," Sin told Irissa and Kendric. "Aven and I have little stake in your quest, save seeing that you return to your rightful place as heir of Rengarth. We and our ambitions of rulership have become as the ravings of grassweavers now—a mute message knotted into the meadows for others to read and grow wise by."

Kendric had heeded Sin's first sentence before the melancholy remainder was out. His tall form was already paces ahead, striding through the entwined grasses.

"Kendric will never accept rule in your stead," Irissa told Sin and Aven as they helped her down the steep incline. "You abdicate your dreams too easily."

"He may have to accept the limitations of rule," Sin answered with a half-cocked smile, "as we have had to."

"Neither of you looks particularly regal," Irissa said with an answering smile. The twins' frank faces crinkled into freckle-dusted grins. It was impossible to dislike the pair; they were as warmly ingratiating as gingerbread figures fresh from the bakingstone.

"I couldn't have invented a merrier set of friends," Irissa consoled them as the three hurried after Kendric. "Knowing you would make staying in Rengarth possible."

"Leaving Rengarth is impossible," Aven noted gently. "You both *must* stay."

"Coming here broke every precedent, why should we not leave if we wish?"

"Because you are not fated to leave," Aven said.

Irissa thought for as long as Kendric was sometimes wont. "We make our own fates. Rengarth is not our native world. And our child has grandparents to see."

Aven shook her locks into a crown of firesnakes. "*We* are our own grandparents, and grandchildren, too. We see nothing but ourselves, Sin and I. That is our fate. We will not leave Rengarth, even though we came to it contrary to all custom, as you and Kendric did."

"You speak so surely. Will you . . . die here?"

"We will . . . cease to exist here," Sin said abruptly. "I see the pattern. There's no room for failed heirs of the same generation. In the old days we would have faded to the far fields, but with all our clan gone, there is no place for us to retreat."

"Nor for us," Irissa said. "Not in Rengarth."

Sin shrugged evasively and took his sister's arm. "Come," he urged. "I want to pass the grassweavers before they stir again and take us for prey."

Shuddering, Irissa glanced sideways. The grasses still twisted into outré interweavings—she could almost read them as giant letters in a manuscript. An underlying hiss thrummed along the dark scalp of ground. Ahead, Kendric's figure plowed through endless marshes of knee-deep grass.

Then, to Irissa's discerning eyes, translucent skeletal forms parted the grasses like the teeth of a comb. Irissa hurried after Aven, after Sin, after Kendric. The blot on the Frostrim now looked like a dark eye socket on Death's crystal-white skull, but it seemed less menacing than the grassweavers boiling unseen around them.

Last, as was usual nowadays, Irissa panted to catch up to the others. Yet she was already preparing to feign instant indignation if they paused to note her tardiness.

Before they could, or before she could rejoin them, a grassweaver loomed out of the green. Forty feet of clear, gelatinous body rose and writhed into a loop. Irissa's feet split just in time to leap the sudden barrier of its translucent sides.

The grassweaver coil looming above collapsed, crashing earthward before her, looping its length around Irissa. She stopped amid the lashing grasses to listen.

Tender stems snapped as the giant loop tightened inch by inch. Grass blades leaned toward her, then bowed as they were cut. Stalk by stalk, the grass fell before an invisible scythe.

Irissa could no longer see the grassweaver's glistening, heaving sides. She could only watch the fringe of unbroken grasses rushing toward her like a knot being drawn tight.

She glanced up. Three backs were wading away, oblivious. The others, visible only from above the knees, floated without feet or lower limbs. They were too distant to hail, and, besides, Irissa hated requesting aid, especially when she most needed it.

Her sword blade hissed through the silk that cradled it, tearing free, she drew it so roughly. Magic stuttered into the chambers of her mind, its facile tongue bloated like a glutton's. Everything felt so *unbalanced* now. Why should the grassweavers spin pointed patterns to guide their party, then trap a member of it in its coils?

"Ancient patterns, though etched without thinking, can act with reason, as you are not doing now," the surly voice within her growled as if awakened cranky from a nap.

"I am not thinking?" Irissa repeated indignantly.

"Not thinking clearly. Obviously, the grassweaver has the advantage on that score. What remaining advantage do you possess?"

"None, unless you include the presence of yourself in that category," Irissa snapped back.

"Five feet away and closing," the voice sang out—or in. *"I've no desire to die throttled."*

Grasses snapped audibly as they broke now, so close came the grassweaver's tightening coil. Irissa glimpsed a rolling wave of glossy matter, colorless as water. Her skin crawled. Something deep within her shrank; perhaps it was her soul.

In the distance someone shouted. Kendric had stopped and turned. Irissa saw his face, slack and unfocused.

Unease shifted in Irissa's center, seeking a balance point and finding the middle ground completely occupied. Her magic threaded a maze of inner obstacles, caged by her own internal growth. She felt trapped within a veritable dovetail of stalagmites and stalactites gnashing shut like teeth.

The Swallowing Cavern housed within herself was dark. Time dripped from dagger point to dagger point, and blood flowed sluggishly, like crimson honey.

Irissa dipped her sword to the ground. A furrow of red trailed it as grasses sliced aside. Around her temples the Iridesium circlet tightened to the rhythm of her pounding pulses. Grasses bled beneath the metal sword point, not crushed or broken at the root, as by the grassweaver, but severed in midstalk. A strange metallic scent wafted from the mingling of their pale yellow ichor and the welling of the bloody soil.

Irissa's head snapped free in some way, as if mowed. She felt the circlet's pressure collapse, felt her inner self swell to encompass the world. A waist-high Iridesium circlet sprang up behind her plowing blade point—a fence, a wall, a magnified replica of what bound her hair to her temples and her magic to her eyes.

The tightening grassweaver's shapeless sides pressed against the new, steely barrier. It squeezed until the pale thready veins of its snakish body grew wine-colored, leaking bruises onto its pellucid surface.

Its motion never stopped, merely rolled imperceptibly forward. Kendric—Aven and Sin behind him, their red hair streaming like comet tails—came pounding over crushed grasses.

The grassweaver's awesome circumference shrank as the leagues-long body flowed on. At last, only a thinning tail circled Irissa's Iridesium wall—a final point trailing around and vanishing into an agitation of grasses hissing farther and farther away.

Kendric pulled up short at the Iridesium barrier, ready to impale his ax blade if it barred him. Instead the dark, rainbow-hued metal collapsed into a tiny mountain range of multicolored powder. Red dust sifted from the tip of Irissa's sword.

Kendric stepped over the glitter-dust ring to Irissa's

side. "You look as drained as your circlet. All the color's left the metal for this crumbled barrier upon the ground."

The circlet felt like iron banding Irissa's temples, no longer light and unsensed. Everything in her felt leaden; even words seemed too hard to find and too heavy to lift once located.

"I wish I could see it . . . in a mirror."

A sun-sized flash brought a self-image before her eyes. Irissa was staring into the small circular looking glass hung from Aven's waist chain. She avoided confronting the gaze of her silver eyes and looked to the circlet at her forehead.

"They're gone—the rainbow-colored highlights that made it Iridesium!"

Her fingertips whitened as they pressed the dark metal, but no lightning wisps of red or green or blue or gold flashed within the band's black circumference. "I don't know what tune my magic plays here in Rengarth, but it sings either too sharp or too flat."

"Rengarth is not kind to Reginatrixes who carry blades and babes," Aven said direly.

"The *Usurper* is not kind," Kendric corrected. "If Irissa's magic runs awry, then Geronfrey tampers with it."

"He is gone; we banished him," Sin said.

"We have seen him banished before and he has always returned; isn't that the true history of your Usurper—his return rather than his exile?"

"Yes, but this time . . ." Aven looked worried. "Irissa should not have come. She requires care the wilds of Rengarth offer no one."

"I can care for myself!" Irissa tried to ignore the circlet abrading her brow like a crown. Whatever had shorn its colors had cropped the ornament down to its most burdensome, earthy elements. Before, the metal had sat on her like silk; now it chaffed, raw as burlap, heavy as lead.

No one answered her. Her words felt hollow, as did her head. Wind knotted Irissa's hair into a brunette tangle that trapped her thoughts. Rengarth—its air and earth and the things that moved them—claimed her, as the dry lake had.

"I need to rest," she finally admitted, "to reclaim my energies."

"Rest." Kendric surveyed the endlessly heaving landscape. "Why does no one inhabit the vastness of this land? Why cluster in cities?"

"Dangers," Sin said promptly. "Like grassweavers."

"Irissa needs shelter."

Sin's arms spread wide. "This is it—the open lands of Rengarth. Either this . . . or the icy edge of those mountains."

Kendric turned to look back. All sign of Solanandor Tierze had vanished.

"Distances in Rengarth are vast," Aven said. "We did not lightly accompany you to the mountains you sought."

He stood there a moment, torn between back and forward, past and future. Anything seemed better than the present predicament.

"Let us go forward," Irissa herself suggested. "I can manage it. I fended off the grassweaver—"

"And burnished off the best of your magic in the process," Kendric said.

"Perhaps. Or perhaps my circlet has only lost some tarnish. Perhaps unvarnished Iridesium is even more effective in its more polished state."

"Perhaps," he repeated. "Ever the word of optimists and arguers."

Irissa sighed, ignoring the new pressure at her temples, and speared her sword blade into its frayed silken scabbard.

"There. No blood was shed but rust, nothing lost but some colorful dust from a metal ornament. I admit I need rest, but so do you all. Perhaps this most traitorous of worlds will lead us where we can rest in peace."

She moved into the party's forefront. Sin's and Aven's

shorter, brighter forms flowed into her wake through the swaying grasses.

Kendric lifted his arms to seek sympathy from the sun-blazed sky. The central sun and its twin reflections neither moved nor softened their glare. All Rengarth remained noncommittal—vastly, sunnily, breezily neutral.

Kendric stalked after the party, wishing he had a sword with which to strike the grass, shred the wind, and scream shining-metal fury back at the indifferent suns.

CHAPTER
25

MOONLESS NIGHT HAD SWEPT ITS EBONY CLOAK OVER Rengarth.

Wind still rippled the grasses; they hissed together like conspiring grassweavers.

Under a lone tree, Irissa and Kendric slept. Or, rather—Kendric slept and Irissa rested.

She lay with her head propped up against the tree's velvet-barked trunk and her chin on her chest, a position ideal for contemplating her swelling torso, had it been daylight. But Irissa could "see" the changes wrought in her body even in the dark. She looked beyond them to the night itself.

Aven and Sin, invisible except for the green Torloc glow Irissa's eyes had imparted to their waist chains before they had left to explore, danced firefly-shy in the distant darkness.

In the nearer dark, there was no company but Irissa's shadowed thoughts and the regular bellows of Kendric's sleeping breaths.

Irissa let her thoughts wander to the rim of mountains behind her—she had lain down facing Solanandor Tierze. Their long day's march had brought the range nearer; certain peaks wore faces like old friends now and colors other than white shaded their snowy profiles.

Aven and Sin had grown more restive as the day passed, but Kendric and Irissa were not used to traveling to the tune of others' anxieties. When sunfall had come, they'd barely claimed a distant spreading tree as shelter before night had webbed both it and them in impenetrable blackness. Despite the absence of sunlight, Rengarth retained its daytime warmth. Even now wind warm as bathwater trickled over Irissa's face as she dreamed wakefully.

Something brushed her eyelashes and she jolted away. Then a voice eddied in the silence.

"Worry makes an ungrateful bedmate," Kendric rumbled beside her. His unseen finger flicked against her eyelashes again. "I thought you might be awake."

"I was watching Aven and Sin." In the darkness, sparks of green light bobbed. "There are no stars to follow."

A rustle became a creak as Kendric shifted to look beyond the awning of leaves. "No, no stars. Rengarth is a world the night can snuff completely out. Little wonder no one can find it."

"We did."

"No, Geronfrey found *us*. I think he still has us."

"Naught has been heard of him since he destroyed my shadow self and fled the city."

"Naught was heard of him in Rule, for decades. He was still there, under Falgontooth Mountain. Waiting."

"For me?" Irissa sounded incredulous.

"For us. For an opportunity."

In the pause before her answer, Irissa imagined she heard crickets singing. "And now he has your sword, your lifeblade."

"Now he has you convinced that my longevity is measured by the length of my sword," Kendric amended. "Remember the source of that prediction—Geronfrey himself. He has reason for luring us to the Frostrim. How are we to find one lost sword among all those lofty peaks?"

"Your sword is longer than most; and it beams a hilt-light."

"What does a foot-length difference mean on such a scale as mountains make?" Kendric answered. "No more, perhaps, than the span of an additional twenty or forty or sixty years makes to a single life—"

"*Your* life," she interrupted hotly. "If Geronfrey is right and your sword carries your life span, any risk is worth recovering it."

"Not any." In the dark, his hand found hers, which clutched the Overstone egg, and shook it gently. "Irissa, leave me to my human destiny. I was born to fade in a few-score years. Prolongation holds no lure for me. I don't see how Torlocs can face their endless dawns and sunfalls as unchanged as a stone decade after decade without longing for the utter dark. . . ."

"You will *leave* me!" she mourned.

"Yes. Inevitably. Once you would have chafed under the idea that I would *not* leave you—"

"That was long ago—"

"Only two years as humans measure it, an eye blink to Torlocs."

"Not to the inner timekeeper," she argued. "How can I bring another into the world—any world—to know it will likely face your loss?"

"We face each other's loss in ordinary ways day by day. Don't begrudge me my forty or fifty—or four hundred—years. I may fall to a sword within two."

"Not if you have your own sword back!"

"That is but a *shadow* of itself! Even the original sword I left in Rule, no matter how magically forged, cannot add a single grain to the sandpile of my life span."

"Having it cannot hurt," she said stubbornly.

"No, which is why I search for it against all inclination. I would rest more easily to see the rainbow reflected in your Iridesium circlet again. I am merely separated from my sword; your circlet has been . . . altered, even while you wore it."

Irissa was aware of a dull headache tightening at her temples, of her body expanding daily to its own inner demands rather than her outer ones. She no longer saw the glitter of Sin and Aven's far-flung excursion. Even Kendric's darkside presence seemed a feeble bulwark against the night within and without, against her own uncertainty.

Then . . .

Irissa pulled herself upright, dislodging Kendric's hand, pulling away from the buttressing tree trunk.

"What is that?" she wondered intently.

"What?"

"That. Ahead in the dark. That . . . veil drifting over the night, or into the night. Has a cloud come to earth?"

Even as she spoke, Kendric saw it. The night had opened a thousand gleaming white eyes. It shimmered before them, a pale face of multitudinous orifices. It thinned and spread, beaming a soft white glow, breaking into myriad forms.

The apparition stretched heavenward, spreading wide and high simultaneously, like an instantly sprouting tree.

Ghostly stairs coiled around contorted towers. Thin window slits of night peered through the opalescent haze. It seemed that a normal night sky had turned itself inside out, that a bright white sheen of moon and stars had puddled into a mass that let only a few quill points of darkness quiver amidst the light. . . .

Kendric scrambled upright, lifting Irissa beside him. Already the darkness had softened. He could see Irissa's face and hands shining alabaster, the leaves overhead silvering into sight as if washed in a downpour of moonglow.

The great, glowing ball of lumination burned whiter until it swallowed them, forcing Irissa and Kendric to shield their eyes from its lightning brightness.

Phantom walls washed over them like waves. Closed doors of bleached wood hinged in silver hurled toward and through them. Flights of translucent stairs rippled beneath them. Silken carpets figured in endless shades of ivory slipped beneath their road-dusted boots and beyond them unsoiled.

Water splashed in ghostly fountains. Perfumes and herbs tanged the air. The clink of commerce mingled with

the chatter of spectral voices. Pale, amorphous forms
brushed by. Kendric stiffened at the expectation of collision, but nothing here touched him. He drew his ax blade
anyway, fearing a sending of Geronfrey's.

The drifting figures pooled into a crowd of glittering,
insubstantial light. White shadows stirred in its center.
Voices caressed his ears.

"Phoenix clan ax work . . . exquisite."

"Unseen for so long –"

*"Sharp along the runes' edges . . . poor forsaken forg-
ing."*

He turned, feeling spun around by the press of shapeless cocoons. He saw Irissa through a glaze of crystallized
light. His ax blade cut the luminous haze with his motions,
but the elements veiling him seemed unhurt.

They had eyes now—fugitive glimmers of color—that
winked out of their encompassing whiteness in shades of
blue and brown, yellow, green, and mauve.

"Kendric."

Irissa's voice—and her hand on his arm—pressed reality into his flesh and senses. Her solid form passed through
the clustered specters. Her silver eyes shone with a living
light not all their ethereal luminescence could rival.

"Questing spirits," she answered a question he had
asked only in his mind. "We have—or the Spectral City
has—materialized around us."

"Materialized?" Kendric pinched at a swirling cloud
but half his height. Contact eluded him, yet a sad childish
laugh pealed as a clump of fog skittered away.

"How do we leave it?" he wondered hoarsely.

Irissa shook her head, dodging a colliding form that
momentarily wreathed her in a smoky embrace, then evaporated into the ambient shimmer of the Spectral City.

Chill and heat gripped Kendric's body in turn, his own
dread and anger—or possibly the city's whimsical touch.

"Geronfrey commands it," he suggested next, when
the fog forms had cleared slightly. The city's expansion had

slowed to a marketplace scene of pallid goods flowing slowly past them.

"He is not so subtle," Irissa answered.

She lifted her arm over her eyes as a mob of marketing specters appeared ahead. Kendric stared them down, stared through them until they flowed beyond him and vanished.

"Do you feel them?" he wondered.

"Only a . . . chill tickle," Irissa answered, "as elusive as blades of grass or spider legs. Even my magic barely stirs to their passage. They are not truly present."

"Then why must we arrive among them?"

"Aven said the city came and went as it pleased. Apparently we happened to be where it pleased to appear tonight."

"Then I am pleased to go elsewhere!"

Kendric stepped face-first into a diaphanous stone wall, expecting it to flow past him like water. This one didn't. It remained rock-solid despite its transparent appearance.

He rubbed his nose and applied a few choice curses to its deceptive ways, until Irissa pulled on his sleeve. She was laughing.

"The city has expanded to its limit. Look, nothing moves anymore. I think, once fully conjured, it answers to everyday rules. To leave it, we shall have to pick our way through its streets as if it were any other place."

Kendric looked around to confirm that the scene—translucent as it was—had hardened into a semblance of reality. Pebblestone streets stood still beneath their feet. Walls no longer wavered. Ghostly citizens passed at a normal pace, carefully avoiding contact with himself and Irissa instead of flowing through them. He reluctantly returned his ax to his belt.

"From the length of time this city raced past us, we'll have a good long walk out of it," he grumbled. "One would think specters could have the courtesy to deposit themselves on unoccupied ground."

"Specters, I suspect, are blithely indifferent to whether their vicinity is occupied or not." Irissa looked wistfully toward a tethered bearing-beast—an albino mount with crystal hooves and glossy wisps of mane and tail.

Kendric was already stalking over to it, his sword-long strides making no sound on the pebblestones. He might as well have been treading snow.

He reached for the looped reins, but they eluded his hands. He patted a shining half-visible flank, feeling naught but a certain roughness in the air.

"No use," he reported on returning to Irissa. "No matter how much a living thing *looks* like itself, it's so much mist and disappointment, not unlike the worlds that await the other side of a gate. I fear that you will have to walk your way back to solid ground."

"I wasn't sleeping anyway," Irissa said cheerfully enough, falling into step beside him.

However unsettling the Spectral City's ghostliness, it followed ordinary settlement rules. Archways opened into courtyards; byways led to thoroughfares and one street led to another; intersections appeared.

At a crossroads, Irissa paused.

"Each intersection thus far has contained a fountain at its center," she noted. "It's an excellent idea for citizens who crave convenient water, but why should specters drink?"

"Good question." Kendric joined her in pausing at the structure's shimmering edge.

Scarves of iridescent water streamed from the fountain's central bowl. When Irissa put her hand to the flow, her flesh gave, but not the spectral water. Kendric glimpsed a tapestry of veins, an intricate construction of bones. He didn't know what Irissa saw, but she jerked her hand free as if burned.

"Dry." She showed him her unharmed palm. "So was the lake I fell into on my arrival."

"Then what purpose has the fountain?"

He leaned to inspect its airy shape from many angles,

then jerked away as a reflection regarded him from the bowl of ghostly water. It wasn't his own.

"What do you see?" Irissa urged.

"A stranger, but a man of flesh and blood. A creature of color in a colorless city. A prisoner of the fountain."

Irissa peered into the bowl for her own satisfaction. A middle-aged face floated on the glassy, unwet water. It was male, as Kendric had said, and the intelligent gray eyes begged for rescue.

She, too, jerked away.

"Does every crossroads fountain contain a prisoner?" Kendric asked as they resumed their march through the city.

She didn't answer, but at the next intersection approached the central fountain and leaned gingerly over the bowl. After a moment she straightened and rejoined Kendric.

"Well?"

"No, a fountain," she answered with grim humor. "And it housed a woman's face—a girl's, really, with raven eyes and hair. All the reality and color in this city seem to have congealed in the fountain mirrors."

"Then we'll never find our way out, but will endlessly tread these silent streets."

"Not possible. This cityscape moves—and without warning, too. At any moment the entire city could decamp and leave us standing where it found us."

"*If* we have not wandered too far afountain," Kendric quipped. "At least it's insubstantial enough to offer us no imminent dangers."

Like most instances of self-congratulation, this one proved prophetic in the opposite direction.

Kendric and Irissa were padding soundlessly but efficiently through the city streets, leaving the familiar behind them for the hope of progress offered by the unfamiliar, when—into this cloud of swirling, incorporeal whiteness—came a distant flare.

Not pallid white light, but a warm, fiery glow.

It advanced upon them as they neared it, a spurt of ardent flame in the Spectral City's frost-rimed heart. Wary, Irissa and Kendric slowed their steps on the silence-upholstered streets. Faint figures wove by wrapped in their air of unseen indifference.

Through them, through the advancing citizens of the Spectral City, beamed a hotter burnished light. Kendric and Irissa parted wordlessly to give it passage between them.

It bore toward them, growing larger and more vibrantly flame-colored with every moment.

Then, as good as upon them, a barrier of spectral souls melted away, leaving the flame's source exposed—Aven and Sin, their vivid coloring afire in this pallid setting, with circlets of green metal glowing around their waists.

Kendric caught each twin's forearm in a grip that was part greeting and part custody. "Flesh and blood! How did you two find your way after us?"

"After you?" Aven's voice chided, but relief underlay it. "We were exploring the dark of night when the Spectral City rolled up and engulfed us in its elusive fog."

"Whoever follows whom," Kendric said, "we are fortunate to share this exile. Four can conquer what two can only contemplate."

"What's to conquer here but delusion?" Sin wondered "You must consider the Spectral City as a . . . detour, Kendric. It will cost us time and boot leather, but it's only a matter of hours before it will fade from view here and appear elsewhere."

"I am tired," Irissa put in, "of walking without reward. Which way points to the Frostrim, so we don't lose what ground we've gained as we wend our way out of this haze?"

The foursome confronted one another, suddenly aware not only of weariness but the fact that each twosome had chosen an opposing direction.

"Perhaps a fountain-wraith will tell us," Aven finally

suggested. Here, her skin seemed less pallid than usual, and her freckles, like Sin's, shone like copper pots.

"Wraiths?" Kendric scoffed. "These faces in the fountain look more real than any citizen we've seen in these faded streets."

"Wraiths," Sin repeated firmly. "In a Spectral City, the images of the residents' past selves are wraiths to them, and that's what you see in the fountains."

"Past selves—!" Irissa was rushing to the nearest fountain, oncoming specters parting for her passage like earth cleaved by a plow. "Then these unwatery bowls must ape Geronfrey's Dark Mirror and harbor their past selves." She leaned over the bowl, her locks trailing in the ghostly iridescent water.

And then, impossibly, she paled.

"What?" Kendric loomed over her, gazing down into the bowl past the curtain of her dark hair. What he saw sobered him as well.

"Only a wraith," Aven comforted, coming to look. Then she, too, was silent.

Sin was the last to crowd around the visionary bowl. He looked but said nothing.

Irissa tilted her head to see if the image shifted, but it remained motionless on a pale surface of apparently running water. "This . . . wraith . . . we know."

"Good, then it may help us," said Sin.

"It is *not* a wraith," Kendric contradicted Irissa. "It is a . . . vision from another world. We know the possessor of this face."

"It's a pretty face," Aven put in, "but wraith-pale. This woman is dead, Kendric," she consoled him. "You can see she belongs to the Spectral City."

"But the other fountain-wraiths are semblances of the specters' past selves—and fully fleshed," Irissa argued. "This manifestation is ghost-pale. Yet I have known her in the flesh, albeit pallid flesh. . . ."

Sin squinted into the bowl over their hunched shoulders. "White as her hair and face and raiment are, her eyes

are living gold. She is at least *partly* some lost Rengarthian's living self—"

Irissa spun away from the fountain, putting her back to
it, her hands curling over its rim for support.

"You are ill," Kendric fretted, as if expecting it.

Irissa pressed her fingertips to the solid-black metal
banding her forehead. "No, confused. You know that we
know the woman in the fountain's face. . . ."

"Yes, but she is a world away and was insubstantial
even when we knew her. She was native to Rengarth. Is it
so amazing she should appear in some ghostly scrying device of a Spectral City in Rengarth? Even ghostly cities
must have anomalies. . . ."

His soothing tones did not calm Irissa. "Even," she
gritted between her teeth. "Do you not hear what you are
saying? E-ven."

He shook his head. "That was the cheapest word in my
discourse, mere filler—"

"Her name!" Irissa urged, as if afraid to articulate it
herself. "Say the name of the woman's face in the fountain,
if you remember it."

Kendric looked apologetically to Sin and Aven, who
were staring at Irissa with the first concern their young
faces had mustered.

"Of course I remember her name, Irissa, as you do.
Neva. The image in the fountain is Neva, the white woman
of Edanvant woods who was spelled by night into a wolf.
Neva."

"Even," Irissa repeated. "Say it again."

He shrugged at the twins.

"Even."

"Again!"

His face grew alarmingly sober, but he complied.
"Even."

There was a pause. Irissa cautiously opened her eyes.
All three were staring at her as if she were mad. She asked
Kendric one more time, without looking at him. "Again."

"Even!" he exploded in frustration. "Even, even,

even! What does one meaningless word have to do with floating faces from our past and Rengarth's past and Edanvant's present and, and—?"

He glanced to Irissa, who waited without looking at him, as if hoping not to see what she so clearly had seen.

"*Aven*," Kendric said slowly. "Not *even*, but Aven. Neva. And Aven."

The twins' heads cocked politely, their faces as mystified as his had been until now. Kendric stared into Aven's freckled features, trying to absorb her youth, color, and even her imperfections into the unearthly face he had grown to accept in Edanvant.

"Neva tried to save my life once, in Edanvant," he recalled numbly.

The twins listened patiently, convinced that both these strangers had surrendered their senses.

Kendric considered the possibilities, aloud. "Neva's . . . spectral self, released from its unnatural bondage in the animal form of the Rynx, came to warn me of danger. But Neva's *corporeal* self, once Neva's and Ilvanis's enchantment had been broken in Edanvant—"

"Awakened here," Irissa finished, revelation underlining her eyes' silver sheen, "as she had been when the Usurper banished her brother and herself to their joint animal form. With the Rynx dissolved, the entire spell unraveled. Time . . . collapsed. Twins spawned twins. And Sin is a young Ilvanis, as he was hundreds of years ago."

Specters eddied around the four frozen at the fountain's eerily silent edge. Aven was stepping backward, her long hair flame-bright in the Spectral City's pale atmosphere.

"No!" Aven backed into the shield of Sin's body. "We are not specters in our own world! We are living beings! We don't remember much of our pasts, but that's to be expected. We were always here in Rengarth, Sin and I."

"Yes," Irissa said. "But . . . asleep for many, many centuries. That's why you only remember your recent activities, why you 'appeared' so suddenly to overthrow the Usurper."

Kendric, who had been thinking, suddenly burst out, "Sinavli! That's the full name you called your brother once, Aven. You two are mirror images of—not each other, as ordinary twins are, but of your . . . older, spiritual selves— Ilvanis and Neva, as we knew them in Edanvant."

Sin's face flushed as furiously red as his hair. His fist whitened on his dagger-sword hilt.

"We are not images of anything but our own selves. We are no specters, living long past our times! We are realer than you and Irissa, for we spring from Rengarth. We have never dissipated our true selves in gates between worlds—"

"It is not fair that we who have never left Rengarthian soil," Aven added, "should defer our heir-right to you, a man birthed by a gate more than a mother and reared in some uncivil outland—"

"Rule was far civiler than Rengarth," Kendric answered, "and I never sought your cursed heirship, which has brought Irissa and myself naught but travail! All that has happened to us through four worlds was spawned by the fever to win Rengarth's rulership. You may have it, with my blessings—!"

A hand clumped Kendric's taut forearm. He assumed it to be Irissa's, and turned to assure her that he would be coldstone-calm in only a moment.

But the restraining form behind him looked spectral, not human—a column of icy garments and faint features. This time, though, he *felt* its touch. He glanced down to confirm this phenomenon and looked up again to the vision's face.

He gazed into the mournful golden eyes of Neva standing beside him.

CHAPTER
26

"ILVANIS," NEVA SAID, REACHING A GHOSTLY ARM TO-
ward Sin.

He backed away, stumbling soundlessly on the rough
pebblestones.

Neva's hand brushed the air as if cutting through cobwebs. "Ilvanis, but not as he is." She turned briskly to
Irissa. "Have you seen Ilvanis here?"

Irissa shook her head. "Only you—and strangers."

"Quickly, then!" Neva's albino robes fluttered as she
whirled to consult the fountain bowl. The airy strands of
unwet water circulated aimlessly as Neva's long fingers
probed it. "This may be the only channel. Ilvanis must not
be stranded alone in Edanvant, or we shall never be whole
again! Help me."

"How?" Irissa demanded, turning the concentration of
her seeress's eyes to the vapors churning in the bowl.

"Call Ilvanis. These others' very presence summoned
me. I thought Ilvanis was with me, but—"

A face formed in the fountain bowl—a man's face,
youthful but wise, his hair pale, his eyes blue.

Neva leaned toward it, but Kendric pulled her back
roughly, relieved to grip solid flesh. "Not Ilvanis, another.
Have you forgotten Geronfrey, who slew your parents?"

"Geronfrey!" Neva, Sin, and Aven hissed at once, retreating in one motion.

Kendric's big hand fanned over the bowl, blocking the
sorcerer's visage. Beneath it, the mists boiled and turned

314

brackish. He felt imps licking his palm with fiery tongues, felt the touch of supple feelers and a sudden icy blast.

Beneath his palm the frustrated magic of a thousand years snapped at the simple shield of his hand. His ring-stones gleamed in conjoined power, then Kendric's fist was squeezing shut on fog. It squeezed until it wadded mist into a cold, hard ball that warmed to his body heat and melted through his fingers.

He squeezed until a depth of genuine water lapped the bowl's sketchy edges. All the colors of his ringstones swirled in the water, fading to milk-foam white.

Eyes opened in the water's surface, blinking milky droplets . . . gray eyes polished to pewter.

"Ilvanis!" Neva clapped her pallid hands. "We have never been separated so long as this . . . please—!"

Sin approached, leaning over Kendric as the assembling face lifted from the opaque water. Milk-born, Ilvanis poured from the bowl onto the street and rose into his real form. The last droplets fell from his tattered sleeves. He stood there dry and dazed, gazing alertly at the milling specters.

Kendric flexed his hand, shaking off pearls of liquid.

"You should have let *me* banish Geronfrey," Irissa said.

Ilvanis and Neva were moving together, as birds used to roosting side by side on the same perch, their white garb feathering into each other's edges. Their eyes fastened on Aven and Sin.

"Two sides of the same coin," Kendric declared, "alienated by time and two worlds."

The four ignored him, eyeing one another with wondering scrutiny.

"We have now managed to unite the anomalies of two worlds," Kendric added sourly.

"And two times," Irissa put in.

She glanced over her shoulder at the bowl. Empty of wonder, she saw through its bottom to the fountain's next tier—a larger bowl for more water, with a rim wide enough to sit upon. The visage of Geronfrey occupied neither level.

"If Geronfrey was in the fountain," Kendric said quietly to her alone, "he still moves upon this world. He still retains . . . ambitions."

"Without an heir?" Irissa said.

"He can get another—somehow. Do you think he saw us, knows where we are?"

Irissa considered it. "Even if he does, I doubt he can reach physically into the Spectral City. And there are six of us now to repel him, all of us magicked."

"And four of us born of an ancient wrong of his," Kendric added, turning to watch Ilvanis and Neva approach their earthier Rengarthian originals.

Irissa observed the uneasy conjunction, too. Despite Neva's and Ilvanis's eerie resemblance to specters, they were fully alive—their whiteness was as much a part of their flesh and raiment as the rich red that imbued Aven and Sin.

The four gathered in cautious fascination, not quite touching, but measuring each other's matching height, exact features, and identical wariness. No one spoke, until Kendric.

"Which way?" he asked. "I suppose with two added to our party, our decisions divide even more. I say we go where the city seems to go—outward from the marketplace—to reach its boundaries."

"Then where?" Neva asked in cool, amused tones. Kendric had always felt she liked him.

"To the Paramount Athanor to find my lost sword. To the Frostrim."

They nodded, Neva and Ilvanis. Aven and Sin kept silent, quenched by their quieter counterparts.

Irissa sighed as she turned to the tunnel of pale city streets melting into misty distance. "Another long journey afoot. I am glad Felabba is not along to complain."

"Not to the rest of us anyway."

"My . . . inner voice has subsided of late," she confessed.

"Then it cannot be Felabba," Kendric rejoiced, "for I've never known that feline to sheathe her tongue unless she was eating."

They moved into the shifting veils that composed the Spectral City's streets and buildings and populace and strode into the mist.

Morning lifted the Spectral City from them as a dome is snatched from a platter. It retracted in a great, arcing silver-white flash, rather like a large bird soaring from sight overhead too quickly to be seen.

Rengarth's central sun, dogged by its duplicates, bobbled on the empty horizon at their backs. Ahead, the Frost-rim blazed with icy glory, casting red and yellow sparks at the sky.

Irissa and Kendric studied the long line of peaks from horizon to horizon. The mountains were closer, but their sides looked more sheer.

"How is she to climb?" Aven's eyes lowered to Irissa's bulky waist.

"A way will find us," Neva soothed.

Sin snorted disagreement, but Ilvanis came to consult with Kendric.

"How invigorating is the Rengarthian air. Do you smell the cinnamon-swallows on the air?"

"I smell a sneeze coming on." Kendric answered shortly, but Irissa lifted her face. Scent sprinkled into it as a flock of bird shadows swam overhead.

Kendric sneezed explosively.

"How do things go in Edanvant?" Irissa asked Ilvanis.

He scratched his narrow nose with a pallid fingernail "Jalonia mourns your departure even as she prepares for the arrival of her new offspring. The Torloc men are restless, and see the sudden vanishment of you both as some outland plot aimed at wresting Edanvant from their rule—"

"They would," Kendric put in. "High-handed, the lot of them."

"But they miss us?" Irissa wondered.

Neva nodded and joined her brother. "Medoc is quite wrathful at the notion of losing his first grandchild. Dame Agneda goes about with her nose red and sews her stitches uneven. Jalonia, your mother—"

"Yes?" Irissa encouraged, regretting how little comfort she had accepted from her mother when she was present.

"Jalonia is torn between mourning the past and welcoming the future."

"That was ever her misfortune," Kendric said. "Poor woman. Her life has been ruled by the comings and goings of everyone but herself."

"Yes," Irissa added acerbically, nodding at the Frostrim slowly warming to day-bright intensity before them. "No mountain climbing for her in midcondition."

"Stay, then," Kendric suggested. "All of you. 'Tis my quest, my cursed sword that is lost."

"'Tis ourselves that are lost, Wrathman," Neva answered. "Some ancient pattern drew Ilvanis and myself back against all possibilities—perhaps the presence of these other two of us. . . ."

Sin bristled, but Aven merely fidgeted. "I felt long ago," she told Sin, "that we were only partial, our memories were partial. Perhaps we should not even have existed, but for Geronfrey's ancient spell shattering in another world."

"I exist!" Sin ground between his teeth. "They"—he indicated Neva and Ilvanis—"are part specter already and no part of Rengarth as it is today. Let them fade and we will inherit their past. I weary of being usurped by every stranger who wanders into Rengarth."

"Perhaps you have inherited our past already," Ilvanis said with a smile. "We have no desire to perpetuate our unhappy precedence, and therefore no need to perpetuate ourselves. Take the future, young Sin; squeeze it of its juices until it is as dry as our past and our memory of it. We will defer to whatever you wish."

Sin spun away. "There is no arguing with someone so

agreeable. And do not think, Wrathman, that Aven and I will let you sneak off unescorted to toy with Rengarth's remotest secrets. You are a trespasser here, despite your muddy Marshlands delivery at the lap of Phoenicia, and so is your consort."

"Reginatrix, now consort," Irissa repeated her growing array of titles. "I haven't been called a seeress in so long that I shall soon take offense at such a common title."

"They are young," baby-faced Ilvanis put in, "and will learn manners soon enough. Perhaps in yonder mountains."

All six looked ahead to the jagged walls of ice and snow stitched to the horizon like a lace edging. The land between here and there sank and swelled with the waves of windblown grasses. Irissa groaned inwardly at the endless oceanic sameness of it all. She would welcome an encounter with the treacherous Bubblemeres, but doubted she would get it.

Kendric overlooked the flatlands to study the cliffsides walling away a vision of his sword skewering a side of ice.

What the twins thought—both sides of them, cold and hot, old and young—remained locked between their unspoken minds.

CHAPTER
27

"I'LL SCOUT THE ROUTE FIRST. WE'LL ALL CLIMB TOMORROW."

No one gainsaid Kendric. The upright ice wall before them loomed so high that the mountainside seemed an earthbound extension of the clouded heavens.

"Either of you keep a rope on those waist chains of yours?" he asked the red-haired twins, knowing the answer.

Sin and Aven shook their glorious heads and shivered. They stood in the chill shade of the Frostrim now, despite three setting suns burning at their backs.

Sunfall was yet a half hour away. Kendric squinted toward a light-washed prominence an Empress Falgon's length up the facade, then studied the pockmarks along the way for footholds.

Something soft insinuated into his palms, nosing into his slack grip as if sentient. He jerked his surprise as a black rope coiled between his fingers. It took him a moment to recognize one of Irissa's long dark hairs transformed into a cable thick enough to support even a Wrathman's weight.

She nodded when he glanced his thanks to her. He studied her face in the fading light; she looked undrained despite using her magic.

"My magical creations outwit my intention lately," Irissa warned him softly. "You may hang by a hair in more ways than one. Trust it no more than mortal rope."

He nodded and looped it over his shoulder, then leaped to the first notch in the ice. The upward path was pitted with stepping-stones thick as beard stubble. Kendric climbed easily, his bare hands ignoring the cold. But the higher he went, the slicker the mountain face became, until it seemed he was scaling some gigantic smooth-shaven cheek of ice and stone.

"I'm not attired to climb," Neva mourned at the mountain's foot, yanking her fur-hemmed white skirt in demonstration.

Perhaps Neva also mourned the loss of her nightly reversion to animal form. Irissa recalled how a white wolf had run Citydell's rooftop ridges as if they were highways. Now such transitions—and challenges—were denied her.

"I wear my handicap within," Irissa sympathized. Lowering her gaze from the black bug Kendric had become on the dazzling cliff face, she brooded on her growing limitations.

Even the passive act of watching and worrying strained her powers now. Multihued spots danced before her eyes. The Iridesium circlet that had lost it colors lost also its cohesion, seeming to disintegrate and spiral around her temples in a cloud of sparks. Her stomach lurched, and a low, inner voice hissed in protest.

"Here, sit down." Ilvanis's hand fell to her shoulder snow-soft. Irissa sank gladly onto a rock despite its roughness, and cricked her neck again to watch Kendric.

He was gone! And so quickly. .

"Where?" Irissa was standing again, heedless of the pressure tightening on her head, the queasy protest of her stomach.

The other four stared up with her.

"Where is he?" Aven repeated in frustration. "I saw him just moments ago."

"Do you see the rope?" Perhaps, Irissa speculated, Kendric dangled out of sight around a crevice edge. Perhaps he would swing into view any minute. . . .

But the mountainside remained blandly vacant. The

Rengarthian suns slipped into bloody withdrawal on the rear horizon, painting the Frostrim's cheeks rosy.

On that horizon far behind them, an amber-orange halo crept up the heavens. It merged with the still-blue sky to produce a duet of azure and peach light.

"Kendric was unwise to climb so near to sunfall," Neva suggested. "Soon we will no longer be able to see him—or his rope—should they reappear."

"*When* they reappear," Irissa insisted.

She was right. In mere moments, the five on the ground saw a snake of cable fling out from the cliff face, then curl back into it for purchase. Kendric's thicker form leaped to the cable, inching up toward the great black eye socket they had noted from afar.

"A cavern," Irissa identified it.

"'Tis like a death head's empty eyehole," Aven murmured throatily, her head thrown far back to watch.

Silent, the five watched Kendric's large figure—shrunk small by distance—scale a slender black thread toward the dread symbolism of that dark, uninviting landmark.

Then, before their unbelieving eyes, other forms began crawling forth from the black socket—thick, wriggling forms that unfolded jointed legs or pincers and began swarming over the icy cliff face.

"Maggots!" Ilvanis hailed them with loathing.

"It's only a mountain face," Irissa denied. "Our morbid imaginations make a skull of it—"

"Mountain-maggots," Ilvanis repeated, his eyes fastened on the sight high above. "They bore through the adamant mountains, living on the dead things frozen in the ice centuries ago—on debased things driven from the cities and fields . . . on alien things fallen to Rengarth from Without—or cast here by Those Without generations ago. They eat the heart of the mountains, splitting ice boulders for the remnants of ancient meat within, picking the bones of these frozen peaks from the inside out."

"And what do they do to living prey?" Sin asked.

Ilvanis shook his silver-blond head. It shone like a

torch flame in the luridly fading suns' light. "Let us hope that Kendric can climb faster than they."

Irissa shaded her eyes to view the dimming cliffside. She had felt so frustrated. No matter how her magic might scale the height, her body was ground-bound by even more than its usual limitations. The anchor of her childbearing wedded her to the earth. She even felt her center of balance weighing deeper within herself as if to drown her in her own powerlessness.

The colorless Iridesium at her temples kept her thoughts earthbound, too. Even the Overstone added its swelling lethargy to her paralysis, pulling her shoulders into a disheartened slump until her heart seemed sure to sink into the pit of her stomach.

All five caught their breaths when a slash of silver flashed lightning-swift near the skull socket—Kendric's ax unleashed to harry mountain-maggots.

The black forms swarming up a declivity after him paused as the first of their number began raining back down in neatly truncated segments.

Oncoming darkness and the sudden descent of halved maggots forced Irissa and the others to retreat from the cliff base. Above, Kendric's casual scouting expedition had become a scramble to the top of the precipice, where he would be able to turn and fight.

Wounded mountain-maggots dangled from the eye socket's dark center like tarry tears frozen before they could fall. Yet small veins of life still struggled up the cliff after an ever-smaller figure that kept the lead.

The only magic Irissa glimpsed was the icewraith's ax flashing metallic death.

"He has driven them all *down!*" Aven shouted, drawing her dagger-sword in an arc that caught the suns' reddest rays.

Lengths of black velvet darkness came eeling down the cliff, crashing to the crusted snow that ringed the mountains like a scab healing from the outside in.

The five retreated in a human wall of their own—

Irissa, Aven, and Sin battling the waist-high maggots with sword point—the unarmed Neva and Ilvanis behind them plundering their memories for antidotes to mountain-maggots.

"They've never been known to attack living prey," Neva assured the three ahead of herself and Ilvanis, who were rapt in beating off the advancing maggots. She tripped on her furred hem, her feet stuttering backward but her thoughts never losing a step. "This is most unusual."

"Excellent." Aven slashed into the dark that was conspiring to mask the creatures. "I've always desired an unusual death."

"I prefer *dealing* unusual deaths." Sin struck like a madman at the half-dozen mountain-maggots slithering over the furze toward them.

Irissa struck as blindly, her thoughts veiled by a black cloud about her temples, her mind on the mountain, her body slowed by its bulk and the relentless weight of the Overstone at her neck.

She lifted the pouch off her breastbone, hoping to relieve the ache. The Overstone elevated, then swung sideways. It remained there, suspended, twisting Irissa off-balance, upheld by thin air as if responding to a Drawstone's pull.

"But Kendric's Drawstone is aloft," she realized. "It can exercise no power here—"

"Forget Kendric until we slay these mindless beasts!" Sin urged beside her. "And step back! One slimes your boot toe—"

Shocked, Irissa retreated. The dark was taking the mountain in stages. Only the peak's topmost cliff shimmered in a last bonfire of sunfall. Darkness and mountain-maggots lapped at Irissa's feet and knees and mind and heart.

She felt Neva and Ilvanis shrinking like snow behind her, too fragile to survive elements as earthy as these voracious scavengers. Even Sin's and Aven's blades had drunk too deep of the blackness to remain visible. The

maggots, eyeless, mindless devourers of death, had somehow backed the party against another cliff of stone and
ice. . . .

The Overstone flung itself over her shoulder with almost demonic energy, twisting Irissa's neck around. Her
body followed in a clumsy turn that amazed the others. The
pouch swung too far, dashing into frozen rock, bruising
Irissa's knuckles against the ice as she clutched for it.

White wings buoyed her on either side—Ilvanis and
Neva catching her sinking form in their elegant hands. Behind her, Aven's and Sin's grunts took on a triumphal tone.
Irissa spread her hand against the stone-cold support and
felt her fingertips melt into a slick, icy surface.

Her ringstones burned into radiant color, and then
their light beams seared through the ice, spreading until a
dawning brightness lit all five faces, each with a shade of a
different, protective stone.

Falling close against her heart again, the Overstone
lightened and warmed. Irissa could feel it throbbing in response to the softening ice beneath her palm.

"Done!" Aven announced, sheathing her dagger-
sword.

Irissa had forgotten the maggots, although a glance
showed them dispatched. She only knew a pull beyond re-
fusing, and saw Ilvanis and Neva glowing as ruddy as their
younger selves in the reflected glow from within the ice
wall.

For the rock beneath the veil of ice was melting. The
ice itself was thinning to a translucent sheet.

Only a rough oval of stone remained within the hollow, glass walled chamber the five stared into—a mottled
lump of rock that cracked as they watched. Crimson veins
danced over the surface—bloody lightning scribing the
fault lines of an alien geography.

A form reddened within the rock's gray heart—a skel-
cton that crimson feathers of flame clothed with an elabo-
rate, serpentine shape

"The Salamander Tewel," Neva said, hushed.

"Then a salamander *did* name the legendary forge," Aven breathed in turn.

"Forge?" Irissa asked.

"Frostforge at the Paramount Athanor," Sin explained, "fueled by a living fire-salamander. An ancient Phoenix clan legend . . . boast, we thought. Now we see it for ourselves."

"Now we see a fire-salamander *egg*," Ilvanis amended. "Inert, unborn. It died with the Phoenix clan—centuries ago."

"Not quite." Irissa felt pressure ease at her temples, felt worry withdraw a few feet.

Between her fingertips, the Overstone sang in a hot and humid voice. It sang kinship. It sang salvation. It sang of a small red egg glimpsed by dreamlight in a cavern under Falgontooth Mountain in Rule long, long before.

It sang of it all—held in the palm of Irissa's hand.

Her free hand lifted to the crystalline wall, tears sheathing her eyes because it was too perfect to touch. Then she let her fingers stroke the fragile icy perfection of it, and part that cold veil to the past.

Fissures cracked the glassy surface, spreading a fine-lined web that flung its tendrils farther and farther until the whole, gorgeous, vein-eaten pane of ice shattered and vanished.

Irissa bowed under the jagged-edged portal that remained, and moved into the liquid heat within. She bent carefully, awkwardly to one knee, clutching the Overstone pouch to her body like a kitten. An egg of rock held the living fire of a much-folded form in its heart. It lay before her and she picked it up.

Stone flaked from the surface as she rose and walked back into the night. She saw two pale faces blazing red from the reflected light in her hand, and two crimson-topped heads turning molten, as if their hair burned, in the same painful light.

Beyond them all, the night withdrew before the sweep of the salamander egg's living light. The egg's rock skin peeled away, leaving a molten form trembling in the cup of Irissa's palm.

Nothing burned in Irissa but the cool probing light of her seeress's silver eyes. Her eyes shaped the salamander, followed the intricate curves of its tiny beak and claws, scales and tails.

It swelled—a red-hot image exploding from infancy to instant adulthood. It leaped the confines of Irissa's hand to the world beyond, branded itself on the snow, burned into the night, and took fiery, living form on a shelf of rock as on a pedestal, thrashing its twin tails into whips of flame.

"Well." Sin cleared his throat. "Now we know how the Salamander Tewel got its name. But this creature's forebears must have perished long before Phoenix clan faded, and the Phoenix have been ebbing from Rengarth for centuries. What use is it?"

Irissa, silent, approached the salamander. It had swollen to Empress Falgon size—a long, curlicued extravagance of fire, feather, and scale. Mountain-maggots would snap into cinders at its presence; ice would weep and even seeresses would keep their distance.

She paused twenty feet away, letting her eyes' subtle silver cool its fevered sides. It squatted, sides heaving, then with a great, timeworn crack began unfolding wide leathery wings that ended in a fringe of scarlet flame-feathers.

Irissa came closer, feeling no heat. It was as if she approached the figment of a dream. "The Paramount Athanor," she whispered as she neared the massive head and the spiral of scales that indicated its ear.

The head, crowned with stiffened hornfeathers, lifted. A sound like a hoarse bellows flared into the night

"Quickly!" Irissa ordered without turning to look behind her. "Mount it."

"Mount it?" Aven squeaked

"Mount it. Its flame fades and it is only briefly animated. Quickly! As my Overstone cools so does its lifeshadow."

She heard footsteps pounding the stones. They stopped as the others confronted the head-high belly of the beast.

"There are . . . outgrowths," Neva demurred.

Irissa's eyes shifted to the stiff petals of flame flaring along the salamander's undulating spine. She smiled.

"Regard the valleys between the outgrowths as saddles and the spines as convenient cantles. Mount."

She heard the others' garb rustle, the men's muttered complaints, and the women's leery sighs. But she heard them mount at last.

Only then did she grasp a sweep of horn projecting from the salamander's head like a scaled tree branch. She stepped upon another limb, arranging herself within its thorny headdress as a bird within a bramblebush, caged by its complexity.

"The Paramount Athanor," she told it again, feeling the Overstone cooling to ice and weighing to lead within her palm.

The salamander sprang straight up—a fancy of flame fanned skyward by a bellows. Its spreading wings never flapped. A bolt of pure heat shot them upward, the salamander's underbelly lighting the pale cliff face as they rose alongside it.

Maggot forms below shrank to rock size and then to clods. The sky warmed above them, as if clouds could melt at the salamander's mere proximity. A hole in the cliff sped by so fast Irissa hardly recognized it as the eye socket that had housed the maggots.

Cold air rushed past, screaming. Irissa's knuckles froze over the Overstone, but she held it fast and held her heat within herself, warming the talisman with a potent blend of magical concentration and physical will. The circlet froze to ice upon her brow, chilling her thoughts.

Images of Kendric mauled, fallen . . . Kendric a dark hole in some snowdrift, played over her mind. She saw the salamander turned to solid rock, and falling. Saw herself

. . . heavy as stone, and falling. Saw leaves of white and red with dazed human faces . . . all falling.

The peak was beneath them and the salamander was— falling.

They plummeted into snow that melted from the heat of their arrival. The salamander flamed away, writhing across the icy mountaintop. Its death throes burned strange runes into the ice as its body twisted toward a crevasse. Beneath the gaudy flames, a skeleton grayed and stiffened.

In one last burst of fire, it curled upon itself, managing only a half circle, and was still. Its form evaporated into a wall of flame that trembled at the crevasse lip, then plunged past it. Wind whistled across the deserted mountaintop, and no stars shone down.

"Welcome," said a confident baritone voice apparently unimpressed by the salamander's spectacular passing, "to world's end and my humble beginnings.

"Welcome to the Far Keep."

CHAPTER
28

IRISSA EXPECTED TO CONFRONT THE WORST—
Geronfrey himself in another of his mountain fastnesses.

She spun around, the Overstone bobbing against her
pounding heart. Instead, she saw Kendric illuminated by
the flames still spilling from the crevasse.

Snow drifted over an escarpment of black rock, scribing elusive sentences on the ground between them as they
hurled together.

They met like clashing elements, she still unnaturally
warmed by contact with the salamander, he all too chilled
from embracing the icy mountainside.

"You are unhurt?" she wanted to assure herself.

"And you—also? Where did you find that . . . creature?"

"Within an icy chamber, waiting for a brief moment of
freedom. Ilvanis says it's a fire-salamander. That they—"

"They gave the Phoenix clan its name. I know."

"How?" Irissa demanded, disappointed that her news
was anticipated.

"The Phoenix coat of arms." Kendric led her to a sul-
len rock face and brushed off a skin of crusted snow.

Irissa instantly saw the design of three intersecting
lines already half revealed. A second brush of Kendric's
palm revealed them to be the blades of six crossed swords
with rune-inscribed hilts.

Wavy flame lines radiated from the weapons, as if they
were fresh-forged. And caught in the cradle that the

crossed swords made was a fabulous animal—a winged serpent with a bird's head rising from the flame and swords.

"In Rule," Irissa noted, "the Far Keep was an irony of your invention. Now . . . here, it has become word made fact. How do you know this is really the place?"

"I know." Kendric moved along the rock face, patting it as he would something living. "This is the tower of a keep excavated deep into the mountain. Rock and snow have accumulated over centuries, burying the keep to the tower top. The swords' device is scribed into all six tower walls. There are six ice-shuttered windows I can't see into—"

Behind them, Ilvanis stepped away to study the windswept pinnacle. "Odd for an icy mountaintop . . . it is warm here."

"Warm?" Sin was indignant. "I find it cold."

"And I also," Aven added.

"Warm," Neva disagreed coolly, fanning her face with a limp hand.

"I find it a bit of both," Irissa said. "Perhaps that's because we rode the salamander—took a thing of fire into a place of ice and snow."

"You all are right," Kendric intervened. "Especially Irissa. Look." He led them around the rough tower to an open space lit by a lurid subterranean flicker.

"A well!"

Kendric laughed at Irissa's astonishment. Used to being the one always astonished, he relished the role of unveiler of mysteries that were not really so mysterious.

"Not quite a well." He approached the circle of ice-mortared stones from which light flickered white and red. A cloud of vapor haloed the light, reminding Irissa that their breaths should be puffing frosty atop the mountain peak, but weren't.

Kendric lowered a bucket over the well's lip and dredged it up moments later. It, too, spat clouds of icy breath. "Water for your bath," Kendric offered.

Irissa shivered and passed her hand through the vapor. "It *is* warm—hot!"

"And here is cold!" Ilvanis, at another well, lifted a steaming bucket and poured its contents to the snow. Before the liquid stream touched earth, an ice dagger formed.

Kendric upended his own bucket. Snow hissed and vanished at his feet; even rock melted as water droplets danced off the stony surface.

"Frostforge!" Irissa repeated a word that had been meaningless when it was first uttered. "Ice and fire forge a bizarre alliance here—that's why the Phoenix clan settled this uninviting spot. Kendric, your Rengarthian ancestors were . . . smiths, just like Halvag!"

Kendric grinned wry agreement. "Perhaps Phoenicia left me in better hands than she knew when she came to the Marshlands." He dusted his hands together, ridding himself of heat and cold and past in one gesture.

"Phoenix clan made the swords, the Six Swords," Neva said suddenly. Her delicate fingers were tracing the inscripted patterns on one tower wall. "Forged of ice and fire, the swords could have vanquished the Usurper, but they vanished, all at once. So did the Phoenix clan and their secrets, one by one."

"Rule!" Irissa knew a moment of blinding insight. "Rule was a depository of the Six Swords, centuries before it became home to you, Kendric! Geronfrey spirited them there in the first battle for Rulership of Rengarth. The Rulians found and used them as hereditary weapons, just as the Inlanders found Delevant's lost gemstones.

"Then Phoenicia found the same gate to Rule that Geronfrey had used to banish the swords and convey himself back and forth—that's how you came to Rule, against all chance! Your Phoenix clan heritage made you the natural bearer of the Marshlands sword. Nothing has been accidental, but stems from events that occurred here centuries ago."

"Nothing is accidental," Neva murmured sadly. "Ilvanis and I fell early to Geronfrey. Now we see our sun-

dered selves before us in the latter-day form of Aven and
Sin. All things, begun, come to the same end. As Phoenix
clan began and ended here, so will we all."

"Neva is right." Kendric studied the flame-rinsed night
plateau. "I have been brought to the place where most of
my kind perished centuries before I was born. There can be
but one end to such a rejoining. I only wish for a sword to
hold in my hand."

"*I* did not begin here, nor will I end here!" Irissa
spoke with grim certainty, her face—hollowed of late,
older—pale as Neva's. "I spoil the balance between past
and future. I provide the messy, uncertain present that
both must pass through before they can claim to be what
was and what will be."

"*Nicely put,*" a familiar voice insinuated into Irissa's
ears. "*I couldn't have phrased it better myself.*"

Disconcerted, she paused as Kendric came to put his
hands upon her shoulders.

"Irissa, this quest is not yours, nor should the price of
it be. You carry your future with you, as I have always
carried my past and not known it. If the salamander had
not perished, I would tell you to mount it again and flee
this blasted peak."

Flickering light from the crevasse and the wells momentarily painted Kendric's features as ruddy as Sin's and
Aven's. His aquiline nose and eye sockets cast blood-dark
shadows on his familiar face.

Irissa, desperate, shook off his hands. "The salamander *has* failed us. And you are right about one thing.
Aven and Sin, Ilvanis and Neva may move toward a fate
that was long ago written on the leaves of their book of
survival.

"But you were of Rule before you were of Rengarth,
Kendric, and of Rengarth before you were of Rule. You
are halved and doubled—in your line, your fate, your
magic. You will not easily fall to the fate of either world,
and I won't accept that. Besides," she added, her manner

cooling to black humor, "you have an imperative reason to survive."

"The babe?" he asked seriously.

"The mountain," she answered. Her silver eyes glittered ferociously. "The fire-salamander has melted, as you point out, and I don't intend to climb down alone. Not in my condition."

Kendric blinked. Talk of fates and fatality seemed suddenly presumptuous and premature. He was, after all, a warrior without a sword, stranded on a mountaintop with a woman with child and four shades of the same two persons who ought to have died long before. It was a situation ridiculous enough to make one believe in the sheer, zestful unpredictability of survival.

"Very well." Kendric clapped Irissa's shoulders with more force than he realized. "First, we find my sword, which apparently has found its way home. Then we find a way down from this summit. At least the air is endurable."

"Too hot," complained Ilvanis.

"Cold," snapped Aven.

Kendric shook his head and bent to confide in Irissa. "You are right. These four half-persons share a halfhearted view of things. They may evaporate into the Spectral City, for all I know. It is up to us alone to muster the wit and will to survive this forsaken keep of my ancestors."

"What does your wit tell you first?"

"Yours offers no . . . guidance?"

"Find the sword, silly children!" the dry voice ordered Irissa in hissing confidence. Irissa put a hand to her midriff, alarmed to find it had swelled even more during recent days.

"Let us explore," Irissa suggested, tossing off the unseen advisor and her condition at the same time. She forced herself to scrabble up the snowy incline to the keep tower despite a fatigue that abetted her recent awkwardness.

She first approached the ice windows, suspicious that where there were openings, there could be gates.

Her palm, pressing the clouded glass, felt no chill. Nor

did the windows yield anything to her penetrating eyes. Irissa let her gaze rake the ice until it wept water. Tears ran down the wavy opaqueness but washed away none of the obscuring haze. Irissa exposed nothing more than the impotence of her powers.

"Here!" suggested Aven, who had scampered like a rockram over the uneven ground to the crevasse.

In the lurid light still thrown from it, the others came to confront a rough staircase of stone. Neva drew her furtipped hem back from the edge.

"Too warm," she demurred.

"Nonsense!" Aven tossed her scarlet hair. "A draft blasts upward like some last cold dying breath from the fire-salamander. We shall freeze if we descend."

They could have stood there debating the climate forever, but Kendric inadvertently intervened.

"My sword!"

Irissa looked beyond the veils of steam edging the crevasse to the fringes of reflected light cast on the nearby snow.

There, in a block broken from the mountain's creeping snowcap, something straight and dark transfixed the ice, left like a needle jabbed into a temporarily abandoned tapestry.

"The fire-salamander could have breathed the ice away, if we still had it," Sin lamented.

"A bearing-beast hoof could have *kicked* the sword tree, but I have not had such since Rule," Kendric answered, "and both creatures are equally lost to us. I will have to free it myself."

Seeing the sword again—against all expectations—flooded Kendric with a foreign surge of optimism. He mounted the incline, oblivious to the cold or heat washing him in alternating waves.

Hip-high, the block was formed of crystalline ice—Kendric could see every nick upon the impaled blade's edge as if he inspected it through Chaundre's Inlands viewing apparatus. Even the frozen ice bubbles made perfect circles and shone coldstone-brilliant, like newborn tears not allowed to pool into a pendant shape.

"'Twould be a pity to mar the block," Kendric muttered, crouching to view the blade from every icy side.

"Mar the block," Irissa advised practically from the sidelines.

Kendric glanced down to her and smiled his confidence. "You sound suspiciously like one I knew from another world—a crochety, wearisome creature. . . ."

"Weary I am," she admitted. "Get on with it, please!"

He knew Irissa feared the sword was spelled beyond retrieval; her condition seemed to have drained her resilience. Even though he was possessed of an almost alien certainty, Kendric dreaded the moment of contact, yet stretched his long fingers until they entwined the protruding hilt.

The leather wrapping flaked apart in his palms. His fingers flared open as light beamed hot from the newly naked hilt, casting the cryptic shadow of inscribed runes onto the pale parchment of his palms.

"So long I have evaded reading your meaning," he murmured at his shadow-tattooed hands. Then he re-tightened his grasp and felt flesh weld itself to metal. The union was so mentally and magically powerful that he doubted that he could ever loose hands from hilt unless he loosed sword from ice first.

In that moment, he felt the molten metal of the sword's making flowing through his veins, a fiery lifeline forging blood to liquid steel. The sword *had* become the shadow of his being—bereft of it, he would wither, as Geronfrey had promised.

Now, caught fast in alien ice, it wedded itself to his hands again. It hung suspended in the moment most critical to a sword and its wielder—the split second after acting as One to pierce the eternal Other.

Kendric smelled the keen, swift scent of death more strongly than he ever had before . . . his own death, leaking to him from a fissure in time—a prophecy or . . . mere ghost of what already was? Life welled into his senses, too, coldstone-clear and rising, bubbling up to drown him in a surfeit of self.

His fists tightened until his skin pinched, and he pulled. Nothing would be swayed, neither life nor death. The sword was impaled somewhere between the two—as he was, without it.

His ringstones brightened to call upon talismanic magic, but his sweat-slick fingers washed one another, smearing the ring's surface, clouding the stones' power.

Only his formidable physical strength still battled to free the sword. Sweat bloomed at every pore and hardened to a hail of coldstones that shattered on the icy block's implacable surface.

Everything around him darkened—bloodstones seemed to rain past him. His white knuckles flowered atop a crimson field of fingers pressured into unrecognizable shapes.

And nothing moved but the fringes of his life bleeding into the sword and then into the ice.

"Drawstone!" someone was shouting from far away, or from deep within himself. Drawstone, he thought, but I carry Chaundre's Shunstone. It is Irissa who bears the Drawstone.

Drawstone. Yes, that could work. He felt a vein tighten in his temple as if to clamp shut on his very thought. Drawstone. He pictured it, unembellished pebble that it was, and polished the plain, hard memory.

Within his hot, abraded palms, the runes began to burn their shapes into his flesh. The pain was unimaginable, traceries of fire and blood sharpening agony to a fine point. Never had he so wished to release a thing; never had it so seized him.

And then, so slowly he wondered if he were being drawn down to impalement in the ice itself, he felt the hilt slip in his grasp. He felt his weight lurch back and the sword inch outward with him.

By such inching battle, the sword allowed itself to be

prized out. Kendric didn't know what he had achieved until its angled point chipped the ice as it suddenly sprang free.

The blade, released to the full power of Kendric's pull, rebounded from the block's side, swiped at Kendric's thigh, and finally trembled to a stop, its point delicately balanced atop a melting lump of scarlet-hued ice.

Kendric uncurled his hands one at a time so as not to lose grip on the hilt. He could not feel his hands. His arms trembled and his heart—his heart pounded like a smith's hammer. Darkness crouched at the edges of his vision.

He lurched down the incline, the sword in hand, his other hand numbly adjusting his baldric to position the sword sheath across his back again.

"Well done."

Kendric felt that the voice came from a distant star. But Neva's golden eyes shone sun-bright with congratulation. Aven and Sin looked pale, even their hair faded to orange, and could say nothing. Ilvanis smiled encouragingly.

Kendric donned his sword and stopped before Irissa.

"Your Drawstone?" he asked, his voice hoarse.

She didn't need more. "A little, at the very end. Mostly it was the draw of yourself. I have never seen you vanquish a more powerful foe."

He frowned. "I felt . . . I fought a shadow self."

No one answered him.

He looked back to the incline. Rivulets of melted ice and blood mingled and trickled into the fiery crevasse.

CHAPTER
29

AN ICY. WALL SLICKENED BY THE CEASELESS BEAT OF fire was the party's only guide as they followed the stairs down into the mountain keep.

Water pooled in the steps' sunken centers, threatening to plummet all six down an endless cascade of ice into the beckoning inferno below.

"Why?" Sin asked abruptly. He and Aven were shivering, their teeth chattering so hard that only a word at a time could escape.

"Why not?" Kendric, in the lead, his sword cocked across his back, had donned new confidence.

Ilvanis and Neva remained silent, their pale forms drooping as if the distant flames sent out unseen feelers to touch them. Sweat flowed as elegantly as beeswax down their tapor white faces and necks.

Irissa, at the rear in hopes that any tumble would at least provide the cushioning of others' bodies if she stumbled, lifted her hair off her neck. Like Kendric, she ran hot and cold· her hands had numbed from contact with the icy wall, yet she felt the same heat Ilvanis and Neva did.

Kendric paused to confront Sin and his question. The Wrathman's face had flushed to an apple's sheen, but it was hard to tell if his high color marked cold or heat.

"Nothing has been accidental," Kendric said. "If I am brought to my forebears' seat, there is more than a sword to wrest from it. Irissa . . . you should have stayed atop."

She recognized the belated regret of one driven, who

does not yet know it. Irissa shook her head in silent demur, heat-curled tendrils tickling her cheeks. The party members all looked washed out and worn out—only Kendric was blind enough, or stubborn enough, not to see it.

"It is your quest and my turn to accompany you," she answered at last.

Between they who had traveled together so long, four heads nodded mutely—two silver-haired and two crimson.

"Besides," Irissa added, "nothing is accidental, as you say. We remain because we are all drawn here for some reason. You at least have a reclaimed sword to show for it."

He nodded. "You sense it, too."

"What?" Neva asked dully.

Kendric shrugged. "It is unspeakable, whatever it is."

"Horrible?" Sin demanded.

"Not so much horrible as . . . inevitable. Irissa?"

She took pity on Kendric's contorted features. Confronting—or explaining—intangible things pained him more than any physical torment. It was enough that he knew, as she did, by some inescapable instinct half magic and half terror, that they were treading toward the heart of a master-gate.

Somehow time and place froze and flamed together in bizarre counterpoint, becoming more adamant and utterly fluid at the same, contradictory time.

"Perhaps our very presence is the key turning an ancient lock," Irissa explained.

"Then we can withdraw!" It was Sin, sounding hysterical. Only Kendric before him and the three others behind pinning him to the staircase kept him from bolting.

Irissa suddenly knew why Kendric had suggested she bring up the party's rear—not a sop to her lagging strength, as she had resentfully assumed, but a strategic deployment of an ally at the rear. His faith in her restored some of her own.

"No." Irissa dropped her hand from the icy wall. She could no longer see her feet and should have teetered, standing alone on this long, jagged path of icy teeth leading to fiery jaws.

Instead some inner vision compensated for her handicaps. Her feet sensed the stair lip through her boot soles. Her mind numbered each remaining riser and positioned each member of their party on them.

"No," she repeated, her voice as authoritative as when she spoke as a seeress. "You four serve as . . . elements of Rengarth somehow —spirit, body, past, present. We need you now. Rengarth needs you more than ever."

"Here?" Sin demanded. "How?"

Irissa paused a long moment. The Iridesium band was warming her temples. It felt leather-supple yet somehow heavier, too, like the Overstone.

Her mind, coldstone-clear, sliced through heat and mist and confusion. She saw the stairs again, and themselves arranged upon it.

"Help Neva," Irissa expressionlessly told Sin. "Her foot is about to slip."

Even then Neva's erect figure was collapsing into a froth of cloth and fur. Neva slipped past Aven, clutching for Sin's extended arms. He managed to brace himself on the treacherous surface to stop her fall.

Kendric watched the incident as impassively as Irissa did, their eyes meeting briefly over the intervening heads.

"Any more questions?" Kendric said.

"I was overheated," Neva apologized, her golden eyes fevered to a shade of orange.

Irissa wondered if she looked as worn and haunted as the others, but then, it was not her land— Rengarth. It was not her battle. She was mere stopgap.

"I'll h-help you," Sin was chattering between his teeth, putting his arm around Neva to escort her down the stairs.

Despite her weakness, Neva straightened to refuse his aid. Sin suddenly grinned until his freckles vanished into the creases of his face.

"Please d-don't refuse. I f-find myself less c-c-cold."

"R-r-really?" Aven turned to regard Ilvanis on the step above her.

Her look made all of them regard the white-garbed man more closely. His figure showed the same diminished strength as Neva's—a melting from its former physical limits, as if something had softened inside him.

"Come walk w-with me," Aven suggested, extending a cold-palsied hand. "Perhaps we can balance our weaknesses."

Kendric nodded at Irissa and turned to descend the stairs. The foursome followed two by two, barely fitting abreast on the narrow treads. Irissa followed in their footsteps, almost slipping on the deeply hollowed steps where Ilvanis and Neva had paused—the heat of their presence had melted the ice down to the next lower riser.

No one looked back to see if Irissa needed assistance. She appreciated that.

In exactly sixteen more steps, Irissa touched solid ground—or, rather, solid ice-paved floor. The group had finally drawn even with the flames—a curving sheet of fire to their left that reflected from an opposite curving wall of mirror-bright ice.

Cold and heat bounced back and forth between the two opposing elements, leaving the party in between panting and breathless in debilitating succession.

In the middle ground before them, where the area flared widest, stood the ringed stones of another well.

"You said this was a tower top," Sin complained to Kendric. "Who would put a well atop a tower?"

"Obviously the Phoenix clan," Kendric returned. "I begin to like them. But"—he peered into the well and reared back as quickly—"it's not a well."

"What is it, then?" Ilvanis revived enough to walk over and inspect it.

A wave of crimson fire belched from the circled stones.

Neva and Ilvanis backed away from the suffocating heat with Kendric, but Aven and Sin leaned into it. Their eyes closed in relief.

"Wonderful. A fire. A furnace." They fanned their hands over the flames, basked in their ruddy illumination, seemed to swell with vigor.

The flames fell back, deep into the well's narrow throat.

A moment later, a white cloud of smoke billowed from the well's mouth, expanding until a forest of ice daggers sprouted in the air.

Sin and Aven recoiled as if stabbed. They backed away, doubled over, coughing and shivering.

Kendric retreated as well, but only to draw his sword. With one sweeping stroke, he scythed the unnatural upgrowth of ice daggers, reducing it to stubble. Cold vapors coughed into the air like steam, bringing dry stabbing pains to all but Ilvanis and Neva. These two edged nearer to the same site that had repelled them but moments before.

Kendric lifted his blade. A crystalline swath of snowflakes inscribed the surface from hilt to tip.

"New runes," he laughed, "for an old blade. What do you suppose is written in this place's icy-hot heart?"

Irissa pushed past the huddled Sin and Aven, Neva and Ilvanis parting for her at the well's edge.

"It welcomes back an old friend," she said, "this mouth that blows both hot and cold. And it is not a well. It is Frostforge."

"A forge?" Kendric rested the iced-over blade on the forge lip just as a fresh wave of fire blanched it steel-blue again. The heat seared away both frost and water, leaving the blade dry and bright.

"This is the Salamander Tewel of the Paramount Athanor that Ludborg mentioned," Irissa reminded him, "for what is a tewel but a vessel, and an athanor but a furnace? I told you the Phoenix folk were smiths."

"Smiths." Kendric looked into the bottomless well of light and dark that played sheen and shadow against the sword blade. "Frostforge. Halvag never dreamed of such a forge in Rule."

"*Of course not,*" the grating voice inside Irissa objected. *"Frostforge shapes spirit, not steel."* The tone was no longer carping, but triumphant. *"Watch your sword, Wrathman—!"*

Irissa could have sworn Kendric heard that last admonition, for his eyes stared obediently at the blade he held over the forge-mouth.

Heat and cold ebbed and flowed in visible alternation. Each marked the steel—first icy frost, then vermilion fire. Each time the metal glowed redder and froze whiter.

Kendric, smith's son that he was in more worlds than one, stood fascinated by the accelerating waves of fire and ice. Then his eyes narrowed in disbelief.

"It's growing—"

"The sword?"

Kendric didn't even glance at Sin. "Not the sword. The steel. It's growing . . . *invisible*! It's fading."

Irissa stepped closer despite a wave of new fire. Frost had silvered—and fire had heated to white-hot—the blade in such intensity of turn that it was indeed doing as Kendric said—becoming invisible.

"Frostforge shapes spirit, not substance," she murmured. A satisfied purr rumbled through her mind. "You carry a mind-made sword," she told Kendric. "It was never material except in your memory and your magic. The forge is stripping it to its soul."

Appalled, Kendric tried to unclench his hands, but the runes emblazoned onto his palms seemed to wed him to it.

"I don't need an invisible sword!" he objected. "I don't require that kind of advantage. Only cowards cringe behind unseen weapons. How am I to use a thing that belies its very purpose?"

Irissa helplessly spread her hands. Even as she watched, the ghostly blade vanished in a puff of frost-smoke. When the air cleared, the fire surged up and vanished into nothing. Kendric's hands clenched . . . on nothing. The onlookers saw . . . nothing.

"I can't let go!" He appealed to Irissa. "I feel it still,

feel even the hot and cold waxing and waning in the hilt. What can I do?"

"Hold it. Keep holding it. If Frostforge stripped its substance, perhaps . . . the same process will reshape it again. Frostforge is a gate of making, not unmaking."

"Gate?" Kendric sounded even more appalled, but he eyed the point where his sword had been as if determined to see something.

"I'm not certain that it is a gate; if so, certainly it is too fatal for mortal or even Torloc. Perhaps if you envisioned your sword—"

"Wish for it again? I will not be chained to an unseen thing the rest of my life. Very well, I will see what I wish to see, I will make and remake this sword of my mind and memory and magic here at the forge of my ancestors and woe to anyone—or anything—that opposes me."

Kendric braced his legs and held his muscle-ridged arms straight before him. He seemed to be wrestling the taut line of a maddened bearing-beast, but there was no beast or line.

Irissa stepped back, already feeling an intensification in the resumed play of both fire and ice across Frostforge's mysterious surface.

Kendric sensed the same fury. His face reflected the onslaught of cold and heat in brutal turn. But he had committed himself physically to the forge and could no more turn from this encounter than a grain of sand can rebuff the sea.

Irissa retreated again as a heat blast singed her eyelashes. Her hand cradled the Overstone, but she knew no talisman could alter these events—not hers, not Kendric's, not anyone's.

This was elemental magic now—flesh battling spirit; life asserting itself against death. Phoenix clan had harnessed these powerful twins of force, had drawn them from deep within the mountain and set them against each other in eternal tandem at the Paramount Athanor.

With each blast of heat or cold now came a low moan—Aven's and Sin's, or Ilvanis's and Neva's. Irissa spared them a glance. The four were as forge-caught as Kendric, fading with frost or fire as each's nature dictated.

They clung to their opposites as if to stifle the agony— pale Neva melting into fiery Sin; blanched Ilvanis fading into Aven's bloodred aura.

Torn, Irissa let her attention dither between the ghastly twosomes and Kendric still alone at the heart of Frostforge.

He seemed cast of bronze, yet Irissa recognized that he resisted each elemental wave with an inner tempering. When the heat rose, something within him froze, becoming almost tangible. As the flames sank, she saw the heat seep into his form, bracing him for the onslaught of cold incarnate.

Although cheered by Kendric's apparent self-defense, she herself felt the heat and cold dashing her senses as slaps from different directions buffeting her until her head swam.

She glimpsed the entwined twosomes almost appearing to contend against each other before the nearing walls of fire and ice. She saw a flame-throated salamander curl into the air and pounce, twining Ilvanis and Aven, capturing Neva and Sin.

Then a salamander born of arctic breath shaped itself into a cutting blade of ice and sliced through the firedrake and its prey. Irissa viewed all that and saw one last, unavoidable thing.

The walls of fire and ice surrounding the forge were panting inward, like a bellows breathing deeper and deeper until both sides should meet in the middle—!

"Kendric!" She could hardly see; she wondered if he could still hear. Irissa stumbled toward Frostforge despite an unbearable heat—or cold. They were one now, fire and ice, and stung with the same venom.

On her left, heat harried her. On her right, ice made a frigid mirror in which she'd be forever frozen. Irissa battled on numb feet toward Kendric. His whole figure swelled and shrank in turn. Was it only an illusion she viewed through a veil of pulsating heat—or a fog of wavery ice?

"Kendric!" Her voice rang fire-dry and ice-cold.

Then she was there, beside the forge, in a cacophony of howling heat and cracking ice. Kendric wavered in her sight, but she saw—for a moment—that his blade was growing visible again.

"Yes!" Irissa shouted.

He glanced up, his face so grim it seemed made of leather rather than flesh. Then his eyes dropped to the spectral blade again.

Moment by moment the sword asserted its dawning presence. By turns of scarlet heat and silver-blue cold, the metal evolved through airy nonexistence into bright liquid and ultimately solid, blue-colored steel.

Irissa looked up at the moment the sword surfaced. Walls of fire and ice bracketed herself and Kendric as hands might clap shut on some trapped insect.

"They're gone! All of them." She spoke to herself but someone other answered.

"Were you not warned, seeress? Frostforge shapes spirit."

"And sometimes substance," Irissa murmured.

"What?" Kendric croaked. He looked up at last, released from his task, his brow grimier than any Rulian smith's.

"They go."

Irissa gestured at the fading walls. Had she only imagined them?

She and Kendric stood in a dusky rock-walled tower grimed with lichen and cobwebs. His sword lay atop a table supported by a rough, rock-hewn base.

Fire and ice faded to tapestries of faint red and pale white on opposite walls. Even the tapestries shrunk to window slits. The walls fractured into the six sides of a tower.

"Ilvanis, Neva? Sin, Aven?" she wondered.

"They were always little more than specters." Kendric sounded as if a saw blade had wedged in his throat.

"Aven and Sin weren't specters!" Irissa moved to the walls, feeling them for heat, cold, life, or death.

"Substance made from specters," he said, following her.

She turned against the wall, pressing her spine into it. Her back ached as if it had been severed.

"They perished here!"

"So did the long-dead salamander."

"What do you mean?"

Kendric looked up at the dim roof narrowing to a high dingy point, down to the bare stone floor.

"They were remnants of a Rengarth that's gone—or should be—as the salamander was."

"And we?"

He gently urged her from the wall. Her senses finally measured its substance—chill and dank . . . the stones sweated a bit. It was only a wall carved from a mountainside and long abandoned.

He led her to the table—gate?—where the sword lay in its ordinary state.

"You were right," he said. "I had to bring the forces around again, restore nature to itself. If the sword had been . . . swallowed, we would have been also—and perhaps all Rengarth."

His calm after such a storm undid her.

"I don't care about all Rengarth! What of us?" She asked more than she said.

Kendric looked carefully into her eyes, more carefully than he had since they had long ago ceased to be lethal to him.

"We are remnants—not of Rengarth, but of ourselves. Mind, memory, magic—that is all the substance we have. Frostforge shapes spirit, and spirit reshapes substance. We, like the sword, have survived one more forging."

CHAPTER
30

WIND HOWLED DOWN THE STAIRWAY, DRYING THE POOLS of water from the risers.

Ice and fire had frozen and burned away, along with all trace of Neva and Ilvanis and their fiery counterparts, Aven and Sin.

Only stone and wind remained—and darkness.

"How will we descend the mountain?" Irissa wondered as she paused at the first step.

Kendric only shrugged his uncertainty and gestured her up the dim stairs. She led and he followed. Now that the ice had melted, the rocky stairs were far steeper. Irissa projected all her energy into each step upward, paused, and pushed on again.

The way was interminable. She heard Kendric's heavier footsteps thudding behind her and wished for the echo of four other pairs. Even accepting the four as separated personas of the same two persons who had long outlived their life spans, even believing that they had been destined to return to Frostforge and dissipate into the disembodied forms they always were . . . Irissa missed them keenly.

Despite the recovery of Kendric's sword and his re forging it to invisibility and back, she saw little gain from their expedition—except for heartache and weariness.

She mounted the last step, tensing for the icy mountain wind and the peculiarly black Rengarthian night. She moved into darkness, but not wind . . . into utter stillness.

"Don't worry." Behind her, Kendric stepped to level ground. "I've reclaimed the sword. It won't leave us unenlightened for long, unless I misjudge its nature."

He had hardly finished speaking before a blinding radiance spilled over their shoulders. The hilt, freed of its leather bindings, spread its light as never before—in an intense, hard-edged arc that cast sharp shadows. Softer shadows limned the shape of cryptic runes upon the unexpected scene before them.

They had returned—not to an open-air mountain peak, but to another tower chamber.

"Six walls, six windows," Kendric recounted as he made a quick inspection and returned to Irissa. He stopped to scratch his chin, on which a dawning beard smudged charcoal-dark. "This chamber was not here before."

"Frostforge," Irissa speculated. "Just as it made your blade invisible and restored it, so it recalled this Phoenix keep to its original form—before ruin ground it into the bones of the mountain."

Kendric approached a blind-white window and drew his fingertips over the sill. "Frostforge restored it without dust or cobwebs, restored it empty and lifeless, as merely the shell of what must have thrived here once."

Irissa pressed her hand against the icy, opaque window. Exterior light pressed back, softening the surface to a candle-warm glow.

"Our only exits are sealed," she noted, "from within and from without."

"Not for long." Kendric unsheathed the longsword. A prod with the hilt accomplished no more than a dull thud upon the window glazing.

Kendric finally drew back and struck the blade two-handed through the substance. It shattered—slowly and soundlessly—as if responding to the sword's touch rather than its force.

Blackness swirled outside the window—and eddies of shrieking wind. The sword had only slit the opaque surface.

Irissa leaned near to peer through the long, narrow rent, then drew back rapidly.

"A way to the mountaintop?" Kendric wondered.

"A way to the Swallowing Cavern," she answered flatly. "Sheer nothing lurks beyond the window—endless, tireless, pitiless nothing."

Irissa shivered, remembering how Aven and Sin had done the same before they vanished, then shuddered even harder. Perhaps the four had fallen into this roiling outside emptiness, not the benign spectral ether they hoped.

Kendric's arm on her shoulders warmed her chilled body. He led her to a low chest at the chamber's center.

"Sit. You are tired and have reason to be," he said. "I will find a speedy route back to Solanandor Tierze if I have to weave the hairs of my head into a magical bearing-beast to fly us there."

She would have laughed at his sincere exaggeration, but noticed just then a new luminescence on the opposite window. Its blank surface was shimmering with a myriad golden motes.

Kendric saw it, too, and rushed it, hoping for an exit.

"Not there, here," a voice behind them said.

They spun together to find that the opposite window had turned into a golden web whose dust was even now drifting floorward. A scarlet-gloved hand was pushing the disintegrating strands aside. The figure that made one long step down into the room was calm, erect, and elegantly smug.

"My thanks for summoning elder Ashasendra, the lost Phoenix city-keep of Rengarth. I, too, wish to leave this frigid place, but would have had to scribe Ashasendra in the ice to evoke it. This way shall be warmer."

Geronfrey surveyed the barren chamber, noted the wounded window with a raised eyebrow, and finally addressed Irissa.

"Your Iridesium has darkened as you have paled,

seeress, testimony to the draining magic of generation, I suppose. You will rise, please."

Irissa, who had intended neither to sit nor keep her back to the presence of Geronfrey, stirred. But Kendric moved first.

"We will stay as we are," he said sternly. "You intrude into our world now. This . . . Ashasendra . . . was the fount of Phoenix clan, as I am its final tributary."

Geronfrey laughed, an outburst that echoed against the windows in turn and seemed to slip through the slitted pane into the louder cacophony outside the tower.

"You thought yourself rid of me?" he demanded.

"You lost your claim to mortality—your only child— by your own ill-meaning hand," Kendric said. "Even if your power persists, what meaning can it hold?"

"Where there is life, there is . . . possibility," Geronfrey said, slowly circling Irissa as she sat on the central chest.

She shifted under the pincers of his azure eyes. His unholy calm disturbed her more. "He is cat and we are mouse, Kendric. Don't give him the satisfaction of our chitter."

"Oh, chitter, seeress. Chitter. Your chitter is right in this: it is not your tower, Wrathman. You may visit, but it is mine and—almost—always has been!"

"Yours?"

"Why do you think I kept an undermountain tower in Rule? It reminded me of . . . home. Ashasendra has been mine for generations, since Phoenix clan forsook it. This . . . chamber is my founding crucible. The well the seeress sits upon leads to the Swallowing Cavern that underlies many worlds and all my magic. No, don't move now, seeress. It is so appropriate that you perch upon the very mouth to my Dark Mirror—"

Irissa had leaped upright, staring with loathing at the shiny black oblong she had taken for a low bench. Under the full beam of Kendric's hilt-light, they both now saw it for Issiri's "birthing box," a tomb made womb made tomb again.

Irissa shuddered and moved away.

Kendric drew his sword. "This weapon may be mind-made, but it is mine again, as is my life span. The blade has drunk deep of Frostforge itself. However many tower chambers you claim, Geronfrey, you can't deny the sword's power."

"No." The sorcerer strolled affably about the room, stopping at the low casket.

With a pass of his crimson-gloved hand, the lid began to lift—or not so much lift as grow transparent, like a veil. A midnight veil.

Beneath the veil lay a shimmer of light-spangled dark water spreading in tangible waves. And then the light coagulated into a floating shape.

"Issiri!" Kendric joined Irissa in staring down at her latent image.

"I didn't know you had such fondness for the dead, Geronfrey." Irissa regarded the sorcerer carefully. His eyes were steady, but his gloved fingers twitched.

"I don't."

"Then Issiri is not dead."

"Only . . dormant."

"Why flee Solanandor Tierze, then?" Kendric demanded.

"She was dead, but I have revived her. Somewhat."

Irissa studied the colors swirling upon the black water in Issiri's shape—flesh tones composed of gold and pink and blue, pastels squeezed from an exhausted rainbow.

Her silver eyes sought the edge of Geronfrey's cheekbone. She had not been so evasive at meeting his gaze since first confronting him as an untried seeress.

"This is where the colors from my Iridesium circlet went, to feed your corpse," she said wearily.

"Not even Geronfrey is so—" Kendric began.

Both ignored Kendric, as if his fledging magic—even

after it had fallen far from the nest and found flight on its own—remained insignificant in the deep, eternal game between sorcerer and seeress.

"Not corpse, but consort," the sorcerer corrected politely.

"You are Ruler of Rengarth no more!" Kendric burst out.

"I will be again, and I will have an heir."

"Many claim the heirship!" Kendric argued.

Geronfrey's smile was taut but effective. "Not so many now. Where are the Rynx-spawn? Where are the old pale pair, the young hale pair my spell split in twain when the Rynx became human again?"

"They . . . faded—" Kendric began.

"They ceased to exist, and with them went whatever long-harbored claims of heirship that clung to their altered persons. No, only two vie for Rulership now—I as hereditary Usurper and you as last claimant from a long-vanished clan. Who testifies to your legitimacy but the dead or vanished? And I have an heir."

"As do I!" Kendric reminded him. Irissa indrew her breath while Kendric contemplated his folly in pointing out an unborn rival to Geronfrey's own heir.

Silence occupied the tower. An imp of wind from Without stuck its half-visible head through the crack in one window and howled until the action ceased to amuse it. They ignored it studiously.

Issiri drifted expressionlessly on the water, flat as a false image.

"My magic—" Irissa began.

"—is drained by your condition and further depleted by the loss of the fire within your circlet." Geronfrey folded his magnificently gloved arms. "This is my tower, as you will understand should you try your magic in it."

Irissa said nothing, having reached within herself and found her inner borders empty and still. Kendric must have come to the same conclusion, for he sighed before he spoke. "You will kill us, I suppose."

"Unnecessary." Geronfrey's gloved hand waved toward the windows. "You will find no exit from any of these six windows. You will remain—and die of your own inadequacy. I am loath to kill you anyway. Irissa is half-mother to my heir—"

Kendric took a thundering step toward the sorcerer, only to find himself confronting empty air. Behind him, Geronfrey completed his thought.

"—and I have been too amused by your struggle to master magic to end it a moment prematurely. So retain the tower of your ancestors, your Phoenix keep. Issiri and I shall reclaim Solanandor Tierze with none to naysay us—"

"Issiri?" Irissa asked sharply.

"Yes, I have a last task before leaving."

Geronfrey's red velvet fingers snapped soundlessly. In the birthing box water, blue and yellow motes swirled into twin pools of green. Eyelashes like weeds dripped into open eyes. Then Issiri herself was lifting from the water, her face, her hair, her long black gown dry as a bone.

She rose slowly, her body so child-swollen that Irissa no longer saw a duplicate.

"You both near your time," Geronfrey noted with satisfaction. "I have accelerated the present somewhat while we dallied here. My windows open on Past, Present, and Future as well as Within, Without, and the Nether Limbo itself."

"You entered by one," Kendric challenged.

"The Future, thus propelling you both farther into it. I will exit by it also." Geronfrey cast a worried glance at the sword-lanced window. "You punctured the window to Without— a miscalculation, Wrathman. Without will not like it, no. Even I shall be glad to escape this tower before Those Without respond to your pinprick."

Kendric glanced nervously to the swirling chaos that was pushing at the torn window like demons rending a seam between worlds.

"Issiri!" Geronfrey commanded with some haste.

Obediently, the figure turned, her empty emerald-green eyes passing over Irissa without a flicker of recognition—not even for her own image.

Geronfrey's gloved palm was waiting for the compliance of her limp white hand. Behind the sorcerer, the golden-webbed window was weaving a many-colored pattern.

Irissa recognized the Iridesium highlights leeched from her circlet. She began looming a matching pattern in her mind, thread by thread. She didn't have a purpose, only a wish to reclaim something of her own. She watched Geronfrey's web grow. Hers expanded with it until her mind was absorbed in color and pattern.

Kendric lifted his sword, sending its light fracturing. In that moment Issiri's vacant gaze crossed his. She leaned toward him as if pulled by a Drawstone.

"Jeweled hilt," she murmured dreamily. "All Quickstone."

He glanced at the glitter leaking through his grasp. The light-bright hilt glimmered coldstone pure, the runes cutting its beams into sharp-edged facets.

"Quickly!" Geronfrey ordered.

But Issiri lingered to address Kendric. "You promised me the Quickstone Mountains—"

"So we stand in them," Kendric answered.

Issiri turned to the window to see for herself.

"More Quickstones encrust my sword hilt," Kendric revised too late.

Issiri had already swiveled like some motion-drawn top losing its momentum and turned toward the webbed window glimmering behind Geronfrey.

Her hand lifted into his. He stepped back into the window, leaping lightly to the sill.

"Wait!" Kendric cried. "Irissa—! Issiri . . ."

A name—right or wrong—couldn't deter her any longer. She turned away until Kendric saw only the black velvet silhouette of her gown and hair, the jewel-strung network glittering atop it like stars in a night sky.

Geronfrey bowed out of the chamber gracefully, his

blue eyes ice-cold. Issiri flowed after him. Kendric never saw her foot lift to the sill, so liquid was her motion. But she stood in the window frame now. Surrounded by the stones, she melted into them. Melted—and stopped.

"Come," Geronfrey's voice urged, beating at all the windows at once. His figure was no longer visible, but obscured by Issiri's. "Now!"

She moved again. And balked again.

"The future waits! Walk into it!"

Kendric saw Issiri's hands lift to touch the tangible web that Geronfrey's passage had melted through. It stuck to her like a second netting, glimmering on her hands and dark-sleeved arms.

Beside him, Irissa lifted her own arms. Motes of light danced all around her hands and face—random flakes of Iridesium sparkle.

"What?" he demanded from everyone and no one.

Irissa didn't look at him, but her mouth was smiling. "He forgot . . . Geronfrey forgot! The window is a *gate* and Issiri is—"

"With child!" The fact of it stunned Kendric. "She bears an Unwilling One, as you did! She cannot pass without its consent."

Distant thunder cracked. Kendric glanced to see the window to Those Without widening. The web within the Future window was trembling now. Issiri tangled herself tighter in its bright lacings, her green eyes besotted with the wonder of her enmeshing.

Kendric was tempted to cut her free. He lifted his sword without thinking and started toward her.

"No!" Irissa ordered, then an Iridesium net settled over him.

His sword slashed upward by instinct, but the springy metal slid from his cutting edge like wet grass from a scythe.

"Geronfrey has lost!" Irissa's voice tensed with concentration. "He cannot take Issiri through, no matter what his magic. By the very irony of having an unborn heir, Geronfrey has lost his heir!"

Rooted, Kendric let the realization warm his cold veins.

A howl not quite wind echoed outside the tower. Then Issiri sank away from the window, sinking with her own tangled weight. A pair of scarlet arms reached back through the window for her.

Webbing turned into whips of flame flaying the gloves from the arms. Only the naked hands remained, reduced to skeleton.

White fingerbones flexed with demonic speed, seizing Issiri's sinking form and forcing it toward the window.

"He can't!" Irissa shouted triumphantly. "He can't take an Unwilling One through."

The rest of Geronfrey appeared again, pushing aside the webbing, his face contorted into a wizened parody of youth.

Issiri's black gown billowed as if shaken by winds from Without. It seemed Geronfrey sought to strip her of her garb in a wild attempt to force her through.

A scream more terrible than any wind could loose tore through the tower and beat at all the windows in turn, begging Past and Future, Within and Without for sanctuary.

It lasted longer than Kendric thought possible. Beside him, Irissa loosed her web and pressed her palms to her ears. She was sinking floorward now. He shrugged off the dispersing strands of Iridesium and caught her in his arms.

The scream ran up and down the scale of disbelief. It ended in a hoarse wail seemingly squeezed from the throat of a dying beast.

Or a newly living one.

Kendric, upholding Irissa from sinking into the web of herself, looked to the window again.

A sack of black fabric was billowing to the floor. Geronfrey stood crouched in the window frame, his bare arms crimson-gloved to the elbow. His skeletal hands clutched something red and dripping. The creature squirmed and spit as Geronfrey swung it to his chest and cradled its bloody head on his shoulder.

"The gate!" he demanded.

"Yesssssss!" came an echo on the wind, dying into another faint, protesting bawl of outrage.

Geronfrey backed into his web, but it rebuffed him. The threads had blackened and each juncture gleamed Torloc green, where a stone of Irissa's careful mental making sealed his exit.

His eyes dashed madly from window to window, finding them blank and closed with icy shutters. Only the spreading vertical seam to Without struck by Kendric's sword remained.

Geronfrey, pressing his hard-bought heir to his bloodied breast, darted across the chamber floor and hurled himself and the unborn infant into the narrow black fissure.

The seam sucked shut behind him with a great intake of breath, as if something huge had just inhaled.

Kendric commanded an empty chamber, Irissa senseless in his arms. He lay her gently on the floor. Pieces of her web trailed from the window like a train, glimmering over her form. Like fireflies, the web-stuff clustered at her head, finally massing into bands of green and crimson and azure and gold and violet that settled into the dark Irideslum circlet.

Kendric brushed the hair from Irissa's ice cold face. The restored circlet warmed his fingers, pulsing slightly. He waited for Irissa's eyes to open, for her mouth and mind to answer all his most profound questions.

Across the room, a fading voice asked, "Quickstone?" Then a whimper.

Kendric blanched and turned from the window with Irissa in his arms, hoping he hadn't heard what he had.

"Yes," the inner voice told Irissa. "You may pass."

She had asked nothing of anyone this time, yet she had been granted something by someone.

She looked around the innermost tower of herself.

No throne commanded center stage. No tiny being donned its encrusted carapace of jewels to grant her boons. She saw a small red light at her center, and another gleam above it, that was all.

High above, in the heavens of her temples, stars fashioned from the stuff of Iridesium highlights swarmed like gnats.

Everything occupied its proper place, she knew—and nothing. She searched the core of herself and found a great black emptiness, sinking.

The Swallowing Cavern, she thought . . . the Swallowing Cavern is Within, not Without. It always was and always will be. No wonder Geronfrey had used it as a road from world to world. No wonder the unmagicked fear it without knowing it.

Irissa crouched, helpless, at the core of her own inner emptiness. Half of her knew that she had passed from waking awareness to someplace between dream and death. The other half pushed—confused, in all directions—at the limitations of her hollowness. She stretched until she touched the boundaries of another.

"Yes," some voice said, not her own.

No, Irissa said without saying it.

There was no escape, either within or without.

She felt her eyelids tremble as light beat down upon them with its own inescapable force. Irissa, knowing more than she had ever wanted to, decided to awaken and try to forget it.

Kendric watched the subtlest muscles of Irissa's face reflect an inner tremor. Eventually the turmoil reached her eyes, which quivered open.

He was relieved to see the sheer silver strength of them reflecting his hilt-light and helped her sit.

"Geronfrey?" she asked.

"Gone. I think for good. And you?"

"Unhurt."

"In . . . every . . . way?"

"In every way I call my own."

"Then the child is—"

"The child still—a mystery to me and itself."

"I was afraid he harbored some ill toward it."

"Geronfrey is more interested in acquiring than taking away. As long as he has what he wishes he is indifferent."

"He has his heir."

Irissa passed her palm over her eyes. When he read their expression again, their color had darkened to pewter.

"Did I . . . see . . . what I thought I saw before I had seen too much?"

He nodded, not quite looking at her.

"Geronfrey took his heir, then, by force?"

Kendric waited a long time before answering. "I should have slain him for it—or tried. He did what I had never dreamed a man could do . . . kept life by taking life. There must have been some magic in it, but I only saw—murder."

Irissa forced herself upright and stared straight ahead so stiffly Kendric could sense her inner eyes looking back. "You . . . shield me from the sight."

"And myself."

"What is . . . left?"

He paused again as if simple words were hardest of all to find. "I don't know. I don't want to know."

Irissa sighed and braced her hand on his knee, pressing down hard to rise.

"No—" he began, but she was pushing herself upright as one blind, facing always into some unseeable distance.

"I thought while you lay senseless. One window opens on the Present," he said. "We know which two lead to Future and Those Without. We can hazard on the remaining four—attack one by might and magic and forge through—"

"What do we leave behind?" she asked.

"Only what Geronfrey did."

"I must know."

His hand on her arm kept her from turning around. "I would have slain it weeks ago, Irissa—should have—then Geronfrey would not have what he wants. He'll come back to claim Rengarth again, in time."

"Everything comes back in time. That is why I must see."

"No—"

But she was turning again and he found himself unable to stop her. He waited until she faced the opposite direction and then measured her breathing. It didn't change.

"Well?" he asked.

Irissa was still for a long moment. "Now that I have seen, we confront a greater challenge."

His head jerked up.

"She still lives."

He whirled, disbelieving.

Issiri—or the face and hands of Issiri—lay draped over the low black casket. Her dark garb spread around her like a pool of black blood. The glittering cage of jeweled netting had rusted black; even the jewels at the intersections had turned to lumps of dully glittering coal.

Only her emerald eyes sparkled in her waxen face. Those eyes focused on Kendric with an expression that made him shut his own.

"She is dead," he grated between his teeth.

"She is dying," Irissa modified. "I felt it when Geronfrey reached through more forbidden walls than any he has breached before—the membrane between life and death. I felt it as a tug upon my very soul. . . ."

Kendric forced Irissa's gaze to his. "She can't have touched your soul! She is a . . . an abomination; a thing nurtured on the most misspent seeds of nature and magic. She had no right to exist, no life to call her own."

"Yet she carried life; you saw it."

"I know not what Geronfrey tore from the frail fabric of her existence—something that moved, that cried, that even said yes to a gate. An heir perhaps, but no true child—how could it be? A son or daughter of shadow, not substance. An empty heir to an empty kingdom."

Irissa listened, then looked down at Issiri. "She wishes to speak to you, I think."

"No!" He turned away, his anguish echoing against four frozen-white windows.

"She doesn't know me, barely saw me," Irissa explained. "There was never enough of her to admit my existence, though she tried to feed on me, and I have always felt hers. But she remembers you; that memory she took from me as much as my slender slice of soul. Acknowledge her, or deny me."

Kendric hurled himself down on one knee beside the casket. The lid had solidified again. Issiri's ghastly face reflected faintly in it.

"What . . . do you want?" Kendric asked. He had seen men die, and women. He had seen bodies wounded to the death and had bled deep from his own injuries. But he had never before seen a soul slaughtered by its very maker.

Issiri's face floated water-lily-white on the obsidian casket top. "Quickstone." Her pale lips shaped the word as if it were fashioned of kisses. The emerald in her eyes ebbed to a shade paler than moss ivory. "You promised me Quickstone. All my pretty glittery things are gone. Everything is gone. You said . . . Quickstone. I remember."

Kendric confronted his lie, a thing so minor and so necessary, so easily justified when he had uttered it. What was an imprisoned man to do when confronted by a simpleton but to exploit the weakness and use it to free himself? Who would expect any behavior but that? Who would condemn that?

Now he saw the sin of Geronfrey written in his own language. Issiri had never been more than a tool to abandon when its use was over—living but dead, real but unreal.

"This is Irissa!" he cried out to the tower windows, as if they should answer. He had no right to slay Issiri, nor any right to save her. She was anomaly incarnate, already fatally wounded in her selfness, yet still—still, despite the awful paradox of it—living her unliving life.

Issiri's cheek rubbed the slick lid top. "Quickstone," she whispered, smiling.

Numbly, Kendric reached for the boarskin pouch. Perhaps he could make part of his lie true. . . .

The Quickstone sat on his broad palm like a dewdrop—delicate and reflecting a world in its tiny window. He pushed his hand before Issiri's face, ignoring the inner voice that said the Quickstone was Irissa's coldstone tear transformed into something uniquely hers and uniquely his.

He *couldn't* offer it to another, especially a stolen self that usurped Irissa's very soul. . . .

Something of the Quickstone reflected in Issiri's dying eyes. They flashed sovereign silver for a moment. Kendric felt the Quickstone sucked from his fingertip, felt it flow into Issiri.

She stared into his eyes as if seeing him for the first time, into herself as if looking within. Her eyes widened in lengths and widths and depths of horror he had never seen measured.

"Nothing," she whispered, uncomprehending. "There is truly nothing. . . ."

Two quicksilver tears rolled from her eyes, drawing all the color with them. Kendric saw Issiri's black pupils swell until they swallowed her face—or his vision. He saw only blackness and the casket top shimmering like roiled water and something sinking into it so dark and fast that it was gone in a moment.

Quicksilver separated into rings on the black surface that rippled outward until they vanished. Kendric put his hand atop the casket. The stone was solid, and cold, and quite impervious.

Another hand touched his shoulder.

"She was me," Irissa said, "but she was not mine to call or release. Thank you."

He rose, slowly, his knee joints creaking like unoiled

armor. He sensed a new emptiness in the tower, and when his eyes questioned Irissa, she only nodded.

"We've still to risk a way out of here," he said, not believing that his voice could sound so ordinary.

She shook her head and pointed to a window behind him.

One ice-drawn pane was melting to sheer, see-through quicksilver. Through it, he viewed the same mountaintop from which they'd begun their journey to the forge.

He even thought he saw the forge—for a fiery glow was warming the summit's snowy cap.

A moment later an emblazoned creature burst over the precipice horizon—a winged firedrake with a bird's head. It trod air, its vast wings beating, waiting.

He looked incredulously to Irissa.

"Aven and Ilvanis, Neva and Sin. And Rynx," she named it. "Frostforge reshaped them, too. They will take us off the mountain."

"You, who quailed at an Empress Falgon, would ride *that* on such a supposition?"

Irissa shrugged slightly. The sad smile that had haunted her features turned impish.

"Well, I'm not climbing down. Not in my condition."

EPILOGUE:
Afterbirth

FLEEING FISH MADE COMMAS OF THEMSELVES AS KEN-
dric's boots paced the glassy floor over their heads.

"I'll be fine," Irissa said from the bed, trying not to
mind that she could barely see Kendric past the hummock
of her stomach.

"I had not thought we would be exiled here, unable to
go anywhere else," Kendric fretted.

"Rengarth is possessive of its people," Scyvilla put in.
The ludborg was bouncing softly against an illuminated wall
where fish circulated in a vividly colored aquarium. "I
found it as hard to leave as to return. But no doubt you
two, with your talents, will achieve as much in very few
years."

"Irissa is bearing our child *now*!" Kendric exploded.
"Neither of us anticipated her doing it alone, far from any
of her Torloc kind. I would give my sword for Dame Agneda at this moment!" he swore, pacing again and sending
fishes flitting in every direction.

"I can perform a crystal casting on the child's future,"
Scyvilla said. "That should distract you both for a while."

"Myself perhaps," Kendric said, "but who and what
will distract Irissa? What is the use of being Ruler over a
land of which I barely know one-tenth, if I cannot command circumstances at the birth of my own child?"

"There are many uses to being a ruler," Scyvilla answered, "but you are not well disposed at the moment to value them. Perhaps I had better withdraw—"

"Withdraw, withdraw!" Kendric ordered testily. "That at least is one advantage of being a ruler I appreciate. Out! Take your crystals and your chatter elsewhere."

Irissa managed a laugh as Scyvilla wobbled toward the chamber door and exited.

Kendric turned, unplacated. "It is not amusing. We have faced many foes, but nothing so unnerving as this."

Her laugh became a sigh as another long prong of pain delved inward. No Torloc dame had mentioned how a seeress was to comport herself during birth pangs. Irissa couldn't help wishing that Kendric would leave so that she could relieve herself of a good, long, self-indulgent scream.

Instead, she managed to smile. "The women of Sola-nandor Tierze have pampered me since our return. They haven't seen a legitimate heir born in years. Our child will be spoiled from the womb onward."

Kendric picked a few exotic fruits off a bedside stand. "They do their best, but no pampering can substitute for a woman who knows you and knows the process you go through. May time forgive me, but I'd even be grateful for Finorian at this moment."

"Finorian? You are that desperate?—oh!"

"What is it?" Kendric hurled himself to the bedside to clutch her hand.

"The same thing it was last time," Irissa managed to pant out.

"Can't you use your powers to . . . hurry things up? Or ease them?"

"I've tried! My concentration is dispersed. I can't focus on anything, especially myself. It's as if there's a barrier—"

He looked to her swelling stomach before he could help himself. Irissa caught his glance, then began giggling until she hiccoughed when another spasm came. She pulled her hand within his to her face, biting hard upon his knuckles until the wave passed.

"I'm sorry!"

"That's fine," he reassured her. "I'm glad to be of use and would prefer a pang or two or twenty to this endless watching and waiting! Where is that wombwitch?"

The chamber door flew open.

Framed in it stood a creature of lengthy limbs and sparse hair, that looked neither man nor woman and barely human. It advanced with a long, jolting gait. Its raiment was fashioned from long beaded strips that chuckled softly as it moved.

"How is our Reginatrix this day?" the wombwitch inquired, looking at Kendric all the while.

He felt somehow his own well-being was under question. "She can tell you for herself. As for myself, I wish you would get this over and done with."

Kendric watched the wombwitch settle beside Irissa, staring into her eyes and stroking her wrists.

"Dilating nicely," the creature announced.

"Dilating—?" Kendric repeated.

"The eyes, the eyes! One can always tell the tempo of a birthing by the mother's eyes. See, her pupils swell, narrowing the silver of the iris to a band as slim as that Iridesium circlet at her temples. I pray you let me remove that, it must be quite discomforting—"

Irissa pulled away from the long thin fingers that reached for the circlet. "I told you I must keep it. It will not harm me."

"But who is to know what will harm you?" the wombwitch fretted. "I have never assisted at a Torloc birthing before, although a Torloc or two have come and gone in Rengarth. And you are a seeress on top of it."

"I am sure I will prove to be a woman at bottom of it," Irissa said dryly. "Let nature end what nature has begun. My magic had no part in this conception, and my magic will do no harm to its fruition."

Kendric leaned over the wombwitch's bony shoulder to study Irissa's eyes. It was true—her silver irises were shrinking to a slim ring around the darker centers, something that had not happened since Irissa had lost her magic three worlds before.

"Will it come back once it's over?" he asked anxiously.

"The pregnancy?" the wombwitch inquired. The creature had no name, being an odd unsocial sort who apparently only appeared when a pregnant woman was ready to deliver.

"Her silver eyes!"

"Ah. Well, I cannot say. I have not dealt with silver before. Usually, however, all returns to normal. I suggest, sir, that you repair beyond the chamber door, as your heir is preparing to make his entrance."

Kendric stood stunned, watching Irissa gasp sharply and then begin panting in earnest.

"I warn you," the wombwitch said, delving under the covers with its facile arms. "This is far too distressing a process for mere fathers to witness."

He retreated to the door. "I shall be right outside," he announced. No one answered, so he crossed the threshold, shut the door, thought better of it, and left it ajar.

Then he stood and regarded the long corridor, thronged with ludborgs and the palace serving staff and assorted officials, all of whom he hardly knew.

Although it was broad daylight, he remembered another ajar door in another place, another man pacing outside it . . . too distressed, or too unconcerned, to enter.

Irissa had lain beyond that other door also, in dire danger from an unknown poison. Yet outside it, Ovrath, her father, who should have been most stricken, had paced and paced. Like a stranger.

Kendric took a deep breath and surveyed the anxious watchers watching him. The flat of his hand pushed the door wide as he reentered the room. Harsh breathing filled the chamber. Fish had fled to the floor's farthest limits, leaving only a swirl of colored water to walk over.

Kendric's advancing bootsteps made the water intermingle in unheard-of shades no one noticed. He came to the bedside, knelt, and clasped Irissa's hand again.

She was pale and sweat-pearled, her eyes midnight-dark. But her lips parted in a smile that was half grimace as he arrived.

"Soon," the wombwitch grunted. It had set up a small firepot, and some aromatic brew was wafting into the air. Kendric inhaled, finding himself instantly calmed. Sounds softened, even light seemed filtered. The pressure of Irissa's fingers around his eased.

His own sweat, more from anticipation than any effort, passed. Whatever the wombwitch was, it seemed to know what it did.

Irissa's head suddenly turned from his on the pillow and she smiled into the distance.

"How nice," she murmured, "that you could come."

Kendric stared into empty space, stunned. Had the scent drugged her?

Irissa was looking past his shoulder now, and nodding in that insane, pleased way. He jerked his neck around. For a moment the dimensions of the room faded as another room surrounded them with its ghostly proportions.

He blinked as Aven, her red hair paled to pink, reached out to pat Irissa's hand in his. He felt a feathery brush and jerked his hand away.

Across the bed, Neva wavered into shape and bent down to take Irissa's other hand.

"She saved me from the Hunter once. It was the least I could do."

"But—" Kendric glanced at the wombwitch, who went about its business without any recognition of the others' presence. "You and Aven and Ilvanis and Sin were forged into the semblance of a salamander—at least that's what Irissa and I thought even as we rode the winds down off the mountain on the salamander's back."

"Oh, we are many things," Aven laughed behind him. "We always have been. Now we are merely friends. Let us be so."

"But how—?"

"Shhh," Neva hushed him a trifle imperiously. "She feels better for our presence." Kendric glanced at Irissa to see her face serene, her body less racked. "Warriors are useful for some things, and women for others."

"Tell him," Aven urged. "He is, after all, our Ruler."

"*Your* Ruler? By Finorian's fingernail, no—I want no responsibility for your come-and-go ways!"

"You have us," Neva said. "This Spectral City is as much a part of your domain as Solanandor Tierze or Liderion. Only the Spectral City comes and goes, as we do. We simply arranged for our city's appearance to coincide with Solanandor Tierze for this momentous event—oh, look, I think the babe arrives!"

Speechless, Kendric couldn't stop himself from gazing to the bottom of the bed. The wombwitch's many-jointed fingers were easing the tip of a small, writhing shape from under the bedclothes.

The sight was too reminiscent of seeing the shadow Irissa's only-born wrested beforetime from her substance.

Kendric tore his eyes away and focused on Irissa's face again. She seemed momentarily unpained, her birth-dilated eyes moving from his face to the two spectral visages that bracketed her.

Suddenly, her face clenched. She pulled her other hand from the immaterial clasp of Neva's and clutched the Overstone pouch at her breast.

"No," she whispered, "don't go yet. I may need you—"

Her whole body pulsed in waves of motion, smooth and powerful. Kendric had never felt so helpless, so ignorant.

He remembered mind-shared memories of his own birth relived through the Crux Crystal, recalled being pierced by splinters of Phoenicia's birth pangs—and hating the knowledge that he had caused them.

Irissa's hand collapsed on the pouch, shattering its contents. A faint bawling cry, like that of a scalded cat three rooms away, spilled into the bedchamber. Something made Kendric want to cry out a warning, but something equally strong stoppered his throat.

Through so many worlds she had carried the Overstone safely, and to destroy it now, with her own hand, at such a moment—!

He watched the ruined contents squeeze from the pouch like a long silver entrail and reached to pull the mess from Irissa's throat.

Something flashed moonweasel-fast by his hand—a supple silver thread. Irissa's eyes and mouth widened with wonder as another half-strangled cry wailed into the room.

The wombwitch was lifting a small struggling bundle in both its bony hands, wrapping some cloth around it. The silver streak darted for it, even as Kendric realized that he must . . . he must . . . stop it!

The infant squirmed in its swaddlings as it was laid atop Irissa's level stomach. The wombwitch beamed, its narrow, pasty face growing ludicrously benign.

Kendric rummaged in the infant's wrappings, indifferent to its looks, its sex. Silver flashed and eluded him. It wrapped a minuscule wrist. As his big fingers pursued it, hampered by awe of the tiny still-wet body they fought over, it writhed away.

A moment later he caught a gleam around the infant's shapeless torso. The thing attached itself to the babe's tied-off umbilical cord and wrapped its waist. Kendric saw a scaled pattern marking its slim length and knew the invader for a serpent. And Rengarth teemed with poison!

He insinuated his fingers under the serpent's chill belly to tear it free, but its grip was ungiving. Like quicksilver, it flowed away in a whip-thin thread. Again Kendric pursued it over the infant body—the throat! It had circled the undefined throat twice, gleaming there like a mocking necklace.

He glimpsed the thumbnail-sized snake's head, the open jaws clasping its own tail, and reached to crush it. His fingers closed on cool, scaled silver again. Then his grasp was empty and the damnable thing had slipped up the babe's face to circle its forehead.

"A crown," the wombwitch chuckled, unconcerned. "As befits an heir."

Irissa was struggling up in the bed linens. Kendric caught her eyes, relieved to see the seeress's silver spreading in them again.

"Irissa—I'm sorry. That cursed Overstone has birthed a monster. It won't release our child."

"Let me see." She reached calmly for the bundle.

He couldn't hand her such a marred child. But the wombwitch lifted it past his numb hands and tucked it into the cradle of Irissa's crooked arm.

She received it rather gingerly, like a piece of broken pottery, and gazed experimentally into the eyes squinting out from a red, puckered face.

Irissa smoothed a bit of downy hair and ran a casual fingertip over the serpent circlet.

"Be careful! The viper lives."

Irissa looked up, strangely. "It's only metal—a kind of Iridesium . . . only the color runs to light, not dark. It's merely a piece of lifeless jewelry."

Kendric leaned in to clasp the cold metal circlet. It remained emplaced, as if the child had been born with it so positioned.

"It moved," he insisted.

"The child wears a circlet like her mother," the wombwitch announced, dismantling her firepot. "It seems a good omen."

Kendric finally apprehended the facts. "She? A *she*?"

The wombwitch smiled, exposing pointed teeth. "Like her mother. Another good omen."

Irissa looked at him, an anxiety in her eyes that was not fear for the child, or fear of the circlet-serpent, but for his reaction.

Kendric frowned and inspected the babe again. The unfocused eyes glittered toward him—pale but not silver at all. The . . . thing . . . around her forehead remained that—a thing. A thin metal circlet, a birth gift from the Inlands Overstone.

He looked up to find Neva and Aven and the Spectral City had faded. They were alone again—he and Irissa and their unnamed child. They were well and alive and had much to learn.

It did not seem a time for questions.

THE BEST IN FANTASY

THE BEST IN SCIENCE FICTION

BESTSELLING BOOKS FROM TOR

THE TOR DOUBLES

Two complete short science fiction novels in one volume!